Light the Night

Light the Night

JOHN CULEA

Victor Books is an imprint of ChariotVictor Publishing
Cook Communications, Colorado Springs, CO 80918
Cook Communications, Paris, Ontario
Kingsway Communications, Eastbourne, England

Cover design by Bill Coburn
Cover illustration by Chris Cocozzo
First printing, 1997
Printed in the United States of America
01 00 99 98 97 5 4 3 2 1

Library of Congress Cataloging-in-Publication Data

Culea, John
Light the Night / John Culea
p. cm.
ISBN 0-7814-0296-4
I. Title.
PS3553.U285L54 1997
813'. 54—dc20 96-9833

To Patti.

You always believed I could do this.

I love you.

Foreword

Drive-by shootings, drug wars, pay-back killings, intimidation of witnesses—right out of our daily headlines comes the power-packed book *Light the Night*. Written as only an insider could do it, this excellent work of fiction runs close enough to reality to make you wonder which of the scenarios had the names changed to protect the innocent.

This story may thrust John Culea into that club of "inside the profession" writers that have thrilled the nation. Like Tom Clancy's insight into the military and John Grisham's knowledge of the legal profession, Culea has walked the trail of the TV reporter. He has lived the reality of the bottom line of the ratings, seen the hollowness of political life, and experienced the effects of daily calamity. The story goes behind the headlines to the terror, tragedy, pathos, and ethical dilemmas that plague our nation.

In addition to the exciting action and the thrilling suspense, this page-turner offers hope. John Culea brings attention to two significant issues: (1) the need for everyone to accept responsibility for public safety; (2) the importance of the spiritual dimension in our lives.

I commanded the Pacific (Venice) Area of the Los Angeles Police Department in the early 1970s. We experimented with a new idea that in those days we called Team Policing. Today we call it Community Based Policing. It involves establishing a partnership between the police and the people of a given community. After a year of working together, the results were astounding. Crime decreased by 24% in the test area. This story revolves around that basic concept. It is fiction, but hopefully it kindles an interest in working together to make our communities safer.

Most importantly, like John Culea, I have a personal relationship with the Lord. I, too, believe that this relationship is strategic in taking the first steps to solve our many problems. Our country has a rich cultural, as well as religious, tradition of acknowledging the providence of God in our public, as well as private, lives. George Washington recognized this as crucial to our survival in his farewell address. Somehow this issue has become politically incorrect and controversial. John treats this important subject with tact and conviction. He clearly presents the ultimate answer to life's problems without being pedantic or preachy. This is a book to enjoy and share with friends. There is good news in *Light the Night*.

Robert L. Vernon
Assitant Chief of Police (ret.)
Los Angeles Police Department

Special Thanks

I've always considered this part of a book terribly boring. Now I know why it's needed. I could never have written the adventure you're about to read without the following:

Encouragement and story critique from my wife, Patti.

Understanding for my love of writing from my daughters, Janet and Heidi.

Years of conversational writing at its best in the form of letters from my mother, Hilda. A lifelong example of discipline from my father, John.

Computer troubleshooting and patient instruction from KFMB-TV senior photographer Ben Cutshall.

Technical advice from Dave Cohen, San Diego Police Department, Jim Stephens, Weisser Sporting Goods in San Diego, and KFMB-TV photographers Todd Ward and Scott Hall. Insight into the world of A.C. Nielsen from Melanie Jones of KFMB-TV.

Kindness from ChariotVictor Publishing assistant editor Elisabeth Brown, who answered a query letter from an unknown, unpublished author. A green light from managing editor Julie Smith.

The greatest help came from my editor, Gloria Kempton. I had a good story, but you made it come to life. You are my teacher.

Friends and relatives frequently questioned me: "How's the book coming along, John?" That, more than anything, showed that the project was not my doing at all, because each time someone asked for an update, I had a chance to share my faith in Jesus. God's leading and the presence of the Holy Spirit were very real.

That's how *Light the Night* came to you. I hope you'll enjoy the adventure.

CHAPTER ONE

Monday, September 11

"This is Channel Three News, at six in the morning, with Paul Thomas, Karen Franklin, and Rita Roberts with weather. News Three, for Southern California, the news that hits home."

A fast-paced musical production open flashed scenes of a surfer, crouched and sliding through an ocean tube. Next was the video of a Hollywood movie premier, followed by shots of a burning building. Children laughing, two people shaking hands, three police cars running code three, and then a montage of aerial shots. Finally, like visitors at your doorstep who wanted to be part of your family for the next sixty minutes, were the smiling people of Channel Three's anchor team. Just hours earlier, Paul Thomas and each of his on-air teammates had dragged their bodies out of bed. Paul remembered looking at the mirror in horror and wondering how that mug could go on the air before the sun came up.

"Good morning, I'm Paul Thomas." The lead anchor on Channel Three's morning news team had won another battle against the alarm clock. And without coffee, too. Not that he wouldn't have liked a hot cup of java, but it always poured through him like Niagara Falls. Since he was on the air for an hour straight and had no chance to hit the men's room, the coffee waited until seven.

"And I'm Karen Franklin. Our top stories this morning—a liquor store holdup by suspected gang members leaves three people dead in Compton."

"And fire takes the lives of an entire family in Alhambra," Paul continued.

"Also, a drug deal that backfires takes the life of an innocent bystander in Culver City," said Franklin.

"Then, ominous predictions about LA's economy, and what happened last night as the city tried to fight crime," Paul finished.

It was the guts of local television news, and it spilled out on the screen. The news philosophy of Channel Three was no different than that of most stations. Someone, somewhere, said it first: "If it bleeds, it leads."

The first segment of the news was arranged in predictable order, with the most recent and urgent story at the top. The formula was simple: grab the audience as they were waking up, show them what happened overnight, but understand that not many people would sit and watch. They were getting ready for work or school, stepping out of the shower, combing their hair, shaving, putting on their clothes. Every once in a while, they'd turn to look at the television, but mostly, they listened; some called the morning news "radiovision."

Today, during the seven minutes before the first commercial break, Paul Thomas and Karen Franklin reported that nine people had been shot, stabbed, or burned to death in metropolitan Los Angeles. The news was the words and pictures of life, but mostly of death. Crime in Los Angeles the past night was actually lower than on previous Sundays, but Thomas figured most people wouldn't feel the difference because LA and its sprawling suburbs were in trouble. No Gallup polls were needed; fifteen million people knew that the number-one problem was violent crime, thanks to the powerful street gangs. In LA, there were at least 600 known gangs, with more than 70,000 gang members. The LAPD and LA County Sheriff's Department had fewer than 250 officers in their anti-gang units.

"Still to come on News Three," Thomas read off the TelePrompTer, "is your car or truck about to be stolen? We'll tell you the models that are most likely to be taken, and new charges are being leveled at the White House about what happened at Camp David a week ago."

Each time a headline was read, a video linked words with pictures.

"Also," said Franklin, "LA county schools ask for help in keeping students away from gang intimidation, and we'll tell you what happened when our neighborhoods took part in the national 'Light the Night' crime fight. Please stay with us."

Mercifully, the first segment was over.

As the commercials for credit repair, Toyota, health care, and breath freshener appeared on the screen, Paul wondered to himself why anyone would want to keep watching after the bloody and depressing first segment.

He leaned back and looked at his co-anchor. They'd been together now just short of a year. He liked Karen's enthusiasm and was glad the wretched hours hadn't gotten the best of her. Two previous co-anchors had left the station for more regular hours—one landed an evening anchor job in Phoenix, and the other quit the business altogether, saying she needed to get a life. Of course, viewers didn't give a rip about the anchor team's schedule. Paul was a TV personality in America's second largest city. If he didn't like it, a hundred other guys were more than willing to take his place for half his salary.

A car, its lights off, moved slowly around a corner in the early morning hours. Maurice "Mo-Jo" Jones, a man in his early twenties, slouched behind the wheel, and two boys, one fourteen, the other eleven, hunched down in the backseat. Jones knew the boys were scared; he'd armed them with semiautomatic weapons. When he'd seen their hands shaking, he'd made sure the guns' safety locks were on.

Mo-Jo was an enforcer, an assassin for Iron Claw, a street gang, but this was his own assignment—it was personal business. He'd taken the Manchester Avenue turnoff from the Harbor Freeway, headed east to Broadway, then turned right. He was now at 89th

Street in a familiar neighborhood. Jones looked over his shoulder at the boys in the backseat and grinned. The youngest was shaking so badly, Jones thought the kid might drop his gun.

"You guys ready?" he asked.

Silence.

"I said, you ready?"

"Yeah," they returned.

The car pulled up alongside the curb and stopped, its engine still running.

"Okay, here's the plan. See that house up there with the white van parked out front?" The boys peered out the window. In the dark, Jones could barely see the van, and he knew the boys didn't have a clue which house he was talking about. But they nodded anyway. "I'm gonna drive by the house. When I get there and give the word, both of you empty your guns. Aim for the windows. Got it?"

"Yeah."

"That house is filled with gang-bangers who would just as soon cut your throat. If you do this right, you may have what it takes to be an Iron Claw."

Jones reached over the seat and released the safety on both of their weapons. "Don't put your fingers on them triggers 'till I tell you, understand?"

Mo-Jo knew he was taking a risk, but figured he'd reached a high enough level in the gang hierarchy that he could do things without the gang's approval. He'd chosen the youngest and most vulnerable gang wannabes to help him carry out his personal vendetta. His target was the home of his ex-girlfriend; he'd seen her with a member of their rival gang, the Insane Rulers. Before starting the car, Jones pulled out a small black notebook from his coat pocket and wrote in it. Then he put the car in gear. "Okay, here we go."

Neither of the boys had ever fired a gun before. They'd been along on drive-by shootings and had seen older boys do it, but this was their first time.

The night was still. Sunrise was thirty minutes away.

As the car pulled parallel with the driveway, both boys leaned out the right side of the car and pointed their guns at the house.

"Do it!"

The boys jumped, and the first shots were wild.

"Hold the guns with both hands!" Mo-Jo yelled.

They did, emptying their guns on the house. Glass shattered, a woman screamed, and a light flashed on. The car sped off.

"Thomas, you're living a charmed life," Wilson Ruggles mumbled to himself as he stared at the television in the bathroom mirror. He wiped off traces of shaving cream, reached for a pair of scissors, and began trimming his neat goatee. He looked closer into the mirror to see if the hair inside his nose needed cutting and decided against it. The image of Paul Thomas was clear in the mirror, but of course, everything was turned around.

Just like what was happening at the station. Ruggles smiled. He was hired to shake things up, and that's exactly what he was doing. In his first year as president and general manager of Channel Three, fifty-two-year-old Wilson P. Ruggles had fired three department heads. He'd also ordered the termination of the last two news anchors when their contracts had expired. Paul Thomas was the next one up for renewal, and if Ruggles had a replacement who could bring in better ratings, he'd love to dump Thomas, too.

Ruggles pushed the skin up on his cheeks to see how he'd look with a face-lift. He grinned. He liked what he saw, but decided cosmetic surgery could wait a year or two. *You've still got what it takes, you handsome devil.*

"Pious pinhead," he said to the TV as he heard Paul Thomas's voice once more. Ruggles turned from the mirror and watched the screen. He wished someone else were doing the news, but like it or not, Thomas brought pretty decent ratings, considering the number of people who watched both in the morning and at noon.

Ruggles walked to his closet, took a blue button-down dress shirt off a hanger, and put it on. The collar was too tight. He knew he'd put on some weight; his pot belly hung over his green boxer shorts. But he was afraid to step on the bathroom scale and see how much.

Ruggles eyed his wife, Mary, still lying in their bed. He knew she was awake; she was only pretending to be asleep. *That's one of the few things you do well, woman.* He was glad not to have to talk with her. What a bore. Ruggles couldn't think of one thing they had in common anymore. And without makeup—*just keep yourself buried under the covers.*

"Ha, ha, ha! Good line," he said, reacting to Thomas's ad-lib about the weather, "but don't expect me to tell you."

Since coming to the station, he'd heard Paul Thomas reveal bits and pieces of his personal life with others on the news set. Ruggles seldom had any direct contact with Thomas, and when he did, it was brief. Their conversations were usually about the content of the syndicated programs Channel Three carried during the day and in prime-time access. Their most recent contact was last Thursday afternoon when Thomas walked into Ruggles's office.

"How can you face the leaders of this community," Thomas asked, "and tell them you're concerned about social problems when you air the kind of garbage that was on the Felix Banner show yesterday? Fathers proud of their promiscuous sons? What's that?"

"I didn't see it, and I don't care what you think."

"Well, maybe you ought to take a look at the sewage you're dumping into the air."

"Where do you get off by coming in here and telling me that? That show is on in the afternoon."

"Yeah, but the promos run during our newscasts. Then I have to come back on and do the news."

"So what?" Ruggles had never seen Thomas so insistent.

"Wilson, people associate me with this station. A lot of our stuff is degrading and offensive—same for most of our news specials in the last ratings period. Sometimes I'm embarrassed to be part of this station."

Ruggles swore at Thomas and told him that no one was forcing him to stay. Thomas had looked around then and asked where Jesus Christ was. Ruggles was confused for a second, until he realized it was Thomas's way of correcting his swearing.

The general manager could put up with that, but deep down, what bothered him most was that Paul Thomas was a Christian who openly shared his faith with people at work and in the community. Ruggles would definitely be more comfortable if Thomas were gone. The anchorman was a constant and irritating reminder of Ruggles's uncertainty about life after death.

Ruggles looked through his closet and found the bright red tie he'd bought in New York during a network TV affiliates' meeting. He still couldn't believe he'd paid $100 for a tie. He was with three general managers from other network-owned stations, and they were in the hotel's men's shop. He thought buying an expensive tie would impress the men, but they hadn't even noticed.

As Ruggles watched Thomas on the screen now, he was reminded of a recent magazine article where Thomas had said that Jesus Christ was the center of his life. Ruggles put on a dark blue suit, slipped into a pair of black Gucci loafers that needed new heels, and muttered, "Bible nut!"

With that, he walked out of the bedroom. Channel Three's news still had five minutes to go, but Ruggles didn't watch—he wanted to get to work early.

"Last night, Los Angeles turned on its lights in hopes of turning off crime." Karen Franklin was reading the final story of the morning news. "We were all encouraged to turn on our porch lights, go outside, and get to know our neighbors."

Paul Thomas listened to his co-anchor read, and watched the

video of porch lights and people standing in their yards. The story was a recap of a once-a-year nationwide effort to cut crime, called "Light the Night." At six o'clock on Sunday evening, people were asked to turn on their porch lights and mingle outside as a way to bring members of the community together and keep an eye out for one another. In past years, during the hours of extra awareness, crime had dropped dramatically. It had happened again last night.

"Police tell us that Light the Night is their slowest night of the year. And in this case, slow is good news," Franklin said, "but they also say that the following night, crime usually returns to normal."

Paul knew what the real story was in Los Angeles. People no longer felt it was safe to walk any street in the city, day or night. Drug dealing, gang warfare, attacks on the elderly, and home break-ins were rampant; no neighborhood was immune. Innocent people were often caught in the cross fire, and gang graffiti was sprayed on buildings everywhere. People felt isolated, like captives in their own homes.

It seemed that each day Paul reported at least one brutal crime somewhere in the city more shocking than one the day before. Police and sheriff's investigators believed that more than half the crimes were gang related, and while no one knew for sure which ones were causing the most trouble, the names of two gangs kept surfacing: Iron Claw and Insane Rulers.

"You've got an extra minute to fill, Paul," an urgent voice spoke into his earpiece. The show's producer was his audio link to the television control room. The cooking segment had ended too soon, and the producer needed his co-anchors to ad-lib until they switched to the network's morning news program.

As Karen finished talking over the video of last night's Light the Night, the camera showed both Paul and Karen on the set together.

"Karen, what if the Los Angeles area turned Light the Night from a once-a-year event into a nightly occurrence? What do you think would happen?" Paul knew she could fill the extra time and wasn't surprised when she responded right away.

"Wouldn't it get old after a while? I mean, the same thing night after night?"

He nodded. "But people would like not having the same kind of crime night after night. Would they tire of no more drive-by killings?" A camera closed in on Karen intently listening to Paul. "Would they tire of no more worrying about their homes being broken into? Do you think they'd tire of no more graffiti in their neighborhoods?"

Karen smiled. "Well, of course not, but how would you keep it going?"

Paul was pleased with how well they worked together. They not only respected each other, they were good friends.

"Thirty seconds until we're off the air," Paul heard in his earpiece.

"We don't have much time left," he said, "but I have a few ideas. We could expand neighborhood watches into citizens' patrols with video cameras. The police could work closely with the patrols, and the mayor and city council could get involved. Our city's newspapers could take part, and Channel Three might be a kind of visual 'war command post' to keep people informed, show what's happening, and target neighborhoods that need help."

"Wrap it up!" the producer said again. "You've got fifteen seconds to say good-bye!"

"It might be worth a try, Paul."

"I think it could work," Thomas said into the camera. "We're all fed up with what's happening. It's no secret that street gangs, two in particular, have us by the throats." He made a gesture with his hand, beckoning to his viewers to come. "Come on, friends, let's quit messing around! Demand that something be done! Give us a call. If you mean business, get down here and talk with us at the station. We're ready to help. We need to hear from you."

Karen gave a quick wave. "See you again at noon."

A split second later, they were off the air.

"Good job filling the extra time, guys," the producer said over the studio loudspeaker.

Paul turned to his co-anchor. "Way to go, Karen. You had some good comments on the year-round Light the Night brainstorm."

"Hope I didn't sound too negative."

"Not at all. I wonder if we'll get any calls."

Five minutes later, as Paul walked from the studio into the newsroom, he knew something was different. Normally, at seven in the morning, the atmosphere was fairly loose. This was the time when people on the assignment desk decided which crews would cover the morning stories. Then, later in the afternoon, as the station got closer to the main newscasts, tension began building. Not so today. The telephone switchboard and the operator at Channel Three were both in danger of melting down. Calls to the station were about one subject: Light the Night. They asked for Paul Thomas, Karen Franklin, the station manager, the news director, anyone. They wanted more information about Light the Night and directions on how to get to the station. Phone lines were jammed. A major story had broken wide open.

A writer rushed by him. "Thanks a lot, Paul. We're swamped with calls."

Paul poked his head into the assignment room and listened to the one-way conversations. As soon as one person hung up on the assignment desk, the switchboard operator would send back another call. The writer he had just spoken to was on the phone. He shot Paul a dirty look over his shoulder. Paul grinned back sheepishly, then retreated from the assignment area.

Paul walked past the newsroom fax machine and saw a pile of messages spilled onto the floor. More messages were sliding out—coming from every part of metropolitan Los Angeles. Paul grabbed a few messages out of the pile and read them. Some wrote words of praise, others called for action, and still others begged for help in their neighborhoods. They'd caught a glimmer of hope and had now turned it into a laser beam aimed at Channel Three.

Curious as to what his most reliable critic might be thinking, and eager to share what was happening, Paul made a telephone call of his own. On the fourth ring, he heard the recorded message, the strong, businesslike voice of a woman—his woman. "We're unable to come to the phone right now. Please leave your name and number at the tone. Bye."

Paul smiled, and when he heard the beep, began to talk. "Hi, Maddie. I know you hate to answer the phone, but it's only me, your friendly, kind-hearted, anchorman-husband, waiting for you to lift the receiver. . . ."

"Paul? You still there?" Maddie sounded out of breath.

Paul laughed. "For a second, I thought I was doomed to answering machine oblivion. You okay?"

"Of course I am. What's up?"

"Did you see any of the news?"

"Bits and pieces. Why?"

"What did you think of the Light the Night stuff?"

"In what way?"

"Well, that challenge—or whatever I said at the end."

There was a pause. "Oh, maybe a little corny," she said finally. "What kinds of reactions are you getting?"

Maddie Thomas. Right to the point. Ask an honest question, and you'll get an honest answer. These were some of the reasons Paul enjoyed being her husband and was glad she was the mother of their two children.

"Looks like we may have struck a nerve," Paul said. "People are calling like crazy."

"Let me guess. You're not getting out of there on time, right?"

"Probably not. I'll call you later. I love you."

"I love you more."

Carol Singleton, a petite, dark-haired woman in her late twenties, was not frowning. This was unusual for her, the assignment editor, especially at 7:30 in the morning. Most days at this time she wore what she called her "game face," a scowl, as she pondered what her top story would be. But there was no doubt about her top story; today she had two possibilities.

The first had happened about an hour ago in South Central LA—a drive-by shooting near Broadway and 89th Street. When Singleton called the police, she was told that, while the family that lived in the house had no apparent gang connection, the crime seemed to be gang related. Neighbors had told a Channel Three crew on the scene that a young woman, known to run with gang members, had moved out of the house three weeks earlier.

One of the bullets had pierced a wall and killed a six-month-old baby boy in his crib. Another bullet had shattered a bedroom window, killing a sixteen-year-old girl who was spending the night with her best friend. Still another bullet had left a forty-two-year-old father of six in critical condition, shot in the head while getting ready for work. Singleton knew the crime was good television—lots of feeling and all sorts of action with cops, paramedics, and grieving neighbors.

The other breaking story was close to home—right outside the station.

"Get out front and start shooting the demonstration," Singleton said to photographer Jack Martinez, who had stopped by her desk for his morning assignment. He grabbed his camera and raced to the lobby.

Singleton's news judgment told her this could be big. The newsroom phones were still ringing nonstop with calls from viewers who had heard Paul Thomas that morning. Many had left their homes and were now outside the station's front lobby. She figured most were strangers to one another; what made the story great was that they were united here in a spontaneous outpouring of frustration. And when there was emotion, it often led to confrontation. Light the Night was a story about people, lots of people, and that meant viewers.

"I think we may need another camera," the photographer told Singleton on his two-way radio. "There are cars lined up all the way down the street."

"I don't have anyone to spare. Do the best you can. Paul's coming out to do some interviews."

Wilson Ruggles approached Channel Three's studios in his company-owned Jaguar and headed for his personalized parking spot in front of the station. His name, "Ruggles", was painted on the space and on the curb. It had faded a bit and wasn't quite the way he wanted it. He decided he'd call the head of maintenance into his office and put him on the job right away.

As he neared the station, though, he saw cars double-parked, and a crowd with picket signs in front of the three-story building that housed the offices and studios of Channel Three. Could they be upset at one of his editorials? Ruggles tried to recall what he had recently said on the air, but couldn't think of anything that would cause protesters to come armed with pickets.

By now he'd entered the station's driveway. The crowd was chanting something, so he lowered his window to hear what they were saying. But it wasn't clear.

His parking spot was up front next to the visitors' spaces. He thought about driving around the building and going in the side entrance, but it was too late.

"Hey, that's the guy who comes on after the news!" one woman shouted and motioned with her sign.

Ruggles braked to a stop in the driveway as part of the crowd rushed forward and surrounded his car.

"We like what Paul said this morning, and we want you to do something about it!" The order came from a woman with a small child in her arms.

Ruggles was trapped in his car. What were they talking about?

He read one of the signs. It said, "Light the Night Every Night! Wilson Ruggles, take a stand! Help us!"

Ruggles grabbed his briefcase and forced his door open so he could climb out. A sign reading, "Channel 3, SOS" was shoved in his face. The paint on several of the letters had dripped before it had dried.

"We're afraid to walk in our own neighborhoods!" an elderly man shouted.

Ruggles put his head down and walked toward the entrance. "Sorry, I don't know what the problem is—I'll get my people on it right away."

"What about Light the Night?"

He waved his hand, as if a fly were buzzing in his face. "Put whatever you're complaining about in writing and send it to me. Now let me through here! I'm a busy man!"

As Ruggles reached the front door, a large man in his fifties stepped in front of him and looked him straight in the eye. The two were nose-to-nose. Ruggles felt the man's hot breath on his face.

"Okay, Mr. Channel Three big shot, you listen to me," he said in a deep, steady voice. "My name is Arthur Jackson. Your man, Paul Thomas, came up with an idea we like. What are you going to do about it?"

Ruggles's knees felt like rubber. People began chanting, "Light the night, light it every night!"

"I—I'm not sure," Ruggles' voice cracked as he spoke. "I mean, I really don't know what you're talking about—sir."

"What do you mean, you don't know?" a young man hollered.

Not a second too soon, Phil Nelson, head of station security, rushed out of the front door and to Ruggles's side. "Be cool, everyone," he warned the group that had now grown to about a hundred.

Arthur Jackson was still nose-to-nose with Ruggles, only now he had ahold of the general manager's suit lapels and the hundred-dollar tie.

"Hey, brother, it's okay." The security guard put his hand on Jackson's shoulder. "Mr. Ruggles here must not have been watching his own station this morning, that's all."

"I find that hard to believe." Jackson released Ruggles's suit as he was pulled away. "But just tell your boss we're tired of all the killings, the shootings, and the gang bangin'. We want him to get off his rear and do something! You read me?"

Ruggles straightened his coat and wiped his hair out of his eyes. Then, using the burly security guard as a shield, he ducked past the crowd and through the station entrance without a word.

When the glass door closed behind them, the shouting outside was muffled, but still threatening. Nelson let out a whistle of relief. "Are you all right, Mr. Ruggles?"

"Shut up! Why didn't you call the police when those idiots first arrived? They might have killed me."

Before Nelson could reply, Ruggles headed toward the security door, cursed at the receptionist, then shouted, "Open the door! Now!"

CHAPTER TWO

Fred Taylor, Channel Three's news director, had spoken by cellular phone to those working the news assignment desk on his way to work. He'd heard Thomas's comments about Light the Night, and at the time, hadn't given it much thought. In his mind, it was good studio interplay between anchors—maybe a little long, but it gave the impression that the newscasters on Channel Three really cared about the community.

Fred was just relieved that Thomas hadn't mentioned the word "church", or said "amen" or "bless you" on the air. When Fred had first been hired at the station a year before, Ruggles had informed him that Thomas was a so-called born-again Christian. After that, Paul and Fred had had several heated discussions about what Fred did not want to hear on the news.

One of their closed-door meetings came to mind. Fred could still hear the words.

"Why doesn't this station give more attention to stories about religion?" asked Thomas.

"When it's newsworthy, we cover it."

"Oh, come on, Fred," Thomas said, "you know that's not true. About the only time this station mentions religion is Easter, Hanukkah, or if the pope's prostate gland is inflamed."

Fred had struggled to keep from laughing.

"Fred, a person's faith impacts every part of his life. Our viewers—"

"I don't care. That kind of thing is private. I just don't want any hint of religion on my newscasts."

Thomas had smiled and had gotten up from his chair. "You don't have to worry about me. But like it or not, I'm praying that one of these days you personally will know what the Good News is all about."

The subject had remained dormant until a month ago when a magazine article had detailed Thomas's personal relationship with Jesus Christ. Both Fred and Wilson Ruggles had hit the roof. The three of them had had another talk behind closed doors.

"You need to understand this, Paul," Fred said as Ruggles rocked back and forth in his office chair. "We don't want to see any more of that religious stuff in print. What you do and say at your church is one thing, but no more Jesus articles. When you speak out in public, you represent Channel Three, and we don't all feel the way you do about religion."

Ruggles had nodded his agreement, but Thomas hadn't backed down. He told them they had no right to keep him from saying what he believed when he was not on the air. "My faith in Jesus Christ is what gives me reason to live," he'd told them. "It's personal, yes, but if I'm asked to share it, like I'm doing now with the two of you, or in a magazine article, I will. But I do promise never to use it in a way that would be unfair to any of you."

Thomas's next comment had stuck with him.

"Fred, I believe my faith in Christ makes me a better news anchor and reporter."

Ruggles laughed. "Yeah, right!"

"How's that?" Fred had asked.

"Because if I report the news in a biased way, I'm not being true to my faith as a Christian."

The men had not discussed it since.

Marcia Willis, a reporter for the *Los Angeles Examiner*, had planned to spend her morning researching and setting up interviews for future stories. Instead, she was sent to check out a ruckus at the studios of Channel Three.

While walking up the concrete steps from the sidewalk, she spotted her photographer emerging from the crowd of demonstrators. She couldn't miss him; his bright smile told her he had gotten what he was after. "Hey, Marcia. I got a great shot of a protester grabbing this guy's tie and holding him up by his throat." He chuckled. "Looked like his eyes were going to pop out. It was Ruggles, the station GM."

"Super. Call the desk and tell them what you have. Find out if they want you to stay here for a while, in case more happens. I'm going to get the reaction inside."

She opened the door to the front lobby and walked to the reception area. There, behind a long desk piled high with envelopes and UPS and Fed-Ex overnight deliveries, was a frazzled-looking, skinny woman in her fifties. Her wire-framed glasses were pushed down on a rather long and crooked nose, and all Marcia could see was her head. The woman was nodding into a telephone headset and thanking a caller. Marcia stepped closer and saw a full cup of coffee next to the switchboard. She figured the coffee had gone cold after the first sip.

The woman looked over her nose through smudged glasses with a cracked lens. "What do you want?"

"I'm Marcia Willis, with the *Examiner*. I'd like to talk with Paul Thomas or Wilson Ruggles." Marcia pointed to the demonstrators. "I'm doing a story about what's going on out there."

"Well, I'd like to know myself. I come to work, just before the morning news ends, get ready to drink my coffee and, blam—everybody in the world starts calling." She stopped and answered another call, then continued. "Fifteen years at the station, never seen the likes of it. Mr. Ruggles starts swearing at me—I don't have to take that. It wasn't this way before he came, I'll tell you that."

Marcia wasn't interested in this woman's problems, but she

also knew she had to get by her to see Thomas or Ruggles. "I know you're terribly busy," she said in her most understanding voice, "but could you tell Paul or Wilson that I'm here?" *Maybe if I use their first names, she'll think I know them.*

The receptionist answered three calls and put two others on hold, then looked up at Marcia. "Do they know you're here?"

Marcia could tell the woman was familiar with the tricks of those who wanted to get past her, but she'd learned some ways to open doors, too. "I think they'll want to talk with me about a story I'm writing on the station," she countered. "Or would you rather I get all my quotes from people outside and say that you denied me access to station management?"

The receptionist answered a call and put two more on hold, then motioned to a sofa. "Have a seat; I'll see if I can get through to either of them."

Marcia walked a few feet to an uncomfortable-looking sofa and stood studying a wall filled with framed photos of Channel Three's on-air people, every hair in place, every smile just right. She noticed two empty spaces—probably victims of the revolving door at Channel Three. She vaguely remembered reading about two news anchors whose contracts weren't renewed, but she couldn't think of their names. Obviously, whoever was in charge of the photos hadn't gotten around to rearranging the lineup. The talent was in alphabetical order; Paul Thomas's photo was in the second row.

She'd never met Thomas in person, but she thought he was one of the rare professionals in TV news. Since moving to the city, she'd watched him over the years, and felt comfortable with his style. What stood out was his ability to interview guests on the set. His questions were often tough, but he was always fair. People at the paper who knew him said that he was a very private man, content to be with his family. The two words that seemed to best describe Paul Thomas, according to those close to him, were integrity and respect. She also knew that his sense of humor could be off-the-wall.

She remembered reading a magazine article about him not long ago in which he'd been very open concerning his Christian faith. According to the story, he'd been with the station for eleven years, but he made it clear that he'd not allowed himself to be defined by either his profession or Channel Three. Marcia hoped he'd give her a few minutes.

After sitting on the sofa and finding it even more uncomfortable than it looked, she scanned the photo gallery again. Interesting mix of faces. Racially diverse, with an emphasis on youth. But something seemed odd. It took her a while, and then she realized that the only management-type on the wall was Wilson Ruggles.

Boom! Instinctively, Marcia ducked as a large panel of glass shattered to the floor. What had happened? She looked up. Someone had thrown a rock through the lobby's front window.

Fred Taylor arrived at the station that morning by the back entrance. When he stepped into the assignment desk area, a phone was handed to him. On the line was Wilson Ruggles's assistant.

"Fred, Mr. Ruggles wants all department heads in the conference room immediately. It's an emergency."

"What's up?" he asked.

"Very funny," the assistant replied, and hung up.

"What's Ruggles in a panic about now?" he asked Carol Singleton, who stood nearby.

"Well, you just got here. We've got a breaking story in South Central, and there's a big flap over Light the Night."

"Okay, fill me in."

She told him what had happened and then pointed to her desk assistants who were on the phones with viewers, all wanting to talk about Light the Night.

Carol rattled off her battle plan. "I've got Martinez up front shooting the demonstrators, and Paul just joined him to do some interviews. We've got calls into the mayor's office and police chief.

This thing just blew up on us. I think it's really going to be a big story. I can't believe the public response."

Fred didn't know what to think, only that he didn't want to start his day in a meeting with Wilson Ruggles. "Have Paul put a story together for noon. We need sound bites with the mayor or police chief. I'd like them both. I gotta see Ruggles."

The wave of public reaction to Paul Thomas's ad-lib had reached city hall. Most of the members of Mayor Brenda Bodine's staff hadn't heard him make the comment about a year-round Light the Night, but they knew about it now. People from all over Los Angeles were calling: what did the mayor plan to do?

"Mayor's office," answered the young man. "No, I'm sorry, the mayor can't talk to you." He had repeated the same lines over and over. "Give me your name and phone number, and we'll try to have someone from your council member's staff call."

Ian Thornberry, the mayor's chief of staff, stood nearby. He was a gangly sort—an eastern elite snob from Rutgers with a sense of self-importance that went beyond whom he worked for. He'd just taken a call in his office from Channel Three's assignment desk and confirmed that the mayor's office was receiving calls about Light the Night. The station was sending a news crew to interview the mayor who was on her way to city hall from a breakfast meeting.

Thornberry was glad Singleton had not asked what the meeting was about, because the mayor was having secret talks with executives of Regal Brothers, one of LA's largest manufacturers. Tomorrow the company would make the announcement—it was relocating its assembly line, sales staff, and administrative offices to Arizona. Company officials could no longer put up with violent crime and gang threats near the plant on Alameda Street. The cost of private security to protect employees and the property was no longer justified, and more importantly, it wasn't working. Mayor Bodine had fought hard to keep the company from leaving, but it seemed to be a losing battle.

Because of this, Thornberry expected the mayor to arrive back at city hall in a rotten mood. With Regal Brothers pulling up stakes, the city stood to lose millions of dollars in tax revenue, and Bodine's administration would be blamed for another major company leaving Los Angeles. The problem for the mayor was also political; part of what got her elected was a promise to revitalize the business climate. But because of crime, just the opposite was happening.

On any other day, Thornberry would have been in a damage-control mode, but now he had an idea. He prided himself in spotting opportunities before they blossomed, and now he had a hunch about Light the Night. *This just might be a "can't miss" political jackpot.* The chief of staff didn't care about Regal Brothers' sixty-three hundred workers and their families. His idea would benefit one person—himself. His plan would keep the company from moving, and then, if the mayor listened to him, he would not only guarantee her re-election, but she could start making plans for the governor's mansion in Sacramento. He would stick by her every step of the way. *After that, who could tell? The US Senate—and dare he even think it—the White House? Why not?* He didn't especially like Washington, but he loved power.

"I want Paul Thomas fired!" Wilson Ruggles's neck bulged. His face was red, his hair was still messed up, and his hundred-dollar tie was at a cockeyed angle. He glared at those seated around the long, shiny mahogany table in an otherwise drab conference room. "I want him out the door this morning," he shouted at Fred Taylor as he slammed his fist on the table, causing the coffee in two cups to slosh over. "Get him for breach of his personal services contract, negligence, disreputable conduct. . . ." He choked mid-sentence, gagging on his words. "Thomas nearly caused a riot!"

Taylor looked around at the others. "Wilson," he said with a sigh, "we can't fire him."

"Why not?"

"We don't have grounds. It would be a big mistake."

Ruggles glared at Taylor, the only member of his staff who didn't roll over when he made a demand. Taylor did have an advantage. He'd been hired by Ruggles; the others were leftover baggage from the old regime.

"Well, then, take Mr. Holier-than-Thou off the air, buy out the remainder of his contract. He's only got another month left."

"I think you're right, Boss."

Heads turned to the far side of the table where Harvey Rose sat. Rose was the young, well-dressed, schmooze-talking man in charge of Channel Three's promotions department. Ruggles liked him—he had come up with some of the sleaziest on-air ads anyone could remember having seen in the entire country. Besides, Rose called him "Boss." No one else did.

"Paul Thomas has been a pain ever since I came here," Rose said. "He refused to do the voice-over for our series on adult bookstores. And last week he told me he wouldn't be a celebrity bartender at an AIDS-awareness fund-raiser. I say dump him. Get him outta here."

"Wait a minute," Taylor said in an irritated tone. "Let's talk about crime and Light the Night. There's a ton of people waiting to find out what we're going to do." Taylor looked around the room. "Some of those folks out there are afraid to walk the streets in broad daylight. That's what needs our attention—not someone's personal opinions about Paul Thomas."

Eleven miles away from the safety of Channel Three's conference room, a Channel Three reporter was interviewing a UPS deliveryman who had found himself in the middle of a shoot-out on Violet Street during the early morning hours. The first hint of trouble had come when someone in this older, residential neighborhood, two blocks from the Regal Brothers' manufacturing plant, heard three pops in quick succession.

"I was in my truck," the UPS driver was saying, "when I heard loud shots—heavy-duty gunfire. A second later I looked over and saw this guy lying face down and motionless on the sidewalk. Another guy was sprawled on his back, across the curb."

"Tell me what you saw next," the reporter prodded.

"Two guys ducked behind a car. The younger dudes with the heavy weapons backpedaled toward that house over there, blasting away as they went. I think one had—I've seen 'em in the movies—an Uzi machine gun."

"Then what happened?"

"The guy with the Uzi was hit in the chest. It really nailed him. He fell into those bushes near the porch. The police showed up then—they came from opposite ends of the street." The eyewitness paused to swallow and catch his breath. "They screeched to a stop, got out of their cars, took aim with their rifles, and began firing. The guys they were shooting at were up by the porch." He stopped.

"Go on," urged the reporter.

The man lowered his voice. "I wish I hadn't seen what happened next. An elderly woman came out on her front porch, and an officer yelled something like 'don't shoot,' or 'hold your fire.'"

The man shook his head. "One of the guys just turned and opened fire on the old woman. Then the cops let 'em have it."

Paul Thomas was watching a videotape of the confrontation outside Channel Three between Wilson Ruggles and another man.

"This is good stuff, Jack," he called over his shoulder.

The photographer stood behind him, a grin on his face, a cup of coffee in his hand.

"Oh yeah, we've got to use the sound up full of Ruggles and that big protester. I'll start writing the story, and we can insert the mayor's sound pop when the tape gets back to the station."

Thomas was putting together a report on the protest and a summary of last evening's Light the Night event for the *Noon News*. He and Martinez were waiting for another reporter to finish taping an interview with Mayor Bodine.

The phone rang in the editing room, and Paul answered it. The switchboard operator asked if he wanted to meet with Marcia Willis of the *Examiner*. She was waiting for him in the lobby. He had a good idea what she might want. "Why not? I'll be there in just a few seconds."

Paul walked toward the front lobby, wondering if he had met her before. Marcia Willis. He'd seen her byline.

At the door to the lobby, he stopped and peeked through the small glass window. A petite woman sat on the sofa. She wore a frilly, powder-blue dress with white lace at the edges. *She doesn't dress like a newspaper reporter.* She wasn't beautiful, but she was definitely in the top 10 percent. *Doesn't look like a print reporter, either.* Paul chided himself for thinking that and opened the door. "Marcia? Hi, I'm Paul Thomas."

She walked toward him and extended her hand. "Hi. Thanks for seeing me." She was no more than five-two.

Paul gave her hand a firm shake. "Sure, but I don't have much time." He motioned to the sofa.

"You're taller than you look on TV," she said with a smile as they sat down.

"Imagine how I'd look if I did the news standing up."

They both chuckled.

"I'm doing a story on what happened here this morning. What's your reaction?"

I was right—I knew that's why she was here. "I'm surprised, but then again, I'm not. People all over this city are ticked off. They've lost control of their lives and neighborhoods. Maybe Light the Night is their last hope."

"Do you think it'll work every night?"

"That's really up to the people, but I think it's worth a try. You know what the Bible says, 'Let your light shine before men.' So it can't be all bad."

"And don't forget that Sunday school song, 'This Little Light of Mine,'" she countered with a smile.

Paul wondered if she were a believer. "Mind if I ask? Are you a Christian?" She hesitated, and he wondered if he were out of line. "Sorry, maybe I shouldn't have brought that up."

"No, it's okay. Yes, I am a Christian. You—you kind of caught me off-guard."

His eyes brightened. "Well, how about that! There aren't too many of us in this business, are there?"

"Not in print journalism. What about electronic?"

"Probably worse. Sometimes you feel like . . ." He paused, leaving the thought unfinished. "Jesus said the Christian life would be difficult, and He was right."

After talking for a while about Light the Night, and what might happen, Paul excused himself to get back to the editing room.

"Would you like to watch us put together the piece for the *Noon News*?" he asked.

"Thank you, maybe another time. Right now I need to get some quotes from Wilson Ruggles. Could you get me in to see him?" she asked hopefully.

Thomas chuckled. "Marcia, if I thought I could do it, I would. Let's just say, you'll have a better chance if you don't mention my name."

CHAPTER THREE

Ian Thornberry figured it would be good, but this was astounding. Right here, in front of his eyes, Brenda Bodine, the mayor of the second-largest city in America, was jumping up and down in her office. "Ian, I knew you were a winner when I hired you."

Thornberry beamed. He'd expected a few attaboys for his idea, but nothing like this.

When the mayor had first walked past his desk that morning, she looked as if the end of the world had come. She was stunned at the news of the shoot-out between the four undercover narcotics officers and the four drug dealers. Two of the Drug Enforcement Administration agents had died—one was a father of three, and the other had been married just a month. The dead woman, who lived alone, was in her eighties and was deaf.

The four dead suspects were members of the street gang Iron Claw. They were part of a drug ring and had been selling cocaine, heroin, and methamphetamines to employees at Regal Brothers for the past six months. In broad daylight, they'd arranged a deal to transfer twenty pounds of cocaine from one car to another.

For reasons no one would ever know, one of the suspects had pulled a gun and opened fire on the agents. The other gang members had then pulled weapons out of their coats. The first question everyone wanted answered: were standard safety procedures followed by the four agents? If not, two had died because of it.

Mayor Bodine had considered going to the scene, as is common for most mayors following a major tragedy. But when

Thornberry learned that the shooting was near the Regal Brothers' plant, he had persuaded her to change her mind. Since the company was as good as gone, Thornberry wanted to avoid any confrontation between the mayor and angry Regal executives that could be shown on TV or in the papers. And now, instead of jumping out the window, Mayor Bodine was jumping for joy.

"You came up with good strategy that helped us get into office, but this Light the Night stuff is positively brilliant."

Bodine had defeated a three-term incumbent in the last election, thanks to crushing, last-minute mailers on her opponent that Thornberry had dreamed up. He'd also uncovered some political dirt that Bodine had used in a debate; that had clinched it for her.

"So why can't we make the announcement today?" she asked, sitting on her desk.

The mayor wanted a news conference this afternoon. She was eager to tell the city she was calling for Light the Night every night.

"I just think it's best to hold off for now," Thornberry told her. "Do the interview with Channel Three. The crew is waiting outside your office—their story runs at noon."

"Ian, Regal Brothers is going to announce they're leaving tomorrow. Light the Night will be moved to the back page of the paper, and the other TV stations won't even cover it."

"That's why you hired me, Madam Mayor," Ian said in an exaggerated tone. He scooted a chair over to her desk and sat down. "Now, I just talked with the PR guy at Regal Brothers. He's decided to withhold the announcement indefinitely. As you might imagine, they're trying to regroup after the shoot-out. Just do the interview. Tell them you want more community involvement, but don't commit yourself to anything right now. Let's see how things go tonight. If Light the Night bombs, we'd look kind of silly calling for one every night. Let's let Channel Three take the risk and do our dirty work for us, okay?"

He got up then, opened the door, and gave a royal welcome to the TV crew. "Come on in, great to see you. The mayor's ready. Doin' a super job. Watch you all the time."

Wilson Ruggles thought he'd regained his composure. He hoped so, since his secretary was bringing Marcia Willis into his office for an interview. While Ruggles enjoyed doing his editorials for Channel Three, he got a bigger kick out of seeing his name in the paper—better yet when his picture ran alongside the story.

"What can I do for you, young lady?" he asked as his secretary ushered Willis into his office. "Where's your photographer?"

"He left. He got what he needed earlier."

"Well, then let's proceed. I don't normally give interviews to newspaper reporters who just show up in the front lobby." Ruggles paused to ogle her and then winked. "But for you, I'll make an exception."

"What are you going to do about the demonstrators out front?" she asked, apparently unfazed at having been undressed by his eyes.

"They got a little rowdy, smashed a window."

"I was out in the lobby when it happened. Was anyone arrested?"

"We're not pressing charges. We encourage input from the community we serve, even if it's overly enthusiastic." He liked the way he'd stressed, "community we serve."

"I'm told that your station, our newspaper, the mayor's office, and the police and sheriff's departments have been flooded with calls from people who heard Paul Thomas's comments about Light the Night."

"Thomas had no business committing our station to anything. He was an idiot to say that." Ruggles leaned forward. "Uh, the comment about Thomas being an idiot is off-the-record, of course."

"Sorry, you didn't say it was until after you'd called him that.

You consider him an idiot, then?"

Ruggles bristled and sat back in his chair. "Wait a second. I let you come in here as a courtesy. And now you're out to get me?"

"I'm not out to get anyone, but you didn't answer my question. Why did you say Paul Thomas is an idiot? That's a strange way to talk about one of your news anchors."

"Marcia, you seem like a smart woman. Surely you know that on-air people have to be careful about what they say. Paul Thomas got himself in trouble by saying some things he shouldn't have."

"Is his job in jeopardy?"

"I don't like where this is going."

"Well, just answer my questions. Do you think Paul Thomas is an idiot, and are you going to fire him?"

"The interview is over."

Willis closed her notebook and stood. "I take it, the answers are 'yes', you believe Paul Thomas is an idiot; 'yes', his job is in jeopardy; and 'no', you don't want to expand Light the Night."

Ruggles slammed his fist on his desk. "Get out of my office!"

"This is *Channel Three News at Noon*. Paul Thomas, Karen Franklin, and Rita Roberts with weather. *News Three* for Southern California, the news that hits home."

"Good day at noon," said Paul on a two-shot with Franklin. "We have three major stories in Los Angeles. The first is a violent shoot-out just hours ago downtown near Regal Brothers manufacturing. And last night a drive-by shooting left a sixteen-year-old girl and a six-month-old boy dead, and a forty-two-year-old man in critical condition in South Central LA."

"And later," Karen jumped in, "people by the thousands are letting us know they want the violence to stop. Paul will have that, but first, our top story—two DEA agents, an innocent bystander and four suspects have been killed in an undercover drug deal. We go to

Channel Three reporter, Alan Ortiz, who has a live report."

Ortiz stood at the crime scene in front of yellow police tape. He told as much as he knew, then brought in the UPS eyewitness who had watched the shoot-out from his truck. While he was talking, the camera panned to several bodies, covered with sheets. Just then, an officer removed the sheet over the woman on the porch, and a crime technician with a camera shot several pictures of the body. On the front lawn, another officer marked the location of spent shell casings with little flags on wires.

Next, Paul introduced a report at the scene of the drive-by shooting. The reporter told viewers that the wounded man, ironically, was an employee of Regal Brothers, and was not expected to survive. He was the father of the dead baby.

Paul was then on a two-shot with Franklin again. "Karen, people are telling us this kind of thing has to be stopped, and from what we've seen this morning, that just might be possible. Something big is happening in our city unlike anything in the eleven years I've been here. We've had peace marches, neighborhood-watch programs, and citizens' patrols, but nothing like this. Here's how it started."

Paul's taped report began with a shot of Karen Franklin on the morning newscast reading the story about the previous evening's Light the Night event. This was followed by a replay of Paul's suggestion that the event be a nightly one, and then his challenge to viewers to speak up.

The video showed the loud demonstration outside Channel Three, an interview with a woman who wanted Light the Night every night, and words from Mayor Bodine. Her comments weren't as strong as Paul had hoped they would be, but useful enough that viewers would know city hall was flooded with calls, too.

The footage of Ruggles and the protester was next. Experience had taught Paul that if those in the studio react to a story, so will the viewing audience. Paul smiled now as he watched the floor crew and his co-anchor. They were mesmerized by the video.

"Look at Ruggles," Karen exclaimed. "He's scared out of his wits." The floor crew was laughing hysterically.

Paul's report ended with a montage of crime scenes from recent weeks. Under the video were the words of people in their various neighborhoods telling what was happening to their city.

"We checked with the police and the sheriff," Paul was saying, "and they tell us that hundreds of you have called their departments. In fact, at one time the police switchboard needed emergency procedures when all lines were overloaded. So please refrain from dialing 911 when you want to let someone know how you feel about Light the Night."

Wilson Ruggles dialed his own version of 911—Fred Taylor's extension. Fred picked up the phone in his office, but had no chance to speak.

"Taylor, did you just see what Thomas put on the air?" Ruggles was spitting into the phone.

"Yeah, I saw it. Actually, I thought it was pretty good. Might turn into something that moves us ahead of Channel Five."

"He's as good as gone, I tell you! I want him fired!"

"Wilson, I've got two other breaking stories right now, and I don't have time to talk. Later, okay?"

Ruggles heard the line click.

"Ian, I knew I shouldn't have listened to you!" Brenda Bodine stood beside her desk and glared at her chief of staff. She picked up an empty coffee mug from her desk and clutched it in one hand. Was she thinking about throwing it at him? She stomped her foot. "That was my idea and I wanted to be first to announce it!"

She had just been informed that council member Francie McMillan was calling for a news conference to push an expanded Lignt the Night.

Ian Thornberry shifted uneasily in his chair, ready to duck if one of the mayor's desktop mementos came flying his way. His political stock had fallen faster than the crash of 1929. He looked at the mayor, who now stood in front of him, her hands on her hips. For one of the few times in his political life, Thornberry was caught off-guard, and now he had to try to salvage what, just a few hours ago, seemed like a can't-miss opportunity.

The mayor continued to glare at him. "This just burns me up, Ian!"

Thornberry leaned back in his chair. He hoped his body language was more reassuring and persuasive than the words he was about to say. "I've cut down the amount of media coverage McMillan will get. I talked with all the other television stations and called the news-talk radio stations and told them what she was going to say. They agreed that the news conference will be publicity for Channel Three and Paul Thomas. I don't think they'll come."

"But the newspapers will be here, and they'll plaster it all over the front page," she whined. "You blew it!"

"I still think we're okay," he said without much conviction.

"How about if McMillan and I do the news conference together?"

Thornberry knew that the mayor thought of McMillan as her biggest competition. The third district council member from Reseda was active in anti-crime programs, and Thornberry considered her the strongest challenger for the next mayoral election. "Her people told me she wants to do it alone," he said.

"Well, can't you convince that publicity hog that having me there would make it look like a bigger deal?"

"I already tried that, and the answer was 'no.'"

"What about giving her my swing vote on that jobs project she's pushing for?"

"Tried that, too. No deal."

"This is really bad, Ian." She walked over to the window and looked out at the city.

Thornberry hadn't figured on being beaten to the punch by McMillan, or her staff. He planned to ride Brenda Bodine's coattails to higher office. Now, McMillan had stolen his ticket to the big time.

"Don't worry," he said as he moved toward the door. "We'll still come out on top of this."

"What do you mean, 'we'?" the mayor said coldly. "Your job is on the line, Ian."

CHAPTER FOUR

"Paul Thomas made a comment this morning that captured the imagination of people all over Los Angeles," Bill Randall, the news anchor at 6 P.M., was saying. "Some think we're ready to not only take back our streets, but make our sidewalks and homes safe again."

Paul was excited and felt a sense of awe as he awaited his turn to go on the air. *It's true, my idea is actually beginning to take the city by storm.*

At six o'clock that evening, Consolidated Edison had reported a slight power surge in metropolitan Los Angeles. More than a million porch lights had flashed on at the same time. Light the Night had returned, and Paul Thomas was leading the charge.

Paul was told that thousands of people had made plans to be outside for much of the evening, but most had delayed that for at least ten or fifteen minutes. They wanted to learn the latest on the drive-by shooting, the DEA gun battle, and Light the Night. So, after they turned on their porch lights, they switched on their televisions for the local news.

The first seven minutes of the 6 P.M. news detailed the DEA shoot-out and confirmed earlier reports that the dead suspects were gang members with links to Regal Brothers. There were unanswered questions about how the agents could have been caught off-guard, but the thrust of the story was the tragedy of this event for the dead agents and their families.

Reporters combined for team coverage and focused on the suspects, agents, and the reaction from local law enforcement leaders. The elderly woman's neighbors were interviewed; it was discovered that the dead woman was the widow of a retired Regal Brothers assembly line foreman.

The DEA story was followed by coverage of the early morning drive-by shooting. Paul had learned earlier that the forty-two-year-old male victim, Raul Fernandez, had slipped into eternity about the same time council member McMillan was holding her news conference on Light the Night. An interview with the man's widow showed a woman completely broken, her husband and baby son taken without warning.

Paul knew that people all over the city were watching. But tonight, instead of a quiet resignation that this was their life and they could do nothing to change it, he sensed a growing anticipation that something exciting was about to happen. Despite the tragedies that had hit the city, overall crime was down the night before, and everyone wanted it to happen again.

Randall was introducing Paul now. The director in the TV control room called for a switch to another camera. Bill and Paul were shown on set in a two-shot.

"Paul, after what we've just seen—a day of terrible tragedy in our city—I know we're ready for what you have."

"Bill, we've all heard of the light at the end of the tunnel." Paul turned to another camera that took him in a close-up. "Right now, lights are switching on all over metropolitan Los Angeles. And each one could mean we're about to leave a dark tunnel of violence that has nearly choked our city to death."

The director called for a special effect that put Paul and a reporter in two boxes on the screen. Above them a graphic read, Light the Night.

Paul continued, "Channel Three's Heidi Taddie joins us now from Santa Monica."

He watched the live shot on a studio monitor and saw that the reporter was at a neighborhood block party. She was tall, slender, a perky blonde in her mid-twenties, and on this night, Paul felt she was a welcome relief from the devastating news of the day. *Good going, Heidi, you're having fun, and you found a great group of people.*

"Paul, I'll be here this evening. These people say they're serious. They've suffered three shootings, a stabbing, two rapes, and four home break-ins in a four-block area in the last month, nearly all traced to gangs—"

"And it's going to stop!" shouted a man standing next to her. "We'll be back out tonight, porch lights on, flashlights charged, video cameras in hand, and two-way radios on-line. And that's just for starters!" A crowd behind him started cheering.

Paul was brought back in a double box shot with the reporter. "Heidi, it sounds to me as if Light the Night is going to continue."

"And it's not just here," she said. "People all over LA are doing this. They say they have some big surprises for gang members who've had it their way for too long. Paul, did you ever think what you said this morning would result in this?"

A special effect zoomed her out of the screen and brought Paul back. "All of us here at Channel Three are amazed at what we've seen and heard from many of you. You want Light the Night expanded. Well, now there's a call for the city to extend it for another six days. Here's more on the story."

A taped report from Paul began with the crowd chanting at the morning demonstration outside Channel Three's lobby. The shots of Arthur Jackson holding Wilson Ruggles by his necktie, Ruggles stammering and sputtering, brought guffaws of laughter from those in the studio.

"I want that guy to be my agent the next time I deal with Ruggles," said Randall's co-anchor Nancy Chen.

Everyone roared with laughter.

"Hey, there's Jackson again," said the floor director.

They had missed the first words of Francie McMillan's news conference. Now Jackson was shown standing behind her.

"... once a year is not enough," McMillan was saying. "Let's light up the Los Angeles area every night for the rest of the week. Let's meet our neighbors and talk about how to change what's killing the soul of this great city!" The petite, dark-haired woman smiled a smile that could melt her coldest critic. She was the most articulate member of the council, including Mayor Bodine.

Jackson was shown next. With quiet dignity, he apologized for roughing up Ruggles. "What I did was wrong, and I want Mr. Ruggles to know I'm sorry. We've got problems, big problems, and starting tonight, with God's help, we'll work on solving them in a nonviolent way."

The two men in their early twenties were dressed in T-shirts, dark pants, and black high-top basketball shoes. They both wore baseball caps turned backward; one said "Sox," and the other cap was blue with the Los Angeles Dodgers logo on it.

The guy with the Dodgers cap backed the pickup truck into the driveway of a two-story house. The sun was just about ready to set, and the two sat in silence for a few minutes. "Anyone see us?" he whispered to his friend.

"Nah, let's do it." The other guy reached for the passenger door, but the driver grabbed his arm and held on.

"What's with you, man? I'm in charge, got it? You move when I tell you to. Let me disconnect the overhead light in the cab, so it won't turn on when the doors open." He hoped his partner wasn't getting sloppy.

They climbed out of the truck and left the doors slightly ajar for a fast getaway. Each of the men carried a blue nylon duffel bag in one hand, and the leader held a small toolbox in his other hand. They quietly slipped along the side of the garage until they came to a door.

A large-sounding dog barked three times, and the leader held his hand up. They stopped.

A woman a few houses away yelled at the dog to shut up.

"Let's see if we have to jimmy the door, or if they've made it easy for us," the one with the toolbox said, and he tried the door. It was unlocked. They stepped inside the garage.

Isn't it something? thought the man with the Dodgers cap. *People put double locks on their front doors and leave the side doors open. Rich idiots.*

Using their penlights, the two men found the door that gave them access to the home.

"I'm sure no one's home, but be careful," said the guy in charge.

He figured this would be a good night—a home in an upscale neighborhood, no gates, no alarm system, and no security guards. Their first break-in was two years earlier—done mostly out of boredom and curiosity. It was easy and exciting, but neither of them knew exactly what to do with their new computer and two television sets. They remembered then about a guy they knew, a member of a street gang called Insane Rulers, who dealt in hot merchandise. When they found him, to their surprise, he bought their stuff right on the spot. Not long after that, they began dealing exclusively with the gang, and six months later joined up. They'd been given the gang names, "Ruler One and Ruler Two," and were known as the "Ruler Brothers."

The leader insisted on only two break-ins a week—on Sunday mornings and Monday nights. Their first big score was on a Monday night; the homeowners were at a pro football game.

They moved around in different areas of LA, sometimes in territory claimed by their rival gang Iron Claw, other times in posh neighborhoods like San Marino, the one they were in tonight. The key was to never establish a pattern the police could follow. So far, it had worked, and the money was good—a lot better than if they were flipping burgers at McDonald's or putting a swirl on Dairy Queen ice cream cones.

Three years ago, they were part of the LA unified public school system. They were gifted on the basketball court and baseball field, but were without a clue in the classroom, and were never academically eligible to play sports. They'd graduated in the same class, but were barely able to read or write. After leaving school and several dead-end jobs, they decided the only thing they were good at was working the street. They joked to other gang members that they were all-stars in the NBA, the National Burglary Association.

"You check upstairs for jewelry, cash, and cameras," the leader told his partner. "I'll stack the stereo equipment and TVs by the door."

The residents were obviously on vacation and had left an open invitation to burglars; three days of newspapers were bleaching in the driveway and the front porch light beamed all day long.

The two had worked the day before. Sunday mornings were easy, although they liked to party Saturday nights and were often hung over the next day. Their Sabbath routine, as they called it, was the same each week. Around eight o'clock on Sunday morning they'd drive to a residential street and park at the end of the block. Then they simply watched for those families who were leaving for church. They were easy to spot—mom and dad were all dressed up, and their children were always fussing or fighting in the car's backseat. They were usually in a hurry, and occasionally the father would reach back and swat one of the kids. It was strange, they thought, how churchgoing folk always seemed to be yelling at each other on Sunday mornings.

Actually, the two men didn't care what the families did or where they went, just as long as the home was empty for at least fifteen minutes. When the family pulled out of the driveway, the men's truck was close behind. No one had ever challenged them. Nonchurchgoing neighbors were usually sleeping in, playing golf, or on unseen, find what they wanted, load up, and be gone in minutes. The police had tagged them the "Amen Burglars."

Tonight was a bonanza. An upstairs closet contained camcorders and still cameras, and in a jewelry box in the master bedroom they discovered a mini gold mine. Downstairs, they'd disconnected a top-of-the-line stereo system and a sophisticated computer setup and stacked them near the back door.

They made only two trips in and out of the house. On the second trip out the side door, the leader of the two spotted a near-new set of King Cobra golf clubs in a brand new leather bag. He slung the bag over his shoulder and headed to the truck. His partner was right behind him. "Hey, so when's our tee-time?"

"Shut up, let's get out of here."

They threw their loot in the truck bed and jumped into the front seat.

"What the—" the driver said in shock. "There's some kind of a club on the steering wheel!"

Suddenly, headlights blinded the two men.

"Police! Freeze!"

How could this be happening? They'd never even seen a cop before and now they were busted? Two officers raced to each door of the truck and leveled their guns at the men.

"Well, look what we have here," the officer near the driver's door sneered. "I think we just caught ourselves the famous 'Amen Burglars.'"

The officer hauled the driver out of the truck and handcuffed him. He looked over at the right front fender where his buddy was also being cuffed and getting razzed by what appeared to be a civilian security patrol.

"I'd say the Amen Burglars had better start saying their prayers!"

"Hey, pal." A security patrol member put his face only a couple of inches from the leader's face. "When you get to prison you can tell all your dirt-bag friends that there's a new sheriff in town—it's the people."

As Paul Thomas wrapped up his segment on the 6 P.M. news, he wondered if he should say what he was feeling. He believed that what people once thought was impossible was actually beginning to happen. Many of the streets and neighborhoods that had been surrendered to criminals were now at least up for grabs. Law-abiding citizens had the opportunity to take control; encounters like the one with the Amen Burglars could become commonplace.

As Paul reached the end of his script, he decided to go ahead and say it. "Friends, let me tell you something," he said, sounding like someone's next-door neighbor. "It's our job as television news journalists to report the news, all the news, and to do it truthfully. But most of the stories we choose focus on the bad things that happen. And that's not telling the complete truth. So there may be a change coming. People are demanding a permanent change. The members of our community are sick and tired of being victims." Paul tried to ignore the picture in his mind of the producer and the director falling off their chairs in the control room. "From now on, those of us at Channel Three will report what you want. If it means Light the Night every night for one week, one month, one year, or forever, we'll be involved. We need to hear from you. Contact your politicians, the police, and the sheriff's department. But most of all, stay in touch with your neighbors."

Paul Thomas turned to anchors Randall and Chen. His report was over, and he was glad he'd followed his heart. For he was convinced that something was happening in metropolitan Los Angeles that had never been seen before.

CHAPTER FIVE

Tuesday morning, September 12

Fred Taylor was at home, still in his bathrobe, when he slipped the morning *Examiner* out of its protective plastic bag and opened the paper to the front page. The headline, "Six Dead in DEA Shoot-out," was day-old news. That was why television news could beat the pants off newspapers. Besides, television was usually the first with pictures. Fred loved the strength of television news; it was immediate, and it carried emotion. But he was also aware that television, with its limitations of time and only one shot at the audience, seldom brought understanding. He settled back on his sofa, a mug of coffee in hand, to see if the *Examiner* had given the story depth or perspective. But his attention was diverted to a small photo he happened to notice at the top of the front page, above the headline. The photo and caption previewed a story in the local section. There, in color, with eyes bulging and tongue protruding, was a close-up shot of Wilson Ruggles in the grasp of protesters. Under the photo were the words:

Ruggles Struggles
To See the Light
Local News, B-1

Fred turned to the local section and saw the same photo, only much larger, of Ruggles being grabbed by the necktie. Underneath was Marcia Willis's article on Light the Night. She had covered the demonstration at Channel Three and the pressure on Ruggles to extend the anti-crime program, but there was much more.

Fred read the story and thought it was a remarkable piece. Sure, Ruggles came off as a buffoon. So what? That was easy. What made it exceptional journalism was that Marcia Willis had captured the excitement sweeping the city.

Fred read her account of the dramatic arrest of the Amen Burglars. Her interview with members of the patrol made him want to stand up and cheer. But it didn't end there. She'd written of other encounters during the night involving people who were looking out for each other. Marcia had written about one of them in detail.

Someone had been stabbed near Delano Park in Van Nuys. Over the year, this neighborhood in the San Fernando Valley had been hit hard by "taggers." Gangs, wannabes, and independent punks roamed the streets at will, marking their territory with spray-painted graffiti.

At 9:31 P.M., a squad car with two police officers skidded to a stop at the scene. Grant Peters, described by Willis as a barrel-chested man in his mid-forties, ran up and identified himself as a resident of the area and leader of a newly organized citizens' patrol.

From what police could piece together, Peters was apparently parked in a van across the street from two teenagers who were spray-painting "SAY-R"—gang markings for Insane Rulers—on walls and cars. Bobby Silva, a member of the patrol, was videotaping them from a window in the van. Other members of the patrol were positioned just down the block and were in two-way radio contact with Peters. They were about to call police when an elderly man came out of one of the houses and confronted the boys, who turned on the man and started beating him.

Two other patrol members ran up to help the elderly man,

quickly laying the boys out. Then, from out of nowhere, another teenager with a knife snuck up behind them. Peters got out of his van to cut him off, but the teenager turned and stabbed Peters in the hand. Peters grabbed the knife, and during the ensuing struggle, the knife pierced the boy's heart.

The Examiner has learned that the dead boy was Danny Escobedo, the story finished, *the sixteen-year-old brother of Jorge Escobedo, leader of the Insane Rulers gang. Escobedo and his gang are known to every law enforcement officer in California. Insane Rulers have replaced Iron Claw as the most notorious gang in the Los Angeles area, perhaps in the state. Jorge Escobedo is a suspect in two murders, is believed to be the drug lord of a heroin ring, and is number six on the FBI's Ten Most Wanted list. A national television program featured Escobedo in a segment a month ago.*

Fred put the paper down, and looked again at the writer's name. Marcia Willis. Her story ended with comments from Ruggles that Paul Thomas should not have said what he did without the station's approval, and that Thomas's job may be in jeopardy. Fred winced when he read that Ruggles had called Paul an idiot. He knew what was coming, and sure enough, minutes later the phone rang.

"If you don't fire Thomas today, I'm going to fire you!" Ruggles exploded. Fred held the receiver away from his ear. "I'm looking at this picture in the *Examiner*. . . ."

Fred heard what sounded like the newspaper being slammed down on something hard.

"This story makes me look like a retard! And that picture with the guy holding me by my tie! I'm the laughingstock of this city!"

"Wilson, let's talk about it when we get to the station. What's printed is printed. There's nothing we can do right now, okay?"

"He's gone, and if you don't do it, you're gone. Got it?"

Before Fred could reply, Ruggles hung up.

"Got it." Fred stared numbly at the phone. It was seven in the morning. He would get ready for work, but before doing that, he would call the *Examiner* and leave a message for Marcia.

Paul Thomas sat behind his desk in his office, a large paper cup of coffee in his hand, the one he had to deny himself each weekday morning until he got off the air. This so-called gourmet java from the cafeteria vending machine was okay, but nothing like Starbucks' coffee, which to him was like a taste of heaven.

He'd had a short turn-around, arriving back at the station less than three hours after he got off the air the night before. It was remarkable what one could do on only two hours' sleep. It was his fault, of course; he'd said yes when Fred asked him to put together a taped package for the 11 P.M. news and be on the set. He was thrilled with what had happened during the continuation of Light the Night. It was more than he could have ever hoped for. Unfortunately, it was one in the morning when he finally got home. Maddie was asleep, so after crashing on the living room sofa, he was back up and into work at four. With his schedule, sometimes two days would pass before he and Maddie saw each other in person.

He smiled, stretched his arms in the air, and then put his hands behind his neck. He'd asked the Lord for a more significant role at the station, if it was His will. Now he had it. Paul remembered what he often told others; be careful when you ask God for something to happen—it just might.

He picked up the *Examiner* off his desk and looked once again at the story by Marcia Willis under the photo of Ruggles and the protesters. *There he is, our fearless leader.* Paul read again the part in the story where Ruggles hinted that the anchorman was on shaky ground and then called him an idiot. *Well, at least I'll go out in a blaze of idiotic glory,* Paul thought as he flipped to the op-ed pages. An editorial headline stood out: "Keep the Lights On."

The writer believed the residents of metropolitan Los Angeles now had a chance to drastically and permanently reduce the kind of horror and heartbreak detailed on page one. The editorial praised Paul Thomas for first suggesting that the event be extended and then promised that the *Examiner* would support councilwoman McMillan's call to extend Light the Night. Finally, the paper pledged to give as much information as possible to readers who wanted to involve their neighborhoods. The name of a contact was suggested for community patrols and awareness groups; the paper suggested calling them "The Light Brigade." Paul liked that idea.

Paul chuckled as he read the last few lines of the editorial. The writer referred to the part of Marcia Willis's story that said Paul might be fired and then posed a question to Wilson Ruggles and Channel Three: *Why would you want to fire Paul Thomas, the Captain of the Light Brigade?*

Paul downed the last of his coffee and left his office. He wanted to see what Fred Taylor thought.

Fred Taylor knew that most people who worked in major market television news lived and died for what was printed on the piece of paper he held in his hand. He wouldn't put it quite like that, but it often decided who was hired and fired.

His assistant had just handed him the Nielsen ratings results, and he was stunned. Fred glanced up and saw Paul standing in the doorway. "Good morning, Paul." He reached for the morning *Examiner* and held it up. "Or should I call you 'Captain'?"

Paul smiled. "'Idiot Captain' to you, if you don't mind."

Fred shook his head. "Quite an editorial—first time I've seen the newspaper say anything good about us. Have a seat."

Paul sat on a small sofa. "What's with Ruggles? Am I about to get canned?"

Fred picked up the ratings results. "Not after he reads the battlefield numbers from last night."

"How'd we do?"

Fred looked at the sheet of paper that to most people was a baffling maze of numbers, fractions, and abbreviations. Two numbers were important: one showed the percentage of all televisions turned on during a given time—a share, and the other measured the number of homes watching certain programs—a rating. In metropolitan Los Angeles, called a market, each rating point was equal to 50,000 homes, or 133,500 people, using the recent census finding of 2.67 people per household.

Five hundred homes in the LA area had electronic meters hooked up to their television sets. When the TV was turned on, the meter recorded the channel and how long it was activated. The homes chosen represented a demographic sample of the city as a whole. Each weekday morning, the A.C. Nielsen company checked the data from the meters, and then the ratings results were sent to stations that subscribed to the service.

Fred studied his two most important newscasts for advertising dollars. "This is incredible. Come here." Paul walked to the desk, and Fred pointed to Channel Three's column of numbers. "Our six o'clock news did a 21 rating and 39 share!"

"Awesome. How about the 11 P.M.?"

"You won't believe it. We got a 26 rating and 48 share!" He scratched some figures on a notepad, then looked at Paul in disbelief. "That's 1.3 million homes." Nearly half of all the TV sets on in the Los Angeles area were tuned to Channel Three.

"Good grief," said Paul. "More than three million people?"

Fred nodded, then opened his bottom desk drawer and pulled out the results of the last rating period. For twenty days in July, Channel Three had averaged a 7 rating and 16 share, losing to Channel Five, which had an 8 and an 18. The numbers from last night were phenomenal, nearly four times higher than the last ratings period. He studied them again. "And look at this, Paul, even your *Noon News* went out of sight." The *Noon News* normally was in the 7 and 21 range. "Yesterday, it did an 18 and 40!"

Paul stared at the numbers. "That's the highest we've ever done at noon."

"By a mile. The best that show once did was a 10 rating."

"How about some expert analysis?" Paul said.

"Well, we had two high-interest crime stories that broke yesterday. But we also had Light the Night."

"So, are you telling me to hold off sending out résumés? Ruggles didn't exactly give me a vote of confidence."

Fred held up the rating results again. "Even Ruggles can't ignore these."

Brenda Bodine was on the phone to Police Chief Daniel Morgan.

"Chief, I need you over here at ten. I'm calling for continuing Light the Night until at least the end of the month. Get your people to outline a plan of action. We're calling a news conference, and I want you to be part of it."

In a corner of the mayor's office, Ian Thornberry sat in an overstuffed chair watching and listening on a speaker phone.

"You can do it alone, can't you?" asked the chief. "I just got a call from Francie McMillan. She wants me to help her with the same thing."

"Daniel, I'm calling in that favor you owe me."

Shortly after Bodine had taken office, Morgan's eighteen-year-old daughter was involved in an altercation at a party, and the mayor had intervened to keep the matter private.

"I'm cashing in the favor now, Daniel, because you know as well as I do that McMillan wants to move into my office. She got the jump on me over this Light the Night thing because I didn't follow my own judgment." She threw an icy look at Thornberry.

The ice slid up and down his spine.

"Well, I'm not going to let that happen again," she continued. "I'm expecting to see you in my office, ready to talk with the news media."

"What would you like me to say?"

Bodine bristled at the question and the tone of the chief's voice. "Very cute, Chief. Now listen to me. I don't have time to beat around the bush. You work for me, not McMillan. You'll tell the media that I'm tough on crime, and you're grateful for my leadership, okay? Or do you want me to script it?"

There was a pause. "How about if I send my assistant chief? He'll probably be your next chief—"

"Daniel, how would you like to be the ex-chief *now*?"

"I'll be there."

From the conference room window, Fred watched the demonstrators outside the station's front entrance. Some in the large group of people carried signs with messages about Light the Night. The crowd was larger than the day before, but the chanters weren't as loud. Today they were praising the station and the city for taking action.

The mood in Channel Three's conference room was giddy. Word of the overnight ratings had prompted much back-slapping, taking the place of the usual back-stabbing, which was the norm since Ruggles's arrival at the station. Fred was relatively new, and when he asked, no one could remember the last time loud laughter had been heard at a staff meeting.

Arlene Zahn, the acting sales manager, had had doughnuts, muffins, and coffee delivered. The comment was made that bread and water were more appropriate for what usually took place in the room. People laughed freely as Wilson Ruggles had not yet arrived.

But then it became quiet in the room, and Fred turned from the window.

"Good morning, Boss," said Harvey Rose, the station's promotions director. Fred had seen Rose keeping his eye on the door, and now he knew why. Rose, a notorious brownnose, wanted to be the first to greet Wilson Ruggles.

"Morning, Rose. Everybody take a chair."

Rose scrambled to sit next to the general manager, while the rest of the staff settled into chairs around the table.

"I've just seen the overnight ratings," Ruggles said. Everyone nodded and smiled at one another. Ruggles held a newspaper which he now threw on the table. "And I've also seen this!"

All smiles disappeared.

"Wilson, forget the story for a second," said Fred. "I think we're on to something with Paul."

"And I'm onto him! He's the cause of this. Because of him," he jabbed a finger at the paper on the table, "I look like some retard. And then, some stupid editorial writer is telling me not to fire—what did that idiot call him?" He fumbled until he got to the op-ed page. "Here it is, 'Captain of the Light Brigade!' Give me a break!"

"Shall we call Paul an idiot, instead?" Fred asked. "That was the word you used to the *Examiner*." Someone in the room gasped.

Ruggles turned red and looked around the room. "All of you hear this. If Paul Thomas isn't fired today," he now glared at Fred, "this station will need a new news director in the morning."

The room was silent.

"I agree with the boss," Harvey Rose said.

Rose shot a smirk at Fred, and Fred felt like stuffing it down his throat. "Shut up, Harvey, you make me sick." Fred paused and then looked at Ruggles, who had taken a seat. "Wilson, this is your station, you run it the way you want." Ruggles gave him a look that said, *You'd better believe it.* "You hired me and you can fire me," Fred went on. "I'll always find another job. But you just said that Paul Thomas caused all of this, right?"

"Yes!"

"Well, if that's the case, what about the overnight ratings? Can we thank Paul for that?"

Silence.

"Mr. Ruggles, I think Fred has a good point," Arlene Zahn spoke up.

Fred stared at her in amazement. Why would she be supporting him? From what Fred knew about her, she seemed only concerned with promoting her own self interests. The juicy gossip about Zahn's past hadn't taken long to reach Fred.

Arlene Zahn was forty-four, married and divorced twice, and had two children, a boy and a girl, now eighteen and sixteen, who lived with her first husband. Her second marriage had lasted six months; she couldn't remember the wedding, only that it was at some chapel in Las Vegas and that she was drunk. She dumped the guy when she learned firsthand of his nasty habit of beating her up.

Zahn was an alcoholic. She'd started drinking in her late teens and soon got in trouble with the law. She'd spent six months at a juvenile detention facility when she was seventeen for stealing a neighbor's car while drunk; she ended up wrapping the brand new Firebird around a light pole.

Her problems were generally overlooked by others who found in her a free spirit and a sense of adventure. Zahn was the life of the party, and while she longed for a permanent relationship with a man, most of her encounters were one-night stands; two resulted in pregnancies which she aborted.

She'd hoped marriage and a family would answer her problems, but when she drank at home, she took her frustrations out on her children. After her first marriage went on the rocks, the court sided with her husband and gave him full custody of the kids.

She began her broadcasting career as a telephone receptionist at an FM radio station heavy into disco. She became the party and event's coordinator for the station and worked part-time in sales; her specialty was getting signatures on sales contracts after late night dinners and several bottles of wine. During this time, she began experimenting with cocaine, heroin, and methamphetamines.

Zahn bounced from station to station and from city to city at a time when opportunities for women began opening up, especially in sales. She enjoyed a degree of success and managed to keep secret her involvement with drugs. At stations where it was known, her sales records caused management to look the other way.

Three years ago, she'd rolled into Los Angeles and found a job as an account manager at KMPC radio, and was there when she learned that Wilson Ruggles had been named general manager at Channel Three. The way she told it, the day he fired the station's sales manager, she saw her chance and began hounding him for an interview. Three days later, she walked into his office and told him she wouldn't leave until he put her in a sales position. She bragged that rather than calling the police, he hired her as an in-house sales assistant.

She immediately went to work in areas she wasn't assigned. Using her charm, she launched a nighttime blitz, wooing, cajoling, and seducing her way into the arms of several major business accounts. All she wanted were signatures on sales contracts—and she got them.

From what most people could tell, Zahn's sales performance so impressed Ruggles that he had fired a productive, twenty-year veteran salesman and gave her his job. Within six months, she was the runaway leader in sales and had been named the acting sales manager. Now she was defending Fred Taylor with apparent sincerity.

How stupid can I be? Fred suddenly realized why she was supporting him. *Arlene, you've seen a Nielsen miracle, and the memory of a 26 rating and 48 share is dancing in your mind.*

"Paul was out of line," Zahn said. "We can take care of that later." The others around the table looked puzzled. "But think about the millions who watched our news last night. Do you know what we could charge for our eleven o'clock spots with those numbers?" Fred noticed Ruggles writing madly on a notepad. "We get $1,017 for each rating point—that's more than $26,000 for a thirty-second spot! Nearly four times what we get now. We can't take their 'hero' away from them."

Arlene, you transparent snake oil saleswoman. You don't give a rip about me or Paul, but you know the way to Ruggles's heart of stone.

The eleven o'clock news had four commercial breaks with four, thirty-second spots in each one. The way Zahn figured it, they could get more than $400,000 in advertising revenue each night, just for one thirty-minute newscast. Fred knew what Ruggles would do.

Chief Daniel Morgan studied the police news release that detailed last night's two murders. The first was a domestic dispute in Hawthorne. According to detectives, a man slapped his wife, then went into the living room to watch TV and read the sports page. The woman told officers she'd tried to talk with him, but he wouldn't put the newspaper down. So she went to their bedroom and returned with a gun. When he still wouldn't answer her, she aimed at the newspaper, pulled the trigger, and shot him in the head. He died before paramedics arrived.

Then, in an area known as Korea Town, the owner of a liquor store was murdered during a holdup. Three witnesses told police officers that two young men, believed to be gang members, shot the man when he tried to stop the robbery. The victim had come to America from Seoul two years earlier with his wife and four children.

Chief Morgan considered himself a realist, a far cry from when he was a wide-eyed, gung ho, crusading police rookie wearing a new badge twenty-eight years ago. Crime was spilling into the streets, and Daniel Morgan was the man who would stem the tide. He'd win the battle against the bad guys.

He glanced at a small picture frame on his desk that contained a wrinkled black-and-white photo of himself, taken his first day on the beat. He shook his head. How naive. In recent years, he figured the best he could do was keep his finger in the dam. But the crime statistics in his hand told him otherwise. Had a window of opportunity opened?

Last night's two murders were tragic—he would never deny that. But on a normal Tuesday night, his homicide detectives would have at least six new murders to investigate. Chief Morgan knew that others might consider his thinking callous. He didn't care. To him, having only two new murders to investigate from the night before was great news.

What stood out even more was the incredible drop in home burglaries, the kind of discouraging crime that hits more people at the grassroots level. On a normal Tuesday night there would be about seventy-five. A year ago on the day Light the Night was held, there were sixty-one home break-ins. Last night there were fifty-three, a 15 percent drop from a year ago, and 30 percent lower than usual.

Auto thefts, aggravated assaults, rapes, and armed robberies were all down. The big news at Channel Three might be the way ratings were going up, but at the LAPD headquarters, the big news was the way crime was going down. *Here's something for your script, Madam Mayor.*

Daniel Morgan folded the sheet of paper, stuck it in his coat pocket, and left his office for city hall. He wouldn't need the mayor to write any script, and there was no need to shoot from the hip. He had some heavy-duty firepower of his own.

"Fred, this is Marcia Willis. I'm at home. I just called my voice mail at work. Thanks for the nice words about my story."

Fred Taylor looked out the window. He liked the soft sound of her voice. "Well, I meant it. Other than complaining to your TV critic or trying to sell a car in the classified ads, I've never called a paper before."

She laughed, and he liked that sound even more.

"So, what's your station's game plan today?" she asked. "Is Paul Thomas fired yet?" He tried to imagine how she looked. *Short, fat, tall? She sounds pushy.*

"Paul Thomas fired? Are you kidding? Not with the ratings skyrocketing like they are."

"Is that off-the-record?" she teased.

He felt a strange flutter in his stomach. *How old is she? Married, single, divorced, kids?* He'd heard through the grapevine about Ruggles blowing his cool with her. "Heck, no. Unlike people who will go unnamed, I try to think before I put my foot in my mouth. I don't care if you use it. It's good for us—tells people who weren't watching that they missed something."

"Would you be available for an interview today?" she asked.

"Why do you want to interview me?" He hoped his question would not cause her to change her mind.

"Well, since Paul is the captain of the Light Brigade, you must be his commanding officer."

Perfect answer, Fred thought. *Clever, witty, and just enough flattery to win me over.* "I'd say I'm more of a sergeant, carrying out the orders for General Ruggles." By the sound of her laugh, she had to be pretty.

"Okay, Sergeant, how about the interview?"

The flutter in his stomach turned into a flop. "Only if I could buy you lunch." He held his breath.

She paused, then, "I guess if I want the interview, I don't have a choice, do I?"

He exhaled, wondering if she had heard him. *She's not exactly falling all over herself for me.* "How about the Green Terrace in Santa Monica—at 11:30?"

"Okay, Green Terrace, Santa Monica—11:30. See you then, Sergeant."

Sergeant. She didn't have to say that. Was she? Does she? We'll see.

Harvey Rose stood and paced the floor of the conference room. He and his staff were discussing how to best continue momentum from Light the Night. He wore a starched white dress shirt with a hard collar and a muted blue tie. His shirt sleeves were rolled up, and his black hair was slicked back. He spoke in machine-gun bursts and waved his arms to bring his points home. In his right hand was a grease pencil, and occasionally he would turn to the easel, about to write an idea down, but he never did.

"Everything we do, every part of this campaign, has one purpose." Rose whirled once again to the easel, but stopped short, and swept the room with deep-set brown eyes. "I want us to look good. Make people think we were the ones behind all of this. I want each of you ready to go with ideas and copy in thirty minutes."

His plan had six parts. He'd briefly gone over it with Fred Taylor and was miffed at the changes he had to make, but overall he had the go-ahead. Harvey knew it was critical to put things in motion as soon as possible. It began with two thirty-second on-air spots. One would show the demonstration at Channel Three.

"I don't want any footage of Ruggles and that protester Arthur Jackson, you hear?" He then told them to find a few seconds of Paul Thomas on the morning news when he first mentioned Light the Night. "Use the part where he asks viewers to contact the station."

He then said he wanted a portion of the live shot with Heidi Taddie at the neighborhood block party. "The spot ends with Ruggles. I wrote his lines last night. You ready to hear it?"

He looked around the table, hoping to see anticipation on the faces of his staff. "Come on, people, show a little enthusiasm for the Harvster. Get this—Ruggles will say, 'You asked for Light the Night, and now Channel Three is helping you hold the light.'" Harvey hesitated, then, "Here's the big finish—you'll love it. The boss says, 'We're ready to shine it on the criminal cockroaches that have had their way too long.'"

There was silence for a moment, and two people coughed. "Uh, that's really good stuff, Harvey," said Andy Fry. Rose wasn't sure if he meant it.

A crew would have the camera and lighting in studio three ready to tape Ruggles in fifteen minutes. Rose told them he would write the rest of the copy when their meeting was over. The person narrating the spot would be 6 and 11 P.M. anchor Bill Randall.

"I want the second spot to show what's happened because of Light the Night," said Rose, "but make sure it looks like we're the ones people should thank."

Harvey told his staff the station had video of Light the Night in action. "We bought home video of those two guys getting arrested. What'd they call them, the Amen Burglars?"

One of his staff members asked, "Didn't our news guys get to the scene in time to show the graffiti taggers getting caught?"

"Now you've got the spirit," said Rose. "Right. We've got great interviews with members of the citizens' patrol."

Rose wanted Ruggles to do the voice-over for the spots, but Fred Taylor said it had to be Paul Thomas. They argued, but Taylor won out; so Fred would owe Rose one. "The promo ends with Mayor Bodine giving LA's support to extending Light the Night."

Rose ordered a print ad made up to go in the next morning's newspaper. He said to make it "caring and catchy." Someone in the room groaned.

He knew that Francie McMillan would agree to be part of a thirty-second spot commending Channel Three for its part in Light the Night. The station would show her on-camera for the opening, and then cover her voice with video of neighborhoods and porch lights.

Rose thought for a moment, then grinned. "How about this? People—people and porch lights. Yeah, that's good. Make sure you get people and porch lights in the copy."

The plan included using interviews with people from the night before and putting them on audiotape, then blitzing radio stations in Los Angeles with as many paid spots as they could get. "Make those spots sound like the Second Coming," he said.

Leslie Gathers was in charge of the radio campaign. "Harvey, does that mean I can mention Jesus in the spot?"

"Huh?" Rose was momentarily thrown off-stride, then realized what she was doing. "I thought I warned you to leave the

Christian stuff out of work."

"Sorry, but you were the one who mentioned the Second Coming."

"Okay, Sister Leslie, why should your Jesus be in the spot?"

"Well, since this is about Light the Night, why not mention Jesus, the Light of the World?" She smiled, which only irritated him more.

"Very clever, Leslie—I just wish you could be that creative for the station."

Rose would handle the two remaining parts of the plan himself. He'd try to get a couple of radio stations to interview Paul Thomas on their morning or afternoon talk shows. He'd thought of getting Ruggles to do the interviews, but decided that might be dangerous, considering what had happened between the general manager and Marcia Willis. Radio people would destroy him on-the-air.

Finally, he would contact Willis and see if he could arrange another meeting between her and Ruggles. If he played everything just right, he could create the biggest promotional campaign the network had seen in years. Light the Night was his chance of a lifetime, and one way or another, the people in New York would remember the name of Harvey Rose.

CHAPTER SIX

As Fred Taylor and Marcia Willis slid into a corner booth, Marcia took a good look at the man seating himself across from her. His appearance closely matched the picture she had in her mind. In his mid-thirties, he was close to six feet tall and about 175 pounds, with dark hair and a ruddy complexion. He wore a dark blue blazer and a red tie. He had a kind face, but seemed to have a bad habit of biting his lip. Nerves, she thought.

"You're not what I expected," he said.

"And what was that?"

A young waiter interrupted them and asked if they were ready to order. "What's your soup of the day?" she asked.

"Split-pea."

"I'll have that and a small chicken salad."

He ordered a cheeseburger, fries, and cole slaw. "And could you put a slice of red onion and a hot pepper on the side?"

His choice for lunch matched his personality. Steady, but with moments of creative fun. They both asked for iced tea.

"Why don't I fit what you expected?" she asked again.

"Actually, you're better than I pictured."

"In what way?" Marcia braced herself for what might be a "line."

"Well, I liked your voice over the phone, but sometimes people turn out to be the opposite of what you think."

If that's the best line he can come up with, this guy's harmless. She grinned. "Sounds like you were afraid a lady wrestler might show up."

He threw back his head and let out a belly laugh. It startled her. Everyone in the room looked their way.

Fred hunched his shoulders and grinned sheepishly. "I'm sorry. But I haven't laughed like that in a long, long time." He leaned across the table. "Tell me about yourself."

"Well, I've worked for the *Examiner* for seven years. "Let's see. . . ." She thought for a moment. "I was born in Nashville and graduated from the University of Tennessee. I'm twenty-eight, single, and . . . ," she beamed, ducking her head, "I'm one of the top reporters for the paper."

"Maybe it's your southern upbringing, but you're very charming," Fred said.

He immediately seemed sorry he'd said that. She pushed back her dark reddish hair and looked at him with enormous eyes.

"Why, thank you ever so much," she said in her best Scarlet O'Hara southern drawl. "Goodness, gracious me, there are still some gentlemen left in this awful, old world."

He blushed slightly. "I deserved that."

The waiter brought their lunch and the discussion turned to Light the Night. He told her how the station was dealing with the public response and offered some general information. But he didn't seem to have his heart in the subject. She knew she didn't.

"Are you married?" she asked. "I don't see a ring."

"Well, that gets right to the point," he said. "I used to be."

"Divorced?"

"No. She was killed."

"Oh, I'm so sorry. Maybe someday you can tell me about it."

"There's not much to tell. I'm still not really sure what happened. We were married less than a year, no kids, but she was six-months pregnant with our first. Some low-lifes shot her while she was out walking our dog one night."

Marcia sat up straight. "Was her name Cynthia?"

"Cynthia Marie Taylor," he said softly.

"Fred, that's awful. I remember the story. There was another reporter on it. I never made the name connection until now."

"We'd only been here a few weeks. Next month it will be a year since she was taken from me."

Neither said anything for a moment.

"Let's talk about something else," he said. "What did you study at Tennessee?"

She told him she was a broadcast journalism major and about how she had tried to get a job in television news after graduation. She'd spent months searching and traveling around the country, but no TV station would hire her without experience, not even the smallest markets. She remembered her feelings at the time; while they never came right out and said it, she was certain they were looking for a woman who was an ethnic minority. She'd then turned to print, and eight months out of school, landed a job with the *Examiner* covering obituaries.

"What would you have told me if I had come to your station looking for a job?" she asked.

"That you needed to get some experience."

"And what about now, Sergeant News Director who liked my story on Light the Night?"

"I'd tell you I can't hire you."

"Why not?"

"I never date people who work for me. Would you have dinner with me tomorrow night?"

Marcia had expected that, but now she wasn't sure what to say. She wanted to accept. Fred seemed like a nice guy, and she'd enjoyed their time together so far. He wasn't the best looking or brightest guy in the world, but he was an interesting conversationalist. Still, she didn't want to get involved with someone who worked in news, especially television news. She'd heard too many horror stories. She looked at him, but didn't say anything.

He leaned back in his chair. "It's the moment of truth. My fate is being decided in front of my very eyes. Will Fred Taylor win the right to wine and dine the damsel of his choice? Or will he suffer humiliation, rejection, and disgrace?"

"Pretty dramatic, aren't you?" Marcia said with a smile.

"TV news does that to you."

"I'd like to go out to dinner with you," she heard herself saying. "But only if it's separate checks. I wouldn't want anyone to think Channel Three was buying off the reporter who wrote the story on Light the Night."

"Dutch treat, it is. I'll pick you up at—" Just then, Fred's pager went off on his hip. The station's number stared up at him.

Paul Thomas stood in front of the yellow police tape. "Last night, there was great celebration in this Van Nuys neighborhood. One of the first victories in the new Light the Night took place not far from here, but today, criminals have struck back."

Paul was field-anchoring for the *Noon News*, which was now winding down. He and the crew had arrived midway through the newscast and were on the air in five minutes. "We're still trying to piece the breaking story together, but this is what we know. The body of a man was found in the entryway of this house on Friar Street. He'd been stabbed to death. Apparently, early this morning, the victim either discovered or was surprised by someone in his house. We're not sure how many people he came up against. The man's wife and two sons were away from home at the time."

As Paul was talking, two members of the coroner's office pushed a gurney with a cloth-covered body out the front door of the house. The camera panned to the gurney. "Dead is forty-three-year-old Grant Peters, the leader of a neighborhood patrol. Last night, Peters and his patrol members helped apprehend two suspected gang members who were breaking into cars and spray-painting graffiti. A third suspect, also thought to be a gang member with Insane

Rulers, was killed during a struggle with Peters."

The camera returned to Paul. "We can also now report exclusively that the walls inside Peters's house are covered with graffiti. And there is an unconfirmed report that something was spray-painted on the dead man's body."

Paul heard through his earpiece that he had one minute left. "Let me talk to some people over here." Paul, using a wireless microphone, approached a group of people gawking at the murder scene over a small hedge. The cameraman followed Paul, the movement adding to the immediacy of the report. "Ma'am, did you know the victim, Grant Peters?" he asked a middle-aged woman.

"Yes, I did. He was a wonderful man, he really cared about our neighborhood. He used to get so angry at the graffiti. I told him, just forget it, but he said someone had to fight back. It's a terrible tragedy—his wife and children . . ." She began to cry.

"It is indeed a tragedy." Paul turned to a man standing next to the woman. "What about you, sir? Your thoughts on what happened?"

"I'm Grant's neighbor, too." His words came in a rush. "And it's your fault—you're gettin' people killed. You TV guys are sick—makin' people think they can fight back—"

"Uh, thank you, sir." Paul turned to the camera, but the man pulled the microphone and Paul's hand toward him.

"Channel Three is responsible for Grant Peters's death!" Paul jerked the microphone free and walked away.

"As you can see, emotions are very high—we urge you not to try to apprehend anyone. Call the police about what you see. That's our live report. I'll have more on this story tonight at six. Paul Thomas, *Channel Three News,* now back to you in the studio, Karen."

Maddie Thomas was on the freeway, returning to her West Los Angeles home from a trip to the vet. Emmy, the Thomases' golden retriever, was overdue for her shots. Maddie stroked the dog's head as she drove. Emmy meant more to the family than the six Emmys Paul had won over the years. Emmy moved to the window and stuck her head out; she barked at passing cars and seemed to smile into the breeze that flapped her ears.

"Emmy, get your head back inside, your barking is driving me crazy." Maddie pushed the passenger window button on her side and chuckled as the glass nudged the dog's head, prompting the animal to pull it back inside the car. "I told you to watch out." Emmy just looked at Maddie, tongue hanging out the right side of her mouth.

Maddie was a button pusher when she listened to the car radio, changing stations whenever a commercial came on. She punched the preset button for the oldies channel. Elvis was belting out "Suspicious Minds." Maddie joined in and Emmy barked out her part.

The song reminded Maddie of Paul. It was his favorite Elvis recording, and it triggered memories of their courtship. They'd met at Moody Church in Chicago. A romance followed, but to her dismay it included hot, sticky, summer afternoons in the bleachers at Wrigley Field watching the Cubs play (or try to play). She fondly remembered the hours at the Chicago Art Institute, as well. Paul had tried to convince her that he enjoyed their frequent trips to the Institute on Michigan Avenue, but she knew he was bored stiff. All that mattered was that they were together. And after eighteen years, they loved each other more than ever. Their daughter, Elizabeth, was in her third year of high school, and their son, Travis, was an eighth-grader. Maddie Thomas gave occasional piano lessons, but had recently thrown most of her energies into a new art form, cloth doll making.

Maddie turned the car into the driveway of her home, a cobblestone entry that extended fifty feet from the street. She drove past the turnoff to the circular drive in front of their house and continued driving straight to the garage. Emmy barked a protective warning.

"My goodness, something has you all riled up."

Emmy was growling—a steady, low, guttural sound. Every

so often, her growl turned into a mumbling bark. The dog was peering over the dashboard. Her ears were pinned back, and the hair along her spine stood straight up.

"Emmy, be quiet."

Maddie pushed the garage-door opener button and drove her blue Pontiac Firebird forward. As the door swung open, Emmy growled louder. Maddie laughed. "It's just the garage door, Emmy, you've seen it open a hundred times."

Maddie drove the car into the garage and then braked. As she reached to turn off the car's engine, Emmy growled louder and bared her teeth.

"Emmy, are you going wacko on me?" But Emmy had her eye on something at the left of the car. Maddie jerked her head in that direction and saw a Hispanic young man. Then, suddenly, a switchblade knife flashed in his hand.

The man grabbed her door handle, but the doors were locked. She screamed, causing Emmy to bark furiously now. Wrenching around, she saw another man behind the car. She slammed the gearshift into reverse and floored the gas pedal, knocking the man up in the air and into the rear window, which shattered. She kept the pedal floored, and the car rumbled backward over the cobblestone driveway, swaying back and forth until it hit the street. Maddie winced at the loud scraping sound it made as it hit the pavement. Finally, the car bounced against the curb across the street, and another car approaching from her right swerved to avoid hitting her. The man inside laid on his horn.

"Are you crazy?" he screamed as he squealed to a stop and jumped out.

Time seemed to stand still then. Neighbors started appearing in their yards while the first man pulled and yanked at the injured man, who was half-running and half-limping down the sidewalk.

A car suddenly roared to a stop in front of the attackers, and the two men jumped into the backseat. Then the car headed toward

Maddie, and Emmy started barking like crazy. Gunshots rang out and Maddie's windshield cracked in front of her. She shifted out of reverse and stomped on the gas pedal. The left front fender of her car slammed into the left rear of their car. Her Pontiac spun in a circle, while the other car bounced off a parked pickup truck, then raced down the street. With tires squealing, it turned the corner and was gone.

Stunned, Maddie sat for a moment, then she reached to pull Emmy close to her. She recoiled in horror; the dog was bleeding and silent.

Maddie grabbed her keys out of the ignition, opened the door, and ran up the driveway. She fumbled with the side-door lock, but it finally opened, and she ran across the kitchen to the telephone.

Out of breath, Maddie quickly dialed 911. The operator told her that someone else had just reported the same incident. She then dialed the hotline number at Channel Three's assignment desk.

"Carol, two guys just attacked me! I need to talk with Paul."

"Are you okay?"

"No, I'm not okay! They tried to kill me—they shot our dog—where's Paul?"

"Are you hurt?"

Maddie took a deep breath. "I don't know—my car's a wreck—"

"I'll call Paul. He's on his way back from a live shot. We'll have him head your way. He's got a cell phone."

Mayor Bodine stood with Police Chief Morgan and Councilwoman McMillan at a dais that had the seal of Los Angeles on it. Reporters and photographers had been summoned to a hastily called news conference; many of them were in the same room just four hours earlier.

"This morning, Chief Morgan and I stood here together and called for another thirty days of Light the Night." The mayor stared into the glare of the media's bright lights. "The overnight police reports showed us that a miracle had come to Los Angeles. The drop in crime was, indeed, miraculous—there's no other word for it." She looked at McMillan. "But it has come with a price, and for that part of our fight, I'd like council member McMillan to say a few words."

Francie McMillan moved to the microphone. "Thank you, Mayor Bodine. I speak for my district as I tell you we lost a hero this morning. He lived in Van Nuys, but our loss is shared by every person in the greater Los Angeles area. This morning, they took away a hero, a man who dared to walk the point in our war on crime. They took away Grant Peters. We said, 'Re-Light The Night', with great determination yesterday. But now, what do we say to Grant Peters's widow and his two sons when they lay him in a cold, dark grave?" She paused. "Well, here's what we say—" Her voice was low, but building with effect. "Grant Peters's life was not lost in vain! We won't let what he did for this city be forgotten! Someday people will look back and say, 'Grant Peters was the one who put us on the right track. Grant Peters was the one who sent the criminals in the opposite direction. Now we need the help of God Almighty to right the wrong.'"

Mayor Bodine returned to the microphone and gestured to the police chief. "Chief Morgan, tell us what people can expect."

Mayor Bodine could not tell from Daniel Morgan's outward expression what he might know about the murder of Grant Peters. "Well, first of all, I want to extend my sympathies to the Peters family, and let them know that we're doing our best to solve the crime. But I'm sure you understand I can't be too specific. If we're to keep the heat on criminals and wipe out crime in our neighborhoods, it will take every man, woman, and child in this city working together. Light the Night is doing some good, but it can also place citizens in situations they aren't trained for."

"So, you're saying Light the Night is responsible for Peters's murder?" a reporter asked.

Mayor Bodine nervously clutched at her skirt and vehemently shook her head.

"Of course not," replied the chief in a tone that said the question was ridiculous. "Everyone just needs to understand what is and what isn't their responsibility."

"Channel Three has been making a big deal out of this," called out another reporter. "Should they be doing that?"

Morgan now looked irritated. "Listen, I want to publicly thank Channel Three for their part in Light the Night. When you're in a battle, you suffer some losses. No one knows that more right now than Paul Thomas and his family."

Several reporters shouted questions at the same time, wanting to know what had happened to Thomas.

Paul Thomas had always dreaded the possibility of arriving at a crime scene to find that his loved ones were involved. He'd talked briefly with his wife on the phone and so he knew about the attack, but driving up and seeing the flashing lights and squad cars outside his home made the hairs on the back of his neck stand up.

"Tell Fred I'll call him," Paul said to his photographer as he jumped out of the van.

"Taylor wants me to get some video. Is that okay?" the man replied.

Paul had also wondered what he would do in this situation. Tell the media to leave him alone? He was the media, and this was a big story. "Bring the camera in, but hold off on shooting until I check with the police."

Paul then ran to the front door where an officer let him in. "Maddie?" he called out as he stepped into the entryway. His wife immediately ran to him and they embraced.

"You okay?" Paul held her at arm's length and looked her

over from head to toe.

"In one word, no!" Tears sprang to her eyes, but from the look on her face, Paul was sure they were angry tears. "Emmy's dead, they nearly got me, my car's a wreck, and—" She frowned as she spotted the news photographer behind Paul, his camera on his shoulder. "What's he doing here?"

"Easy, Maddie. I know you're upset, but we need shots for the—"

Her eyes met Paul's. "Shots? I'm the one who was shot at. Get him and that camera out of here! This isn't one of your stupid little news stories; this is your own family!" She motioned to a living room wall. "What about that? Will you tell your children, Paul, or will they see it first on the news?"

Obscenities and gang markings covered one entire wall. The obscenities were clear, and when he saw the letters "SAY-R," he knew who had been there.

"Mr. Thomas?" A man in a suit approached him. "I'm Lieutenant Ted Banks of the PD. I need to show you something upstairs."

"What is it?" Paul looked at his wife, but she shook her head.

"I haven't been upstairs yet," Maddie said. "But, while you're up there with your cameraman, why don't you make a documentary out of all this? You might win another Emmy and dedicate it posthumously to our Emmy."

"Maddie, you've made your point."

"It's more of what you see on the wall here and in other parts of the house," the lieutenant said. The three began walking up the stairs.

Paul turned on the stairway. "Maddie, I'll be right back. See if you can locate the kids at school, then call your parents. I'll try to get ahold of mine in a minute."

The three men climbed the spiral staircase, and when they

got to the landing, they walked down a hall and into the master bedroom. "I wanted you to see this before your wife did." Lieutenant Banks pointed to the couple's king-size bed.

The bedspread was covered with big black letters.

"P.T.—U R NXT!"

CHAPTER SEVEN

Fred Taylor was getting ready to watch the six o'clock news in his office with assistant Tim Hires.

"Tim, we're part of one of the great stories of our time, and Paul Thomas is the guy who started it."

Tim nodded. "He's the talk of the town."

"What would you think of taking Paul off the morning and noon news for a while?"

"I can hear that brain of yours at work," Hires said. "Tell me more, oh, cutting-edge leader."

Fred grinned. "I want Paul to devote all of his time to 'Light the Night.' I'd like you to work closely with him and expand his segments at six and eleven."

"Who takes his place with Karen?"

"Rotate a couple of reporters in, so they don't get the idea they're permanent. Let Karen solo at noon. Have her say Paul's on special assignment, which he is. I don't want it to look like a demotion for Paul, especially with Ruggles saying we're going to fire him."

"How's Paul's wife?" Hires asked.

"Not very well. I guess she freaked out when Paul brought a cameraman home after she was almost killed. I called this afternoon, told her we'd arranged to have a bodyguard in the house each day while Paul's at the station. We've got a twenty-four-hour rent-a-cop outside their home."

"What'd she say?"

"Not much. She's ticked off, says we're using Paul and

putting them in danger. She's worried about their kids. Can't say I blame her."

"How about Paul?"

"I'm not sure. He didn't say much, except to apologize for his wife. Right now he's the biggest star in all of Los Angeles. I don't think it's gone to his head, but you never know."

It was 6 P.M., and Fred looked out his office window. "Turn on your lights, folks, and sit back and watch Channel Three."

Fred watched as the video taken inside Paul's house flashed onto the TV screen; it showed the graffiti and the threat on Paul's life. Fred knew Paul had used the video against Maddie's wishes.

This was the third night of Light the Night, and while Paul couldn't give the exact number, he announced that there was an increase in citizens' patrols from the previous evening. Scores of people were coming out of their homes to meet their neighbors. Channel Three reporters were discovering that most people wanted to talk about the shocking murder of Grant Peters. His funeral was still two days away, but all over the Los Angeles area, people spoke about him as if he were their friend.

Paul told the viewing audience about a coalition of churches that had turned this night into a night of prayer services and outdoor rallies. Hundreds of church members lined the sidewalks in areas known for prostitution. As the cars cruised by, the drivers were stopped and given gospel tracts and invitations to Sunday services.

A Channel Three photographer showed prostitutes, male and female, as they were befriended. Church members stood near them on the streets and began singing, then invited them to sing along. Many cursed the church folk and slipped into the night, but a few remained and joined in song. A close-up shot showed one prostitute managing only to hum the tune as an arm of Christian love was wrapped around her shoulder.

Channel Three's team coverage of Light the Night carried a reminder to the millions of people who were watching. "Please remember that officers and deputies can't respond to every call," said Paul. "There's no way crime can be completely stopped in an area where fifteen million people live. Tonight, people will still get hurt, stores will still be robbed, homes will still be broken into, but just like last night, with your help, the number of crimes will be much lower than in the past." Paul pointed his finger into the camera. "Criminals, gang members, anyone expecting business as usual, know this: things have changed—this isn't your city anymore."

Fred exhaled a sigh of deep satisfaction. He was grateful for everything the captain of the Light Brigade was doing to make LA streets safer for all. And he knew it was not without cost to Paul's personal life and family. Anonymous messages and threats were constantly being left on his answering machine; some addressed him as "Captain of the Looney Brigade."

Paul Thomas was driving home after the six o'clock news. Fred had told him about his new assignment and new working hours immediately after he was off the air. He'd taken a moment to call Maddie and tell her the news, then he'd headed out the door.

He had mixed emotions about temporarily giving up his morning and noon anchor duties. When Paul had first come on the morning news, it was trailing Channel Five badly, but after several years, Channel Three had a two-to-one lead in the number of viewers. Those who worked the dreaded early shift shared a bond of some kind; they were dedicated people who had to do more with fewer resources than the other newscasts did.

On the other hand, Paul agreed with Fred. Being the primary reporter for the beginning of Light the Night would no doubt advance his career. It was the middle of September and plans were being made to have Light the Night in place just before the key November ratings period.

Paul rounded the corner on Camden Avenue where he lived. The private security car was parked across from his home. He was glad Fred had insisted on the bodyguard inside the house as well.

Paul turned into the driveway and felt the rolling bumps of the cobblestones under his tires. The garage door swung up, and he drove in, parking beside Maddie's blue Firebird. He tried to imagine the horror his wife had experienced just six hours earlier. As a Christian, he wanted to be able to forgive those who wronged him or his family, but how could he feel that way toward the human waste who had tried to kill his wife?

Sorry, Lord, he said in an honest prayer, *I don't think I can do that right now. You'll need to help me with that.*

Memories of Emmy filled his mind. *Bless her heart, she was just an animal, but my, she brought joy to our home.* The last time he saw her was the previous evening. She'd greeted him at the door when he arrived home from work, her toy rope in her mouth, a not-so-subtle way of telling him she wanted to play tug-o'-war. He played with her for a while. Emmy tugged and jerked the rope back and forth, her tail wagging, giving a low growl while her jaw was locked on the rope. And now, Emmy was gone. A chill went through his body—Maddie could be gone now, too.

His wife was at the back door when he came into the house.

"My, my, my!" he said. "Are you a welcome sight."

They embraced and enjoyed the closeness of their bodies for a moment.

"Sorry I lost it this afternoon," she said, "but I'm still ticked off at you, Paul Thomas."

Paul noticed a man in the family room. "Is that your watch-dog?" he whispered. "Or is it a watch *gorilla*—that guy's huge."

"Its name is Vinnie," she whispered back.

The man began to put on his jacket. "Hi, Mr. Thomas. I'm Vinnie. Off-duty LAPD—doin' a little moonlighting for your station. I guess I'll be goin'. What time you leavin' for work tomorrow?"

"Not until two . . ." Paul looked at Maddie and smiled, "in the afternoon."

"Okay, I think four of us are rotating on your protection. Someone else will be here tomorrow. See ya. I'll let myself out."

Paul and Maddie watched Vinnie's walk, which was more like a muscle-bound waddle. "What do you think? Six-foot six, 250 pounds?" Paul asked.

"Maybe at birth," she said as Vinnie closed the door.

Paul took her in his arms. "Well, I'm glad you haven't lost your sense of humor."

"My life, maybe, but never my laugh. How you doing?"

He held her at arm's length. "Me? You're the one who played demolition derby in front of the neighbors."

They laughed.

She told him that she'd reached both of their children before they heard the news on TV. They'd come home, had something to eat, and were spending the night with friends. "They're really scared, Paul. I didn't do the greatest job explaining what this is all about. Because I don't really understand it myself."

"Yeah, I'm not sure I do either. What about your parents? Did you call them?"

"I called, didn't give all the gory details. Just said I was okay."

"Same with my folks."

He caught a whiff of something cooking, but there were no plates or silverware on the counter near the kitchen where they ate most of their meals. "Want me to set the table?"

"No! We're eating in the dining room," Maddie said with purpose in her voice.

He glanced into the dining room. "Candles, the good china, crystal, and linen napkins? What's the occasion, Mrs. Thomas?"

"Well, for starters, we can be like regular people tonight. With you off the morning news for a while, no need to get up at three. Right?"

He had always hated getting up that early—it was the most difficult part of his job. "Maddie, with the way you look and with what you've cooked, we may be going to bed early, anyway."

"I wasn't too subtle, was I?" she said with a flirtatious smile.

"Lead me astray, right after dessert."

"I'm dessert," she said.

"I may not make it through the first course."

It was an evening of gentle conversation. The meal was not exotic. His wife knew what Paul liked. She'd made a casserole with ground meat, tomato sauce, cottage cheese, noodles, and cheddar cheese melted on top. It was fast and a success.

They shared some tears as they grieved over the loss of their dog. Maddie had said she should have known something was wrong by the way Emmy was behaving when they approached the garage. Paul tried without much success to tell her not to blame herself.

They had dessert twice, once at the table and then again upstairs.

Later, they lay on their backs, side-by-side in bed. The sounds of a forest rainstorm came from a CD player and filled the room. Paul reached over and gently put his arms around his wife—she was warm to his touch.

"Maddie, I want to know one thing."

"What's that?"

"How can so much pleasure and excitement come from one man's rib?"

She laughed. "Didn't someone say God used the rib because it was close to Adam's heart?" She snuggled closer.

"I love you, Maddie."

"I love you more."

Paul said a silent prayer of thanks for the remarkable friend, wife, mother, and lover he held in his arms. She was a gift from above. He was convinced that when God created the marriage bed, He had put their names on it.

CHAPTER EIGHT

Wednesday, September 13

"Chief, it's the mayor."

Daniel Morgan thanked his secretary and picked up the telephone in his office. He knew what the call was about and had the numbers Brenda Bodine wanted. "Good morning, Mayor."

Morgan always found it best to be formal with mayors; he'd worked with three since his appointment to chief. His upcoming retirement was more important to him than getting chummy with a politician who might be swept out of office with the next shift of public opinion.

She got right to the point. "So what happened last night? How'd we do?"

Morgan looked at the piece of paper in his hand. "Not as well as the first night . . ." He heard her groan. "But compared to a year ago, it's very, very good."

She put her hand over the receiver to say something to another person in her office, then Morgan heard a cheer in the background.

"Chief, that's tremendous," Bodine said. "Which crimes did not go down?"

"Mayor, they all went down."

"Did you say all?"

"Yes, just not as dramatically as the first night."

"Well, I expect it to continue, Chief—and you're the one who will see that it does. I want this to be our little project, do you hear? Just you and me."

"The numbers are public, Mayor."

"I know, but you don't have to pass them around."

"Might you be talking about the honorable council member from the third district?" Morgan knew who the mayor had in mind, but in a rare moment, gave a verbal needle.

"I'm not amused by that, Chief. Just remember, you work for me, not Francie McMillan."

"Okay, Mayor, but I hope you understand the crime numbers can't be looked at as a trend."

"That's how I see it."

"It's only been forty-eight hours. I'm not a miracle worker."

"Chief, God separated light from darkness in one day. You've done it in two. Keep it up, and keep in touch. Bye."

At that moment, across town at Channel Three, Arlene Zahn waited for her daily fix. She was oblivious to everything around her. She knew others joked about her behind her back, but she didn't care. Every weekday morning, a mug of coffee in her hand, she hovered over the fax machine in the sales offices of Channel Three.

Arlene admitted it—she was addicted to that little report that slid out of the fax machine every Monday through Friday morning. She also knew it could be her worst enemy. It could create a glorious high, or deliver a devastating low. If the news was good, her spirits soared. If the news was bad, her mood soured until she drank away the memory.

She waited now for yesterday's Nielsen ratings. The first paper was sliding through the machine, and after Monday's surprising numbers, she was almost afraid to look. Almost.

She grabbed the paper, and as soon as she saw the results, she picked up the phone and dialed Fred Taylor's three-number extension. "Fred, this is Arlene," she blurted when he answered. "You guys did it again!"

"What did we do, tick off another one of your clients?"

"No! The ratings from last night—we did it again!"

"Okay, tell me."

"It's better than Monday. At six we had 100,000 more homes, but wait until you see what we did at eleven."

"What's with the *we*, Arlene? When the ratings are down, it's always *my* newscast. When they're up, it's *ours*."

Arlene ignored him. "At eleven, we did a monster 28 with a 52 share! That's 1.4 million homes, Fred. More than half of all the television sets at eleven were on us." Arlene felt light-headed. She was on a Nielsen high. "That's nearly four million people!"

"Easy, Arlene, don't flip out on me."

"Fred, this is what it's all about." She looked at the numbers again. "Here's the best part. We're burying the other stations."

"How bad?"

Arlene told Fred that Channel Five, which had won the last ratings sweeps in July, was now trailing badly. Its numbers had dropped from the night before, and Channel Seven had done even worse.

"Whatever you do, don't change a thing," she said. "If it's that hokey Light the Night stuff, pour it on."

"I'm not sure if it was just that, Arlene. We had the DEA gun battle, then that drive-by shooting, and Paul's wife got attacked. There were a lot of things."

"Well, who knows, maybe the gang will try to shoot her again."

"Arlene?" Fred paused. "Tell me something."

"Okay."

"Were you born with a heart?"

"I was born to be number one, Fred. Nothing else matters."

In another part of the station, Wilson Ruggles stared at his copy of the overnight ratings on his desk. His hands shook with excitement, and his eyes kept returning to two numbers. Twenty-eight and fifty-two! *This is why they brought me here. And this is why I held out for a percentage of any ratings increase.*

Ruggles figured the corporate bigwigs might be looking at the numbers at headquarters at that very second. He remembered his first interview at Channel Three. He had always resented how he was treated then. *I wasn't your first choice for this job, gentlemen. You made that clear. You said you wanted someone tough, that you'd heard bad things about me. Well, look hard at those ratings.*

Just then his intercom buzzed.

"Mr. Ruggles, Harvey Rose has Marcia Willis here for your interview."

"Yeah, all right, give me a minute or two. I'll let you know when I'm ready."

Ruggles wanted to give the impression that he was busy, so he pulled several folders out of a drawer, spread some on his desk, and tossed the rest on the floor near where the reporter would be sitting. He then wadded up a few pieces of paper and threw them on the floor. That ought to impress the broad. He loosened his tie, unbuttoned his collar, and rolled up his sleeves, then picked up the phone and hit the intercom. "Okay, show them in."

The door flew open.

"Good morning, Boss!" Rose said loudly as he and Willis stepped over and around the file folders to two chairs near Ruggles's desk. "Ms. Willis is here to discover once more what a great guy you really are, so she can go back and report to her readers."

"Don't lay it on too thick," Ruggles said. "What's on your mind, Miss, Mrs., or is it Mizzzzzz Willis? What shall I call you?"

"I'm not married, and not comfortable with 'Mizzzzz,' but if you want to call me 'Miss,' go ahead. Otherwise, Marcia will do."

"Single, huh?" he said, raising his eyebrows. "How nice to hear. Then, Marcia it will be. Please sit down."

"Are you going to fire Paul Thomas?"

"Marcia," Rose interrupted, "I thought this interview was

going to be about Mr. Ruggles."

"It is. He told me two days ago that Paul Thomas's job was in jeopardy. So what's your decision Mr. Ruggles? Are you going to fire the captain of the Light Brigade?"

"It's okay, Rose, I'm used to this tactic from print people."

He folded his arms across his chest. "We never divulge contractual agreements between the station and our employees, Marcia. Paul Thomas is no different from anyone else who's legally bound to Channel Three."

"Could it be that the ratings of the past two days have changed your mind?"

"We've had pretty good ratings, but how we interpret them is our private business."

"Pretty good?" she repeated. "How about the highest in the station's history."

"Who told you that?"

"Harvey Rose, that's who."

She held up a piece of paper. "It's on a news release. Right here. Says it's from Channel Three, but I guess it could be a fake."

"Boss, I thought you'd want the city to know how many people are watching us."

"Yes, Marcia, Harvey's right. The numbers right now are spectacular. We're very pleased. What Harvey may have failed to tell you is that I'm the one who ordered the changes that have put us back on top."

"Doesn't Fred Taylor get any credit?" she asked.

"You know Fred Taylor?"

"I've met him. He's a smart guy, a gentleman, too."

Ruggles glared at her. "Are you implying something?"

"I think you could learn a few lessons in civility."

"Oh, do you?" Ruggles struggled to keep his left eye from twitching. Nervously, he rose from his chair and walked to the window. Feeling a mixture of lust and loathing, he turned and looked at

Marcia. Dressed in a sweater and a skirt that gathered around her ankles, there was no hiding her figure.

"Is this an interview or an inspection?" she asked.

Always ready with the smart comeback, aren't you? Ruggles detested Marcia—his sexual fantasy was now overpowered by a feeling of hatred. "You work in a dying part of the media, so save the lesson about civility for your print dinosaurs." Ruggles was accustomed to intimidating people. "Here in the world of TV, gentleman Fred Taylor, captain Paul Thomas, brownnose Harvey Rose, and every other person at this station do exactly what I tell them. Nothing goes out over the air without my approval."

"If you think that impresses me, you're wrong," she said. "But I'm curious if you have a semi-intelligent answer for this, Mr. President and General Manager. If it's true that you're in control of everyone around here, then are you the one who told Paul Thomas to suggest expanding Light the Night? Hmmmmm? Was it your idea that sent the ratings out of sight?"

Ruggles felt his jaw tighten.

"I don't think it was, Mr. Ruggles. I'm a newspaper reporter, and it's obvious you don't have any respect for my profession, but here's what I think. I believe you have a big problem that's really bugging you. You don't like Paul Thomas, perhaps because he's a decent and caring gentleman. Or maybe that he's a—dare I say it?—Christian."

Ruggles felt his eye begin to twitch again as Marcia continued. "But what's eating you alive is that Thomas is a solid journalist who has succeeded in television news with credibility and trust—two words I doubt you can even spell. You don't like him, so you buried him on the morning news. Well, now you need him, and that really bugs you."

"Get out of my office."

She looked around. "Is there an echo in this room—seems as if I've heard that before. I'll gladly leave, but one last question, sir. If you don't renew Paul Thomas's contract, do you think, by chance, Channels Five or Seven might have an opening for the captain of the Light Brigade?"

"Out!"

"I'm going." She looked at Rose. "I'll find my way, Harvey. Should be easy, I'll just go in the direction of fresh air." She walked toward the door, stepping on his folders as she went. "Sorry to mess up your vacation plans," she said as she went out the door. "Aloha."

Ruggles glanced at the floor; he'd pulled the wrong folders from the filing cabinet. A smiling hula dancer looked up at him from the cover of a tour brochure.

Paul Thomas felt strange going to work in the afternoon; he had been on the 6 A.M. shift for seven years. He was in a little early today to meet with Fred Taylor, Tim Hires, Alex Stone, Carol Singleton, art director Gladys Knorr, and Harvey Rose. They wanted to come up with a strategy for covering Light the Night on the 6 P.M. newscast.

"Harvey, with the exception of that closing line you wrote for Ruggles, I like the two thirty-second promo spots you've been running," said Taylor.

"I've got a new one in production right now," said Rose, ignoring Taylor's jab.

"Okay, how can we get our viewers to tune in to Channel Three for the latest on Light the Night?" Taylor said. "Any thoughts?"

"I had an idea." Paul opened a computer printout and laid it on the table. "On my way to work, I went by police headquarters. A guy in media relations gave me this. It's a crime summary of what happened last night."

They all stared at him—their expressions said, "So what?"

"We could have a map made up for tonight," he said. "Gladys, when you have time, maybe you could design one of those three-dimensional table relief maps, like the one you used to see in old war movies. You know, where the generals moved model tanks to show where an attack was going to be." He looked at Taylor.

"I'm listening."

"Who out there is most interested in Light the Night working in their neighborhood?" Paul asked.

"The people who still have crime," said Carol Singleton.

"Right!" Paul hoped he could put his vision into words. "We turn a portion of the set into a Light the Night war command post. On a map, and eventually on a table model of the city, we show where people need to band together. I'm not sure how you do it, maybe with computer animated drawings." He looked at Fred. "Our technical people could run with that."

Taylor's expression showed he liked the idea.

"We can go as far with it as we want," Paul went on. "Make it look like the Pentagon during Desert Storm—make it look like America is at war, which it is."

Everyone looked at each other, but no one said anything.

"If we did this, wouldn't we be directing the criminals right to the most vulnerable neighborhoods in the city?" asked Hires.

Fred laughed. "So you think they don't already know?"

"I think it's a good idea," said Singleton.

"So do I," Fred agreed. "But not just for all that Hollywood set design stuff. I like it because it gets those people watching who haven't had a drop in crime where they live. That's still most of the city right now. We don't want to just hold our audience, let's add to those numbers. I don't know about you, but I think it would be kind of fun to own this market."

"The boss would love that," said Rose.

"Oh, come off it, Harvey," said Singleton.

"We'll put you in charge of telling Ruggles the good news," Fred said.

Rose ignored him. "Paul, I think what you've done is fantastic. We should all thank you."

Fred looked at him in amazement. "Nice of you to say that after what you said about Paul two days ago, Harvey." His voice dripped with sarcasm.

"I'll work on the map for tonight's newscasts, Fred," Gladys said, "and get our computer nerds busy. Maybe they'll have a clue what Paul's up to. Give us a few days on that Pentagon stuff. I've got to rent some war movies to see what you guys are talking about."

They all laughed.

Paul felt old feelings returning. The spark he'd had in the beginning of his television news career was being rekindled. Years of being a role player, of seeing others given prime assignments and anchor jobs—it was all behind him. His career had been born again. *God wants His best for me, and now I have it.*

At about 7:30 that evening, Jorge Escobedo and his men walked to Ramon Rojas's home. Rojas was a custodian who worked at Our Mother of Perpetual Peace Roman Catholic Church, where Danny Escobedo's funeral service would be held the next morning. The wake was this evening; the Escobedos wanted both services private and over as quickly as possible.

Jorge knew that police intelligence officers and FBI agents planned to position surveillance units in the area, so he had sent ahead two members of his gang, Tony Romero and Felipe Manuel, to the parish priest, Father Salvador Garcia. Escobedo told his men to do whatever was necessary to get him inside, undetected, even if it meant killing a priest, or holding a nun hostage. When the two gang members returned, they had told him that the priest wasn't afraid of their physical threats. In fact, when they pushed him, he'd challenged them on the spot to a fistfight. But Father Garcia didn't want violence in his church, and so he'd come up with an idea.

A secret underground passage led from the church to a garage next door. Father Garcia told Romero and Manuel they could use the tunnel to smuggle Jorge in, but he could stay in the church for only fifteen minutes. The priest then gave them directions to the custodian's home. Rojas was a retired shipyard worker who agreed to help Father Garcia.

Jorge was nervous as he walked to Rojas's front door now. He kept looking around for any sign of an ambush. The plan was that Rojas would take Jorge to the church, while Romero and Manuel remained at Rojas's house.

"What are we going to use for wheels?" Jorge asked.

"Rojas's car." Romero pointed to a white 1988 Buick Skylark in the driveway.

Jorge looked at the car and shook his head. "No 'Ruler' would ever be seen in that pile of junk."

Romero and Manuel laughed.

Just then Rojas came out of the house. "I'm Rojas. Which one is Jorge?"

"I am," Jorge said. "No double-cross, Rojas, or you and the padre are dead. *Comprende?*"

Rojas nodded. "I'm ready. Let's go."

They walked to the car. Rojas opened the trunk, and Jorge climbed inside. Five minutes later, Rojas drove the car into the garage, opened the trunk, and Jorge got out. Father Garcia then led him to a trap door in the garage. The door was under a piece of plywood, and when Father Garcia slid the board aside, three large, black spiders crawled away in different directions. The entrance was crisscrossed in cobwebs.

"Hey, man," Jorge said, "what's down there?"

"Okay, Mr. Tough Guy who's wanted for murder, you want me to call the cops to clear away the spider webs?"

"Shut up," he said, pushing the priest. "Get in there."

The priest began climbing down the ladder, and Jorge followed. The only light was from the priest's flashlight. The tunnel smelled old and damp, and water dripped on the two men as they walked. The sound of their footsteps echoed, and Jorge felt something dart up against his foot, then skitter away.

"You got rats in here!"

"All kinds of rodents visit us. Some have two legs."

Jorge let that one go. He needed the priest to get to his brother. The tunnel took a left turn. Their footsteps and the dripping water were the only sounds.

"Here's our way up," said the priest, shining his light ahead.

Jorge saw an opening above a ladder and climbed to the top. He found himself in a musty smelling storage room, as he waited for the priest to climb the ladder. Father Garcia left the hole uncovered and motioned for Jorge to follow. "You've got fifteen minutes—I'll be in the room. When I tell you to leave, you leave. Got it?"

Jorge, not used to taking orders, mumbled that he understood and walked a few feet to the room where he would find his brother.

His mother cried when she saw Jorge standing in the doorway. *"Jorge, Jorge,"* she cried, *"por culpa de su bandilla, mi hijo Danny esta muerto* (because of your gang, my baby Danny is dead)."

Jorge gave her a blank stare. "This is between Danny and me." He walked past her to the casket where he looked down at the lifeless shell of his brother. The body of Danny Escobedo was dressed in a black shirt and black pants. He looked at peace, perhaps for the first time in his life. He was in a cherrywood casket, the most expensive one at the funeral home. Jorge Escobedo had given his gang members $8,375 to pay for it—all in cash.

"What a waste, Danny," Jorge said. "I told you—stay away from the car break-ins and tagging. That was small-time. Now you're dead. *Stupido!*" Jorge reached out to touch his brother's hand. It felt like cold plastic. *Look at you, in a wooden box with a hole in your chest.*

He had nothing to say to his mother. His father was gone, killed a year after Danny was born, shot during a drug deal that went bad. Jorge was Danny's role model.

"I had big plans for you—you looked up to me."

"And now, you're looking down at him in a coffin," Father Garcia spoke behind him.

Jorge whirled around. "What do you know?"

"I know that I bury one of you gang members every week. When are you going to learn?"

"Learn what? How to be poor like you? How never to know a woman, like you?" Jorge looked at Danny, then back at the priest. "I was his idol. He wanted to be like me."

"And some day, soon, you'll be just like him, in a box. You're nothing."

Jorge walked to the priest and poked his finger in his chest. "Nothing, huh? I have everything—money, power, women—all because I follow my rules."

The priest slapped Jorge's hand away. "Tell that to your mother tomorrow when we put six feet of dirt on top of your brother."

Jorge smiled and looked into Father Garcia's eyes. *You're lucky I don't stick a knife in your belly right now. But the time is not right.* He had vowed to remind Los Angeles again and again about what happened to his kid brother, and who was responsible for it. Yesterday, three of his gang members had botched the first part of his plan at Paul Thomas's home, but there would be other chances. He could wait.

"In more ways than one, Escobedo, you've run out of time." Father Garcia motioned to the door. "Let's go."

The two men retraced their steps to the tunnel. Five minutes later, Jorge was in the trunk and on the way back to his gang.

Bill Randall was in Fred Taylor's office, complaining about the direction and content of the six and eleven o'clock newscasts. Fred knew his lead anchor was worried about only one thing: Bill Randall.

"I just learned about these special segments we're doing with Thomas. I can't believe you're giving him a window of ten minutes in the first half of the 6 P.M. to do his stuff. You've got him introducing live shots, asking the reporters questions, and doing voice-overs for the best video."

Fred listened without saying anything.

"Why don't you just let him stand at the map for a minute or two and let me toss to our reporters in the field? Now I see he's coming back for another segment in the back half. For cryin' out loud, Fred, people will think Thomas is the star of the show!"

Fred still didn't say anything.

"I mean, the first and second night were one thing, but now he has his own segments at six and eleven? Why not give him the show?"

"That idea has occurred to me," Fred said in an even voice.

Randall's eyes nearly popped out. "What? *I'm* your lead anchor. With me, we've done close to a 30 rating both nights!"

"Yeah, and before Paul Thomas said what he said, we were doing a seven with you as the star."

"I'm not taking any more of this abuse. You'll be hearing from my agent!"

"I can hardly wait." Fred eyed a clock on the wall. "Bill, in case you didn't know, when the big hand is on eleven, and the little hand is on six, that means you have five minutes to airtime. Now get into the studio."

Panic rose in Randall's eyes as he hurried from the office.

When the opening to the newscast ended a short time later, and a camera took a wide shot of Channel Three's set, Fred saw Randall clipping his microphone to his tie. The temperamental anchor man had just made it to the studio in time.

A day in the life of metropolitan Los Angeles was being compressed into an hour's newscast, and Fred was pleased with the result, so far. "Nice map. Good graphics. Fine idea."

"Good flow." Tim Hires leaned back in his chair in Fred's

office. "Paul's really in command."

"Why not? He's the captain of the Light Brigade." Fred laughed softly.

Three televisions were on, but only the sound on Channel Three was up. Fred held a remote control in his hand, ready to bring up the sound on the other stations if it looked like they had something of interest. Until now, the screens of Channels Five and Seven remained silent.

"Look at the crud they're going with," said Fred.

Tim agreed. "They're acting like Light the Night doesn't exist."

"I love it."

The men watched as Paul gave a recap of last night's events. One story brought howls of laughter from Fred and Tim, and they knew the thousands of people watching at home were loving it, too.

Near Encino, there had been a standoff between a car prowler and an unwelcome resident in the area—a skunk.

Patrol members had caught the whole thing on tape and brought it to Channel Three. They'd offered it free to the station as a token of their thanks for Light the Night, but Fred gave them $100 for it.

The car prowler was surprised by the citizens' patrol. The patrol members had chased the young man through the neighborhood, which was close to the Sepulveda Dam recreation area. Those who drove through there early in the morning could usually count on smelling a skunk or two. The animals were all over the place, and County Vector Control seemed unable to catch them.

In his attempt to escape the citizens' patrol, the car prowler hopped a fence and hid in a shed in someone's backyard. But one of the patrol members had spotted him. When the pursuers arrived at the shed and saw an open padlock hanging on the door, they quickly locked the prowler inside.

The tape showed patrol members doubled over in laughter.

In the background, cries of help came from inside the shed. The man had disturbed not one skunk, but an entire family. He was getting it from dad, mom and their skunk-ettes. Some of the young ones were probably pulling their triggers for the first time.

"The family that sprays together stays together!" one of the patrol members shouted.

A terrible commotion rose from inside the shed as the man screamed and threw whatever he could find at the nocturnal pole-cats. The man was let out when the police arrived and soaked him with a garden hose, all duly recorded on home video.

"As amusing as that story is, many of you are wondering why you haven't seen any drop in crime where you live," said Thomas when he'd finished his skunk story.

A map of the entire Los Angeles area was electronically positioned behind him. "With the help of police and other city workers where you live, in the weeks to come, we plan to target those areas and help you get rid of what's destroying your neighborhoods."

He pointed to two areas of the city that were highlighted in red. "Last night, North Hollywood and Van Nuys were hit hard by crime. Earlier we told you about the three fatal shootings in those areas. But those of you who live there know what else happened."

A special effect enlarged the highlighted areas. Graphics appeared listing the streets where crime had happened. "You had a rash of home break-ins, several muggings, and two liquor store holdups. There was also a drive-by shooting, but thankfully, no one was hurt during any of these altercations." Then Thomas told them the good news. "Beginning tonight, and for as long as necessary, the LAPD will be shifting more units to your neighborhoods. We understand that eight citizens' patrols are now in the final stages of training and will be on the streets for the first time tomorrow."

He then switched to a live shot set up with a community leader. About thirty people stood behind him. "We're going live now to North Hollywood where we'll talk with Oscar Felix who's an honorary lieutenant in our effort to 'light up' that area. Oscar has something to say to the people in his neighborhood, and then we'll take some questions and comments from others who live there."

It was interactive television on the streets, a talk-back segment in which people could feel involved. It went well. People asked questions about how to set up patrols, and Thomas had the answers.

"This is good, Tim," said Fred. "Even though it's about North Hollywood, I'm interested in what they're saying. And if I feel that way, then all those Joe Lunchbuckets out there in other parts of LA feel the same way."

Hires gave thumbs-up.

"I think it ran about a minute too long, though. Have the producer cut it down some tomorrow."

"No prob-lem-oh."

"And tell Paul I thought he was terrific tonight. I've got to get out of here a little early. Are you set for the eleven o'clock show?"

"Yeah, should be a good one. But why the early exit? That's different."

"It's none of your business, but if you really want to know, I have a dinner date."

When Paul got back to his office after the 6 P.M. news, he counted thirty-four phone messages on his machine. He called Maddie first.

"You were great, Paul. I'm really proud of you."

"You're the only critic I listen to."

"One thing—Bill Randall was sure cold to you on the set."

"You don't miss a thing, do you? Who knows and who cares? Will you wait up for me?"

"I'll be the one on the right side of the bed."

"Now how am I supposed to concentrate on the eleven o'clock news when you say something like that?" he said with a laugh. "Who's your bodyguard tonight?"

Maddie whispered, "He looks like the Son of Vinnie."

"See you later."

"I love you, Paul. Be careful."

He hung up and dialed into his voice mail.

"You have eighty-three messages." *This is ridiculous.*

He began listening to the messages and writing down the names and numbers. Paul soon realized he just didn't have time to answer them all, a problem he'd never had before. He'd ask Taylor to get him some help tomorrow. *Speaking of Taylor, I can't believe he left early. Good for him. Wonder who she is.*

Most of the phone messages didn't need a response. They were supportive viewers thanking him for Light the Night and encouraging him to keep up the good work. A few asked specific questions; if he had time, he'd get back to them.

The fifteenth call, though, was chilling. "Paul Thomas," the deep voice began, "I can't give my name over the phone on a recording. But I need to talk with you. I wasn't going to tell anyone about this, but I just can't keep it secret any longer. It's about who killed Grant Peters. It's 6:45 right now. I'll be at a pay phone at ten tonight. If you want to know more about this, be at your desk at ten o'clock sharp." *Click.*

CHAPTER NINE

Marcia had agreed to meet Fred at Wild Harry's, a casual Hawaiian-style restaurant in Santa Monica. The name scared away some people, but the restaurant was really quite tame. The owner was a muscular, flamboyant guy who worked the tables as if he were on a comedy circuit.

"Marcia, *daaahling*, you look splendid on this one-three of September," he gushed.

"Harry, meet Fred Taylor."

"Well, since you've spurned my every advance, now I see who I'm up against." The owner's eyes sparkled.

"Good to meet you, Harry. Marcia said you were one-of-a-kind. Now I see why."

Harry roared with laughter. "The best table in the house for the two of you. It's your destiny!"

Harry disappeared, and a moment later the waiter came by the table to take their orders. Marcia selected the mahimahi, and Fred decided on the grilled marlin. They ordered drinks.

"Are you hungry?" Fred asked.

"Famished. I lost my appetite after meeting Channel Three's gift to broadcasting."

"Then why don't I lose any weight? I see Ruggles every day."

She laughed, then asked, "So, how did the battle go today?"

His look turned serious. "That's scary."

"What is?"

"I'm sorry—nothing. I . . . "

"What did I say that was scary?"

"Your question—'so, how did the battle go today?' Those are the same words Cynthia used every time I came home from work."

She looked at him, but didn't say anything.

Fred shook his head. "What a stupid thing to tell you. Boy, you can see I've been out of circulation. I'm sorry."

"Don't be," she said. "It's no big deal. Actually, I'm flattered that you told me."

Harry arrived as the waiter served their dinners on sizzling platters. "My, my, it's mahimahi for the woman of 'mahi' dreams. What a complete surprise!"

It was Marcia's favorite, and she ordered it often when she stopped by after work.

As they ate, Fred told Marcia that this was his first date since losing his wife. Then they talked about everything from music to sports to travel. Their jobs seldom came up in the conversation, and Marcia was quite happy to do without shoptalk. They were in agreement on how much they detested going to parties with their coworkers.

"Seems like all they do is gossip, backbite, or tell stories that have been repeated a million times," she said.

"TV is no different," he said. "Probably worse with the ego factor."

It seemed to Marcia that the two of them had the same game plan on this particular evening—they just wanted to know a little more about each other. Nothing was forced or rushed. There were even moments of silence, and while at certain times with certain people silence was awkward, tonight these moments were comfortable.

Harry put his own finishing touch on their dinners—double-chocolate mousse, on the house.

"Marcia, *daaahling*, what shall I tell the chef? Do I say two mousses, or two mice?" He let out an enormous laugh, and then with a dramatic bow, did his best Arnold Schwarzenegger impression and said, "I'll be back."

"Harry's a special guy," she said.

"And you're a special woman."

Marcia wondered what Fred was thinking. He seemed to be enjoying her company.

"I have a question," he said quietly.

"Not sure if I have the answer."

"What is it about you? I keep bringing up Cynthia, but there's some subtle difference between the two of you that I can't figure out."

She smiled, then looked up and closed her eyes.

"Did I blow it again?" he asked.

She looked at him and sighed. "No, you didn't blow it. I just said a prayer of thanks."

"For what?"

"Fred, I'm a Christian. Everything in my life centers on Jesus Christ. Maybe this is the something you see." She had already sensed that he had a deep longing in his life.

"Sounds like I'm talking to Paul Thomas."

"What?"

"Never mind. I just didn't expect this."

"You asked. I have to be honest. I'm a reporter for the *Examiner*, after all."

They both laughed, which seemed to break the tension that had crept into their conversation.

Fred looked at his watch. "Listen, Marcia, it's getting late. Let me take you home."

Well, there you go, Willis—the big brush-off. "Sure, thanks for the evening. I had a great time, but remember our agreement—dutch treat."

"Newspaper people may tell the truth, but you forget—I'm

a TV-type, and we lie."

He grabbed the check, and those special moments they'd shared were left at the restaurant.

Paul Thomas was in his office at 10:02 when the phone rang. He waited until the second ring and then picked up the receiver. "Paul Thomas."

"Mr. Thomas, I called you earlier and left a message."

Yes, he's called back. "I know. I recognize your voice."

"You know who I am?" the caller said with alarm.

Don't scare him away. "No, I just remembered what you sounded like. You said you know something about Grant Peters's murder."

"I've got videotape of the whole thing."

Videotape? Paul was stunned. "How did you get it?"

"I shot it myself."

"Do the police know about this?" Could the call be a hoax?

"No, I was afraid to go to them."

Paul tried to keep his voice steady; he didn't want the caller to know how excited he was. "Listen, I give you my word—this call is between you and me. Who are you and how did you get the murder on tape?"

"My name is Bobby Silva. I'm the one who videotaped the scuffle between Grant Peters and Danny Escobedo. Look, Grant was my best friend. After the cops left and they'd taken the kid's body away, Grant asked me to do something for him. He was afraid the gang would come after him for what he did." He paused.

"Go on." Paul looked at the clock on his wall. *Get to the point.*

"Well, Grant wanted me to set up the camera in the van in front of his house that night. He thought they might hit his place with graffiti, and he wanted it on tape. So I set it up, but I kind of dozed off."

Paul's shoulders sagged. The guy fell asleep and missed it.

"What happened next?" he asked, trying to conceal his disappointment.

"I hear some loud talking, so I wake up and immediately hit the camera's record button. I've got it aimed at the front door when suddenly the door opens and it's Grant, wrestling with some dude dressed in black. They're fighting for a knife, and two guys jump him from behind and hold him by the shoulders. Then this guy in black takes a knife and stabs Grant in the stomach. Man, it was awful! I'm scared. I don't know what to do. I forget the camera is rolling by itself."

"So then what happened?" Paul could hardly believe he was hearing all this.

"Well, the two guys leave, but the one in black rips off Grant's shirt and takes a can of spray paint and writes something on his chest. But here's how I know who did this, especially the guy who killed Grant. The two guys who were holding him split and ran like crazy. But the dude in black, he's in no hurry. He just casually walks out of the house, closes the front door, and struts to the street, right to my van! I'm freaking out, I tell you! He comes up to the van, looks right in the mirror window, smiles, and combs his hair. I thought for sure he'd see the blinking red light on the camera."

"Did you recognize him?"

"Sure, I seen his picture on that national TV show."

Paul knew, but wanted Silva to tell him. "Who was it? Who killed Grant Peters?"

"Jorge Escobedo. I'm positive."

Paul immediately called Fred Taylor on his car phone.

"Fred, Paul. Get to a pay phone and call me right back. I don't want anyone hearing what I have to tell you."

"Okay, I see one just ahead."

A moment later, Paul's phone rang, and Paul told Fred about the call from Silva.

Fred was leery. "Have you seen the tape?" he asked.

"It should be here in about ten minutes. He's bringing it to the station." He glanced at the clock on his wall—10:15. "Fred, if this guy is on the level, I think we should go with the video at eleven, minus the gory stuff."

"Do the police know about it?" Taylor asked.

"No. I thought we should notify them just before the news, then air the video. We don't have much time. We still have to transfer the tape from VHS to Beta."

"Okay, I'm trusting your judgment on this. Go with it if you think it's legit, but make sure we protect the guy's identity, and put up a super that makes it clear we weren't the ones who shot the video."

"We were going to do that as soon as we got the go-ahead from you."

"Work close with Myrna on this, okay?"

Myrna, his producer for the eleven o'clock news, was standing in Paul's office listening to the conversation. He gave her an okay sign, and she clapped her hands.

"Myrna's right here, Fred. Watch us from home."

"Hope you'll have something for me to see."

"We will. See you tomorrow. And by the way, can't wait to hear all about your big date."

"Never mind that, just get the video on the air."

Bobby Silva still wasn't sure he was doing the right thing. But his best friend had been murdered in cold blood, and he had seen it happen. As he walked toward the lobby at Channel Three, he thought, *This is for you, Grant.*

A Hispanic guy was waiting for him at the front door. He was dressed in a black shirt and black pants and was big, perhaps 6'3" and 220 pounds. *Did Escobedo send him? He doesn't look friendly.*

As Bobby walked to the door, he put his hand in his right

jacket pocket and gripped his revolver. *Make one move toward me, pal, and your next one will be to the morgue.*

"Hi, I'm Reuben Miranda, a writer for Channel Three. Paul asked me to meet you and bring you inside. Do you have a videotape for us?"

Bobby lightened the grip on his gun and took his hand out of his pocket. The tape was in his other pocket. "I want to see Paul Thomas."

"Sure, come on inside. We don't have a lot of time."

Bobby looked at his watch. It was 10:37. They walked down a hall to a flight of stairs which led to the newsroom. *So, this is what it looks like.* Computer terminals were everywhere, but most were not in use. As Bobby gawked around the newsroom, a tall man and a woman approached from the right.

"Bobby Silva? Hi, I'm Paul Thomas and this is Myrna Oliver, our eleven o'clock producer. Thanks for coming. Could we see the tape? We've only got a few minutes."

"You sure no one will know who shot the tape?" he asked.

"Not from us, positive," Thomas said.

"What about my getting paid for the tape?"

Thomas gave an exasperated look at Oliver. She nodded.

"We'll pay, but first we've got to see what you have," he said, glancing nervously at his watch.

"Myrna!" Bill Randall stormed into the newsroom.

Bobby grinned from ear-to-ear. *Bill Randall. In person. Wow, the guy I see every night.* "Hi, Mr. Randall."

Randall ignored Bobby and spoke to the producer. "Why don't I have all of my scripts yet? How do you expect me to get ready?"

Bobby thought that sounded like a reasonable request. *Randall's the main guy. They should take care of him.*

Randall frowned. "Of course, with all the time Paul has been getting, I'm probably written out of most of the newscast."

"Bill, we've got a breaking story on our hands," said Oliver. "We don't have time for this."

"Bobby, we need the tape right now," said Thomas, glancing at his watch.

"Okay, this is for you."

He reached into his jacket and pulled out his gun. Everyone jumped, and Bill Randall hit the floor. "He's got a gun!" someone yelled.

"Call the cops!" screamed Randall from under a desk.

"Sorry, wrong pocket." Bobby grinned sheepishly, and with his left hand reached into his other pocket, pulled out the tape and gave it to Thomas.

Randall slowly got to his feet. "Who is this nut?" But Bobby was too embarrassed to be insulted.

Thomas handed the tape to his editor. "Gary, start transferring this as we watch it."

The editor grabbed it and ran to a nearby room where he pushed the VHS tape in the machine and started recording video onto a newsroom Beta tape.

Bobby followed Paul Thomas's eyes as he looked at a clock on the wall. It was 10:44.

Thomas and Oliver watched the screen, while many of the others in the newsroom looked over their shoulders.

"Oh, wow, a shot of a house," Bill Randall sneered. "Big deal!"

Bobby looked at Randall with new feelings.

"Shut up, Bill," said the producer.

Bobby smiled. *Yeah, shut up.*

"Fast-forward the tape, Gary," said Paul. "Bobby, how far 'till we see Peters and Escobedo?" He glanced at the clock again—10:46.

"Pretty soon. I tried to cue it up to that point, but must not have advanced it far enough."

"Wonderful," Randall said in disgust as he walked away.

"I've got to check my makeup."

"See if it can cover your ego," said the producer.

Bobby laughed at the slam, then saw what they were looking for on the tape. "There it is!"

"Regular speed, Gary," said Thomas.

It was silent in the room as they watched the murder of Grant Peters. Several people gasped when they heard the victim cry out for help. Tears streamed down Bobby's face.

"Oh, my gosh, he's coming toward the van!" said one of the writers.

"Here's what I want, Gary," Thomas said. "Take the video from the point of the struggle and where Escobedo stabs Peters. Let the tape go until he walks to the van, looks in the window, and starts combing his hair. I want to freeze the video at that point. Sound okay, Myrna?"

"Yes. What about your script?"

"No time. I'll ad lib over the video, based on what we know. Do you have the graphic ordered that says 'Home Video'?"

"Yes. I've got you at the top. Think you can make it?"

"Yeah, we've got plenty of time."

Bobby looked at his watch—10:52.

"This is *Channel Three News* at eleven with Bill Randall and Nancy Chen. Eric Brock with sports, Andrew LaPointe weather and Paul Thomas, captain of the Light Brigade. *News Three* for Southern California, the news that hits home."

Myrna Oliver thought Bill Randall seemed rattled as he opened the newscast. He'd just yelled an obscenity when he saw that Thomas was added to the production open without his knowledge.

"Myrna, the tape room says we don't have Paul's video yet," the eleven o'clock director said, sitting next to her in the control room.

"It'll make it," she said, wondering if it would.

"Topping our news tonight—exclusive video of the murder

of community leader Grant Peters. Here with details on this breaking story is Paul Thomas."

Randall and Thomas were shown on a two-shot, but Randall wouldn't look at him.

"Come on, Bill," Myrna mumbled, "try to make it look like you're interested in the story."

"Tape's still not in, Myrna," said the director with urgency.

Fred Taylor was like the millions of others watching the news on Channel Three that night—only he had an idea what might be coming. Paul Thomas was on the screen and was getting ready to talk about the murder of Grant Peters. Fred wondered if they got the video in time. He edged closer to the TV from his sofa.

". . . Now, this late-breaking development. Within the last thirty minutes, we have been given a videotape that shows the murder of Grant Peters. The scenes are very disturbing and we have—"

He paused. Fred knew the director was telling Paul to stretch until the video was ready.

"I've just learned the tape is on the way. The scenes are quite graphic and we have chosen not to show a particularly gruesome moment in the murder. We also are not revealing how the tape was shot or those who were involved in the shooting of it. We have notified the police and will share with them the video you are about to see."

"Come on, come on—get the tape on," Fred muttered.

"Grant Peters was murdered sometime in the early morning hours on Tuesday," Thomas continued. "He was the leader of a citizens' patrol in Van Nuys that confronted two suspected gang members who were spray-painting graffiti on cars. They also attacked an elderly man. That's when Peters saw Danny Escobedo running to the group with a knife in his hand. Police say Peters headed off the boy, they scuffled, and Escobedo was accidentally stabbed in the chest. He died at the scene." Thomas paused once again, and a graphic appeared on the lower third of the screen—"Home Video." "Okay, we now have the tape. This is outside Grant Peters's house several hours after Danny Escobedo was killed. In the open doorway you'll see Peters being held by two men. Another man will stab Peters."

Fred Taylor couldn't believe how clear it all was. A bright porch light illuminated the murder scene. It was horrific.

"Now, the two men who held Peters will run from the scene, but the murderer is in no hurry. He rips open the dead man's shirt and with a can of spray paint, sprays something on the victim's chest."

The video then showed the murderer dragging Peters's body far enough inside the house to close the front door.

"He now closes the door and casually walks toward the camera," Paul said in a steady voice.

"Here is the face of a murderer," Paul's tone was angry. "And what does a cold-blooded killer do after he has taken the life of a husband and father of two children, a man who cared about his neighbors?" Thomas paused as the man approached the camera.

Fred got up and walked closer to his television screen.

"The murderer combs his hair. What else would you expect from a person with the mind of the devil?" Thomas paused. "And now he looks into the mirrored window. We'll freeze the video at this point."

The man's face was in still-frame. He was smiling.

A chill shot up and down Fred's spine. *I'm a hardened news person,* he thought. *What must this be like for millions of viewers?*

"Here's who we believe killed Grant Peters," said Paul. "This man is Jorge Escobedo, older brother of Danny Escobedo. Remember his face, remember the name, remember the smile. He is Jorge 'Cruel Rule' Escobedo, who may represent everything that Light the Night is fighting against."

CHAPTER TEN

Thursday morning, September 14

Fred Taylor stared at the face of Jorge Escobedo; the photo was taken off the television screen during Channel Three's eleven o'clock news, and was now on the front page of the *Examiner's* late edition. Alongside it was a larger shot of Escobedo and two men holding Grant Peters before he was murdered. Under both photos were the words: *Courtesy: Channel Three News.*

The paper gave a sketchy account of what had aired the night before. Paul Thomas and Myrna Oliver were quoted briefly, but little else had made it into the story before the *Examiner's* late edition went to press.

The phone rang. It hadn't stopped ringing since he had arrived in his office this morning. He answered some calls and let others go into his voice mail. Everyone wanted to talk about the video of Grant Peters's murder. Fred picked up the phone now, if for no other reason than to stop the ringing.

"Fred, this is Marcia Willis. Some kind of video you guys have on Peters's murder."

It was good to hear her voice. He knew Marcia was playing catch-up. Just like every other reporter in the city who had been "scooped" by Channel Three, she was trying to find a new angle, more information, anything that would put a fresh touch on the story.

"Who took the video? Was it the same guy who shot the stuff with Peters the night Danny Escobedo was killed?"

Fred felt uneasy. Her guess wasn't that perceptive, and it was correct, but Fred wasn't about to reveal Bobby Silva's identity as the photographer. "You know I can't tell you that."

"Yeah, but I had to ask—had to get your no comment' for my story."

Fred didn't say anything. It was strange—he felt comfortable talking with her over dinner, but now it was different. She was the competition. "Marcia, what aired on TV is public. We gave your paper permission to use the shot on the front page. But everything else is ours. It's confidential. Not even the police can touch it."

"Well, how did whoever shot the tape know to be at Peters's house?"

"I can't answer any more questions, okay? Gotta go." He hung up, then chided himself for being rude to someone who'd rekindled familiar and wonderful feelings in him just last evening.

A call on his direct line brought him back to the present. On the other end was the network bureau chief. The Peters video and Light the Night would head the national news that evening. Could they interview Paul Thomas? If he wasn't at the station, could they go to his home?

What took you guys so long to figure out this story is enormous?

Paul hung up the phone and turned to Maddie.

They had been taking advantage of Paul's new hours and were enjoying a leisurely breakfast in the kitchen nook of their West Los Angeles home when the phone had rung a few moments before. Maddie had made his favorite thin pancakes, then completed her attack on his health by browning some sausage.

"Maddie, Carter Davidson wants to interview me, live, on *Nightscope*."

"Carter Davidson?"

"The one and only."

Maddie walked to the coffeemaker and poured herself another cup. "Why do you want to do it?"

Paul was puzzled, but knew his wife well enough to guess she was taking a reality check. "I don't know why—I guess because I've never been on national TV before. I think it would be kind of neat, being seen around the country. Might get me more respect at the station, and I know it would drive Bill Randall completely out of his mind."

"Is that your best answer?" She stirred some cream and sugar into her coffee and walked back to the table.

"Yeah, what's wrong with it?"

"If that's why you're doing it, I think your motives are wrong."

Paul felt a surge of anger. "Oh, come off it, Maddie. We're about to hit the big time—lighten up." Paul couldn't believe their conversation had suddenly gone in the tank. "Just two minutes ago, we were celebrating—now you're laying some guilt trip on me."

"All I'm saying is, don't let this get the best of you, Paul. Don't let it change you for the worse."

Maurice "Mo-Jo" Jones was cruising in the San Fernando Valley, traveling east on Sherman Way in Reseda. A short man to some, a runt to others, he now felt like the biggest, baddest dude in all of Los Angeles. He glanced out his window at a passenger in the car beside him, hoping the guy would give him a bad look. *Don't mess with me, man, or you dead.* The man in the other car looked away.

Mo-Jo was on orders from his gang's leader to settle a territory dispute. Mo-Jo, an enforcer for the gang, knew the ground rules; kill anyone who wore the wrong color clothing, or be killed by the other side. Mo-Jo and his Iron Claw brothers wore blue—Insane Rulers wore red. He was "cuz"—they were "blood." His orders were clear—take out a "blood."

An elaborate "chop-shop" scheme had brought thousands of dollars a week to the Iron Claw gang. Up until recently, it had worked without a hitch. But the scam needed all phases to work, and now it had broken down at the beginning. Insane Rulers were stealing cars that "belonged" to Iron Claw. Mo-Jo was looking for a "blood." His orders: deliver a message to Insane Rulers to back off. That message was a bullet.

Mo-Jo switched off the doom-doom, doom-doom beat of rap music blaring on his car stereo as he turned right on Amigo. He glanced from side to side and passed through the intersections of Gault, then Hart. It was familiar territory. He had been in the area the past two nights. It was frustrating because each time he spotted a potential target, Light the Night citizens' patrols kept him from getting close to his intended victim. Mo-Jo had decided his "search-and-destroy" mission would have to be done during the day.

Mo-Jo patted his coat pocket where he carried his black book. It was a record of, as he called them, "Mo-Jo's greatest hits." Under his car seat was a gun with a silencer. He was ready to make a new entry in his book.

He headed south on Amigo and reached Bassett Street. Excitement, mixed with a rare case of nerves, built as he passed through the intersection. He wasn't used to working in the daytime; he enjoyed the cover of darkness. But he was told to kill, and killing was how he'd earned his reputation. Mo-Jo was fast, clean, vicious, and he always made his hit.

It was Mo-Jo's business to know what went on in the Reseda-Sepulveda area. This was his turf. He liked the tension he felt in the neighborhoods, the fear he saw on peoples' faces, the way they stayed to themselves and left him alone. It had taken a while, but there was no doubt who controlled the neighborhoods.

Occasionally, he would hear about how the place used to be. He would shake down old-timers who would tell him that for years it was a place to be proud of. The streets were rich in history. Precious memories of neighborhood events had found their way into family scrapbooks that overflowed with photographs. People who moved away always thought of it as "back home." But in recent years, the Northridge earthquake had cracked this fine neighborhood, and drug dealers had broken it. Much of what was rebuilt became fresh canvases for gang graffiti and targets for drive-by shootings. It was never an affluent neighborhood, but its rich history was now bankrupt from violence. The memories being created now were full of violence and grief, and the only photos of many of the residents were mug shots on police blotters. "Back home" was now just "back there." And nobody appreciated the change more than Mo-Jo.

Amigo Street was the home of Arthur Jackson, the protester whose confrontation with Wilson Ruggles had made Channel Three's news and the pages of the *Examiner*.

"Arthur, would you get off that phone?"

Clarice Jackson needed help. Her husband, a retired master chief petty officer in the Navy, was now a mini-celebrity, but she wasn't impressed.

"What do you need?" he called from the living room.

"Well, I don't need you talkin' with everybody about being on TV. James will be here soon, and I'm trying to bake his favorite pie. Put some clean sheets on his bed, will you? And throw some of your junk in the garage. That room is small enough as it is. Goodness!"

"Aye-aye, sir," she heard him answer back good-naturedly.

Clarice knew how important their house was to her husband. He had used his GI loan and reenlistment bonus to buy the house while stationed on a ship in Long Beach. They had scrimped and saved for the down payment and, not wanting to give it up, had even rented it out three times when his duty assignments took them overseas.

Arthur walked into the kitchen. "It'll be good to have James home again, won't it? Just like old times."

"Uh-huh. I just wish the neighborhood was like old times. Did you hear the gunshots last night?"

"No, but let's not get into that again, Clarice."

"It's happened three nights in a row. You didn't hear them?"

"I must have slept through it."

"That's because you're getting used to it. How long before the bullets come through our bedroom wall?"

"I'm not giving up on this neighborhood, Clarice, and you know it. This is home."

Clarice wondered why she even brought the subject up anymore. The conversation always ended with Arthur telling her the military had been good to them, and that he wanted to give something back to a community that needed leadership. She waited, and sure enough, it came.

"The Navy was good to us, Clarice. Now it's time for me to give something back."

"Our neighborhood desperately needs leadership, right?"

"I couldn't have said it any better."

She smiled. *He never catches on that I know the speech.* "I just hope those streets you're trying to save don't eat you alive."

Arthur Jackson served on two local advisory groups, was active in church, and was recently urged to run for a seat on the school board. Some told him he should think about being a candidate for the city council if Francie McMillan ever went after the mayor's job.

Clarice shuddered at the thought. She hated politics. "Well, all I know is I'm glad our kids had the good sense to get out of here." She began coring some Granny Smith apples. "By the way, the security bars on the front door screen are coming loose."

Arthur walked out of the kitchen. "I'll fix them after I get James's room in order."

Clarice sighed. She could hardly wait for James to arrive. She and Arthur had been married for twenty-nine years and had three sons and a daughter. One by one, they had left home and now, all but their youngest son, James, had married and were raising families of their own. The home on Amigo Street had been quiet for many years, but soon twenty-two-year-old James would be back. He was coming to Los Angeles for a job interview at Regal Brothers. James was the pride of the family; he'd made it through the University of Missouri in just three years and graduated Phi Beta Kappa. He was working for an advertising agency in Chicago and had been contacted about a newly-created position in Regal's marketing department. Regal was actively recruiting minority applicants, and James Jackson was told he was their number-one choice.

The first thing Mo-Jo Jones saw as he continued driving on Amigo Street was a man in a red baseball cap and a red St. Louis Cardinals jacket. He was using a coat hanger to open the door of a white car. A big car. A new car. It could be sold for a big price.

What are you doin', fool? Mo-Jo was looking for someone in red, but didn't expect him to be stealing a car—and in the middle of the morning. Mo-Jo pulled in behind the parked car. The guy with the coat hanger was much taller than Mo-Jo, but then almost everyone was.

"Hey, bro, what's happenin'?" said Mo-Jo.

"I locked myself out of my car."

"This your car? Come on, man. There a lot of dollar here."

"Well, it isn't exactly my car." The man smiled. "It's a rental. Picked it up at the airport and now I'm locked out."

Jones looked at him. "Ain't seen nothin' like this in the 'hood, 'cept some pimp's car. You jivin' me?"

The man gave Mo-Jo a nervous frown.

Mo-Jo grinned. "Okay, bro, I believe you. Tell you what. I know a little about gettin' into cars. Show me how you usin' that hanger. When I first saw you, it looked like you had it in the wrong place."

The man turned to the car and pushed the hanger into the small crack in the window. "It's really frustrating. I seem to catch something, but when I—"

A muffled *fffttt* stopped him in mid-sentence. The bullet from the .38 revolver entered the back of his head, and blood spattered the window as his dead body crumpled against the driver's door and slid to the pavement.

Mo-Jo looked around. He was sure no one had seen the killing. He had one last thing to do before leaving. He tucked the pistol with the silencer back inside his waistband, then took a piece of cloth from his pocket and wrapped it around his index finger. On the bloody window he finger-painted, "CLAW 1144 (police code for dead body—he knew this stuff) SAY-R." He had delivered his message.

Councilwoman Francie McMillan was called out of her meeting for a phone call. She picked up the phone at her desk.

"Francie, it's Arthur. Our James is dead." Arthur began to cry.

When she heard the news, her shoulders sagged, and she gripped the desk. She found her way to an overstuffed chair and sank down into it. "Your J. J.?"

Over the years, Francie had spent many evenings with James in the Jackson home on neighborhood and campaign business. She was instrumental in his contact with Regal Brothers. The company had asked her for the names of people she might recommend for a special position being created, and she had given them only one name: James Jackson.

Arthur told her as much as he knew. James had apparently arrived near their home early and had parked his car two blocks away, probably intending to walk to their home and surprise them. Police believed he had somehow locked his keys in the rental car. A clerk for the rental company at LAX remembered James because he'd upgraded him to a luxury model when no mid-sizes were available. A witness to the crime said James had come to his house to borrow a coat hanger.

"Someone gunned him down in the street, Francie. It was cold blood. We never got to see him."

"Oh, Arthur, Arthur. And Clarice, sweet Clarice. Let me pray with you—may I?"

"Sure."

"Dear Heavenly Father, our hearts are broken. J. J., wonderful J. J., is with You; we know that, but You allowed him to be taken so quickly. I ask that Arthur, Clarice, and their family would feel Your loving arms of comfort. Give them strength. Almighty God, have mercy, in the name of Jesus. Amen."

"God, bless you, Francie," Arthur sobbed.

"Arthur, do the police have any leads?"

"Some ideas, that's all. I told James not to wear that jacket around here, but you know how he loves the Cardinals. The cops think it was a gang hit."

"Why?"

He composed himself and told her about the gang-writing on the bloody window. "Can't say much more. Let me call you later. I haven't even thought about the funeral, but we've got to start."

"Please tell Clarice and the children I am so, so sorry, Arthur."

"Francie?"

"Yes?"

"Things are different now." He paused. "The war came into our home today."

Francie put the phone back on the hook and released the tears she had held inside while Arthur was on the line.

The funeral for Grant Peters was going exactly as Ian Thornberry had planned. It was a media spectacle. Cameras were in place, and soon Mayor Bodine would stand up to give words of comfort to Peters's family and loved ones.

Ian sat in his pew in the front row and, out of the corner of his eye, watched the veiled young woman in black fight back tears. Two boys sat on either side of her—one looked about ten and the other was in his early teens. Directly in front of them was a closed casket, draped with flowers surrounding a color photo of Peters's smiling face.

Friends were now eulogizing the deceased. The family had not wanted the mayor to speak, and they'd nearly had their way. But Ian coaxed, pushed, cajoled, and pleaded with Peters's widow. Why, she'd asked, should a politician whom she'd only met that morning speak at her husband's funeral? Ian was relentless and finally convinced the family that if the mayor spoke, it might help bring Jorge Escobedo to justice. Based on Channel Three's video, a murder warrant was out for Escobedo's arrest, and Ian had told the family the mayor would make a public plea for his capture. The truth was, he had simply worn them out. Grief usually won over logic.

Every seat in the First United Methodist Church was taken. One row of pews in the front of the church was set aside for the family, and three more behind them for the news media. An overflow crowd of about three hundred stood quietly on the lawn and under trees in a light drizzle. They were listening to the service over a loudspeaker rigged up at the last moment.

Grant Peters's widow had told Ian she did not want TV cameras inside the church during the service. But, once again, he got his way. He told her that if the mayor's comments were going to have maximum impact, they needed to be shown on television. So a camera was set up in the balcony. It was operated by Channel Three as "pool" coverage for the other stations and networks. Channel Three had preempted regular programming and was televising the funeral live.

Ian watched Brenda Bodine walk toward the platform. She

was about to read what he'd written for her. *Brenda, no!*, he wanted to shout, *first stop and say something to the widow. Remember what I told you!*

As if she had heard him, she turned and walked over to the family. The television camera zoomed in on what appeared to be a comforting moment between the two women.

Ian grinned.

Bodine then walked to the pulpit. "On behalf of the city," she began, "I would like to express my heartfelt sympathies to the family of Grant Peters." The mayor then looked directly at the family.

Remember to use their first names. Rosemary is the widow, Tommy is the oldest, Philip is the little guy.

"To Rosemary—and—Tommy—and, ah, your entire family, we share your pain."

Oh, well, two out of three isn't bad. Come on, Brenda, this is our big chance!

"We all grieve over the loss of Grant Peters, but in death, he has given every citizen of this city new hope. I learned just an hour ago from Police Chief Morgan that crime is dropping in Los Angeles."

Great! You used the late info I gave you.

"Grant Peters did not die in vain. He'll be remembered as the person who taught us that just saying no wasn't enough. He's the person who taught us we had to say yes! Yes, we'll get involved. Yes, we can fight back. Yes, we won't quit, and yes, we'll win! Grant Peters is one of our greatest heroes. Grant Peters will be remembered as the man who gave the streets back to the people."

Several people began to applaud before remembering with embarrassment they were at a funeral.

"But there is still one person we need to remove from our streets. I use the word person only because he looks like a human being. He's not a man, he's a monster. That person is Jorge

Escobedo."

She now looked directly to the balcony and into the television camera.

"We need the help of all of you to find this monster. I give you my vow, and that of our entire police department, that he'll be caught, tried, and convicted for the murder of Grant Peters. I will also do everything in my power to see that the poison he has spread in our city will one day fill his lungs in the gas chamber."

Yes! Ian Thornberry pumped his fist, then sat back in his pew, grinning from ear to ear. When members of Peters's family turned to look at him, he quickly put his hand over his mouth to hide his smile. But his eyes were full of glee. *Sacramento, here we come.*

Televisions were on throughout the offices of Channel Three.

"Too bad about that guy, but what a break for us." Arlene Zahn was in her office speaking to Harvey Rose. The entire station had stopped mid-morning to watch the coverage.

"Everything's going our way," answered Rose. "But how much are we losing by preempting the soaps for the funeral?"

"A hundred thousand or so, but I got Ruggles to see we're building our audience for later tonight. We'll get it back and then some."

Rose put his hands behind his head. "We need another shocker, something outrageous to happen."

"I already suggested that to Fred—another attack on Paul's wife."

Rose chuckled. "That would do it. What did Fred say?"

"He was ticked—asked me if I was born with a heart."

"No sense of humor, huh?" said Rose.

Arlene leaned forward. "I was serious, Harvey. We've got momentum, and we've got to keep piling it on." She reached across her desk and picked up the ratings from the night before. "Look at this." She held the paper out to him and pointed to the figures. "We did great at 6 P.M., a bit higher than yesterday—we're destroying the other stations. However, we went out of sight at eleven—four million people tuned in!"

"How much of our commercial time is locked in?" Rose asked.

"I've canceled about half the spots on the eleven o'clock news at the old rates, but I couldn't dump them all, at least not for now. It's killing me."

The price for advertising time at Channel Three was already set by the results of the July ratings period. But because the audience now was more than four times what it was a month ago, the station had canceled agreements with some advertisers. If they were willing to pay $28,476 for a thirty-second spot that had been priced at $7,119, they could still have it. Otherwise, the ad time was sold to another sponsor. This is what had happened during the Gulf War. Longtime sponsors who had kept their spots at the old price were happy until Arlene told them they had to buy additional time at oddball hours.

"Did you have anything open at eleven?" he asked.

"We killed your in-house promo and a public service announcement, but I could have sold ten more spots at top price without leaving my office."

"So, if we keep this up through the November book, what's the price for a thirty-second spot?"

She tilted her head back and let out a deep sigh.

"We could get $30,000 each, probably more. Four two-minute commercial breaks means sixteen spots, and that, my friend, is $480,000 a night, just for the eleven o'clock news."

Rose scribbled some numbers on a piece of paper. "That's 2.4 million a week. Obscene!"

"And enough for Ruggles to make me permanent sales manager."

"And me, program director," Rose said. "That job is mine."

"Just do the job you have now, Harvey—"

"The head guys in New York will go nuts when they see this!"

Arlene considered his last words. "Someday, I'll be one of those head guys, Harvey. Bet on it."

They looked at each other and smiled.

"Thank you, Grant Peters," he said.

"Harvey, you're cold. But you're right."

CHAPTER ELEVEN

"It's sixty-two degrees with light rain falling in most of Los Angeles, ten minutes past one. You're listening to KFI, 710 Talk Radio, and I'm Lester Hawkins."

Paul Thomas sat across from Hawkins in the studio. Harvey Rose had arranged for him to be on the program and had asked Paul to stop by the radio station on his way to work.

"I'm joined by none other than the captain of the Light Brigade, Paul Thomas of *Channel Three News*."

Paul winced at Hawkins's sarcastic tone. "We're ready to sign you up," he replied with a smile he hoped listeners could hear.

"Forget it. This whole Light the Night thing has looked bogus from the start. Smells like a TV promotion to me."

Hawkins was often at odds with local television stations. Almost everyone knew that Hawkins wanted very much to be on TV, but he'd been told more than once to look in the mirror. Radio suited him much better.

"Les, give the neighborhoods credit. I wish we'd come up with the idea earlier, but all I did was say something off-the-cuff, and the people ran with it."

"Well, if this is so great, what's this stuff I'm reading about you being fired?"

"I'm still on the payroll, but it can happen to the best of us, even you, right?"

Hawkins obviously wanted to engage Paul in an argument.

"Okay, I agree some crime in LA is down the past few days. So what? You think your citizens' patrols with their Mickey Mouse camcorders is the answer?"

"Come on, Les, you know they aren't my patrols. They're just part of the answer."

"Are you saying this Light the Night thing is strictly a public service? Hasn't it helped your career and the station's ratings?"

"Sure, but since more people are watching us, that should tell you we're doing something right. Do you have a problem with Light the Night?"

"Be real, okay? How can people go up against gangs that are armed to the teeth?"

Paul's mind flashed to the murder of Grant Peters, the attack on his wife, and the threat against his own life. "What do we do, wimp out? Do we just give up?"

Hawkins didn't answer. "Fifteen minutes past one. I'm Lester Hawkins, KFI 710 Talk Radio. Channel Three news anchor Paul Thomas, the captain of the Light Brigade, is my guest. We'll let you talk with him after this commercial time-out." A music bumper was heard, then Hawkins looked at Paul and gave him a sneer. "We'll let the rubes at home sound off, but I'm not through with you."

"Take your best shot," Paul said. "But try to keep your punches above the belt."

Two minutes later, they were back on the air, and all phone lines into the station were jammed. Some callers criticized Hawkins for the way he was treating Paul. One man agreed with Hawkins, saying Light the Night was a gimmick that would soon fizzle out. Paul had heard Hawkins instruct his telephone screener to find that kind of call. The overwhelming majority wanted to give Light the Night a chance and chided Hawkins for being so negative.

"Okay, I've heard enough. It's obvious the Paul Thomas fan club has some kind of organized call-in to make him look good—"

"Wrong, Les!" Paul interrupted. "That's a cheap shot—

you're insulting your listeners. There's nothing set up on my part. Yours, perhaps, but not mine. This is all spontaneous, and you know it." As he spoke, Paul saw Hawkins smile. *He got me into an argument—just what he wanted.*

"Oooooh, aren't we touchy this afternoon? Can't take a little heat, huh, Captain? Well, before you go back to mission control, and I think this whole thing is being controlled by Channel Three, answer this."

"Fire away."

"If Light the Night is not a Paul Thomas, Channel Three ruse, why aren't the other TV stations going all out on coverage?"

"Ask them. All I know is that at eleven o'clock, our news is on in more than a million homes. We're giving four million people something they need."

"Well, why did your station televise the funeral of Grant Peters live? Did they need that?"

"It helped bring the city together. Grant Peters is a symbol of what we're trying to do."

"A dead symbol?"

"A courageous symbol, Les."

Paul knew he'd landed a knockout punch. Hawkins was reeling. "Just don't enlist me in your 'Blight Brigade.'"

Now Paul put Hawkins down for a verbal ten-count. "Don't worry, pal, you wouldn't measure up." Paul hesitated, and Hawkins responded silently. "Les, I know you've always wanted to work in television. I wish we were on TV right now."

Hawkins was making an obscene gesture.

"Does that gesture mean Channel Three is number one?" And Paul winked.

Fred Taylor stuck his head into Paul's office. "You handled yourself well with Hawkins today."

Paul looked up from his desk and nodded. "Thanks, Fred.

Hawkins ticked me off. I was tempted on the air to make him a private in the 'Wimp Brigade.'"

"Yeah, I know. You did the right thing."

"Fred, I need help on this voice mail and the letters that are coming in." He pointed to three boxes of unopened mail in the corner next to a bookcase. "I'm just glad I listened to my voice mail last night so I could get Silva's call."

"I've got Tim working on it."

"Well, I need it now. I can't clear my messages." He pointed to the box. "And who knows what might be in those letters? Could be tips on Escobedo, could be anything."

"Okay, I'll find out, but not now. Listen, I know you're waiting for a call from *Nightscope*, and the network people are in the lobby. After you get things squared away, we need you in the conference room."

Thomas shrugged and went back to listening to his phone messages. Fred proceeded down the hall, only to be intercepted by Bill Randall.

"Fred, I need to talk with you in your office."

Fred groaned. What now? "I don't have much time. I've got a meeting."

The two walked into Fred's office, and Randall closed the door behind them.

Great, a closed-door session with the "star."

"Fred, I just heard Thomas on the radio with Lester Hawkins, and I think we're going overboard with Light the Night."

"Oh, you do, huh? Well, I don't."

Fred didn't have time to make small talk with a news anchor who had quickly turned into a pain. The first six months after his arrival at the station, Bill Randall was fairly easy to work with. His large ego hadn't caused many problems at Channel Three because he was the principal anchor—the star, as he liked to call himself. But now he obviously felt threatened; insecurity was tattooed all over his face.

"We're wasting too much time on not one, but two segments. Viewers are going to get bored."

"Listen, Bill, I heard this same whining yesterday. It made me sick the first time. Your problem is not Light the Night; it's Paul Thomas."

Randall's eyes blinked.

"I really don't care what you think," Fred went on, "because we have more than four million people watching us. Sorry to break this to you, but you aren't the main reason half of the TVs in Los Angeles are tuning in to Channel Three at six. People want to know more about Light the Night, and Paul Thomas is going to give it to them. You have a role to play, and you're still an important part of the news team." Fred paused. "Did you hear that last word, Bill? Let me spell it for you: T-E-A-M. Be a man, be a player. We're winning right now, winning big. Be part of it—for your own good."

Randall stood silent.

Fred gathered some papers into a folder, then looked back up. "I'm late for a meeting I should have been at ten minutes ago. You can stand here with your mouth open if you want, but our conversation is over."

Paul Thomas had been on the telephone for fifteen minutes now. The network was briefing him on what to expect for his *Nightscope* interview. It would be produced live on the East Coast, but taped for broadcast in other time zones. The program's theme was the fight against crime, and network host Carter Davidson wanted to ask Paul about the media's role in bringing people together.

"What was I doing before this thing broke?" Paul said, repeating the producer's question. "I was anchoring the morning and noon news." He smiled at Carter's response. "Yeah, you could say my life has changed. I never thought I'd report a national story, let alone be the story." Paul listened as the producer made sure he understood where he had to be. "Okay, I've got it—in place at 8:20, the segment goes on at 8:36. Just Carter and me?" Paul nodded. "Okay, see you then. I've got some network people here."

Next was an interview with a network news crew that had just arrived at the station. They were even now setting up lights in his office while he finished his phone call with *Nightscope*.

"Paul, I'm Connie McDougall and I'm field producing the piece on Light the Night." A petite brunette reached out to shake his hand.

"Good to meet you, Connie. The last four days have been incredible."

"And I understand it all started with you."

"Yeah, an ad-lib turned into an avalanche—hey, that's not bad," he said with a laugh.

She laughed, too, then turned as a heavyset man entered his office. "Paul, meet Darnell Fulton, our correspondent on the story."

"Seems like I know you, Darnell. I like your work; you're a pro."

"Hey, thanks. Sounds like you're the main guy in the story of the year. If all goes right and we get this piece done in time, the whole nation will know who Paul Thomas is."

Paul couldn't explain the strange feeling that had suddenly come over him—first the *Nightscope* producer and now a network correspondent about to interview him. He decided to just enjoy it.

"I heard about your ratings," said the correspondent. "Hope your contract is up pretty soon. I'd imagine you could ask for the moon."

"As a matter of fact, it is about up. I hadn't thought about it until all of this. I'm not sure if I could get the moon, but if things continue, I should be able to get most of the craters."

They all laughed.

Paul walked into the room just as plans for the 6 P.M. newscast were about in place. The producers and assignment people had already gathered at their regular meeting that morning, but now Light the Night had brought them together again for last-minute adjustments.

"Sorry I'm late," Paul said. "You know the network—they ask a hundred questions and they'll probably use twelve seconds."

Fred Taylor pointed to his right. "Paul, listen to what Gladys put together."

Paul turned to the art director who looked as if she had been up half the night. "Well, after fast-forwarding through a hundred war movies until three this morning, I think I have what you want," she said, rubbing her eyes. She unrolled a blueprint-sized paper and spread it on the conference table. It showed a portion of the news set from two different angles. "Here's Paul's 'War Command Post.'"

Everyone gathered around the drawing.

Paul looked it over, then smiled. "You'll get a Distinguished Drawing Cross for this, Gladys. It's perfect."

"It should be. When we build it, you could direct World War Two from here."

"Good work, Gladys," said Fred. " I like it."

"Looks pretty official to me," added someone else.

"When can you have it ready?" asked Fred. "Today is Thursday."

"We bought most of the material this morning. I figured any design changes wouldn't make much of a difference in what we use to build it, so we've got a little head start. If you can get me two people from engineering, then okay a ton of overtime, and let me hire two carpenters and a painter, we might have it ready to go by late next week."

"What would it take to get it finished by the eleven o'clock news Monday?" Fred asked.

The art director's eyebrows went up. "Monday? I, ah—that would take a miracle."

"Can you do it?" asked Paul.

She looked around the room. "Well, all we can do is give it a shot."

"Pull the trigger," said Fred. "Do it."

"Great newscast, Tim." Fred Taylor walked around his desk to his chair and sat down. He'd seen exactly what he wanted.

The closing credits for Channel Three's 6 P.M. news were rolling too fast for the names to make much of an impression. The intent was to show the audience the number of people needed behind the scenes to bring the news into their homes. The station's theme music came to a dramatic end, and the news was over.

"Everything fell into place," said Hires.

"Right from the top, we grabbed their attention and for sixty minutes never let go." Fred clapped his hands. "It was perfect!"

James Jackson's murder had been the lead story. Police believed it was gang related and that Jackson had been mistaken for a gang member. Channel Three had learned the suspect's car was stolen. An eyewitness saw a man leaving the scene in a dark blue Mustang, later found abandoned in an alley. Inside, officers found the blood-soaked cloth the murderer used to write his message on the window of Jackson's car.

The coverage of Grant Peters's funeral was a natural follow-up to the Jackson murder. The reporter had been told to keep his narration to a minimum and to focus on the words of those who eulogized Peters. It was a hard-hitting and emotional report, and Mayor Bodine was featured prominently.

What followed next in the newscast was the reason Fred thought the Channel Three news team was wiping out its competition.

Just before Paul's first Light the Night segment was a heartbreaking report on the funeral of Raul Fernandez and his infant son. The story showed a loving family saying good-bye to a God-fearing man and a precious baby. The beauty of the report was in its simplicity. No need to be sensational or fancy—just show the people and tell the story.

Then came Paul Thomas. After three emotionally draining stories, the more than four million viewers desperately needed something to lift their spirits. They wanted to see the good guys winning some of the battle, and Thomas gave it to them.

He went first to an overnight story. An electronic map behind him highlighted the suburb of Temple City. Special effects zoomed the map out, and in its place was a powerful videotape shot by an unidentified woman.

"Watch what all of us can do," Thomas said. "It's simply people working as the eyes of the police."

The tape showed the outside of a Lucky's supermarket. "Police say the woman had just returned to her car after buying some groceries. As she was about to drive away, she looked back into the store and saw two men wearing ski masks. She used her cellular phone to call 911." Paul paused for effect. "She happened to have a camcorder that she'd used earlier in the evening at a birthday party. Her vantage point was excellent—she was parked directly in front of the store." Again, Paul paused to create suspense. "This is an armed robbery. It's late in the evening, and two men in ski masks are taking cash from each register, along with watches and wallets from customers. One of the men is armed with a handgun."

The video showed the other man filling what looked like a pillowcase with whatever people gave him.

"It's not a sophisticated holdup, but these often are the most violent."

The robbers turned their attention to a man who appeared to be the store's night manager.

"Now the two men are apparently demanding access to the store's safe. One of the men hits the manager with the back of his hand. We've learned that the manager told them cash accumulated during the day is put in a safe that can't be opened until morning."

Sirens could be heard in the background.

"The person shooting the tape called police immediately. Look at the bottom of your picture. Her video shows officers arriving and positioning themselves near the entrance by some shopping carts. Other officers entered the store from the back. Now watch what happens when the suspects realize the cops are nearby."

The video showed the robbers bolting for the front when officers started shouting from the back. The suspects obviously expected the glass doors to open automatically—they didn't. The store manager had apparently pushed the emergency lock button. Both men crashed headfirst into the closed doors and fell backward. The robber with the gun immediately fired into the doors, and the window shattered. A burly male customer in a hard hat then shoved a grocery cart in the direction of the two men. It hit the armed suspect in the back of the legs. He dropped his weapon, was knocked into the cart, and wedged in tight. The officers in front of the store, guns drawn, made the second suspect change his mind and surrender on the spot. But there was one more scene to be played out.

"We don't recommend this, but I have to say, this is my favorite part of the whole story," Paul said.

The tape showed an older woman walking up to the robber who was stuck in the grocery cart. She yanked off his ski mask, shook her finger in his face, and said something to him which he took exception to. So she walked a few feet to a shelf where she picked up a banana cream pie. Then she calmly walked back to the man and splattered it in his face.

In the second half of the 6 P.M. news, Fred had watched as Paul concentrated on two new areas that continued to have a high crime rate—Long Beach and Compton. Part of Channel Three's master plan was to have some form of Light the Night in every neighborhood in the LA area by Thursday, November 2. On that day, the most important ratings period of the year would begin.

At Paul's suggestion, Fred had okayed a new feature listing the day's ten newest Light Brigade citizens' patrols. Paul narrated over videotape of a group shot of men and women standing for what looked like a classroom photo session. Many were armed with video camcorders; they were bringing their tapes to Channel Three to be shown on the evening newscasts.

The newscast put Fred and Tim in high spirits.

"Did I tell you I've had three camera companies call and ask if we could mention their names on the air?" Tim grinned. "They're offering the patrols free cameras."

"What did you say?"

"Thanks, but no thanks. I told them if they want mention on the air, they'll have to buy commercial time."

"I'm sure the sales department will thank you," said Fred. "Is Paul all set for *Nightscope?*"

"Yeah, everything is in place," said Tim. "The *Nightscope* stuff shouldn't interfere with his eleven o'clock segments. There's only one person I'm really worried about."

"Who's that?"

"Randall. He gave me a ration of grief this afternoon about Paul. He thinks you're going to make Paul the six and eleven o'clock anchor."

"How can I not think about it after what's happened this week, Tim?"

"Well, are you?"

"I don't think so, for now. For the time being, we keep Paul right where he's at, in the spotlight. If we move him to anchor, I think it dilutes his impact. This way Randall reads all the stuff around Light the Night, and that keeps Paul closely identified with his brigade."

"I still think Randall is going goofy on us."

"You may be right. Keep an eye on him, okay?"

"Got a straightjacket handy?"

Fred thought for a second. "You might order two."

"Who's the other one for?"

"Wilson Ruggles."

"Thirty seconds, Paul," said the floor director.

A taped report by a *Nightscope* correspondent on crime around the nation was just about over. It was prepared especially to set up the live interview with Paul, and it included the dramatic drop in crime in metropolitan Los Angeles since the beginning of Light the Night. The reporter made it clear that all of the recent events began with a casual comment Paul had made on the air. Paul felt a glow when he heard himself praised.

Appearing with Thomas was Kathleen O'Malley, a media critic for a Philadelphia newspaper. The two would be on the air simultaneously in a boxed special effect. Paul was only told about O'Malley's part in the interview five minutes beforehand. Typical TV news ambush. Paul never liked being interviewed—strange, since he'd been asking people questions his entire career. He didn't think he was uncomfortable in the interview setting—he just felt he never said enough or either said too much. And afterward he'd always think of great lines he could have used. Yet, if he were honest with himself, he supposed he was uncomfortable with a microphone in his face.

This was worse. He would be talking to a camera on national TV and to someone he couldn't see. His only contact was through an earpiece. Paul was used to pouring out his emotions to a camera for the news, but this was different. It felt weird.

Carter Davidson was on-camera in the network's New York studio. "So, our question tonight—can people, ordinary citizens, stop crime?"

"Stand by, Paul," spoke a voice from New York into his earpiece.

"The person who planted the idea in the minds of those people is news anchor Paul Thomas."

Paul nodded and smiled. *Try to look comfortable.*

"Also with us is media critic and Philadelphia newspaper columnist Kathleen O'Malley."

She, too, nodded, but didn't smile.

"First to Paul Thomas. Thanks for joining us. I wonder, would Los Angeles have seen a drop in crime without your television station pushing Light the Night?"

"Carter, we did two things. First, we listened to people. They were fed up. Then we helped them rally together. They've cut crime, we haven't."

"What you're doing, though, is nothing new, is it?" asked Davidson.

"Taken individually, no. But the citizens' patrols forming in the neighborhoods, many arming themselves with video cameras and two-way radios, that's new. Already, in one week, overall crime in this area compared with last year has been cut in half. That's amazing."

"Let me bring in Kathleen O'Malley," said Davidson.

The shot of Paul pulled back on the screen to a box next to O'Malley, and then she was zoomed back full behind Davidson.

"Ms. O'Malley, what's your opinion of Light the Night and Channel Three?"

O'Malley was a woman in her mid-thirties—short hair, dark eyes, a wide mouth, and not unattractive. "I have a problem with a television news station that seems to be creating its lead story every night. It's confusing. Is crime the story, or is it Channel Three's captain of the Light Brigade? Isn't that what they call you?"

Paul was zoomed back in his box, and now the three of them were on-screen together.

"What about that, Mr. Thomas?" Davidson asked.

Paul smiled. "Yes, that's what they call me. But as a print journalist, Ms. O'Malley, you should be pleased. The title they've given me came from a newspaper, the *Examiner*."

She didn't look pleased. "Are you creating the news?"

"I think you've missed the point. Crime isn't the main story here, people are. That's what Light the Night is all about—people making crime go down. If I can help them do that, if Channel Three can help, then that's what we'll have on our news."

O'Malley fidgeted in her seat. "Okay, Captain, how about your wife being attacked? That conveniently brought sympathy and helped boost your station's ratings."

Paul bristled at the suggestion. "Kathleen, we've never met until tonight, but that's a truly stupid thing to say. Frankly, I'm embarrassed for you. To imply that I might have staged the attack on my wife is an outrage."

Her eyes darted from side to side.

"Yes, I'm scared about threats against my family," Paul went on. "Who wouldn't be?"

"Why make them a target?" she countered.

"There's a war going on out here. Brave people were brutally murdered this week. However, we have our first glimmer of hope in years. Residents of the LA area are making crime go down, and I'm not about to give up." He paused. Should he say it? Yes. "To be honest, as a Christian, I've left all of this in the Lord's hands."

"Paul Thomas, Kathleen O'Malley," Carter Davidson broke in, "we've run out of time, but we need to have you two on again soon. After a break, a look at crime in one rural community and how citizens there are coping. We'll be right back."

"We're clear," a floor director told Paul. "Good job."

"Whew." Paul looked at a man who was taking off his headset. "Thanks. Pardon the lack of humility, but I thought it went great. Can you see any scratches? That gal from Philly sure went after me."

"Isn't that supposed to be the City of Brotherly Love?" asked the man.

"Now you know why they don't call it the city of sisterly love."

Much of the nation had just watched and listened to Paul

Thomas. When *Nightscope* aired out west, he would be known from coast to coast. He congratulated himself. *For the first time, you actually said what you wanted to say. Thank you, Lord.* Other thoughts crowded out his prayer—thoughts of a new contract. He chuckled. *Wait 'till Bill Randall sees this.*

Bill Randall introduced the lead story. "Our top story tonight, a dramatic shoot-out inside a Brea shopping mall. Three robbers are dead, killed by armed citizens who were on their second night of a secret security patrol." The camera showed Randall and Paul on a two-shot. "Here, with details, is Paul Thomas."

"Bill, this was a case of 'us' against 'them,' and 'us' made a statement tonight."

The shopping mall showed on the screen. Three covered bodies lay on the ground while a crowd of anxious people strained to get a closer look from behind police barriers.

Paul went on to report that in recent months this mall had been plagued by muggings, vandalism, car break-ins, and even a kidnapping inside a Nordstrom store. Those who lived nearby wanted to do something ever since a neighbor's daughter was brutally beaten in the mall's parking lot. The Brea police were unable to increase patrols in the area, and the mall's management was reluctant to spend money on additional security.

"Light the Night was all the people needed," said Paul. "On Wednesday, eight men and two women formed a citizens' patrol. Two of the members were law enforcement officers—a woman with the LA County Sheriff's Department, and a man, a deputy marshall. Without the knowledge of management, the patrol began surveillance inside the mall. Three hours into their patrol, the two off-duty officers came upon an armed robbery in progress inside a jewelry store. They apparently identified themselves as off-duty officers and ordered the suspects to 'freeze.' Here's what an eyewitness says happened next."

An excited young woman spoke into the camera. "I was in the store, and one of the robbers, I think it was the woman—yeah, it was the woman—she aims her gun at them, and starts firing." The eyewitness pushed her hair out of her face. "Well, then, the two—what were they—off-duty cops—whatever, they blasted away at the robbers. I was, like, frozen. I couldn't move. The ones who got shot, they all fell backward. The men landed on the carpet, and then, I'll never forget it, the woman goes crashing into a jewelry case. And you know what she does before she dies? She yells—" But the eyewitness's graphic words were "bleeped" by the station.

In this case, the edge went to the people.

Paul narrated other stories in the first segment, none with quite the degree of drama as the mall shoot-out, but all ending with absolute certainty that the criminals had lost and the people had won.

One group of citizens heard the cries of an older woman as she was attacked by two men in her Redondo Beach home. When they got to the scene, they called the police, but while the officers were on the way, some anonymous fists managed to break a nose on one would-be rapist and close one of the eyes of the other. When police asked how it happened, patrol members said the men tripped. Edge to the people.

In Koreatown, near the scene of Monday's murder of a liquor store owner, Korean-Americans defended themselves against a group of Iron Claw gang members. The gang had weapons, but the citizens' patrol had black belts in tae kwon do. Police called it "no contest." Five ambulances were needed to transport the thugs who had suffered an assortment of broken jaws, fractured arms, and cracked ribs.

Police ruled the incident self-defense.

The day had started with the heartbreaking funeral for Grant Peters. It was ending with the sense that what Peters fought for was within reach. Paul knew something was definitely changing. A shift was occurring in who was in control of much of the LA area. One side of the city was gaining an edge. Recently, many of Channel Three's newscasts often showed a lighter side of people gaining the upper hand over criminals. However, on this night, there were no burglars locked in sheds with skunks, no robbers with pie on their faces wedged in shopping carts. On this night, deadly encounters had occurred. The edge belonged to the new "sheriff" in town, the people.

Paul concluded his Light the Night report with a commentary. "John F. Kennedy wrote a book called *Profiles in Courage*. We're seeing a new chapter written in Los Angeles, and you are doing it. Something remarkable is happening, not just in our neighborhoods, but in our hearts. This morning we were reminded of our losses. Tonight, because of your caring and your courage, we are counting our victories. There's a great movement of the people right now and all of us here at Channel Three are proud to be part of it. I'm Paul Thomas. Keep on shining, everyone. Bill?"

The camera showed Paul, Randall, and Chen on a three-shot. Randall quickly mumbled, "Good night."

CHAPTER TWELVE

Friday, September 15

It was only a few minutes before six, but to Paul it felt like a leisurely Saturday morning. At this time, just four days ago, he was on the air anchoring the news and about to make his Light the Night suggestion.

A misty, early morning fog had tucked in most of coastal Los Angeles and several miles inland—it was good sleeping-in weather. The window in Paul and Maddie's bedroom was cracked open about two inches, and the shade was pulled all the way down. He liked the bedroom dark, but she liked the window open so she could enjoy the morning sun—this was their compromise.

"How'd you sleep, Captain?"

Paul felt the warmth of Maddie's body as she nestled closer to him. "Captain, sir, if you don't mind," he said, putting his arms around her.

"How about Idiot Captain, sir? I watched *Nightscope* and wanted to punch that Philadelphia broad right in the mouth."

Paul chuckled. "Actually, I think she decked herself with her own foot." He paused. "You still have doubts about me going on *Nightscope?*"

"We haven't seen how it's going to change you. The jury is still out."

Down the hall, they could hear their two children getting ready for school. Elizabeth was blow-drying her hair in the bathroom, and Travis was rummaging around in his dresser, opening and closing drawers, obviously not finding what he was looking for.

"What time are the painters coming this morning?" Paul pulled back the covers, walked to the window, and opened the shade. He couldn't see beyond the back fence because of the fog.

"They said about ten."

"Sorry I couldn't get someone sooner. That junk on the walls is gross. What did the kids say?"

"They're scared to death. What did you expect them to do, just shrug it off?"

"Not that again, Maddie, okay?"

Maddie sat upright in bed. "Paul, I wasn't going to tell you this, but I'm being followed."

He sat on the edge of the bed. "When? Where?"

"It started yesterday morning when I went to the grocery store. And I swear, someone was looking over the fence right after you left to do that radio show."

"Are you sure?"

"Yeah, I'm sure. And I'll tell you this—even if we had a hundred rent-a-cops out front and twenty Vinnies, I think when that creep, Escobedo, decides to get us, he can do it any time he wants."

The morning fog extended from West Los Angeles inland four miles to the rich hills of Bel Air, where Jorge Escobedo had risen before dawn. He was dressed in a maroon silk robe and had just poured himself a cup of Kona coffee—black with no sugar. The *Examiner* lay on the sofa next to him. He'd just read again the words Mayor Bodine had spoken at Grant Peters's funeral. All night, he had replayed her words over and over in his mind. He feared no threat from her or the police, but hated her for calling his brother's killer a hero. He'd already decided the city needed another reminder of Danny Escobedo's death. Plans were in the making for that, but first, he had some gang business to take care of.

He looked at Tony "Big Ears" Romero who sat across the

room from him. They had grown up in the same neighborhood; Big Ears was one of the few people Jorge trusted. Romero had a regular network of reporting gang members, girlfriends, prostitutes, pimps, and even an LA police officer who kept him informed on what was going on in the city.

"So, who killed him?" Jorge asked.

Jorge and Romero knew the murder of James Jackson was a mistake. The blood-scrawled threat was a message to Insane Rulers and demanded an immediate, deadly answer. Even though one of Jorge's gang members had not been taken out, whoever pulled the trigger had intended to kill an Insane Ruler. The gunman had to die; it was part of the rules of gang warfare.

"Maurice Jones did it," Big Ears said.

"Who?"

"Mo-Jo."

Jorge slowly nodded. The street name brought a clear picture to mind. "Mo-Jo is about to become 'No-Mo.'"

Fred Taylor was already in his garage, about to get in his car and drive to work, when he turned around and went back inside his house to make a phone call. He'd thought a lot about Marcia Willis since their time together two nights ago. He couldn't seem to get her out of his mind.

She answered the phone on the third ring. "Hello."

"Marcia, Fred Taylor—hope I didn't call too early." For a moment, there was no answer. He was embarrassed by the silence, fearful she was about to give him an earful.

"Well—hi, Fred. This is a surprise."

"What are you doing?"

"Uh, actually, I'm getting ready for work."

"Oh, yeah, of course." Why couldn't he think of anything clever to say?

"Paul was pretty good last night on *Nightscope*." She was

throwing him a lifeline.

"Yeah, I thought so, too." He hesitated, then, "Listen, Marcia, I don't quite know how to say this. Well, I was, shall we say, a little short with you on the phone yesterday." He waited, but she didn't say anything. "Anyway, this isn't about business. . . ."

"What's it about, Fred?"

"It's about us—or me—you. Ah, shoot, I'm terrible at this."

Silence.

"I'm listening."

His words came in a rush. "Would-you-maybe-like-to-take-a-drive-with-me-Sunday-morning? And-have-a-picnic?"

"I would if we could add something."

"Like what?"

"Like you coming to church with me first, then we take the drive and have the picnic."

"Sure," he found himself saying. *Oh, brother, what have I gotten myself into?*

Daniel Morgan was at Parker Center police headquarters in downtown Los Angeles, a building made famous by Dragnet's Jack Webb. Harry Morgan had played Joe Friday's partner, and now another Morgan was the real-life top cop in LA. He was seated on a small sofa in his office on the eighth floor, which looked out over a panoramic view of the city he had tried to protect, without much success—until now.

The past four days were the most remarkable of Daniel's twenty-eight-year career in law enforcement. He'd been involved in some revolutionary crime-fighting programs, but nothing like what he was seeing with Light the Night.

Across from him in a matching chair sat his right-hand man, Assistant Police Chief Rex Ford. "Come on, Dan, what have we been preaching all these years?"

Daniel let out a sigh of bewilderment. "Yeah, yeah—citizen

involvement, neighborhood watch—blah, blah, blah."

"Well, you got it. Now enjoy it, man."

Daniel looked at the assistant with whom he'd worked for the past five years. Rex Ford was a bright, loyal, energetic presence on the force. In his early fifties, the multi-decorated cop was an inspirational leader whom Daniel believed could one day easily be LA's greatest chief.

"Never thought it would happen, Rex—never expected this." Daniel held the morning crime numbers in his hands. He scanned the printout from top to bottom. There were seven categories, seven types of crimes reported to the FBI by all police agencies. The first four were crimes against persons: murder, rape, robbery, and aggravated assault. The remaining three were crimes against property: burglary, larceny, and motor vehicle theft.

Daniel first studied yesterday's figures, comparing the number of crimes committed with the number committed a year ago. He moved his eyes slowly from the top down to the bottom twice, just to make sure he didn't make a mistake. The phone rang then, and Daniel looked at Ford. "There she is, right on schedule."

Ford nodded, then got up and said, "I'll let you two crime fighters share your victories in private."

The phone rang a third time. "Just think, Rex, I may retire sooner than you think, and you'll get to do this." Ford gave a mock salute and slipped out of the room as Daniel picked up the phone. "Chief Morgan, here."

"Okay, Chief, how's my Friday going to start?" It was Mayor Bodine.

"You know I could fax this stuff to you," he said.

"I like hearing it. Don't keep me in suspense—tell me."

"Every category of crime is lower than on the same day a year ago."

"Every category? Even car thefts?"

"Everything went down at least 5 percent."

"Beautiful! Chief, that's great! Fantastic!"

Before he could thank her, she asked, "What are you going to do about the weekend?"

"Officers will work closer with civilian patrols, and we're shifting a few units into new areas. Other than that, not much change."

"Okay. Unless something big breaks, I'll talk with you Monday. Make it a safe weekend, Chief."

"Fine by me."

Channel Three's Friday staff meeting was about to begin after an hour delay. Wilson Ruggles had stayed at his desk this morning after the meeting was scheduled to begin, convinced someone would call from New York, especially after seeing Channel Three's ratings yesterday. It was 10 A.M. now, and all department heads were already in the conference room as he walked in.

"A monster ratings, top-of-the-morning to you, Boss!" Harvey Rose spoke up, earning his first brownie point of the day.

"Morning, Rose. Let's get started." Ruggles stood at the head of the conference table and looked at each member of his staff, who were obviously waiting to hear words of praise. "This will be short." All eyes were on him. "You've seen the ratings by now. I'll give you my feelings in two words."

"Well done! Right, Boss?" said Harvey.

Wilson looked at him, then scanned the room. "No. The words are: so what?"

Everyone in the room looked a little stunned.

"From the looks, I get the feeling you were expecting me to say something else."

"Wait a minute—look at this." Fred Taylor had brought a copy of the ratings with him to the meeting. "Another 300,000 viewers are watching at six o'clock, and we have a 32 rating at eleven. That means more than four million people are tuned in at eleven o'clock, the highest rating in the station's history. Wilson, are you looking at the same numbers? Lighten up, man—this is new territory. For crying out loud, give some credit where it's due."

"Nothing counts until the November book. So far, this is just—"

Wilson's secretary burst into the room. "Mr. Ruggles," she said, out of breath, "it's New York."

Wilson savored the moment. "Well, looks like the meeting is over. I wonder what they're going to say. . . ."

As Wilson sauntered toward the door, he heard Fred Taylor mutter, "Maybe New York will tell you, 'so what?'"

Moments later, Harvey Rose stood in front of a chalkboard in his office. "I want three different thirties," he said. He'd ordered his staff to have fresh promotional spots ready by the weekend. It was a way to remind viewers of Light the Night, even though the captain of the Light Brigade would not be on the air. "The ones we put together on Tuesday were good, but they're dated, and a ton of stuff has happened since."

"What about using the video of that creep Escobedo in one of them?"

"Yeah, Andy. Put in that part where Paul says Escobedo has the mind of the devil—I liked that."

Leslie Gathers suggested a spot that showed several citizens' patrols in action.

"Good idea," Harvey said, "but I want everyone to know it was Channel Three that caused all of this to happen, understand?"

"Sure, Harvey," she replied. "I thought of including Paul at his 'war command post' talking about the patrol that we're showing."

"Harvey, we've got so much to pick from. You think three spots are enough?" asked Andy.

"Only three—I don't want to throw too much at our audience. We're not talking about brain surgeons out there."

"What about the funerals?" asked Leslie. "I think we should show some of the losses—honor the victims. Let people see why we're doing this."

"Okay."

"Who does the voice-over narration?" asked Andy.

"How about Wilson Ruggles?" Harvey asked, without much conviction.

Leslie spoke to the point. "Harvey, do you want the spots to be good, or do you want to look good?"

"All right, I don't have time to argue."

"Well, what about the narration?" Andy asked again.

"Paul can do two and give one to Randall. Maybe that will get him off my back. He's driving me crazy—says he's going to lose his job to Thomas."

While Harvey Rose worked at ways to promote the station, Wilson Ruggles entertained visions of moving up the corporate ladder. He reached for the phone, then sat back in his chair, ready to savor every congratulatory word.

"Ruggles here."

"Wilson, Rolando Burton—just wanted to let you know we're watching what's happening out your way." Burton was president of the network-owned stations.

Ruggles frowned. He had expected the chairman of the board to call. Burton was a lower-level executive.

"More than four million people out here are watching us," he said, hoping Burton would comment on the ratings.

"We were all impressed with Paul Thomas on *Nightscope*. He's good. Where do you have him?"

"He's doing special segments on the 6 and 11 P.M. news."

"Well, where did you have him before this thing started?"

Wilson cleared his throat. "He was co-anchoring our six and noon news."

"Six in the morning?"

"Yes, sir—R. B."

"Well, I'm glad you have him where more people can see him. I'd say up until now, he was wasted."

Wilson couldn't stand it any longer. "By the way, what do you think of the ratings?" He held his breath.

"The ratings? You've had four excellent days, but they don't count yet. Let's see what you've done by the end of November. Seems like I remember a lot of promises from you about instant success."

"We had the highest rating in the station's history last night."

"Ruggles?"

"Yes?"

"So what?"

As usual Paul Thomas was stuck in freeway traffic on his way to work that afternoon. But he didn't mind so much—it gave him time to think. So much had happened in five days.

Light the Night was a war against crime. Millions of people were banding together to reclaim what Paul had reminded them rightfully belonged to them. And little by little, they were getting it back. Now they were determined to keep it.

And so people were equipping themselves. New civilian patrols all over the Los Angeles area had nearly depleted the stock of flashlights, batteries, camcorders, videotape, two-way radios, pagers, cayenne pepper spray, and mace in the stores. Gun shops had a run on all types of firearms.

Store owners were on the telephone to suppliers, frantically trying to get new orders flown in. In demand were bulletproof vests, night-vision binoculars, closed-circuit TV systems, even handcuffs. Hardware stores now had waiting lists for security lighting systems and double-bolt door locks; the stock of lightbulbs was running low.

Light Brigade T-shirts, sweatshirts, neon shoelaces, and

baseball caps were hot-selling items, and businesses from restaurants to sports teams were offering discounts to anyone who wore anything with "Light the Night" on it.

People were lining up at the the LA Humane Society to adopt large dogs, especially German shepherds and Dobermans. Neighborhood patrols needed the added protection of a snarling set of fangs. It was a seller's market. Prices for the dogs most in demand tripled on Tuesday. By Wednesday, there wasn't a guard-type dog left for sale in all of southern California.

Paul had had fun with the story, showing some patrols with a comic look. A Channel Three photographer found a group in Pasadena with two-way radios, cans of mace, video cameras, matching uniforms—at the head of the group was a German shepherd puppy.

Another neighborhood patrol in North Hollywood was led by a toy poodle wearing a rhinestone collar. The patrol's leader summed it up: "She's not exactly fearsome, but she does one thing really well—she barks."

On Friday afternoon a coalition of churches, representing one-third of LA county, announced a variation of Light the Night. Congregations, parishes, and members of synagogues and mosques were organizing a "See the Light" campaign. It would include a combination of increased security around church buildings and surrounding neighborhoods, plus a social outreach to the needy, the homeless, and the lonely. Some churches planned to use See the Light as an evangelistic theme.

Paul was pleased with the editorial in Friday morning's *Examiner*. The paper had captured in ten column inches what the entire Los Angeles area felt after five days of open warfare in the trenches. Gains and losses were both listed, but the focus was the new feeling of confidence in the hearts of people who had been numbed by years of defeat. The editorial concluded with these words:

"For years, Los Angeles and its surrounding suburbs have

been in the middle of a civil war. One hundred and thirty years ago it was Yank versus Reb, the Blue of the North against the Gray of the South—a bloody battle over turf with millions of innocent people caught in the crossfire.

"So what's the difference between Blue and Gray then and 'Crips' and 'Bloods' now? What's the difference between snipers and plunderers then and career criminals now? Then, it was a fight to abolish slavery. Then, it was two sides fighting for control of the land. Today, we fight to free ourselves from the bondage of drugs and violence. At stake is whether or not we will ever simply live in peace in our neighborhoods.

"The great Civil War was fought for four long years. Our civil war has lasted longer than that, but in four days, Los Angeles has not only stood its ground, but we have seen the other side blink. The enemy won't give up easily, but they will go down in defeat."

Waiting in traffic didn't usually excite Paul, but he couldn't deny his excitement this Friday afternoon as he pulled into the station's parking lot.

That evening, he stood in front of the cameras. Channel Three's lead story was the dramatic shoot-out at Brea Mall the night before. Once again, members of the Light Brigade had stopped crime on their own. But, for the first time since Light the Night had been extended, Paul Thomas was reporting criticism.

"Today, leaders of the American Civil Liberties Union filed a civil lawsuit against those who killed the three robbery suspects. The ACLU claims the dead suspects' civil rights were violated. Tonight, Sheriff's Deputy Sharon Mansky and Deputy Marshal Erwin Fuller are on administrative leave following the shooting deaths of Sherman Polson, Willie Stedman, and Janelle Hill, who were killed while robbing Diamond's jewelry store. But the lawsuit raises questions that may dim the impact of Light the Night."

Paul now faced his most serious conflict between his role as reporter and his role as crusading advocate. He was angry at the lawsuit. He recapped the event, bringing viewers who might have missed the story up-to-date, but as he did so he wanted to ask members of the ACLU, on the air, how they would feel if their loved ones had been killed by the armed robbers. Video then began of the incident.

"The lawsuit alleges that the officers were part of an illegal, vigilante posse operating on private property," said Paul.

An angry mall manager appeared on-camera. "I knew nothing about the patrol's presence. If I had, I certainly would not have allowed them on the property."

"But what about the fact that an armed robbery was stopped?" a reporter asked.

"That's not the point—our security at the mall can handle any emergency. We don't need a bunch of roaming Charles Bronson death-wish types scaring off shoppers."

An attorney with the ACLU followed, condemning the actions of Mansky and Fuller. The lawsuit was also directed at the city of Brea and Los Angeles County, claiming the officers were allowed to use their service revolvers and act in a reckless manner while off-duty.

Next came interviews with several family members of the dead suspects.

"They killed my baby! They murdered my little Willie in cold blood!" wailed Willie Stedman's distraught mother. "He had it rough. Everybody was against him, but he was a good boy."

Stedman, a member of the Insane Rulers gang, had pistol-whipped the jewelry store owner. He had spent half of his adult life in prison. His police record included rape, auto theft, burglary, and attempted murder. He'd fathered three children with three different women and abandoned them all. He was thirty-two when he died and was on parole, having been released from prison only three days before.

"I want justice! Somebody's going to pay for this!" cried the stepfather of Janelle Hill, the woman believed to have fired first at the officers. "She didn't know they was going to rob no jewelry store. She was just along for the ride. Why'd they want to shoot a defenseless woman? Somebody going to pay big-time!"

Janelle Hill, twenty-six years old, was the mother of two children with no idea who or where the fathers were. Twice convicted of welfare fraud, she was on probation for writing bad checks. She was living as the common-law wife of a known drug dealer, but he'd moved out a month before. She and Willie Stedman had recently met in a bar and were sleeping together.

"Sherman Polson is a mystery man, an individual who seemingly had everything going for him," said a person identified as Polson's high school adviser. "Of all the kids who have come and gone through our school, Sherm would be the last one I'd expect to be mixed up in something like this. It's a tragedy."

Sherman Polson was an honor student in high school, a gifted musician, painter, and a star runner on the cross-country and track teams. He was offered scholarships at three major universities away from home, but chose to stay in Los Angeles. He'd enrolled at Long Beach State and had done well for a year and a half. Then midway through his sophomore year, he dropped out. He said he needed a break, but some thought it was because of a failed romance. Others suspected drugs, and then he joined the Insane Rulers gang. He came from a traditional family and had an older brother and sister; his parents had never heard of Stedman or Hill. No one was sure of the full story, only that he was dead at the age of twenty.

"We tried to get an interview with the county sheriff," Paul continued, "but he declined comment because the case involves a lawsuit. The same with the county marshal." Paul turned to another camera. "We were denied permission to interview shoppers in the mall, so we went to the mall's street entrance. We asked people how they felt about armed, off-duty law enforcement individuals patrolling inside the mall."

"I have no problem at all with that," said a driver in his mid-forties. "Look at what the officers prevented. Who knows what would have happened if the robbers had gotten out of the store?"

A young woman alone in her car was next. "Well, it's kind of scary, but I've been hassled here before. The only mall security people I've seen are old geezers with potbellies. I say, 'go for it.'"

The driver of a pickup truck was next. His wife was tending to an infant in a carseat between them. "To tell you the truth, I don't like it," he said. "It's good they were police officers, but who's to say the next ones won't be a bunch of gun freaks looking to blow someone away? I don't want my family near that."

The last interview was with an older woman. "What do I think about it? Well, better them than us. We've been rolling over and playing dead for years. It's about time the bad guys started rolling over and being dead."

Paul knew that some viewers had been impacted over the past five days more than others. The ones he wanted to talk to personally were those left to carry on—the surviving family members and friends of crime victims. Paul used his first segment to pay tribute to them.

A photo of a smiling man, holding a newborn baby, appeared over his right shoulder. "Raul Fernandez and his baby son were murdered in a drive-by shooting early Monday morning. He was killed while getting ready to go to work—an honest, loving man, whose greatest joy was his family. There were no gang members in his home. The only visitor was a school friend of his daughter's, who was also killed." Video of the crime scene appeared on the screen. "Raul Fernandez never lived to see the end of this week, to see a near-miraculous drop in crime. Light the Night is for his family and the family of their daughter's friend."

Photographs of the three DEA agents who were gunned down by drug dealers now appeared over Paul's shoulder. "Then hours later, on a quiet residential street, three men on the front lines of drug enforcement were murdered. They died trying to stop the poisoning of our city." Video of the scene and a cloth-covered body flashed onto the screen. "Caught in the crossfire was Agnes Howard, an elderly woman, whose life passed out of her while she lay across a welcome mat to her home." The camera came back to Paul now; he could hardly keep his composure. "Light the Night is—" He cleared his throat. "Light the Night is for them."

On the screen now was a photo of James Jackson in a cap and gown at his college graduation. "Light the Night is also for James Jackson, mistaken for a gang member, and executed two blocks from his home. He was a highly recruited, brilliant young man who was in Los Angeles for a job interview." Video appeared of Arthur Jackson as he took part in Monday's demonstration at Channel Three. "His father, Arthur Jackson, was at our station Monday morning demanding action in the fight against crime. Three days later, his son was dead." Paul looked straight into the camera. "Light the Night is for them."

A photo of Grant Peters filled the screen next. "Grant Peters was probably the first person killed while actively taking part in Light the Night. He and his friends were trying to stop some punks from beating an elderly man, and during the struggle with Peters, a street gang hoodlum named Danny Escobedo was stabbed. We're sorry for Escobedo's family, but our video tape clearly shows Escobedo trying to kill Grant Peters. That night, Escobedo's brother Jorge and two of his slugs returned to Grant's home, and finished what Danny had started." Video of Peters's murder was shown now. "They murdered Grant Peters, but they didn't know that a video camera was on them from beginning to end." Escobedo could be seen walking toward the camera. "When he's arrested, and he will be caught, this video will help us end the life of a murdering maggot." The video ended. "Light the Night is for Grant Peters."

"I know many other families are feeling deep hurt tonight," said Paul. "We don't mean to lessen your pain by leaving out the names of your loved ones. You, too, have been victims of violent crime this week. It's just that the stories of some become public, while others do not."

"Later in our newscast, we'll show you some clear-cut winners in the fight against crime. And we'll continue our spotlight on neighborhoods that can expect some extra help tonight."

"Tough segment, Tim, but I think we pulled it off."

Fred Taylor and Tim Hires were in their usual position this time of night—watching the newscast in Fred's office.

"I thought Paul was brilliant, the way he paid tribute to the victims' families."

"Concur," said Tim. "I thought he was going to get choked up a couple of times."

"I know I did," said Fred.

The two watched the closing credits, and then Fred switched off the set.

Tim sighed. "What a week."

"Never had one like it in my life." Fred began throwing papers and reading material in his briefcase; he was relieved it was Friday. "What are we doing over the weekend, besides giving Paul some time off?"

"I'm calling in a couple of crews on overtime to give us some extra coverage. This will be the first full weekend of Light the Night—we want to keep the momentum going."

"Especially for the ratings," said Fred.

"You sound like Arlene."

"That's cold, Tim, arctic cold."

Tim shrugged. "Yeah, sorry—couldn't resist. Anyway, Paul's going to hit it up hard tonight, encouraging people to stay with Light the Night, and not let up."

"That's good. Tell me more about the eleven o'clock show."

"We've got some crews going back to Brea Mall to check the

mood twenty-four hours after the shooting."

"They probably won't let our camera inside."

"We were thinking of using the hidden lipstick camera."

"Well, be careful about the legal stuff. Sounds like that mall manager is pretty goosey. We don't need a lawsuit."

"I've already talked with the crews about that."

"Tim, if I get fired—or I should say, *when* I get fired, because that's the fate of all news directors, you'll be an excellent replacement."

"You think I'd take the job if Ruggles were still here?"

Fred laughed. "You're smart."

Maurice Jones drove aimlessly and tried to think of a way to repair the damage he'd brought upon himself. It was just after ten on Friday night, and he felt sick to his stomach as he remembered what he'd done and what he had gone through that afternoon. Fellow gang members looked at him differently now—he knew he'd messed up, and so did everyone else who wore his gang's colors. He was an outcast.

Mo-Jo had not only murdered someone who wasn't an Insane Ruler, but the victim was the son of a neighborhood leader and friend of a council member. He'd compounded his deadly blunder by identifying his gang with the killing. He would now pay for his mistake. Why did I write that stuff on the window in the guy's blood?

Life as a gang member was all that Mo-Jo knew. It gave him identity, family, purpose, power, and his own version of respect. It also brought him money to live better than he had ever hoped for. But he'd failed to carry out specific orders, and so he would now face the consequences.

That afternoon, Mo-Jo had stood in front of Main Man, Iron Claw's leader. He was the one who had given the order for Mo-Jo to kill a rival gang member.

It had turned out even worse than Mo-Jo expected. It was not physical punishment, but a mental execution. He'd stood in front of Main Man for an hour. He still felt goose bumps on the back of his neck as he thought about it. Sometimes they stared at each other. Sometimes Mo-Jo was left in the room alone and told to look straight ahead. Whenever the door behind him opened, he expected a bullet in his head or a knife across his throat.

Main Man's final words echoed in his mind.

"We don't know you. Stay away from all Iron Claws. Do not contact us. Understand?"

"Yes."

"One more thing. You're no longer Mo-Jo. We've given you a new street name."

"What is it?"

"Doe-Doe."

Mo-Jo's eyes closed with embarrassment.

"You can take it two ways. Either dodo, like the stupid bird, or doe-doe as in John Doe." Main Man stepped in front of him so that they were nose to nose. "But you're worse off than a John Doe. See, you don't even have a first name. You're beyond anonymous—you're unclaimed."

Mo-Jo—Doe-Doe—left the room feeling like a dead man.

Now he was out on the streets, fending for himself. A furnished condominium and a car the gang had provided for him were taken away, along with most of his possessions. He'd thrown what little he had—a couple of guns, a knife, and some ammunition—in the back seat of an Oldsmobile Cutlass Supreme he had stolen after leaving Main Man.

How could he regain the confidence of his gang, his family? It had to be spectacular, and it had to be done quickly. But for now, he needed to find a place to stay. He headed toward Watts, where he could find a cheap motel.

For Paul Thomas, the week was minutes away from its conclusion. The eleven o'clock news was winding down.

"But, of course," Paul said, "the manager can't deny regular citizens access, so we figured a way to get you the story."

Video of the Brea shopping mall appeared on the screen. Paul had accompanied a news crew to the mall, but remained apart from them. His face was recognized everywhere, and he didn't want to blow their cover. As expected, the crew was denied permission to bring the news camera inside the mall. The manager didn't want shoppers to see news crews near the stores.

"As you can see from this home video provided to Channel Three by people in the Light the Night program, the mall shows no signs of people being frightened away. Just the opposite. We checked several stores and were told that the mall was busier tonight than it has been on most evenings."

Following were interviews with shoppers who told why they were there. People came out of curiosity; some wanted to see the jewelry store where the shooting took place, and others had never been to the mall and wanted to see what it was all about.

"And then, listen to these three shoppers," said Paul.

"Hey, I feel safer after the shooting," said a young woman. "The bad guys know what's waiting for them."

"I think it's great that they got those robbers," said an older man. "It's about time."

"The people who tried to hold up that jewelry store know what it means to 'Shop 'Till You Drop,'" one woman said, and everyone in the studio howled with laughter.

Paul came back on-camera then. "You may be wondering how we got those interviews if we couldn't bring our news camera into the mall. Well, thank goodness for an anonymous citizen with a home camcorder who rolled the tape while we asked the questions." He hesitated. "You know, I just thought of something. In appreciation to those of you who provide video for the Channel Three news team, we want to give you framed certificates. We'll keep your identities confidential, but you'll be named honorary members of the Light Brigade photo team." Paul spread his hands in a gesture of surrender. "It's probably corny, but why not? Just another way we can keep on shining."

An extraordinary week was over.

CHAPTER THIRTEEN

Sunday, September 17

Fred Taylor felt like he was walking to his own hanging and was wearing the noose around his neck.

"Good morning," he heard Marcia say to a passerby on the sidewalk. They had driven to Orange County, and in the distance he could see where the lynching would take place.

He tugged on his stiff shirt collar and wiped the sweat from his brow. The white shirt was new, as was the black and yellow tie he'd bought the day before. The shirt still had fold marks in it; he hoped he'd removed all the straight pins.

"Good morning," he heard again. The two of them were nearing the large church now with its odd-looking, steeple-like tower. Two massive, curved pieces of wood met above the roof and then jutted thirty feet into the air. This was where he'd meet his doom. Perhaps the tower is where they string up sinners.

They kept walking. He was amazed they'd had to park so far away. Smiles and pleasant greetings were exchanged as they walked by those heading in the same direction. Most were dressed in suits and dresses, some in more casual clothing. They looked like nice folk, but he felt even more uncomfortable when he noticed they all carried Bibles. He'd come unarmed.

"Fred, don't worry," Marcia soothed him. "Once you get inside, and the service starts, you'll be fine."

She reached her soft hand out for his, and that gave him a boost of courage. Fred wished his hand weren't so sweaty. He felt a strange flutter in his stomach. "Thanks, I'm a little nervous. I haven't been to church in twenty-five years."

When they finally reached the front door, a greeter did what greeters are supposed to do—he flashed a big smile, gave a firm handshake, and said "Good morning." Fred mumbled a hasty, "Mornin'" in return.

"Congratulations, Fred," Marcia said as she squeezed his left hand.

"What did I do?"

"You made it inside without getting sick."

"Do I look that bad?"

She laughed. "Worse, but you'll be fine. Just follow me." Four double doors led from the foyer to the sanctuary, and Marcia headed toward the ones on the far left. The organist was playing, but Fred had never heard the song before. "Where do you want to sit, Fred?"

"In the car."

She laughed again. "Come on, tell me."

Fred looked at the large sanctuary, now about half filled with people. Marcia had told him it seated twenty-five hundred people. Fred was glad no one turned to point a finger at him.

"Where do we sit?"she asked again.

"In the back row," he whispered, "as far from the preacher as possible, okay?"

Marcia motioned to her right. "There it is—a seat with your name on it. And if you want some gum, there might be some underneath."

Fred roared with laughter and quickly covered his mouth with his right hand, mortified at his outburst. He turned beet red as some people nearby frowned at him. But Marcia's joke had eased his nervousness, and once the service started, he felt okay about coming. Fred felt a sense of peace as he sat next to Marcia now and listened to the choir. He wasn't sure if this was temporary, or if something long-lasting had begun in his life. Marcia was tough to figure out; he couldn't tell if she were thinking beyond the present or just letting him enter her life for a brief time. Some of what the preacher said confused Fred, but he just might come back at another time to hear more.

He wondered if this shaky first step into "God's house," as they called it here, would amount to anything in the days and weeks to come. He hoped so.

Paul and Maddie sat near the front of the church in Pasadena where they had been members for nine years. Pastors of churches throughout the LA area were using the week's main topic of conversation to their advantage, and Paul's church was no exception.

The minister of their church, a low-key, insightful man with a gift of teaching, was reading from the Gospel of John. "Jesus said, 'I am the light of the world; he who follows Me shall not walk in the darkness, but shall have the light of life.'"

The pastor walked away from the pulpit, then turned to look back over the congregation. "How ironic," he began. "This week, we have seen what happens when porch lights are turned on, and people look out for one another. We feel safer, and—" he pointed to Paul and smiled, "if we can believe the captain of the Light Brigade, law breaking has been cut in half."

Many in the sanctuary chuckled. Paul knew he should be embarrassed, but he loved the attention.

"It's wonderful to see thousands of people feeling good about our neighborhoods being a bit safer," he continued. "But what a tragedy we don't have the same zeal when it comes to the true light of the world. Jesus does more than make us feel safer. If you accept Him, He saves you for all eternity!"

Paul and several others in the church said, "Amen!"

CHAPTER FOURTEEN

Monday, October 9

"The time is 7:05, and it's fifty-three degrees in Los Angeles. You're listening to KFI, 710 Talk Radio, and I'm Angie Marsh. Here's the latest news."

Wilson Ruggles was on his way to the station, eager to begin a new week and see the start of a major renovation project. He'd temporarily moved into a vacant office that was once occupied by the sales manager he'd fired a year ago and not yet replaced. With ratings and sales at record levels, Wilson was spending nearly $200,000 of the network's money to create for himself a drop-dead office.

"LA's crime rate continues to be our top story," said Marsh. "Police say this past weekend was the first in the city's history not to have a homicide. Officials credit Light the Night with the decline in violence and say a new program will be announced today to counter an increase in daytime crime."

Wilson listened with great glee, knowing that all of this meant higher ratings, more money, and hopefully a move up the network ladder. He couldn't wait to see the numbers from the night before.

"Also in the news, Mayor Bodine has confirmed that the city is actively involved in the relocation of a major corporation's headquarters to Los Angeles. She could not identify the company, but said the move would mean several hundred new jobs. She also said a major reason for the move is the drop in our city's crime rate."

Sports and weather followed, and then some commercials,

and Wilson's mind drifted to how he might decorate the right wall of his office. Suddenly, he heard Paul Thomas's name and realized Lester Hawkins's talk show was now on. He could hear the sound of a rustling newspaper in the moment of dead air.

"Okay, I've got it. Yeah, right here in Dino Ballard's column."

Ballard was the *Examiner's* radio and TV critic, and his column every Monday featured the latest happenings inside television newsrooms.

"Dino says that Paul Thomas, our wonder-boy captain of the Light Brigade, has been offered a huge, multi-year contract to jump to Channel Five. As of today, he's working without a contract at Channel Three. Hey, Wilson Ruggles, how about one of your geeky editorials on that, huh?"

Wilson glared at the radio. *You two-bit radio hack! I know your general manager and . . .* But then Hawkins's main point before calling him a geek finally registered. *Fred never said anything to me about Thomas's contract.* Hawkins had ruined the start of Wilson's day, and the first person Wilson planned to collar was Fred Taylor.

Francie McMillan drove her late model car down Wilbur Avenue. Certain parts of the neighborhood had a freshly-scrubbed look, and seeing it for herself helped her understand what her staff had tried to tell her. The district needed more paint and rollers; stores couldn't keep their shelves supplied. Citizens were covering gang graffiti, and more often than not, it was staying off. Francie wrote a note to herself on the pad next to her: call the regional manager of Home Depot.

Francie was known for her tough stand on crime, but had softened a bit when she found out that some of the seasoned graffiti artists who had moved on were returning to neighborhoods and teaching art to boys and girls at local recreational centers. Maybe this thing is working. Francie had heard recently that new pride was evident in neighborhoods that for years had been beaten by defeat and defaced by spray paint.

Just like any politician worth her votes, Francie knew the importance of being seen in public in her San Fernando Valley district, but she also made it her business to go into the neighborhoods. Not many in her third district knew it, but she took frequent trips up and down the streets to get a feel for what was happening.

She approached an elementary school now and saw a group of children waiting at a crosswalk. She stopped her car as a student crossing guard carrying a long pole stepped into the street. *Cute little kid. I hope we can give you the education you deserve, honey.* As Francie watched the children pass by in front of her, she thought about the recent change that had come to many of the schools. It had begun in the homes, moved into the streets, then into the classroom.

Francie was herself a product of the Los Angeles public school system. She was appalled at how it had deteriorated in the past few years. The Los Angeles school system, once the model for the nation, was filled with students who could barely read and write. Hundreds of parents were pulling their children out of public schools and schooling them at home. And it wasn't just in Francie's district—schools all over Los Angeles were dying for lack of parental involvement. But who could blame parents for staying away?

The fall semester had started out tragically this year. At a Culver City middle-school open house, a shooting had broken out between the Iron Claw and Insane Rulers street gangs. Two gang members were killed, and three parents and a math teacher were seriously wounded.

At an elementary school in Elysian Park, just blocks from where the Los Angeles Dodgers played, the mother of a fourth grader was stabbed while walking across the school parking lot. Police were still looking for the suspect.

The school dropout rate the year before was among the highest in the state, and the students who did graduate had difficulty finding jobs. Very few possessed the skills or had earned the test scores to get into college. With nothing productive to do, no fathers at home, and little self-respect, many young people had turned to gangs and drugs. But now something was happening.

If she could pinpoint one defining moment that seemed to chart the course for hope, opportunity, and promise in many schools, Francie believed it was the start of Light the Night. It had begun with something deep inside the soul. Light the Night had brought about a new attitude. Neighborhood patrols were present both day and night around schools in high-crime districts, which gave teachers, students, and parents a new feeling of security. A "one-strike-and-you're-out" policy was in effect; one weapon, one assault—and a student would be expelled for the year. It was remarkable how much less discipline was needed and how much more actual teaching could take place in an atmosphere of safety.

Francie drove slowly around a corner, glancing at the street sign as she did so—Victory Boulevard. She made a note on her pad to use that in the future.

When she finally walked into her downtown council offices, she waved off two of her assistants who had urgent messages, as well as her chief of staff. She wanted to make a telephone call before she did anything else.

She dialed the number of two friends she knew were closely watching the events of the past month. They did so with heavy hearts, having buried their youngest son four weeks before. His murder remained unsolved.

"Arthur, this is Francie. How are you and Clarice doing?"

"God bless you, Francie. How kind of you to call."

"I know it was a month ago today. You're in my thoughts and prayers."

Arthur's voice was choked with emotion. "Some days are better than others. Today is one of the tough ones. But our Lord is in control."

"He is, Arthur, and I think He's also helping us put a stop to what happened to J. J."

"That would be good. I'm ready to get back into the battle. I want James's killer caught."

"We'll get him. Give my love to Clarice, you hear?"

"Sure will, and Francie, remember—I'm ready."

"I believe that."

"Fred, what's this stuff I heard on the radio about Paul Thomas?"

Wilson Ruggles was seated at the head of the conference room table. Fred looked around at the rest of the department heads. Each of them looked relieved that Ruggles's wrath was not directed their way.

"What stuff?" Fred asked. "Who were you listening to?"

"Who do you think? Lester Hawkins. He hates my guts, called me a geek." A snicker came from somewhere in the room.

Ruggles looked around, then exploded in rage. "Big joke, huh? You people make me sick—you're clowns, all of you. I get enough surprises around here, I don't need it from Hawkins. Fred, what happened? Why haven't we re-signed Paul?"

"No excuse, I blew it," said Fred.

"You blew it? Oh, that's just terrific. What do you mean, you blew it?"

"His contract was about up. I knew it, but when things started going crazy with Light the Night, I didn't put a reminder in the file."

"You moron! How could you do that?"

Fred looked at the station's business manager. "Isn't our business office supposed to remind us morons of these things?"

"Well, what are you going to do?" Ruggles asked in a panicky voice. "Is Thomas leaving?"

"I tried calling him at home, but he was out jogging."

"Can we sign him to a new contract? Have you at least

talked about it with him?"

"Nope. Until Light the Night, I didn't exactly think he was one of your priorities."

"Well, he is now."

"Aren't you the one who ordered me to fire him a month ago?"

Ruggles ignored the dig. "Did Thomas get an offer from Channel Five?"

"It wouldn't surprise me. Their head guy is pretty aggressive."

The color drained from Ruggles's face. "Find Paul Thomas," he said in a low voice, "and get his signature on a contract today." Ruggles picked up a paper from the table—the ratings from Friday, Saturday, and Sunday—and then let it drop from his hand. The paper fluttered back and forth and settled on the table. "Because of our numb news director, everything we've achieved is about to be destroyed."

Fred bit his tongue. As much as he detested Ruggles and the way he treated people, the man was right this time. He'd screwed up big-time.

Ruggles picked up the ratings. "Until I learned about Thomas, these made me feel pretty good."

"Great numbers, huh, Boss?" said an upbeat Harvey Rose.

Ruggles gave him a dour look. "Enjoy them while you can, Rose. If Fred hadn't sabotaged this station, no telling how high the numbers could have gone."

"Wilson, Paul hasn't left us—we've still got a shot at keeping him."

"Knowing how desperate Channel Five is, that's unlikely." Ruggles looked at Arlene Zahn. "Give us the report from the sales department, Arlene."

Zahn got out of her chair and walked to an easel that held several poster-sized flipcharts. "Thanks, Wilson. I, too, am stunned at losing Paul." Fred felt her icy stare and looked away. "I agree that we have to do everything we can to sign Paul to a new contract." She turned over a sheet and showed them the first chart. "We're completely sold out for the six and eleven o'clock news," she said, excitement now in her voice. "And in another week, we'll cancel the remaining spots for longtime sponsors sold at July rates."

"What about losing goodwill with those people?" asked someone from accounting.

"Get your goodwill at Goodwill," she snapped back. "There's too much money on the line to give anyone a break."

"How much are we pulling in at six?" asked Ruggles.

Zahn flipped to another chart and pointed to the numbers. "We have a 32 rating for that hour. That's more than four million viewers. We sell thirty seconds of time for roughly $30,000." She took a deep breath. "With about thirty spots, our 6 P.M. newscast is bringing around $900,000 a night."

Gasps could be heard around the room.

"And what about the eleven o'clock news?" asked Ruggles.

Zahn flipped over the 6 P.M. chart and replaced it with a new one. "Ta-da!" she sang. "We have a 40 rating at eleven. That's nearly two-thirds of the audience!" She tilted her head back. "A 66 share!"

High fives, backslaps, and handshakes abounded.

"That's $650,000 a night for just thirty minutes," Arlene shouted over the celebration.

"I get my ratings fix on Route 66!" A giddy Harvey Rose looked at Ruggles and chanted, "We're number one, we're number one, we're number one! The boss is number one!"

"Shut up!" Ruggles yelled hysterically, and slammed his fist on the table. "Shut up!" His eyes swept the room, then narrowed on Fred.

"If we don't sign Paul Thomas," Ruggles said, "the only

numbers that each and every one of you will have to worry about will be who's next in the unemployment line." Ruggles poked a bony finger into Fred's face. "Find him and sign him. Now!"

CHAPTER FIFTEEN

Tuesday, October 10

"This is *Channel Three News* at 6 P.M., with Bill Randall, Nancy Chen, Paul Thomas, and the Light Brigade. . . ."

Fred Taylor was watching the news alone in his office and brooding about Paul's contract. He was still unsigned. Breaking news stories, last-minute speaking requests, and promotional shoots kept Paul on the go, and Fred could never catch him. Fred had mentioned the contract to Paul more than once, but each time Paul just said not to worry. *Easy for you to say—you don't have Ruggles breathing down your neck.* Fred planned to corner Paul as soon as he got off the news. *I'll drag him into my office, if I have to.*

Thomas was on the screen now, positioned at his war command post. It was completed just a day after the near-impossible September 16 deadline. It was a magnificent idea, Fred thought, never seen before on any news set in the country. It not only looked good, but best of all, it worked.

A studio camera mounted above the set shot over Thomas's shoulder onto a three-dimensional model of Los Angeles. Buildings were to scale, and streets, freeways, shopping centers, parks, and schools were clearly marked. But it was all an illusion. Automatic computer-aided drafting made it look as if Paul were walking in the area he was reporting on.

Fred wondered if video from a breaking news story would make it on the air. That afternoon, an anonymous caller told Paul that someone was going to set fire to a furniture warehouse on Olympic

Boulevard at four o'clock.

The caller's description matched the profile of a serial arsonist loose in Los Angeles. Fire investigators believed gang members were responsible for the burning of businesses as retaliation to those companies that would not pay for "protection."

After notifying the sheriff's bomb and arson squad, a Channel Three camera crew was allowed to accompany investigators who were staking out the building. Deputies wanted to catch the arsonist actually lighting the fire, not just possessing flammable material or having the intent to commit the crime. They were prepared to arrest him as soon as they saw a flame in his hand, and were equipped to extinguish the fire immediately.

Thomas had set the stage by moving three toy vans, representing the sheriff's deputies, into place on the model next to the warehouse. One of the toy vans showed the position of Thomas and his cameraman; it was marked with Channel Three's logo.

Paul was into his last sentence, obviously waiting for the video to be rushed into the projection room. "What we hope to show you is remarkable video of an arsonist not only caught in the act, but catching himself on fire. We caution you—the video is very graphic."

The video and Thomas's narration were on the air. Fred blew out a sigh of relief that his people had gotten the video in on time. He'd been told the raw footage was especially gruesome, and so he'd instructed his producer to use restraint. With the frantic rush to beat the deadline, he hadn't known what footage would reach the air.

Paul told viewers the suspect shown on the tape was an ex-con, an arsonist, and a member of the Insane Rulers. He had been released from prison only three months earlier. "Here's our suspect, walking on the alley side of the warehouse. You'll see him position himself to light the first point of the fire." Paul paused as the video rolled. Fred was surprised that the surveillance camera was so close to the suspect. "But as our man strikes the match," Paul continued, "he hears officers yell at him. He's startled, and drops the match and knocks over the container of flammable liquid. Again, a word of caution—you may not want to watch this."

Deputies were shown rushing to arrest the suspect, but stopping in their tracks when a huge ball of flame engulfed the arsonist, setting his clothes and hair on fire.

Fred winced. *We should have edited some of this out. It's way too gory.*

"Deputies risked their lives to douse the flames," Paul went on. "But they couldn't get there fast enough. Thirty-two-year-old Gilbert Stacy suffered burns over 70 percent of his body and is in critical condition."

Fred put his feet up on his desk, placed his hands behind his neck, leaned back in his chair, and smiled. *If we don't have Paul Thomas, we don't have that story. The tape was too gruesome, but sometimes, so is life. I gotta sign him.*

His telephone rang now. He expected to hear from many viewers who were upset with Channel Three. Fred would agree with them and say the tape should have been more carefully edited. Then he'd thank them for watching. That approach usually kept viewers happy. And if he lost a few, there were more than four million others. *That is, unless we lose Paul.*

Jorge Escobedo was watching the six o'clock newscast, and in horror, saw his boyhood friend and gang brother, Gilbert Stacy, turned into a human torch. Jorge had masterminded the plan to burn down the warehouse, but until now, he hadn't known what had happened. After seeing the flames and hearing his friend's screams, he was convinced he'd never see Gilbert alive again.

Jorge glared at Paul as he talked into the camera. *Because of you, Gilbert will die. How did you know? Who tipped off the cops?*

Jorge thought back to the arrest of the Amen Burglars. They were his gang brothers. Again, he glared as Paul Thomas smiled into the camera. *Because of you, they are in jail.*

He remembered his brother, Danny, dressed in black, his eyes closed, and hands that felt like cold plastic. Jorge could still smell the sickening odor of the flowers on his brother's casket. Paul Thomas was still on the screen. *Because of you, Danny is dead. You started this war.*

Jorge had followed Thomas's crusade for the last month, but he was more involved than just watching him on television. He'd ordered the attack on Maddie Thomas in retaliation for the murder of his brother. Jorge's men had botched the attack, and he'd had Paul and his family under surveillance ever since then. Jorge knew every move Thomas, his wife, and their two children made; he could have had them killed a hundred times over.

At the wake for his brother, Jorge had made a vow—he would remind the city of Danny. Now he needed just the right moment to make the city remember his brother's death. And since Paul Thomas was responsible.... He sneered at Thomas's image on the screen. *Captain of the Light Brigade. El Capitan. You will die, and the city will know I did it.*

"Paul, another great effort." Fred Taylor was waiting for Paul as he came out of the studio after the news. "Let's go to my office—we've got to talk."

The two men walked down the hall together.

"From the tone of your voice, it sounds like I'm under arrest," Paul said, thinking he'd get a smile out of Fred.

"In a way, you are," Fred returned with a straight face. "I need to put you under house arrest."

"What did I do, Officer?"

"Well, you continue to do absolutely first-rate stuff. The arson story was incredible, and only you could have gotten it."

"Thanks—glad we took a chance on it. Jack's video was incredible."

"I want to talk about you, Paul. We don't want you to leave, and I have some ideas I think you'll like. . . ."

They walked past the open door of Bill Randall's office. He was hanging up his coat, and Paul waved to him.

"Paul, I've talked with Ruggles. The station is prepared to be very generous with money, a new assignment, and a long-term deal."

"You mean I'm going back to the 6 A.M. news?"

"Yeah, right."

They both laughed as they walked into Fred's office and closed the door. On a table near a small sofa sat a pitcher of what looked like iced tea. An assortment of fruit, crackers, sliced cheese, and three dips were arranged on a plate next to the pitcher.

"Hey, looks like you're serious," Paul said with a grin. "This is a first."

"We've had a lot of firsts around here." Fred motioned to the table. "Help yourself. I'll be right back."

Fred disappeared into the restroom, and Paul sat down on the sofa. He knew what was coming, but was surprised at how nervous he felt. *You've got the advantage. Enjoy this—it'll probably never happen again.*

Paul's contract at Channel Three had expired almost forty-eight hours before. He couldn't help thinking now about Craig Wellington, Channel Five's general manager, who had made him an offer the day before.

Two weeks earlier, Paul had received an unexpected telephone call from Wellington. He had asked if the two of them could have lunch. Paul had seen Wellington at media events over the years, but the two had never met personally. There was no reason; Paul was a minor player in the pecking order of city news anchors.

They'd met the following day at Wellington's country club. Everything about the man was first-class; he was well respected in the community and a devoted family man with three children in college. He seemed genuinely interested in what was best for Paul and his family.

While they ate, they talked of their mutual interests outside of television. Wellington followed the big three in sports—football, basketball, and baseball. Both of their wives were talented artists; Maddie was a cloth-doll maker, and Wellington's wife enjoyed ceramics. They both frequently traveled, especially to Hawaii. Paul enjoyed hearing Wellington describe in detail some of the island's golf courses.

Eventually, their discussion took a natural turn to personal issues. Each had a deep love for family, but they also shared a common faith in Jesus. Wellington was an elder and teacher in a large church in the area, the same one to which Marcia had taken Fred Taylor.

"Paul, I asked you out to lunch because I'm aware that your contract at Channel Three is up for renewal. We both know your station is not just kicking our tail, we don't have much left to sit on."

"It has been pretty amazing."

"We've put together a package I think would be good for both of us. Are you interested?"

Paul was definitely interested. They'd talked a little more, and then yesterday Wellington had called with Channel Five's offer. It was beyond anything Paul believed was possible. He was almost embarrassed by it, except that it would mean financial security for himself and his family for the rest of their lives—and he could leave television news in five years. He wanted to write, and he wanted to teach.

Channel Five was prepared to make him the principal anchor on the station's 6 and 11 P.M. news. The man currently in that position, a longtime fixture in the market, had already discussed his retirement with Wellington and would agree to step down.

The contract was for five years—a guaranteed $6,000,000. Incentive bonuses were tied to the ratings and could boost the package to $10,000,000. But there was more—much more. The list was mind-boggling and included:

1. A trust fund providing two full, four-year college scholarships for Paul's children.

2. Two new leased luxury cars of Paul's choice each year.

3. Six weeks of vacation with airfare, hotels, and rental cars paid by the station.

4. A $5,000 yearly wardrobe allowance.

5. A paid lifetime membership at Wellington's Riviera country club.

It was an astounding offer, and Paul had almost agreed on the spot. Wellington said that he hoped Paul would continue to share his Christian faith openly off the air and use his judgment about comments on the air. He remembered Wellington's words, "I know you would never offend non-Christians, but I also see nothing wrong with viewers knowing you have a strong faith."

Fred returned now, sat down in a chair opposite Paul, and poured himself a cup of tea. He looked at Paul. "You've heard from Channel Five—now I'd like to give you our offer."

Paul said a quick prayer and took a deep breath. "Fred, I don't want this to be a bidding war between you and Channel Five. Frankly, their offer was more than I think anyone's worth."

Fred didn't say anything.

"What's most important is where the Lord wants me to be and what He wants to do through me."

"You sound like Marcia," Fred said.

"Marcia Willis of the *Examiner?*"

"Yup."

"Are you still seeing her?"

"Two or three nights a week—first time I've felt this way about a woman since Cynthia."

If Taylor was so intent on talking about Paul's contract, why did he bring up Marcia Willis? Paul sensed the Holy Spirit directing his words. "You said I sounded like Marcia. What did she say to you?"

"It began on our first dinner date—she talked about Jesus."

"What did you think about that?"

"To be honest, it scared me, and then it ticked me off."

"How come?"

"Well, it's something I've never understood, and no one has ever really taken the time to explain to me. You know—life after death, heaven, hell—who goes up, who goes down."

"Why did it tick you off?"

Taylor leaned forward and put some cheese, crackers, and grapes on a plate. "She seemed so sure, like she'd found the truth." He poured some more tea and then leaned back.

Thank you, Lord, for what you're doing right now. "Do you think she has the truth?"

"Yeah, but I'm not sure where I fit in. You won't believe this, but I've actually been going to church with her. . . ."

"Well, what do you think?" asked Paul.

"At first, I didn't understand much of it. The pastor uses terms I've never heard before. Marcia has been explaining some things, but some of it still bothers me."

"Like what?" Paul thought Fred seemed a little uncomfortable. "Hey, man, don't feel embarrassed. Go ahead."

"Well, she talks about sin, Jesus dying on the cross—and that Christianity isn't a religion." He paused and thought for a second. "She says it's a relationship with God."

Fred took a sip of tea, and then tilted his head as if he were about to say something, but then he stopped.

Paul didn't want to pressure him. "This is pretty heavy stuff, Fred."

Fred took a deep breath. "This has been building for a while. I've been feeling something really strange. Marcia's a special person. You're probably gonna think I'm wacko, but is what I'm feeling love?"

Paul smiled. "Could be, but do you want to know what I think?"

"Maybe."

"I think what you're also sensing is the Holy Spirit."

Taylor looked at him in amazement. "Come on, Paul, are you saying I've got spirits inside me?"

"I'm not saying it—the Bible is. The Bible says the Holy Spirit convicts the world of sin and the need to get right with God. I think that's what you're feeling."

Fred began to say something and stopped again.

"Remember what you said a minute ago about who goes up and who goes down?"

Fred nodded.

"It's all about eternity. Do you know where you're going—"

Taylor looked at the clock. "Eternity will have to wait, I guess," he said. "Ruggles is going to give me you-know-what if I don't settle your contract. Let me explain our offer."

He handed a copy of the contract to Paul, then began reading it point by point. Channel Three's deal was for five years and included the following:

1. A salary of $5,000,000 with the first three years ($500,000, $750,000 and $1,000,000) guaranteed. The remaining two years and $2.75 million were the station's option to exercise.

2. A position as the station's principal anchor on the 6 and 11 P.M. newscasts. (The remaining nine months of Bill Randall's contract would be bought out and he'd be released.)

3. A company car for the first three years of the contract.

4. A clothing allowance of $3,000 a year, increased from the $2,000 he was currently receiving.

The two men looked at each other. Fred was clearly nervous and trying to read Paul's reaction. This was a moment unlike any in Paul's career, and he found himself loving every second of it. It was intoxicating. A seven-figure contract. Unreal!

"Come on, you're killing me, Paul. What's the verdict?"

"Fred, this is a lot of money, and you've been in my corner more than anyone."

"But?"

"No answer right now. I need to pray and talk it over with Maddie."

Fred seemed to deflate. He shook his head. "Let me lay it on the line. I gotta have you. We've built this whole thing around you."

"No one's that important," Paul replied, but only half believed it.

"You are. You're the franchise."

"Give me a couple of days."

Fred sighed. "Okay, but promise me something."

"What's that?"

"I don't know what Wellington offered, but if you decide to go with Channel Five, give us a chance to make a counteroffer. I think you owe us that."

"No bidding war, Fred. They've made their bid, and now I've seen yours. That's what's on the table."

Paul got up and walked to the door. "I've got work to do for the eleven o'clock news. Give me time on this, and thanks for our talk." Then he winked. "Let me know when you've decided about eternity, okay?"

"Just don't take forever deciding on your contract."

That night, when Paul told Maddie about the two offers, it was clear which one she thought was best. Channel Five was giving them the opportunity of a lifetime.

"What's there to consider, Paul?" she asked. "Why are you even thinking about Channel Three's offer?"

"Maddie, there's more to this than security and money."

"I don't get it," she said. "We should be celebrating instead of debating. We've prayed about this. You feel so good about Craig Wellington—it's just the opposite from that weasel, Wilson Ruggles."

"You're right, but a couple of things make it really hard. First off, Channel Three let me take Light the Night and run with it—and it turned into something enormous. Then—"

"Paul, you were the one who came up with the idea. Now look at all the money they're making off it. Have you forgotten Wilson Ruggles was ready to fire you?"

"All right, you win that point," he conceded. "But there's one person I just can't get past."

"Who's that?"

"Fred Taylor."

She didn't say anything.

"I believe Fred is close to accepting Jesus, but if I leave, it may not happen. How could I live with that?"

She shook her head. "Remember what I told you—about not letting all of this change you for the worse?"

"Yeah, you weren't too happy with me when this whole thing started."

Maddie smiled. "Now I don't know what to think."

CHAPTER SIXTEEN

Wednesday, November 1

"Thanks so much for inviting me. When you're around people who know how to use an expense account, you don't get any rubber chicken!"

Paul laughed along with everyone else in the room. As the luncheon speaker for the monthly meeting of the Greater Los Angeles Chamber of Commerce, he'd stood at the head table for the last forty-five minutes and shared his thoughts on the economic impact of Light the Night. Invitations from business and community groups had been coming in faster than he could keep up with them.

"Any other questions?" he said.

"What about the mood of the city?" a young woman asked.

"I don't get the sense of economic despair that I used to feel around LA," Paul said. "Defense Department cutbacks, the earthquake, the riots—these all sent tourism down the tube. Companies were moving out of the state. But in the last month, I've seen a surge in business activity. It's remarkable."

"What do you think is the reason for the change?" one man asked.

"Plain and simple—the attitude of the people. Every night we see neighbors taking to the streets and making new friends. You've probably had it happen where you live—that is, unless you have a moat in front of your estate." Laughter rippled through the group. "When people get to know each other, become comfortable with each other, they begin to help each other." Paul paused. "For example, a Long Beach electrician was out of work for six months. He was with his neighbors one evening, and the talk turned from safe streets to home projects. Someone knew a person who needed major electrical rewiring done at his business. Well, that unemployed electrician was back working the next day."

"How about young people, especially minorities?" asked a man in the back of the room.

"Young people are learning about jobs the same way," Paul said. "They're finding entry-level positions, apprenticeships, and trainee opportunities. A lot of it is spreading by word of mouth. That's what happens when we get to know our neighbors and trust each other."

Paul praised the businesses that linked with Light the Night. They were either finding new customers, or projecting a better image with the ones they had. Consolidated Edison, the local gas and electric utility, was using the theme in its advertising. On a smaller scale, one enterprising manufacturer couldn't make children's night-lights fast enough—every kid wanted one for the bathroom and the bedroom.

"So, are you saying it all comes down to crime?" one man near the front asked.

Paul smiled and shrugged. "I wish it were that easy to say. All I know is that it began to happen when people started winning their streets back. Overall, crime continues to drop in all major categories. And wouldn't you know it, that has created a new problem?" He paused, teasing the group.

"Okay, tell us," someone finally yelled out.

"Well, we've concentrated so much on stopping crime at night, day crime is now up."

"So what are you going to do, Captain?" someone asked, and the audience laughed.

"I'll tell you—you're the first to know. Next week, Channel Three and the LAPD are jointly sponsoring a 'Brighten the Day' campaign."

Paul saw a number of people nod their approval. Then someone called out, "What happens if Channels Five and Seven find out?"

"Are they still on the air?" Paul quipped.

A howl of laughter went up as Paul waved and left the platform. As he began to shake hands with the leaders of the group, though, he began to regret his last comment. *Not good to gloat—you never know when it's your turn to bring up the rear.*

Moments later, as Paul headed back to the station on the freeway, he knew that hope had been replaced with a happening—people were feeling safer and going back to work, students were beginning to learn, neighborhoods were creating fond memories. Business people from around the nation were arriving each day to see the new Los Angeles for themselves. Some were now considering moving here, or building a branch in this area that not long ago was given up for dead.

A hint of fall was in the air. Trees in southern California, lame in comparison to the foliage of the northeast, nonetheless strained to give every ounce of color before dropping to the ground. Spring was still six months away, but a new birth of another kind was happening on this autumn day.

The mayor's news conference was delayed a few minutes while the cameraman for Channel Three set up his equipment. Newspaper reporters could be heard all over the room grumbling about special treatment for the electronic media. Brenda Bodine stood to one side of the stage and watched all of the activity with interest.

"I'm just sure they would wait for me if I were late," said a sarcastic-sounding woman print reporter, loud enough for the mayor to hear.

One newspaper reporter glared at Channel Three's reporter.

"As soon as Paul Thomas's Junior Light Brigadier gets her act together, we can start."

The Channel Three reporter looked around, smiled weakly, then dropped her pocket tape recorder.

Ian Thornberry walked to the podium now and stood in front of five microphones that were taped together. "Let's get this started. Thank you for coming. We're sorry for the delay, but I think everyone is ready now. Mayor Bodine will make an opening statement, and then she has a major announcement. Mayor?"

Brenda Bodine stepped to the podium. "Good morning. I've asked Preston Cesario, the president and CEO of Regal Brothers manufacturing, to be here today." She gestured to a man who stood a few feet away. "There's wonderful news for our city. Preston's company is canceling its plans to leave Los Angeles."

The reporters, many of whom had written of Regal's plans to leave, looked at each other in surprise.

"This is great, immediate news," Brenda continued, "and it sends a message to the rest of the country that things are changing here. We've worked closely with Regal Brothers over the past several months." Brenda paused and looked for Channel Three's camera. When she found it, she looked directly into the lens. "Frankly, until Light the Night began, Regal Brothers was as good as gone."

Brenda glanced at Thornberry, who smiled his approval. She had followed his instructions to look at Channel Three's camera, but not mention the station by name.

"On September 11, Preston Cesario gave me his company's final decision. Because of the crime rate in Los Angeles, especially around Regal's plant, he told us he had no alternative but to move somewhere else. Well, it's now six weeks later, and crime has been cut by two-thirds in seven major categories. Two-thirds! And there's more. I've asked Preston to share the other good news with you." The mayor felt a shiver of excitement as she stepped back; this was one of those days politicians live for.

Cesario moved to the microphone and cleared his throat. "Thanks, Mayor Bodine. Regal is proud to be a partner with Los Angeles, and we're pleased to announce immediate plans for a major expansion. We'll be adding two new product lines, and that means at least 3,000 new jobs over the next six months." Brenda approached the microphones, and Cesario stepped back, but then he moved forward again, and added, "In your last campaign, Mayor, you promised that crime would be cut. All of Los Angeles can see you've done what you promised. With what we've seen in the past six weeks, we believe this is our home. This is where we want to grow."

Brenda hadn't expected that from him, but of course, she was quite pleased. Now came what was called a photo opportunity. She looked to her right and saw Thornberry bringing what appeared to be an oversized check to the podium—the kind seen at sports tournaments for a winning golfer or tennis player.

"To show our support to the mayor and police," Cesario said, "I'd like to present this check from Regal Brothers for $1,000,000 to the city's Jobs Corps training program."

Mayor Bodine beamed and accepted the check as strobe lights flashed.

"Thanks so much, Preston. Wow, what great news. I can't tell you how happy I am you've chosen to stay—and now this generous gift. This will help educate and train so many people." The mayor looked at Thornberry, and he nodded. "Before we open this up for questions, I have one more bit of good news. My economic development team has informed me that we're about to sign agreements with six of the country's top-fifty corporations. They will either expand operations and come to Los Angeles or establish headquarters here. In each case we were told that our reduction in crime was the deciding factor in their move. I'm terribly grateful to the wonderful citizens of Los Angeles for making this happen."

"What are the names of the companies?" asked a reporter.

"We need a little more time to work out the details before I can tell you that, but believe me, it's a done-deal. We're talking about several thousand more new jobs." Brenda Bodine couldn't remember another news conference that had gone so well. Certainly, nothing could go wrong now. "This is a wonderful day for Los Angeles. I'll take a few questions."

"Mayor Bodine, Janet Larson from *Channel Three News*. I'd like to ask you about something unrelated. . . ."

"Oh, this should be a winner," a Channel Five reporter mumbled.

"Please go ahead, Janet," said the mayor.

"I've seen the tape of what you said at the funeral of Grant Peters."

Brenda watched Thornberry's face fall on the floor.

"You threatened Jorge Escobedo and made lots of promises. Why hasn't he been caught?"

The room was silent.

"Why hasn't James Jackson's killer been caught?" Larson asked.

The mayor looked to Thornberry for help.

"What about Raul Fernandez's killer? And his baby son's murderer?"

Someone coughed, and Thornberry slipped out of the room.

"We're listening, Mayor," said the Channel Five reporter.

"Well, uh—let me see if I can—your name is Janet, I believe. Janet, those are excellent questions. First, about Jorge Escobedo—"

Suddenly, the television lights went out.

"Hey, what's going on?" yelled a photographer.

Battery-operated emergency lights in opposite corners of the room went on, but provided only enough light for everyone to get to the exits.

Thornberry returned to the room from a side door. "Stay calm. This is very strange. I don't know what happened, but the news conference is over. Thanks for coming. The background info on Regal

Brothers is outside. Call my office later, and we may be able to tell you what happened to the power, but the rest of city hall seems unaffected."

To Brenda's relief, Thornberry's emergency contingency plan had worked. Together, they slipped out of the room.

Wilson Ruggles leaned back in his chair, feeling quite satisfied with himself. The network had returned for a follow-up story on Light the Night and was interviewing him. The focus of the story was television's impact in reducing crime in large urban areas. City leaders across the country were now closely watching what was happening in Los Angeles.

Correspondent Darnell Fulton was wrapping up the interview. "Channel Three was the catalyst for Light the Night, but what was the key in keeping the campaign going?"

"We had to involve neighborhoods all over metropolitan Los Angeles, but not all at once. You couldn't do that in a region this size—so we highlighted several areas of LA and our suburbs each night on the six o'clock news."

"Where do things stand now?"

"As of tomorrow, we'll have at least one neighborhood in every city participating in Light the Night. Some areas have them on every street. There'll be a citywide celebration tomorrow at 6 P.M. We're going all out to cover it."

What Wilson did not say is that the timing of the plan coincided with the beginning of something much more important to him than cutting crime. And he knew that Arlene Zahn, Harvey Rose, Fred Taylor, and everyone else at Channel Three felt the same. If they didn't, they wouldn't be working there much longer, he'd see to that. Tomorrow—Thursday, November 2—was the first day of the crucial twenty-day ratings period for the November "book." The "sweeps" would cover twenty weekdays and four weekends. Then, six days after Thanksgiving, Channel Three's management would be ready for a multimillion-dollar, post-turkey-day ratings harvest.

Wilson, Zahn, and Rose believed that once most neighborhoods had some Light the Night involvement, all of metropolitan Los Angeles would sit back and watch the results on television—and their sets would be on Channel Three. Rose had placed two full-page ads in tomorrow morning's *Examiner* congratulating the people of the city for what they had done. The ad would read:

You've lit the night and made the day shine bright.
Thanks for making things right.
All is in place for our fight,
so sit back and watch Channel Three
at six and eleven tonight.

Rose was having Wilson do a videotaped version of the ad, which would air up until six the following night. Radio spots were already on the air, and special printed fliers were being circulated to neighborhood watch patrols throughout the LA area.

Wilson had recently learned that Arlene Zahn was making her own plans for the ratings sweeps. She had notified Channel Three's clients that previous advertising commitments were canceled. Once the ratings started, time sold would be on a day-to-day basis. Wilson didn't like the idea at all, since the station's ad rates were now at record levels, but gave in when she told him how much money they could make. Still, he had one more meeting scheduled with her to discuss this and to make sure she wasn't making a mistake.

Others had cautioned Wilson about Zahn's plan, Fred Taylor and Paul Thomas among them. But their concern was news strategy, not advertising revenue. They believed it was risky to give the impression that everything for Light the Night was in place.

"How important has Paul Thomas been in all of this?" asked Fulton.

"Thomas has been a good team player, but you have to remember, without a plan, without a master design, nothing happens. Paul followed my instructions, and now you've seen what we've accomplished."

"I understand he's still working without a contract. Why is that?"

Wilson was startled by the question—it had come out of nowhere. And he was angry with himself for forgetting to ask Fred about the status of Paul's contract. "He's still with us. What does that have to do with this interview?"

"Isn't he a major player in Light the Night?"

"As I said before, he has a role."

"So, I guess if he doesn't have a contract, you consider him expendable."

Wilson squirmed in his chair. "Just a little oversight. We'll take care of that soon."

"What would happen if he went to your competition? Could you plug in another role player?"

Wilson stood up. "That's for me to decide. As for you, your interview is unplugged." He removed the microphone from his $100 tie, flipped it onto his desk, and headed to Fred Taylor's office.

The waitress stopped at the table with a full pot of coffee in her hand.

"Some java to start things out?" she asked mechanically.

"Sure, thanks," said Arthur Jackson.

"For you, ma'am?"

Marcia Willis put her hand over her cup, shook her head, and smiled. "Hot tea, please."

They waited for the waitress to leave before resuming their conversation. Marcia was still working on the James Jackson murder. She'd met with Arthur and Clarice the day their son was killed and realized it was more than just another crime story. Since then, she'd developed a deep, personal interest in the family and wanted to find the murderer.

"Marcia, we know who killed James."

"Who's *we*?" She was stunned. "My police sources know nothing."

"That's why a group of us hired a private investigator. We're ready to break this case wide open. We're gonna get the evidence. I don't think the police can do it. But we have to go in without a search warrant. A private investigator can seize evidence without a warrant, and it's admissible in court."

"That doesn't violate the Constitution?" she asked in amazement.

"Uh-uh. As long as the person acts on his own and without police direction."

"Can you tell me who did it?"

The waitress returned with Marcia's tea. Arthur poured cream into his coffee and stirred in a teaspoonful of sugar. When they were alone again, Jackson spoke. "We'll need your help on what to do when we go public. But for now, I want to tell you something that's off-the-record."

Marcia hated those words, but she closed her notebook and put her pen on the table. "You know this is torture, but go ahead. Off the record, what happened?"

Arthur looked around and lowered his voice. "Word from the street is the leader of a gang called Iron Claw ordered the hit."

"They wanted James killed?"

"No, James was just wearing red, and they thought he was part of a rival gang called Insane Rulers. Nothin' but gang business—one gang invading another's turf."

"Who shot James?"

"A lowlife, two-bit loser from Iron Claw named Maurice 'Mo-Jo' Jones. Turns out, he's the one who did that drive-by shooting a couple months ago that killed a guy, his baby, and I think, a girl. Thought he was shooting an old girlfriend. The creep."

"What's next?" she asked, wishing this were not off the

record.

"Well, Jones knows he's a dead man, twice. It's just a matter of who gets him first."

"How so?"

"Jorge Escobedo and his Insane Rulers are gunning for him, 'cause he was out to kill one of them."

"Who else wants him dead? You?"

Arthur thought about that for a moment. "Whatever form justice takes, I'll be satisfied. No, it turns out Jones's own gang wants him dead, first for writing the name of the gang in—" Arthur stopped to compose himself. "—for writing the gang's name in James's blood. Then, after they kicked Mo-Jo out, they learned he has some kind of diary."

"What's in it?"

"A list of the people he's killed, and who ordered the killings. He's a real nut-case—carries his diary with him to stroke his ego. People who've seen it say it links the gang's leader, a guy whose street name is 'Main Man,' to James's killing."

"Where's this guy Mo-Jo now?"

"Let's just say we know where he's at and how to get that diary."

All of what Marcia had just heard was front-page material. But to print the story would mess up everything. "When are you going to get the evidence?"

"Soon, but we have to be careful. We think Escobedo is close to making an even bigger move."

"What do you mean?"

"Word is that the person he wants dead more than anyone is Paul Thomas, because he thinks Thomas caused his brother's death. Then, after Paul put that video on the air of Escobedo murdering Grant Peters—well, Escobedo is just waiting for the right time to get Paul and the guy who shot the tape."

"Arthur, can I put any of this stuff in the paper?" Marcia

asked in a frustrated tone.

"Not yet, but here's something you can use. An all-out war is about to break out between the Rulers and Claws."

"This is on the record, right?" She picked up her pen and began writing.

"Yeah, you can print this. Light the Night is cutting into the gang's profits. Cars are harder to steal, prostitution is being chased out of neighborhoods, and home burglaries are way down." Even though this wasn't news to Marcia, she kept writing. "Some major drug busts have disrupted the flow of money," Arthur went on. "Cocaine, marijuana, crystal meth, and something new."

"What's that?" asked Marcia. So far, what she'd learned wouldn't make the local section, let alone the front page.

"It's all about the control of the big moneymaker, 'China white.'"

"Heroin?" She wrote down Jackson's comments as fast as she could. She had two page-one stories—this one now, and Mo-Jo's another day.

Arthur nodded. "Ninety percent pure poison. You snort or smoke it, just like cocaine, only the hook is like a whale harpoon. A $20-a-day habit can turn into a $4,000-a-day habit in one month."

"Slow down, Arthur, let me get this all down." She was writing frantically.

"The Chinese drug cartel for LA wants to deal with only one distributor. Our sources say he's told the Insane Rulers and the Iron Claw to fight over who gets it."

"A civil war between gangs?" asked Marcia.

"You could call it that." Arthur sighed deeply. "Like I told Francie McMillan, when the war came to my home, I enlisted in the battle."

Paul drove along scenic Mulholland Drive and thought about his two offers. After leaving the chamber luncheon, instead of driving straight to work, he'd decided to take the Hollywood Freeway and head north to Highway 101. He wanted to be alone with his thoughts, and the Santa Monica Mountains would be the perfect place to go to think.

For more than two weeks now, he and Maddie had prayed about which station he should choose. They'd talked for hours about it. Their conversation the night before was typical of the past sixteen days. It wound one way, and then another, much the same as the hairpin turns Paul was now maneuvering in his car. He signaled and eased off the side of the road to a scenic viewpoint. He needed to talk about his decision one last time. He reached for his cellular phone and dialed his number.

"Hello?"

"Hi, sweetheart. You and Vinnie doing okay?"

"Oh, yeah, I love having a walking refrigerator following my every move. Are you at the station?"

"No, actually, I'm calling from the car. I'm up in the mountains, overlooking the city."

"Sounds dramatic. Don't jump off any cliffs."

Paul laughed. "After I talk with you, I'm calling Channel Five."

"Have you made up your mind?"

"No, I thought you might have the magic words."

"I can't decide for you, Paul. Hold on a second." There was silence on the line, and then she came back. "I'm looking at the paper you drew up last night. The one with the pluses and minuses for each offer?"

"Yeah, I remember. One station was pretty lopsided, wasn't it?"

"That depends on what's most important to you."

Paul sighed. "Okay, that's what I needed. I've decided. Thanks, I love you."

"I love you more." She hung up and Paul smiled. Just like

Maddie not to ask. She figured if I wanted to tell her, I would.

Paul dialed Craig Wellington's office.

"Hi, this is Paul Thomas. Could I talk with Craig, please?"

The secretary's voice sounded excited. "Oh, yes, thank you, Mr. Thomas. I'll let Mr. Wellington know you're on the line. Please hold."

Like I'm going to hang up? Paul startled himself by laughing at his own joke. He took a deep breath and waited for Wellington to answer.

"Good afternoon, Paul."

Paul got right to the point. "Hi, Craig. I've made up my mind."

There was silence. Paul wondered if Wellington was as nervous as he was.

"You've kept a lot of people in suspense," Wellington said. "I know what would be best for us, but what have you decided is best for you and your family?"

Paul took another deep breath. "Craig, when I met you the first time, I was ready to go to work for you right then. And I feel the same way now."

"Great! We'll put you on the air tomorrow—the first day of ratings!"

"I'm going to stay at Channel Three."

Paul waited for Wellington's response. He was angry with himself for misleading Wellington; he hadn't meant to.

"For a second, I thought we had the captain on our side." Wellington's voice was subdued, disappointed.

"This may sound strange, but it has nothing to do with you, or even the business. You made the best offer."

"Well, I'm glad we at least gave you something to think about." Wellington's voice was stronger.

"That's why this whole thing is so crazy. You're the kind of person I want to work for, not Ruggles."

"Well, I don't quite get that. But I know you must have your reasons. Can I make one more offer—sweeten the pot a bit?"

"It's not about money, Craig. You and I talked a little about this. It comes down to following what I think is God's direction, not mine."

"Well, since you put it that way, I'm out of the running. Can we try again, when your new deal runs out?"

Paul laughed. "Sure, but you'll need a TV station in Hawaii, because that's where you'll find me."

Wellington wished him good luck, and they hung up. Paul looked out over Los Angeles. *Lord, please help me if I got Your directions mixed up.*

CHAPTER SEVENTEEN

Arlene Zahn walked into Wilson Ruggles's office and nearly lost her balance on the plush, new carpet.

"Whoa, feels like you've got six inches of padding here," she said. "You could sleep on this."

Wilson leered at her tight-fitting sweater. "I hadn't thought about that until you mentioned it."

"If that's what it takes to make me sales manager, why not?"

Wilson didn't expect that. He coughed and cleared his throat. "Yeah, well—ah, let's take care of business first."

She looked at him with steely eyes. "On the phone, you mentioned some concern about what we're charging for the 6 and 11 P.M. news. What's the problem?"

"Arlene, how can we turn down more than a million dollars a day?"

The ratings for the news were the highest in Channel Three's history. At 6 P.M., nearly five-and-a-half million people were watching. The eleven o'clock news had 73 percent of the viewing audience, which meant nearly seven million people were tuned in.

"Here's how I can turn it down, Wilson. I think we can get more." She pulled a chart out of a large envelope. "Look at the curve. For six weeks it's gone straight up every night at six and eleven. Right now we have a 41 rating and 64 percent of the audience at six. Thirty commercial spots at $38,500 each means $1,155,000 a night."

She switched to another chart that showed the 11 P.M. performance. "At eleven o'clock, we have the highest number in the nation—a terrific 52 rating, which means $52,884 for each of our sixteen, thirty-second spots. That's about $850,000 a newscast."

"I know," said Wilson, "and I like that. But let's not get greedy. We can always adjust later, can't we? No one else operates on a day-to-day basis."

"You're right, but no station in the country has our numbers, either. Let's just keep the 'tab' open and get as much as possible."

She pointed to another chart that showed the 6 and 11 P.M. side by side on the same graph. "How can we put a ceiling on our rates when the curve is doing nothing but increasing every day? I think we can add another million dollars a day if we keep it open to the highest bidder."

Wilson wouldn't mention it, but he was thinking about some other numbers, namely his new home mortgage payment that he would have to start paying in seven days. Five weeks ago, he'd signed papers on a new home, a $4,000,000 estate on Shadow Mountain Drive in Pacific Palisades. Escrow closed tomorrow, and the movers were in the middle of packing the contents of their home. He would take possession of the estate over the weekend. The purchase was heavily financed, his financial obligation complicated by the fact that his current home was still for sale. He had to come up with nearly $40,000 a month just for the mortgages, property taxes, and insurance on both homes.

"I think you know that my contract with this station is tied to the ratings," said Wilson, "and right now with what we're charging for commercial spots, I'm in a good position. That's why—"

"And I'm saying, you can be in an even better position," she interrupted. "I know about your new mansion—"

His head snapped back in surprise. "How did you find out about that?"

"Wilson, I've had to fight for everything I've gotten in this cutthroat business. I've had to scratch and step on people to survive.

I've maneuvered people, mostly men, and when necessary I've done some things on the side with them. So, don't be surprised that I know about the two mortgages that are hanging around your neck. Higher ratings mean you can make those payments. And if you make those payments, it moves me closer to being the permanent sales manager of this station. None of this acting crud."

"Oh, yeah, and what if I decide you're not the right man for the job?"

"Save the macho stuff, Wilson. What are you going to tell New York when they find out Paul Thomas has gone to the competition?"

"Has he?" Wilson asked in shock.

"You see, you don't even know. I can't lose, Wilson. You either name me your sales manager, or I get something better."

"What's that?"

"When they fire you, I'll get your job."

Fred Taylor looked at the two names he'd written on his desk calendar—one was Paul Thomas, the other was Bill Randall. Next to Thomas's name he'd written "3:00 P.M.—CONTRACT." Paul had called from his car phone and said he'd made up his mind about his contract and wanted to tell him in person. Fred had the uneasy feeling that he was about to lose his ratings "star."

The other "star" had called that morning. Bill Randall wanted to talk. He'd said it was urgent, so Fred had told him to be in his office at 3:30, now thirty-five minutes away.

"Hi, Fred. I'm a little early." Paul stood in the doorway of Fred's office. "Okay to come in?"

"Sure, have a seat." Fred studied Paul's face, hoping to get some sign that he'd decided to stay.

Paul walked in, looked around, and feigned surprise. "What, no fruit or cheese? I figured you'd at least have some leftovers out from our last meeting."

"You called this meeting, Paul. With what we've offered, you could buy an entire deli on credit."

Paul laughed and sat down in the same place on the sofa where he'd first heard the station's offer. They looked at each other; Fred was serious, and Paul wore a smile.

"You look relaxed," Fred said.

"I'm at peace, but thanks for noticing."

At peace, what does that mean? Fred wondered. "I don't know if that's good or bad news for me. Tomorrow the ratings begin for real, you're unsigned, and right now I've got butterflies the size of a California condor. What are you going to do?"

"Fred, I'm just one person—one player on your roster."

"You know what I told you before—you're the franchise."

"I've already called Craig Wellington and given him my decision," Paul said, still smiling.

"Was he pleased?" *Come on, Paul, you're killing me. Quit dancing around this and tell me.*

"He wanted what was best for me and my family—remarkable man."

Fred nodded. "So I've heard." *I don't care about Wellington. What about us?*

The two stared at each other, and Fred wiped some perspiration from under his nose.

"So, what's best for you, Paul?" *Tell me, now!*

"That I stay here . . ."

Fred felt a rush of relief.

". . . with a few changes in the contract."

"More money?" asked Fred.

"No. In fact, you may want to pay me less."

"Less? Why?"

"I'm not comfortable being named the lead anchor at six and eleven."

"You don't want the job?"

"Not the way things are now."

Fred was amazed. "I don't get it."

"It's not fair for Bill Randall to lose his job with the ratings so high right now. He's a jerk, but it's a matter of principle. I know I'd feel that way."

Fred was speechless.

"If you want to change the dollars in the contract," Paul went on, "I'll understand. But there's one thing you should know—this decision was made for reasons other than money."

Fred shook his head, got up from his chair, and walked to the window. "Let me get this straight. You say you don't want the six and eleven anchor job here, which I assume Channel Five offered you."

"I don't want to get into Channel Five's offer. It doesn't matter because I said 'no.' What we're talking about is that I can't take Bill's job just so you can keep me here. Things could change, but not now."

"What do you suggest?"

Paul got up from the sofa and joined Fred at the window. "Keep me on the six and eleven with our special segments," he said. "'Light the Night' still has a long way to go before it's fully played out."

"I haven't the slightest idea what's going on in your head." Fred was stunned. "All I can say is, I'm the happiest guy in the world that you're staying."

"I feel good about it, too," Thomas said. "But what I'm not pleased with is that stupid newspaper ad that's going to be in tomorrow's paper. I saw an advance copy, and it says that everything for 'Light the Night' is in place. You know that's not true. Why did we do that?"

"Two words—Harvey Rose. He showed it to me as a courtesy. I said I didn't like it, but as a department head, he has the final say."

"Well, I don't like it either. I think it'll backfire on us."

Fred's phone rang, and he walked over to his desk to answer it. He listened, then, "I don't care if he's waiting. Tell him he can sit there until I'm ready. Please, no more calls."

He hung the phone up and turned to Paul. "That was Randall, our loose cannon, who thinks you're after his job."

Paul shook his head. "Let's get back to my situation. Give it some time, and let's see how things work out. I'd be willing to consider something else, perhaps the 5 P.M. news. It's been struggling with ratings the past few years, and it's common knowledge that Strickland is looking to leave."

Fred sighed. "It's your call. I surely wouldn't have made it. Randall is a complete fool, and I wouldn't miss him for a second. I don't know what Ruggles will do about your salary. The offer was made with the understanding that you'd move into the anchor chair, but if you don't want it, there's a problem. We were prepared to pay you more than what Randall is getting. However, my guess is that Ruggles will be so glad you're staying, he won't change it."

Fred picked up the folder that contained Paul's contract. "Ruggles has been on my back all morning. Let's hope this gives him some other moron to ride. I'll talk with him, then get accounting to revise this for you. Should have it to you in a couple of hours. That okay?"

"Sounds good to me."

"You won't go off and sign with Channel Five while I'm gone, will you?" Fred asked, feeling giddy.

"No, get out of here. Tell Ruggles that Captain Idiot says 'hello'."

Fred turned toward the door, then stopped. "Paul, tell me one thing. You mentioned reasons other than money. What are they?"

Thomas smiled. "A couple of weeks ago, we talked about a decision you need to make—where you're going to spend eternity. Remember?"

Fred nodded.

"I want to stay here to see that you make that decision."

Fred looked down at the carpet and then up again. "Paul, I'm still shaky about the religion stuff, but man, I'm happy you're staying. I'll call you when I have the contract and you can sign it."

They shook hands and walked over to the door. But when Paul opened it, Bill Randall nearly fell into the office.

"Hey, Bill, how's it going?" Thomas put his face about three inches from Randall's and whispered, "Thanks for guarding the door, pal. Wouldn't want anyone listening to our conversation, would we?"

"What do you mean? I wasn't listening."

Thomas grinned. "Of course not, that's why your left ear looks like you slept on it." Randall's hand shot up and rubbed his ear.

Fred, the folder under his arm, pushed past Randall and Paul. "I've gotta talk with Ruggles right now." Over his shoulder he called, "Bill, I'll see you in your office when I'm done."

"I need to see you now!"

But Fred had turned his attention to Arlene Zahn who was walking his way. "What's the word on Paul?" she asked.

"Looks good for us, but nothing definite yet."

"Well, do something—I've got clients holding their money until they know what he's doing."

"Is money all you think about, Arlene?"

"What else is there?"

"Taylor! Come in here!"

Yes, master. Ruggles had spotted him in the hall. As Fred walked into Wilson's office, his shoes nearly disappeared in the carpet. It was the first time he'd been in the renovated office.

"What's his decision?" demanded Ruggles.

Fred told him nearly everything about the discussion he'd had moments ago, with the exception of Paul's assessment of Fred's spiritual needs.

As he listened, Ruggles's face contorted as if he were on a

roller coaster—happy, excited, suspenseful, puzzled, then shocked. "Well, now I've heard it all."

"So, what's your decision?" asked Fred.

"Sign him, of course!"

"His salary?"

"Cut it in half."

"Wilson, I think we nearly lost him to Channel Five. He could still go over there. Are you sure you want to do that?"

Ruggles waved his hand as if to dismiss Fred. "Yeah, we need him. Same salary, but only one year guaranteed."

Fred turned and left the room.

Fred and Randall arrived at Fred's office at the same time.

"Okay, Fred, once and for all, I want this thing settled."

Fred went in first and sat behind his desk. Randall followed and slammed the door.

"What exactly do we have to settle, Bill?"

Randall moved a chair close to Fred's desk. "I've been hearing and reading a lot of garbage about Paul Thomas and his contract." His face was turning red, and the veins in his neck began to bulge. "How do you expect me to carry the load when Thomas is trying to get my job?"

The only load you're carrying is a head full of air that's propped on your shoulders. "How do you know he's after your job?"

"Well, it's obvious he turned you against me. You've made him the star of both newscasts, and he's gone out of his way to make me look bad on the air."

You do that well enough on your own.

"How can you replace me when our ratings are the highest in the country? It's not fair."

"Who says you're being replaced?"

"Well, I just, I just know. The two of you meeting, you going to Ruggles, you coming from accounting, ratings start today—"

"Randall, let me tell you something—I think you're losing it. Right now, you don't even have one oar in the water. We've had this talk before. I was sick of it then, I'm sick of it now, and I'm sick of you."

Fred wiped his hand across his face in frustration. "I may have to write this out in crayon on a brown paper bag for you, but try to read my lips. You are the 6 and 11 P.M. news anchor for Channel Three. You're also an idiot. Now get out of my office!"

Paul dialed the numbers and counted the rings. One, two, three, four. She's going to let the answering machine kick in. At the tone, Paul began speaking. "Hi, Maddie—me again. Just wanted you to know about what I did on the contract. Give me a—"

"Paul?" Maddie sounded out of breath. "Paul, are you still there? What did you decide?"

"I told Fred I was going to stay." Paul tried to imagine the expression on her face. She's probably finding a chair to sit in.

"How do you feel about it?"

Just like her, noncommittal to the end. "Like I just gave away three or four million dollars."

"A million here, a million there—so who's counting?"

Paul laughed; it was just the kind of answer he needed.

"But, are you happy?" she asked.

"I don't know. Right now, I'm just relieved that it's over. At least, I hope it is."

CHAPTER EIGHTEEN

Thursday, November 2

"This is *Channel Three News* at 6 P.M. with Bill Randall, Nancy Chen, Paul Thomas, and the Light Brigade . . ."

Every day at this time, Fred Taylor watched the news from his office, but this was no ordinary day. For him, this was like the first game of the World Series, the opening game of the NBA championship, the Super Bowl. Up until now, everything was pre-season, but today, the counting began—day one of the ratings period known as the November book had started.

"Here we go, Tim," he said to his assistant. "Fasten your seat belt."

"Sure glad we still have the captain on the bridge," Tim said.

Fred shook his head. "Don't remind me. Without Paul, we'd be dead in the water."

"Good evening everyone. I'm Bill Randall, and our top story is a celebration—a victory for the people."

"And I'm Nancy Chen. We're all sharing something special tonight—something that seemed impossible just six weeks ago. Mayor Bodine has declared this Light the Night Day. That wording sounds a little strange," she ad-libbed, "but the results are not. There's new hope for Los Angeles."

"To give us a better idea of what's going on right now," Randall continued, "let's bring in the captain of the Light Brigade, Paul Thomas."

Paul was shown with Randall and Chen. "Are you hearing

clicks all over the city right now?" he said.

Paul looked directly into his camera, and he cupped his right hand to his ear, as if he could hear it himself. "It's the sound of porch lights, security lights, camcorder lights, and flashlights clicking on all over metropolitan Los Angeles."

Fred looked at Hires, then back at the television. "Forget the lights, Paul. I want to hear TV remotes clicking on to Channel Three."

Fred watched as Paul moved to another part of the studio for his Light the Night segment. Channel Three's art department had come up with a new wrinkle—a computerized graphic of the entire city beneath Paul's feet, complete with night traffic flowing around his shoes.

The news department's resources were stretched to the limit. Five separate live shots would run during the newscast, and Channel Three crews were set up around the city to capture the mood in the neighborhoods.

"We lost our signal on two of the live shots just before air time," advised Tim.

Fred didn't answer; it was out of his hands. He was watching Paul, who looked to Fred like a ringmaster at a circus. *Let's hope this is the Greatest Show on Earth.*

"First up tonight," said Paul, "we're switching live to Santa Monica." The special effect made it appear that he was walking to the city's west side. When he stopped at Santa Monica, a laser beam exploded with video of the area. "Back on September 11, the first day Light the Night was expanded, we had a live report from Idaho Street. Let's look at some video of that night, just forty-five days ago, and see what people in Santa Monica promised."

A special effect pushed Thomas and his war command post set off the screen and replaced it with video of a live report from September 11. "We'll be back out tonight," a neighborhood leader was saying, "porch lights on, flashlights charged, video cameras in hand, and two-way radios on line. And that's just for starters."

Another special effect pushed the old video off the screen and zoomed in on Paul in one box and an aerial shot in the other. Twinkling lights of the city filled the screen. "Now you can see what's happening a little better," said Paul. "We're looking down on Santa Monica from Chopper Three, and as you can see, thousands of people are in the streets celebrating." The camera zoomed in for a close-up shot. It was dusk, but clearly visible were people on every street in the neighborhood. On the screen, a graphic read, "Chopper Three Live."

"Somewhere in all of those people is Channel Three's Heidi Taddie, who was in Santa Monica on September 11. Heidi, give us a feel for what it's like out there."

The special effect dissolved out of the aerial shot and moved to the reporter. "This is almost like a street festival. What do I mean, *almost*, it *is* a festival. I'm with Ernie Fields, the man you just saw. It's like this in the entire neighborhood—people have reclaimed the streets, and they don't want to go back inside their homes." She turned to her right. "Ernie, we talked with you six weeks ago. Tell us what you're thinking now."

"Man, this is great!" A cheer went up from his friends, and he grinned at them. "We haven't won this thing, but we're gettin' there, right?"

His friends cheered again and began chanting, "Light the Night, Light the Night, Light the Night!"

"Paul, we'll be here for the rest of the evening," the reporter said, "and have another live report at eleven. There's food, games, good talk—what more can you ask for?"

"Heidi, I'm wondering if anyone is inside their homes watching us?"

She thought for a second. "Well, I guess this is a time when all the lights are on and nobody's home."

Paul laughed. "Okay, we'll get back to you."

The camera now showed Paul walking in the computer-generated graphics to the San Fernando Valley. "We'll now take you to a neighborhood hit by tragedy when Light the Night began." He pointed to Van Nuys. "This is where Grant Peters and his citizens' patrol were on that first evening. They had a violent confrontation near Delano Park with three teenage gang members. The boys were vandalizing cars and assaulting an elderly man, and during a scuffle with Peters, sixteen-year-old Danny Escobedo was accidentally stabbed to death."

Computerized video of the front of Peters's home in Van Nuys tumbled toward the screen. "What comes next is nothing more than a cowardly act of revenge by Jorge Escobedo, the brother of the boy who was killed. Here you see the home of Peters, where gang members returned and murdered him."

To Fred, the video was just as chilling this time as it was the first time he'd watched it.

Paul's voice wavered for a second, and then he spoke in a measured tone. "After murdering Peters and spraying his body with paint, Escobedo left the house." The video showed Escobedo walking along the sidewalk toward the camera. "As you'll see, this piece of human waste was only intent on combing his slimy hair. And everything was taped by someone in a van outside the home." Escobedo's face was locked in a freeze-frame—that smile, that evil in his eyes. It gave him the creeps.

"You're looking into the face of a killer," Paul continued. "If you're watching, Escobedo, this is your ticket to the gas chamber."

A special effect tumbled Escobedo's face off the film, and Paul was back on-camera. "We're going to switch live to Delano Street, not far from Grant Peters's home and Delano Park, where reporter Alan Ortiz is standing by with some of the men who were with Grant Peters on that first night."

"Put Alan on the wall with Paul," said the director.

Paul turned to a video wall, where the reporter stood with a number of men on either side of him. "Alan, what have members of

Peters's patrol done since his death?"

"In the six weeks since Peters was killed, the patrol has added more than two hundred volunteers, Paul. Not exactly intimidated, would you say?"

Two of the men were interviewed—one said that Peters's death was a call to arms for people in the neighborhood, and the other boasted that more than one hundred people were on a waiting list to join the patrol. All that held them up was a lack of surveillance equipment.

The reporter looked around at the people near him. "Paul, I heard Heidi mention the incredible number of people in Santa Monica. I can't imagine there are any more people there than here in Van Nuys."

"Okay, Alan," Paul said. "Let's see what you're talking about. If I can do some directing from our news set, can we get another shot from Chopper Three to see for ourselves?"

The helicopter pilot maneuvered the aircraft over Delano Street. Intersections were blocked off, and it was wall-to-wall neighbors in full celebration.

"As I'm watching this," said Paul, "I have to remind myself that this is not a weekend, but a Thursday night—the middle of the week. People have to go to work and school tomorrow, but I don't see many signs of it letting up. What about that, Alan?"

"If anything, it may get even more crowded. You've got to remember—not everyone is home from work yet."

The reporter walked to a line of tables along the sidewalk; it looked like a church potluck dinner. He reached down to a plate full of chicken and grabbed a drumstick. "There's plenty of food here—no reason for these people to go inside to eat. They're just having a ball. We'll be here and have a live report at eleven. Back to you, Paul."

"Good job, Alan. Save some chicken for the people still on their way home, okay?"

"They've got a slice of pie reserved for you."

Paul laughed. "If it's lemon meringue, I'll be there after the news is over."

Special effects removed Ortiz from the wall, and Paul was alone again with the computerized city beneath his feet. "That's our first Light the Night segment." Paul walked back to the anchor desk and stood next to where Randall sat. "Bill and Nancy, when we return in our second half-hour, we'll go to three other neighborhoods. Each of them is using a different approach to crime fighting. We'll see what's working and what's not."

Fred clapped his hands. "Outstanding! *Perfecto!*" He waited for Randall's response to Paul's newscast. But Randall was leaning back in his chair and staring at Paul. "Come on, Bill, say something." Fred glanced nervously at Hires. "Uh-oh, what's going on?"

"That was quite a segment, Paul," Randall said finally. "I thought the captain of the Light Brigade had assumed command of the newscast."

"Has Randall gone nuts?" Fred exploded. Paul appeared to be taken aback for a moment. "Randall had better be joking." But Fred quickly discovered that he wasn't.

"Ah—well," Paul faltered. "Me take over? Ah, not at all, Bill. You know the captain would never do that to the general of the newscast."

"Good answer, Paul," Fred said, relieved. Then, as if both men could hear him, he pleaded, "Now, please move the newscast along."

"Well, Paul, I'm glad our viewers know where I fit in," Randall continued. "And since I'm part of the strategy for Light the Night, I think it's time to publicly thank the man who shot the video of Grant Peters's murder. I was there when—"

"No!" Paul shouted. "Don't give his name!"

Fred reached for the phone and punched in the numbers to the control room. "Go to commercial!" he ordered when the phone was picked up. But the show's producer had already given the order.

"Tell Randall I want him in my office as soon as he's off the air! And no more side-stuff between him and Paul." He slammed down the phone. "Idiot! I tell you, Tim, he's an idiot!"

"I don't believe it," Hires said, "and on the first day of ratings."

Fred rubbed his hands through his hair. "I can't fire him now. You don't do that during the 'sweeps,' but when the November book is over, he's gone."

To Fred Taylor's relief, there were no more outbursts between Randall and Thomas as the newscast continued. It was Fred's hope that viewers would come away from watching Channel Three with a sense of optimism. To have Randall and Thomas fighting on the set in front of four million people would create a disaster. As it was, Randall's outburst had spoiled an otherwise perfect newscast.

As the news continued, viewers were reminded that, while things had improved, all was not completely right with the city or the world. In an armed robbery at a sporting goods store, a large cache of weapons was stolen, and a gunman had wounded one of the clerks. A fire that killed a night watchman at a large warehouse was linked to gangs. And in a car-jacking, a woman was dragged from her car, then shot and killed.

Fred turned to his assistant. "Tim, we wouldn't have paid that much attention to a robbery, fire, and car-jacking six weeks ago."

"Why not?"

"It was common back then. Now, we're actually surprised it happens."

"You're probably right. Have you seen the latest *Time?*"

"Yeah, I was just reading it. We're under the microscope."

"And the microphone."

National magazines, major newspapers, television networks, and tabloid TV shows had reported the story in-depth. What they found was that the unprecedented drop in crime was due to much more than porch lights being turned on.

"Paul was telling me today that some citizen safety patrols are like a civilian militia. Many are better armed than the cops."

"No matter how things change, they stay the same," said Tim.

"Why do you say that?"

"Okay, a little history lesson. You know I studied that in college before switching majors. Anyway, some of the patrol leaders say this is like colonial America. The militia was the only defense against Indians when the Brits weren't there."

Fred was impressed. Light the Night had gotten off to a good start. But he was also concerned about where it would all end. Some patrol members were wearing uniforms, military rank insignias, and camouflage outfits. Many of them had developed sophisticated communications and intelligence networks, and had shared information with neighboring patrol units. State law made it illegal to form a formal volunteer militia; that was the constitutionally granted duty of the National Guard. Even so, a few of the more militant patrols planned to send selected members to Hong Kong for training with the Royal Hong Kong police. In Brentwood and Beverly Hills, private helicopters equipped with laser beams for night patrols were now in use. And in homes all over the LA area, residents had posted signs that read: "Have Gun, Will Shoot."

"Mr. Ruggles, it's Mr. Burton on line one."

Wilson Ruggles's secretary's voice sounded to him like fingernails on a chalkboard. He was nervous about the first day of ratings, especially with Arlene Zahn's change in the way she planned to sell commercial time.

The 6 P.M. news was about half over. Wilson had downed three double scotch on the rocks after watching Bill Randall and Paul Thomas nearly go at it on the air. He'd called Fred Taylor immediately and was briefly assured that everything was under control. But even after the booze, he still felt edgy. Now Rolondo Burton was on the phone.

"Hello, R. B. You're working kind of late, aren't you?"

"Work? Oh, no, I'm at home. Listen, Ruggles, I called about your numbers. We're pleased with how things look."

Well, at least a halfhearted word of praise. "Thanks—hope we'll do even better starting tonight."

"You're doing something right out there. Don't try to fix it if it's not broken."

Wilson wanted to blurt out that big money was about to roll in, but he was nervous that Arlene Zahn's scheme might backfire. The change he'd okayed violated network policy. "I think it'll work out well," was all he said.

"Good. Based on your numbers now, what could you charge for thirty seconds at 6 P.M.?"

"About thirty-eight five."

"And at eleven?"

"Close to fifty-three thousand, but I really think we could get more."

"Don't get greedy, Ruggles; those numbers are unheard of. That's—" Burton paused. "That's about forty million in twenty days, just for two newscasts. I don't have to tell you that's more than our local station is doing here."

Wilson considered the general manager at the New York station his rival for moving up the corporate ladder. He detested the man. "Sounds like LA is making New York a little nervous," he said, enjoying getting the best of his counterpart.

"Competition is good—you two aren't exactly blood brothers."

"That's no secret," Wilson said.

"Well, that's not what I called about. I just want to emphasize that your news performance is going to help boost access programming and prime time revenue."

Wilson swallowed hard. He thought again of all that could go wrong. "That could be a lot of money, sir."

"I know. Whatever you're doing, don't change it. Lock those numbers in, and you'll find me very generous."

"Yes, sir, we'll do our best."

"Just do it."

Bill Randall stood in front of Fred Taylor's desk.

"Who do you think you are?"

Randall wore a defiant look, but didn't answer.

"Is there anything rattling around in that head of yours?" Fred asked.

The two glared at each other.

"I made my point," Randall said finally.

"Yes, you did, you egomaniac. But listen and listen good, sweeps or no sweeps—pull a stunt like that again, and the only point you'll see is my finger pointing to the door. What you did tonight is grounds for us to fire you on the spot and terminate your contract. You violated at least three clauses in our agreement with that little temper tantrum against Paul. You hear me, Randall?"

Fred waited for a reply, but Randall turned and left the office.

Paul Thomas looked up from his desk as Bill Randall walked past his doorway.

"Hey, Bill." When he didn't receive an answer, he went to the door. "Bill, wait—we've got to talk." But he heard Randall's office door slam. He returned to his desk then and called home. After the second ring, Maddie answered. "Is this the real light in the captain's life?" he asked.

"Only when the captain turns me on."

Paul laughed. "Just thought I'd check with headquarters for any special mission you may want me to go on."

"How about explaining what mission Randall was on? What was that bit about you taking over?"

"He's lost it, Maddie."

"I thought you were going to clobber him when he almost blabbed who shot the tape of the murder."

"That was close. I tried to talk with him just now. It's not just pathetic, I think he's psycho."

"What's Fred going to do?"

"I don't know. I've got to talk with him."

"Well, if you ask me, you may get Randall's job anyway. It looks like he's doing his best to fire himself. Did you sign your contract yet?"

"Not yet. It's got to go through some legal hands before I get it back."

"Don't let Ruggles pull a fast one on you. I don't trust him at all."

"How you doing?" Paul asked, changing the subject. "Is Vinnie there tonight?"

"Yeah, my bodyguard is protecting the television upstairs."

"What do you mean?"

"He's watching some basketball game. He told me he's a big Knicks fan—from New York and all that. Better upstairs than lurking around here."

"You think you're still being watched?" Paul asked.

"I don't know. Maybe I'm paranoid after that garage fiasco. But when I was outside in the yard today, I thought I saw someone peeking over the back fence."

Paul felt helpless. "Just make sure all the doors are double-locked, and keep Vinnie awake. The kids okay?"

"We're all fine, Paul. I shouldn't have mentioned it."

"I love you, Maddie. I'll see you in a few hours."

"I'll leave the light on for you."

"Mine is always on for you."

She sighed. "Sure you have to do the eleven o'clock news?"

Fred Taylor's feud with his loose-cannon anchorman was forgotten for the time being. He and Marcia were walking hand in hand, on their way to see a movie. He'd picked her up after work, and they'd gone to a restaurant in Santa Monica for a quick bite to eat. They'd talked some about the newscast, as well as Marcia's day at the newspaper, but then as always, they shared about their personal lives outside of work.

As they approached the ticket window, Fred asked, "What do you want to see?"

"Any movie, as long as it's a G or PG. Is that okay?"

Fred knew her reasons, but wanted to hear them, anyway. "So, why no PG-13 or R-rated movies?"

"The language bothers me, especially how they often use God and Jesus' name—although, even PG is no guarantee anymore."

"I've never really noticed that."

"I think if you hear it enough, you get desensitized."

Three PG movies were listed at the ticket office, and Fred asked Marcia to pick one.

"I got to pick the rating, now you choose the movie," she said with a smile.

He decided on a spy thriller, and after paying for the tickets, he turned to her. "Do you really think, if you hear something enough, you get desensitized?"

"I'm sure of it," she said as they made their way into the theater. "How about you?"

Fred struggled to keep from saying something he'd felt for the past week. He knew this was not the right time or the right place to say it. They were standing in line behind a purple felt-covered chain barrier, and people were now filing out of the theater. Those in line, waiting for the next showing, strained to hear comments from the moviegoers, hoping for a good reaction.

"I said, how about you?" Marcia repeated.

"Marcia, listen—I've been thinking. If I told you something, and said it enough, would you be desensitized to the words?"

She wrinkled her nose. "It depends on what the words are, I guess."

"I don't expect an answer, but the words are, 'I love you.'"

Before Marcia could answer, they heard applause. Fred looked into the smiling faces around them.

"That's so nice," said a young woman.

"Better than a love story," an older woman agreed.

Fred felt himself blushing. He looked at Marcia, who was smiling.

"That's really sweet, Fred," she said. "Those words get a G rating, for 'Great.'" She leaned forward and kissed him gently on the cheek, then whispered in his ear, "Give me a little more time for an answer, okay?"

It was an evening made for a politician—the perfect opportunity for Brenda Bodine to be seen relating to the public. Ian Thornberry had mapped out a route that would take the mayor to ten neighborhood celebrations. They made a whirlwind tour of three districts from 6 to 7 P.M., timing each so that the mayor would be on live during the newscasts of Channels Three, Five, and Seven. Ian was still miffed at Paul Thomas for not putting the mayor on during Channel Three's first segment; it was the station with the most viewers. Reluctantly, Ian took the mayor first to a Channel Five live shot in South Central LA. Then, accompanied by a police escort, they were whisked to a Westchester neighborhood for an interview with Channel Seven. When that was over, he barely got the mayor to Venice in time for her live interview on Channel Three's second half-hour.

It was now close to ten o'clock, and the mayor was on a platform, flanked by community leaders and talking to hundreds of happy residents in Lincoln Heights. It was one of the areas with the biggest drop in crime, and a district that had gone to Bodine's opponent in the last election.

Milk it for all it's worth, Mayor, Ian thought, as he stood to the side of the platform.

"This is a great night for Lincoln Heights and all of Los Angeles," said the mayor. "The streets once again belong to us. I salute your effort and promise that we will never, ever again be at the mercy of the punks and brainless ilk who held us in terror for years. We are winning!" People cheered for the woman who had been most voted against.

Ian edged his way to the platform to usher her off. A bigger audience was waiting for the mayor elsewhere. As she waved to the crowd, he stepped up behind her. "We've got to go now. I've got you on Channel Three's eleven o'clock news. Paul Thomas is going to interview you live in North Hollywood."

Mayor Bodine threw both arms in the air. "Thank you! I love you all. God bless our city!"

Ian escorted the mayor off the platform to her waiting limousine.

A helicopter lifted off from Channel Three's parking lot. The captain of the Light Brigade was about to do a live remote from Chopper Three for the eleven o'clock news, which included an interview with the mayor.

As the Bell jet helicopter made its way over Los Angeles, Paul looked down on streets that seemed jammed with more people than were seen on the six o'clock news.

"Looks like people don't want to go back inside, Steve," Paul told the pilot through his headset.

"Never seen anything like this before," the pilot agreed.

"Are you getting some tape of this?" Paul asked his cameraman, who nodded.

"Paul, this is Myrna. Can you hear me?" It was Channel Three's eleven o'clock news producer.

"Yeah, go ahead."

"We're about five minutes away from the top of the show. Let me give you some late stuff you can put in your live shot."

Paul opened his reporter's notebook. "Okay, I'm listening."

"First off, the mayor isn't quite set up. Her people called us from her limo. She's getting close. So we'll move that interview to the end of the newscast. Can you handle that?"

"Yeah, no problem. It's probably better there anyway. Where has she been tonight?"

"Glad you asked—that's part of the story. She's been to Westchester, South Central, Venice, and now North Hollywood. But she's not alone on the tour."

"What do you mean, *tour*?"

"Every politician in this city is making the rounds, cashing in on Light the Night. Two congressmen just happened to be in town. Then you've got every council member, supervisor, and school board member mugging for the cameras. It's incredible, like hogs to slop."

"I'll be sure to quote you."

"Yeah, right. Are you set?"

"Ten-four. I'm in the opening tease, right?"

"Straight off the top. Good luck."

"You, too. How's Randall?"

"Don't ask."

"Oh, that's comforting. What—is he going to shoot me down?"

"We're keeping sharp objects away from him. Talk to you in a couple of minutes. Gotta go."

All the pieces had fallen in place for Ian Thornberry. Mayor Bodine had missed the first segment of the newscast and was waiting to be interviewed by Paul Thomas. The police were keeping the crowd back. As Ian watched the newscast on a small monitor in front of the mayor, he congratulated himself. During the past five hours, he figured Mayor Bodine had been seen on three different television stations by more than seven million people. Most of them were watching Channel Three, and in a few minutes, the mayor would be live on Channel Three's eleven o'clock news. He would have liked her to be at the top of the newscast, but Ian could live with this. *Hey, as long as we get on the air. I couldn't buy this kind of publicity.*

"As you have seen, this was quite a night for metropolitan Los Angeles." On the lower third of the screen, superimposed over a medium shot of Paul, were the words, "Paul Thomas, Channel Three's Captain of the Light Brigade".

"Today was officially designated Light the Night Day, and the person who declared that is Mayor Brenda Bodine. Right now, I'm in Chopper Three, and we're over North Hollywood." Paul looked out of the helicopter, as if he could see the mayor.

"Bring up the mayor's live shot," ordered the director from the control room. A special effect placed Paul in a box, and a shot of Mayor Bodine was zoomed into another box and placed next to Paul on the screen.

"We're joined by Mayor Bodine. Good evening, Mayor."

The mayor looked up in the air. "Hello, Paul, I can hear your helicopter. Can you hear me?" Ian stood off to the side, smiling. *Very good, Brenda, you used my line.*

"Loud and clear, Mayor. I understand you've been to several parts of Los Angeles tonight. Give us your perspective on what you've seen."

"I've never seen so many people feeling so good about where they live. One of the priorities of my administration is public safety, and tonight, I think we've shown that we no longer have to walk our streets in fear. We've seen something new and exciting."

"Paul, she's going political on us," the producer spoke into Paul's earpiece. "Wind it up and get to your commentary. We're running short."

"It's my hope that this great city—"

"Mayor Bodine," interrupted Paul, "we do have a great city. Thanks for helping us close out a memorable day."

"Thanks for having me on."

"Roll special effects," said the director.

Paul looked at the camera and smiled. A video montage of video of the day's events spiraled in a special effect across the sky behind Chopper Three. "We just heard from Mayor Bodine. She and many others are saying that we're seeing something new in Los Angeles. With all respect to the mayor, I don't think so. No, what we saw today, and what we have experienced over the last six weeks, is actually something very old." Scratchy, black-and-white video of Los Angeles in the 1950s appeared behind Paul now. "We hear people longing for the so-called 'good old days.' Well, we just went back to the good old days, because tonight, our neighborhoods had the same feel that existed thirty, forty, fifty years ago. Only then, those people didn't think about it. They just enjoyed life without the constant threat of robbery, rape, and murder. Oh, sure, they had serious crime. There was Al Capone and his gang, and we'll always have thugs and lowlifes. But still, you could sit out on the porch and watch the world go by without worrying about someone driving by and shooting you. You got to know your neighbors and their children, and people helped each other. We weren't glued to television sets or VCRs. We didn't isolate ourselves from each other. We were civilized then, and we were civilized tonight." He paused. "I kind of like having the good old days today. How about you? From the captain to his Light Brigade, let's do it again tomorrow. Paul Thomas, *Channel Three News*, thanks for watching. Good night, Los Angeles."

"No time to go back to the anchors," said the show's producer. "End it."

"Fade to Chopper Three wide," said the director. The closing shot was a panorama of millions of twinkling Los Angeles lights. A graphic on the lower third of the screen read: "Produced by Channel Three News."

Paul Thomas breathed a sigh of relief. He'd gone right down to the last second. He tried to imagine the fit Bill Randall must be throwing in the studio. Paul had gone ahead and closed the newscast and said goodnight, something normally reserved for the anchorman. *Oh, well,* thought Paul, *what does Fred say when the newscast is over?* He remembered. *It's on the way to Mars.*

Day one of the ratings was over.

CHAPTER NINETEEN

Friday, November 3

Thursday's numbers were shocking.

"I can't believe it, I can't believe it," said the man who held a list in his trembling hands.

Chief Daniel Morgan stood behind his desk and just stared at those gathered in his office. "What in the world happened yesterday? This is the best I've ever seen—it has to be a record."

Everyone in the room had a copy of the numbers, and each person was smiling from ear-to-ear.

The police chief had called a special meeting of his assistants. Each one held a copy of the previous day's crime totals.

"Look at this," the chief said. "One murder for the entire day—the woman who was shot in the car-jacking. One armed robbery and shooting at the sporting goods store, no rapes, nine burglaries, five auto thefts, and six assaults. Amazing!"

Compared to a year ago, it was a miracle. The officers looked at the two columns:

Crime	Yesterday	One Year Ago
Murders	1	9
Rapes	0	8
Robberies	1	10
Aggravated Assaults	6	14
Burglaries	9	73
Larceny	4	36
Auto Thefts	5	52

"Have any of you ever seen anything like this before?" the chief asked, knowing they hadn't. "Did any crimes go up?"

Daniel's assistant chief spoke up. "We had an increase in drunk-driving arrests, public intoxication, pickpockets, that kind of stuff."

"Well, that doesn't surprise me. Seems like all of LA was in a party mood last night." He looked at his traffic chief. "I guess traffic control kind of overwhelmed you, huh?" The man nodded. Chief Morgan looked at the numbers again. "Do you think this Light the Night thing is going to put us out of business?" He smiled. "Of course not, but if this continues, it will sure make our job a lot easier."

"Anything else, Chief?" his assistant asked.

"No, I just wanted to have you all in at once." He held up the paper. "Who knows when we'll ever see anything like this again? Go on, get back to work. I'm sure the mayor will be calling."

The light had been on in the sales offices of Channel Three since before dawn. Arlene Zahn sat at her computer creating a list of advertising rates she could charge for that night's 6 and 11 P.M. newscasts. In a few hours, when the ratings for last night's news arrived, she'd notify sponsors and tell them how much they would have to pay for tonight's news. *Arlene, you're revolutionizing TV sales. You'll be the talk of the network today.*

Her list began at 40 for the 6 P.M. and 50 for the 11 P.M. news. Going into the ratings, the early news had a 41 rating which would have brought in $38,458 for thirty seconds of commercial time. The late news had a 52 rating, which meant advertisers were ready to pay $52,884 for a half-minute of ad time. But believing the audience would continue to grow, Arlene had canceled those agreements and switched to day-to-day charges. Her list began low, but her eyes lusted when she looked at the numbers she expected to begin charging for tonight's 11 P.M. news. They read as follows:

Rating	Cost for Thirty Seconds
53	$53,901
54	$54,918
55	$55,935
56	$56,952
57	$57,969
58	$58,986
59	$60,003
60	$61,020

Arlene couldn't wait to add to the list if the ratings went beyond 60. What if it soared to 90? Could it go to 98? If that happened, 100 percent of the televisions in use would be tuned to Channel Three. *This is what life is all about.* Imaginary conversations ran through her mind. *Hello, Arlene, this is Mr. Big Shot at CBS. Are you under contract to Channel Three? You aren't? Wonderful. We'd like you to fly to New York immediately. We're interested in having you join our team.* Arlene laughed out loud. *What might you have in mind, Mr. Big Shot?* She laughed again. *Vice president for network sales? Oh, come now, you can do better than that.* Arlene rubbed her hands together in glee.

She leaned back in her office chair and stared at the laser printer against the wall, waiting for the ratings to appear from the station's computer. Every morning, Monday through Friday, the Nielsen ratings service electronically called up the viewing patterns of homes taking part in the survey. The numbers were fed into its computer system in Dunedin, Florida, and then sent to television stations across the country. The results would soon arrive in, Arlene Zahn's office.

She began chanting quietly, "Ratings, ratings, ratings."

Wilson Ruggles prepared to leave for the station. He splashed on some musk aftershave that he knew his wife, Mary, couldn't stand. She was sitting up in bed, but didn't say anything for a change.

"Are you feeling all right, Will?" she finally spoke.

"No, I don't feel good at all about the ratings."

"Why not? You don't talk to me a lot about what's going on, but I thought I heard you telling someone on the phone that the numbers were the highest in the station's history."

He gave her an icy look. "Just keep your big nose out of my business. I thought the only numbers you were interested in were the ones on your Visa card."

"That was below your usual insults, Will. You know, it's really sad. Not too many years ago, we used to enjoy talking about your work. I try to understand you—I am your wife."

"Oh, now I get the big guilt trip laid on me."

"No, I'm beyond that." She sighed. "It's just that with the station doing so well, and moving into our new home, I thought—"

"You thought wrong! I might be in a better mood if I hadn't let Zahn talk me into that day-to-day stuff."

"What day-to-day stuff?" she asked.

"It's too complicated. You'd never understand." He walked toward the bedroom door. "Is anyone going to look at our home today?"

"I don't know."

"Well, find out! Call that lazy realtor of ours and tell her to get her act together. Put some pressure on her—do something to help me. In case you forgot, we move this weekend, and I have to come up with an extra forty grand a month."

The early November sun shone brightly through Paul and Maddie's bedroom window. The shade was pulled up all the way, and the window was open about eight inches. A hint of winter blew into the room.

"Hey, what's with the open window and sunshine?" Maddie

asked. "I thought you liked your bedroom dark and breeze-free."

"I know you enjoy your sunshine and fresh air in the morning," Paul said. "So before I slipped into bed last night I prepared your greeting for the new day."

"You're a sweet man, Paul. Sorry I couldn't stay up to see you when you got home last night. I liked you up in that helicopter, but the news ended in a hurry. It was kind of neat to hear you say goodnight. I bet Bill was upset."

"That's putting it mildly. He threw two computer terminals against the wall. And you know that photo of me in the lobby?"

"That, too?"

"Yup, smashed to smithereens."

"At least he was gone when you got back to the newsroom."

"Maybe I should have Vinnie looking out for *me*."

She laughed and snuggled closer. "The kids are off to school. How about if we start our day with a bang?"

"My fuse is lit."

The sound of the laser printer jolted Arlene Zahn awake. She'd dozed off in her chair. She jumped to her feet now and ran to the machine—numbers were visible on the document in the tray.

The first page gave the results from early morning through 5 P.M.. She'd look at that later. The big money was riding on what she'd find on the second page. *Come on, come on, come on.* She wanted to pull the document through the machine. She walked to the window and looked out. Her office had no view, unless you enjoyed looking at an overflowing trash bin. The office she coveted was the one Wilson Ruggles had just renovated on the second floor. She often thought about how her name would look on the door: "Arlene Zahn, Sales Manager." Her future was certainly, even at this moment, creating itself through the numbers coming through the printer.

Back at the machine, she picked up the second page and looked first at the ratings for the 6 P.M. news. Her eyes widened and her knees felt weak. She sat down on the nearest thing she could find—a coffee table. The hour-long 6 P.M. news had done a 29 rating, down from 41, a drop of 600,000 viewers from the night before. Channel Three stood to lose roughly $300,000 in lower rates for the thirty commercials scheduled for tonight.

Ratings for the 11 P.M. were even worse—there was a loss of 700,000 viewers. It had done a 38, down from the previous night's 52. The commercial time for tonight's eleven o'clock news would bring in roughly $225,000 less than Channel Three stood to receive had Arlene not canceled previous agreements.

What have I done? I've cost the station more than $500,000 in one day!

In her panic, Arlene grabbed the phone and knocked the receiver across her desk into her coffee mug. The brown liquid splashed in every direction. She cursed, then dialed Harvey Rose's home number. *You'd better still be there, you piece of crud.*

"Harvey, Arlene," she said when he answered.

"Hey, Arlene, give me the good news!"

"Shut up. We're in big trouble. The ratings are down 30 percent at six and 27 percent at eleven."

He gasped. "Down? There's gotta be a mistake."

"It's here in black and white. You're the mistake, Harvey."

"I'm—I'm in shock," he stammered. "What happened?"

"How should I know? You're the ratings expert. Get here ASAP. I want to talk with you before I face Ruggles."

"How do you explain it, Fred?"

Fred Taylor and Tim Hires sat on the sofa in Fred's office with the door closed, huddled over a copy of the ratings.

"No matter how scientific they say it is, sometimes you just have an oddball day," Fred said. "There are days when your numbers go haywire in one direction or the other, especially if you're up against some big game or the Olympics. But this is the biggest drop I've ever seen."

He tossed the paper on the table in front of him, then leaned forward and picked it up again. "And we weren't the only ones to drop—everyone else did, too. Look at Channel Five. At six their rating went from a 6 to a 4, and Channel Seven only had a 2 when they did a 5 the day before."

"I'll tell you what I think, Fred. That stupid Light the Night festival the mayor cooked up really blew us out of the water."

"Could be. Remember Paul asking Heidi on the air if anyone was inside watching the news?"

"Yeah. At the time I didn't give it much thought, but the streets were even worse at eleven—it seemed like everyone was outside."

Fred looked at the numbers again. "More than a million of them."

"What are we going to do?"

Fred put his head down and began massaging the back of his neck. Then he looked up and smiled. "What else can we do, except stay with our game plan? We keep doing what's been working. So, we got sacked on our first possession. It's now second-down and nineteen yards to go—as in nineteen more days of ratings."

His assistant grinned. "Okay, Coach, I'll make sure the players get your message. One question, though—what are you going to tell Ruggles?"

"You don't tell him anything, Tim, you just listen."

The late-model red Mazda convertible, top down, squealed in reverse out of the driveway of the plain-looking condominium. Harvey Rose hit the remote button for his garage door and was a block away before it closed. He lived forty-five minutes from the station, but he would try to make it in thirty.

What he had just heard from Arlene Zahn was baffling. *How could the ratings drop that much when they had gone up every single day for six weeks now?*

He had no answer—something that rarely happened to him. That's not to say his answers were always correct—often they weren't, but Harvey Rose seldom cared about the truth. It was a combination of events and some devious moves on his part that had landed him the job of promotions director, a position few people his age could claim, especially in Los Angeles. He was an assistant, working on the station's print ads, when Wilson Ruggles was named general manager. Harvey had tried a couple of different approaches and soon found that Ruggles liked to be called "boss," and that he was open to those who could give him inside information about the station's department heads. Ruggles was out to make changes. It didn't matter whether or not a person was doing a good job, or how long someone had been with the station—he wanted his own management team. He wanted to say, "I created it."

Ruggles felt that the station was too conservative, especially in its news coverage. Harvey had given Ruggles a list of suggested news specials, and had detailed an ad campaign for promoting outrageous topics during the next ratings period. A few were blatantly pornographic: "How to Pick Up Women in A Bar," "Understanding Prostitutes," and "Witchcraft—A Way of Life." Harvey knew it wasn't likely that all of the stories would be done—that wasn't the point. He had counted on Ruggles to ask the then current promotions director and news director what they thought about those subjects. And that's what Ruggles did. Then, when they told him they had no intention of airing or promoting that kind of material, Ruggles found the excuse he was looking for—he fired them on the spot and told them to be out of the station in one hour. A sympathetic Harvey Rose helped his boss, who had been at the station for sixteen years, clean out his desk. He consoled him and watched him cry, then helped him carry his belongings to his car, where the two of them shook hands, and Rose took his gate pass. They said good-bye, and Harvey watched him drive out of the parking lot. Then he walked back into the station and moved into the man's office.

Harvey was twenty-nine and single, with a college degree in mass communications. His father was a legend in advertising, and Harvey had his dad's ambition, but not much else. His father was highly respected for developing a long list of products made popular with innovative and appealing ad campaigns, while Harvey was making his mark with unmitigated sleaze.

Now he was on his way to work and the makings of a ratings disaster. He'd tried his best to push and promote Light the Night, but he was never truly caught up in the hoopla. He was at his best working on topics and ad campaigns that dealt with the dark side of life—the more sensational and repulsive, the better. Light the Night was too positive and upbeat. Paul Thomas was everything he fought against, because if the truth were known, Thomas and his principles reminded him of his father. The only reason he had even a spark of interest in Light the Night was because it would move him up at the station and in the network. Now, everything had apparently changed.

He looked at the morning paper beside him on the seat of his car, still lying open to the full-page ad he'd written. Only the top half was visible, but it was enough to make him sick. "YOU HELPED US MAKE HISTORY! Last night you were part of the largest audience ever to watch a newscast in this great city. CHANNEL 3 loves YOU!" It was signed, "Wilson P. Ruggles, President and General Manager."

The top half of Ruggles's face peeked over the fold. Harvey had used an eight-by-ten photo of the boss for the ad. The eyes were staring at Harvey now, the same eyes he dreaded seeing in a few hours. He looked away, but still saw them in his mind. Beady eyes.

In frustration, he grabbed the entire paper and threw it behind him, but a gust of wind blew through the window and caught it in midair, scattering all five sections into three lanes of traffic. Suddenly, he heard a siren, looked in his rearview mirror, and saw flashing lights. It was a California Highway Patrol car. The officer wrote Harvey Rose a $500 ticket for littering, and a $200 ticket for speeding, "thrown in," the officer told him, "for good measure."

As Wilson Ruggles drove to work, he thought to himself that on Monday, he would be traveling from the opposite direction, coming from his new $4,000,000 Pacific Palisades estate. But the number that kept going through his mind wasn't $4,000,000—it was the $40,000 a month he needed to pay for it.

He turned on the radio and heard his nemesis, Lester Hawkins. "Chief Morgan says the crime totals yesterday for LA were the lowest since the early 1960s. He believes that Light the Night is directly responsible."

Wilson smiled. *And we're the ones who started it, Lester the loser. How about a little credit for Wilson P. Ruggles, president and general manager of Channel Three? Oh, I forgot, I'm only a geek.*

"Okay, I was a little hard on the captain of the Light Brigade, but you've got to admit, Channel Three lucked into this thing. Did you read Dino Ballard's column this morning?"

Wilson heard the sound of a rustling newspaper.

"Here it is. Ballard says he's learned from inside sources that all of this would never have happened if Channel Three's cooking segment hadn't run short that first day. Paul Thomas apparently made his little suggestion only to fill time!"

Wilson slammed his hand on the steering wheel. *Who gave that to the paper? Harvey Rose? Randall? Traitors!*

"I've seen interviews with Channel Three's GM, Ruggles, and he gives the impression that the whole thing was his idea. What an unmitigated idiot! And did you see that cheesy photo of him in the paper this morning, thanking the city for helping his station make history? Channel Three loves you?"

Wilson looked to his right. The newspaper ad with his picture was on the passenger seat. He liked it. But now he reached across and turned the paper over.

"Wouldn't it be something if no one was watching last

night?" asked Hawkins with a laugh. "Next week they could run full-page ads of Ruggles on his knees outside Channel Three begging the Light Brigade to turn him back on."

How could that happen? No way. A shiver ran up and down Wilson's spine, but it had nothing to do with the crisp morning air. He was thinking how awful it would be if Hawkins were right.

Fred and Tim sat on an antique swan settee on one side of Wilson Ruggles's lavishly furnished office. Arlene Zahn sat near the window in a ninteenth-century French chair with elaborate needlework patterns, while Harvey Rose stood next to a Louis XIV-era tortoiseshell bookcase, as far away from Ruggles's desk as possible. They waited for Ruggles to come out of his private bathroom.

"Good morning, Boss!" shouted Rose as Ruggles finally emerged.

"Shut up you—" He stopped in mid-sentence as he saw Fred's assistant. "What are you doing here?"

Tim looked at Fred.

"Tim should be in on this," Fred said. "I'll take the heat, but I need him to know what's going on."

Ruggles walked behind his desk and sat down in his chair. "Well, here's what's going on." He held up his copy of the ratings. The paper rattled as he shook it at them. "After seeing yesterday's numbers, I've got three nooses—one each for Zahn, Rose, and you, Taylor. If Hires wants to swing with you, I'll make the loop on yours a little wider."

"Oh, good line, Wilson, very funny," said Fred. "I bet you spent all night thinking that one up." He pointed to the wall. "Knowing you, you probably had them build some gallows behind this Lebanese paneling, or wherever it comes from. If so, call the hangman."

"Hey, come on, we're all upset," said Zahn. "Let's try to figure out what we can do about this."

"You've already done enough!" shouted Ruggles. "Because of your brilliant idea, we're going to lose $500,000 tonight!"

"It's just one night, Wilson," she answered.

Fred looked at Zahn. *Okay, Arlene, you've got the ball. Now run with it.*

"Here's what I think," she continued. "We got clobbered by that bogus citywide Light the Night celebration. You saw it yourself, Wilson. The whole city was outside until our news was over." She turned to Fred. "Right, Fred?"

Fred nodded. "That's what Tim said to me when we first saw the numbers—could be true."

Zahn had come into the meeting carrying several posterboard charts. She now propped one of them in her lap. "Here's why I know I'm right. Look at the numbers for the shows after our eleven o'clock news. They were about the same as the night before, nothing like the 27 percent hit we took at eleven."

Nice explanation, Arlene, thought Fred. *But why are you coming to my rescue? What's in it for you?*

"I tell you, tonight Fred is going to bounce back and put us on a roll again."

"So, we're back to my news department again, huh, Arlene?" said Fred. "If we get on a roll again, it'll be *us,* right?" He couldn't tell what she was thinking as she stared back at him, but he figured it was probably obscene.

"I think Arlene is exactly right," said Rose.

"Oh, you do, do you? What about that ridiculous ad in the morning paper? 'Channel Three loves you'? I suppose that was your lamebrain idea?"

Rose waved a hand. "Ah, no sir, very embarrassing. I'll try to find the person who did that. Someone on my staff must have sent that ad to the paper without my—"

"Not true, not true!" shouted Ruggles. With a sneer he added, "I saw the working copy of that print ad a few days ago when

I walked through your offices, and one of your staff told me it was your idea. When I left, I heard someone say you'd called the ad—let's see if I can remember all the words. You called it your 'guaranteed pay raise from Wilson Ruggles—the man who came to Channel Three only because he couldn't count to four.'"

Fred couldn't control himself, and broke out in laughter. Ruggles looked at him in shock. "I'm sorry, Wilson. I shouldn't laugh, but that's probably the most creative thing I've ever heard Harvey say. Listen, Arlene is right. Let's not panic over the first day of ratings—we've got nineteen weekdays to go. We've all been in this business long enough to know that some crazy things can happen. Hopefully, yesterday was one of them."

Zahn quickly agreed. "Fred's right. I think when we see Friday's numbers, we'll look back on this meeting and laugh, even Harvey over there who still looks like he's ready to puke on Wilson's Persian rug."

"Boss, I'm sorry about that ad, and what I said. Anyway, I've got different print ads running this weekend, and my staff is ready to work all night to get new promos on the air."

"I really don't care why this happened," said Ruggles, "and I'm not in the mood to hear your grand plans to fix it. But listen and listen good—right now, all of your jobs are on the line." He looked at Fred's assistant. "You, too, Hires. Taylor just put your job up for grabs. You all know when the ratings end—November twenty-ninth, six days after Thanksgiving." He pointed to his desk calender. "When I turn the page to that day, if we're not dominating this market, I'm looking at four turkeys who can line up to have their heads chopped off."

"Monday, you'll feel better," said Fred, ignoring his threat.

"That doesn't help now, and it's going to make for a lousy weekend." He turned to Zahn. "Is there any way we can have Nielsen send us Friday's numbers tomorrow?" But before she could answer, he said, "Nah, why make the weekend any worse? I gotta move into our new place."

"When's the housewarming, Boss?" asked Harvey.

Ruggles looked at him. "Rose, if your nose was any browner, we couldn't see your face."

Fred laughed, and to his surprise, so did Ruggles.

Marcia Willis was at her office computer when the phone rang.

"Hi, Marcia, this is Fred. How ya doin'?"

"I'm fine—about halfway through a piece I'm working on for Sunday."

"Want to give me an advance copy?"

"Why should I do that? You know TV stations always steal our stories and put them on the news as if they're theirs," she teased.

"You know our business well." He paused. "Listen, do you mind dragging me to church Sunday morning?"

She looked at the receiver and laughed. "Of course not. That's a first for us, you asking me to go to church."

"That's a first for me with anyone," he said with a laugh.

"Which service do you want to go to?" she asked.

"How about all three?"

She paused. "Are you sure this is the Fred Taylor I know? What's going on?"

"Same guy," he said, "but I may need divine intervention. I just got out of a meeting with Ruggles. Our ratings last night went in the toilet. Seriously, though, I want to go. Let's make it 9:30 and maybe lunch and another drive. That sound okay?"

"Sure, Fred. Hope your numbers are better tonight."

"I do, too, but I've got a strange feeling something weird is happening. Anyway, I'll pick you up at 8:45?"

"Okay," she said, "see you then."

"Hey, you sure you don't want to tell me what big story you're working on for Sunday?"

"Only if you tell me who shot the video of Grant Peters's murder."

He sighed. "I guess I'll have to wait for your story until I read Sunday's paper. See you then, Marcia."

"Bye, Fred." Marcia hung up the receiver and clapped her hands. "Thank you, Lord!"

CHAPTER TWENTY

Sunday, November 5

"You were right about us stealing your story," said Fred. The headline on the front page of this morning's *Examiner* warned, "Dark Days Ahead for Light the Night." It was Marcia's story.

Fred and Marcia were walking along the sidewalk to the entrance of the church that had so intimidated him just two months ago.

"Oh?" she said, with that lilt in her voice that he loved.

"Yeah, it'll be our lead tonight."

"Might be nice to share some of your zillions with us—we do half your job."

Once again, Fred was impressed with Marcia's work on the story. From police sources, anonymous tips, and Arthur Jackson, she had written about a plot brewing between two rival gangs in the city. During the past week, three outright hits had occurred—two members of the Insane Rulers and one Iron Claw were murdered, each shot to death. The victims were in charge of drug trafficking, prostitution, stolen goods, and vehicle thefts in the city. Their murders were not random drive-by shootings, but clean, quick, well-planned assassinations with no witnesses. Gang markings were left behind.

Marcia had also detailed an early Saturday morning break-in at a National Guard Armory. Investigators thought only one person was involved, which was remarkable, since a number of M-16 rifles were stolen, along with ammunition, hand grenades, bullet-proof vests, and a set of high-tech night-vision goggles.

The story revealed what she'd learned from three separate

sources about the current battle between the gangs. It was apparent to authorities that there would soon be a fierce struggle over who would win the right to distribute the deadly heroin known as China White.

Without naming names, she went on to say that several well-known people in the community were on a gang hit list, people who were targets because of their role in the anticrime campaign. Her story also made it clear that three people were responsible for the killings at Raul Fernandez's home, and that key evidence had been found in the murder of James Jackson.

"So that's what you were working on when I called," Fred said as they walked hand in hand to the church sanctuary. "I bet you know a whole lot more than what was in that article."

"You bet correctly," she said.

"And that you're not going to tell me, right?"

"You're still the competition, Fred—even if I'm holding your hand."

Fred felt himself blushing. "I hope you aren't on that hit list because of your article."

"That thought crossed my mind," she said, "but I've given it all to the Lord."

They entered the church foyer and heard the organ playing.

"What's the name of that hymn?" he asked.

"'I'd Rather Have Jesus'."

"I'm happy with you," he said.

"Jesus is better. Where do you want to sit?"

"How about toward the front?"

She looked surprised, then smiled. "Another first for us, Fred—up until now, you always wanted to sit in the back."

"Does that mean I'm getting closer to God?" he asked.

She thought for a just moment. "God is as close as we let Him be."

Maurice Jones stared at the walls of his motel room and felt the world closing in on him. Since getting kicked out of the Iron Claw, he'd been on the move—staying with friends and living out of stolen cars. If he managed to scrounge some drugs or pawn some stolen property, the money went for meals, booze, women, and a cheap motel, not necessarily in that order. This dump was a new low for him, and his money was running out.

The more he thought about it, the angrier he got at how he'd been treated. He sniffed—the room smelled like an armpit. *I put my life on the line for the Claw, and now look at me—runnin' like a dog, and in this rat hole.*

He'd stolen a Sunday paper, only because he followed several college football teams. Three neighborhood friends had gone on to be star players. Two were at NCAA Division I-AA schools, and one was on a full-ride scholarship at Texas Tech. Another guy he'd known since sixth grade had received an academic scholarship at Michigan State, but walked onto the football practice field and made the team as a defensive back. Mo-Jo wanted to see how their teams did on Saturday.

He flopped down on the lumpy bed of the Sleep-Tite motel; he was in room number six of a seedy sixteen-unit string of bungalows in Watts. There were potholes in the parking lot and potheads in most of the rooms. *They shoulda burned this down in the riots.*

Mo-Jo lit a cigarette, attached his Walkman to his head and before turning to the sports section of the *Examiner*, glanced at the front page. The words Light the Night caught his attention, and he read Marcia Willis's article once, then again, especially the part about the murders of Fernandez and Jackson and the evidence. *What evidence? I wiped the prints off the gun, and Main Man took it.*

Mo-Jo took a final puff on his cigarette and stubbed it out in an ashtray. He got to his feet and rubbed his hands across his face. *Evidence? What are they talking about?* He looked at the room and what little he had, then lifted the flaps of a box he'd covered with his jacket. At the bottom lay some special night-vision goggles he'd stolen from a National Guard Armory. But they had nothing to do with the murders of Raul Fernandez or James Jackson—the same with the M-16s, ammo, and grenades in his car's trunk. *Evidence?*

He looked again at his jacket and remembered what was inside one of the pockets. *Oh, yeah. Mo-Jo, you the man, and you have the evidence. They don't.* The beginning of a plan had started. Mo-Jo—and that's what he would always call himself—Mo-Jo had an idea. If it worked, he could regain the respect and power he'd once had. He also promised himself it would be a thousand times more, in a totally different way.

CHAPTER TWENTY-ONE

Monday, November 6

Friday's, Saturday's, and Sunday's ratings were tallied in Florida and sent to Channel Three. The data was down-loaded into a computer, and the numbers were now coming through Arlene Zahn's laser printer. She sat in her desk chair, nursing a throbbing headache from a drinking binge over the weekend. Harvey Rose sat on the floor across from her, leaning up against the wall. They were the same distance from the printer and watched as six pages were pushed through.

"Three, four, five," said Arlene, counting each printed page.

After number six nestled in the bin, the machine kept running for a moment and then stopped. Arlene and Rose looked at each other in silence.

"I saw them first on Friday," said Arlene. "Maybe I jinxed us. You look today."

Rose stood up and slowly walked to the printer. He picked up the pages and shuffled through them until he came to Friday's numbers. "Okay, here they are. Channel Three, 6 P.M. news—a 21 rating."

Arlene moaned. "Oh, no, down from a 29. What did we do at eleven?"

Rose read slowly. "Channel Three—"

"I know we're Channel Three, idiot! What's the number?"

"At eleven, we did a 26."

She covered her face with her hands. "It was 38 on Thursday." She shook her head and looked to the ceiling. "In two days, we've lost half our audience. Let me see that."

Rose handed her the pages.

She stared at the numbers. "More than two-and-a-half million viewers—poof, gone at 6 P.M. Nearly three-and-a-half million at eleven," she snapped her fingers, "gone."

More importantly, she knew what it meant in dollars. Her decision had cost the station $500,000 in lost revenue on Friday, and more than $400,000 tonight. Nearly one million dollars in two days. She pulled open a desk drawer and took out a bottle of Johnny Walker red-label Scotch. She took a swig straight from the bottle.

"What do we do, Arlene?" asked Harvey.

"'What do we do, Arlene?'" she whined in return. "You're the expert in getting people to watch. You tell me!"

"How about having some kind of give-away? You know, a thousand dollars in the first half hour, and a thousand in the second. Have people call in."

"This isn't radio. We don't take the seventh caller—you can do better than that."

Harvey began to pace. "The people in New York are going to kill us, Arlene."

She sat upright in her chair. "Harvey, as worthless as you are, you just said the magic words."

"I did?"

"You're right, New York is going to want someone's head for this—but it won't be yours or mine."

A look of relief came over his face. "Why not?"

"Ruggles is the one who gave the okay for this. I talked him into it. But when New York wants to know why I did it, I simply point to Ruggles and say, 'He made me do it, honest.'" She saw Harvey smile. "Paul Thomas may be the captain of the Light Brigade, but Wilson Ruggles is the captain of this ship, and I ain't goin' down with him."

"Mr. Ruggles's office."

Wilson watched as his beleaguered secretary listened to the voice on the phone. A knowing smile began to replace the strained look on her face. "Yes, sir, Mr. Burton, he's right here. I'll tell him you're on the line."

"Oh, Mr. Ruggles, there's an urgent call for you," she said through the open door.

"Who is it?"

"Mr. Burton."

Wilson knew this was coming. "I'll take it—close the door." He waited until she'd done so, then picked up the phone. "Hello."

"Ruggles, I have a piece of paper in front of me. What's written on it is really quite remarkable."

This is going to be worse than I thought. He's not only going to chew me out, but he's going to ridicule me. "Why is that, sir?"

"Oh, I don't know." His words were laced with sarcasm. "I want to know the secret of how a station loses six million viewers on two newscasts in two days."

Wilson thought about Arlene's and Fred's explanations, but he was concerned about the smoke coming out of the phone. Any answer seemed feeble. "I don't know," was all he could say.

"You don't know!" shouted Burton. "What kind of an answer is that?"

He swallowed hard. "Sir, we're not the only station that's lost viewers. For some reason, people have just—well, they've just stopped watching the news."

Burton's tone changed. "Then, find the reason. Do some telephone surveys, call our consultants—we pay them enough."

Wilson picked his spirits up off the floor. Burton's suggestions were like a stay of execution. *I can put the blame on someone else. Maybe a survey will show that it's not my fault.* "Very good ideas, sir, excellent! I was about to do just that."

"You know, we've been talking about you over here."

"Really?"

"Absolutely. The numbers you had going into the November book caused us to do some reevaluating about your future."

Wilson felt a shiver of excitement. "I—ah, I won't let you down. You can depend on me."

"This is serious," Burton said. "I'm just glad we locked in those rates before we began the book. You've got a station to run. Do it the right way, you hear?"

Wilson's tongue froze as he thought of how the rate charges had been changed, and of the million dollars the station had lost since Friday.

"Ruggles, are you still there?"

"Yes, sir," he replied weakly.

"Well, get moving," said Burton. "I want a report tomorrow morning, only I don't want to have to call you, understand?"

"Yes, sir, I hope we'll have better news then," said Ruggles.

"We don't *hope*, Ruggles. We *do*."

Paul and Maddie were enjoying a late breakfast together. Paul had scrambled some eggs into an omelette using, as he called them, "the big three"—Swiss, Monterey Jack, and cheddar cheeses.

"I like the green onions you put in," Maddie said.

"The chef gladly accepts tips," he said with a grin, "but prefers more intimate thanks from his favorite customer."

"What do you think the ratings will be today?" she asked.

He gave her a surprised look. She rarely brought up the subject of his work, and never asked about the ratings. "Boy, this is serious," he said. "When Maddie Thomas ignores an outright proposition and wants to talk about the ratings, I'm in deep doo-doo."

"I know it was only the first day, but from some of the things you said, it sounds as if you guys were standing in it on Friday."

He took a bite of his omelette. "Wonderful choice of words

while I'm eating."

"You're the one who first mentioned it."

"Okay, yeah, I'm a little worried. I think the Light the Night celebration hurt us, and we made a huge mistake by giving the impression everything was in place." He looked at her, not sure what she was thinking. "By now Ruggles knows if the ratings dive was a one-day fluke or if it carried over on Friday."

"Why don't you call Fred and find out?"

He shrugged. "It won't change anything. I'll know when I get in. I can call you if you want."

"I'm just glad you signed your contract."

Paul didn't want to tell her what had happened. Partly so as not to upset her, but mostly because he was embarrassed that he had-not followed through on a multimillion-dollar deal. *Stupid!*

His contract wasn't immediately returned to him, and it wasn't valid until Ruggles signed it. He asked Fred about it, and learned that Ruggles was holding it up. He got busy then, getting his segments ready for the news, and forgot about it. Then, when the disastrous ratings results came in—*well, what do you do, go in and say, "Hi, the bottom just fell out of our newscast, but how about giving me that guaranteed contract?"* He'd let his family down, but couldn't admit it out loud just yet. *Maybe this will turn around, and I won't have to tell her.*

Paul reached across the table and put his hand over Maddie's. "I'm just glad you said 'I do' eighteen years ago. That's the best contract a man could ever hope to get."

Wilson Ruggles stormed into Channel Three's conference room. Voices immediately hushed. Most of his department heads were standing against a wall, and he watched them scramble to find chairs farthest away from the front of the table where he sat. The lone exception was Fred Taylor, who sat on his right.

"I just got off the phone with Burton," said Wilson in a low, growling voice. "I don't have to tell you how upset he is with our ratings. I've threatened all of you, but that did no good." He glared at Harvey Rose. "Rose, your print ads and on-air spots did no good. They stink, and so do you." He turned to his right. "Great work, Taylor—no one is watching our news. I want to know why."

"But, Boss, we still have more than three-and-a-half million people at eleven," whined Rose. "That's three times what we had before Light the Night began."

"Yeah, and we had nearly seven million last Wednesday! Any of you chair-warmers have any bright ideas on how to turn this thing around?" Without waiting for a response, he pointed to Ken McCrory, the head of the station's research department. Wilson wanted to shift the problem to someone else. "McCrory, I want an emergency phone survey, or whatever you do to find out why people in this city are turning away from TV news like we've got the plague. Also, work with our consultant on this. How fast can you have the results pulled together?"

McCrory, a skinny man in his forties, was affectionately nicknamed "Daddy Nerd." He was the quintessential research man and was generally regarded as the best in the business. Just last month, he had turned down an offer to go to the network. As had been the case many times before, he'd decided to stay at Channel Three because he didn't want to move his family to New York. Wilson rarely called upon him in meetings, but after seeing the ratings from Thursday and Friday, he needed McCrory to go into action.

"I can begin a telephone survey immediately, but we also have to do some calling at six and eleven to find out what people are doing at those hours," he said. "It'll be an all-night project, but I'll have the results in your hands by eight in the morning."

"There, that's what I like, a person who knows what to do. We need more 'yes' men around here."

McCrory got up from his seat, but before leaving the room, he said, "Wilson, you know as well as anyone here, I'm no 'yes man.' I just give you data. What you do with it is your problem."

Wilson knew that most in the room would have liked to have left with McCrory. He turned to Fred. "And how about you? All that's on your shoulders is the fate of this entire station. What inspired plan do you have for tonight?"

Fred put his hand to his mouth, as if to restrain himself. "All we can do is cover the news just like we've done in the past. But our early news is up against *Monday Night Football*."

Wilson groaned. "Well, you'd better come up with some trick plays of your own, because tomorrow I'm going to be a Tuesday-morning quarterback."

"You second-guess me every day of the week, Wilson. Why should Tuesday be any different?"

"I've heard enough. The meeting's over." Wilson looked at Arlene Zahn. "You may have wondered why I didn't single you out in this little get-together, Miss Sale of the Century."

"Thank you for sparing me your wrath, oh, Benevolent Dictator."

Wilson glared at her. "Be in my office in two minutes."

The room emptied quickly, and there was little talk among those who retreated to their offices. Arlene Zahn followed behind Wilson, and as he walked into his office, his secretary met him. "Dino Ballard of the *Examiner* called."

"Good for Dino Ballard. I don't want to talk with him." He went to his desk chair, and without looking at Zahn, he said, "Close the door!"

She did and then sat down in a chair beside his desk.

"You've cost this company nearly a million dollars in two days," he said in a voice that he hoped promised grave consequences. She gave him a tough look in return. "But more than that, what you've done could ruin me."

Zahn remained silent.

"If you're thinking this is just a matter of someone else losing their money, think again."

"How so?" she asked.

"If things don't change, this company will take you to court for gross negligence as well as violation of your personal services contract."

"The station wouldn't sue me—I'm a woman. Besides, I don't *have* a personal services contract. Remember, Willy-boy, I'm just your acting sales manager. I asked for a contract and *you* wouldn't give me one."

Wilson knew he had taken a verbal shot, but recovered. "You may be right, but there's no one to prevent me from suing you."

"On what grounds?"

"For starters, irreparable damage to my career," he said. "I'll keep you tied up in court for years. Attorney fees will bankrupt you." She didn't say anything as he got up and walked to his bar. "Care for a drink?" he asked, putting ice in two glasses. "I know what you like, and you've never cared what time of day it is."

She nodded and licked her lips as he poured a double scotch for himself and a triple for her. "Arlene, you know all about my financial bind—you made that pretty clear last Friday." He walked over to her, holding her drink in his hand. She reached for it, but he held it back, shaking it slightly so she could hear the sound of ice against the glass. For an alcoholic, it was a form of torture. When she licked her lips again, he handed her the drink. "Well, I know some things about you, too, about your sordid past, and some of what you're involved with now on the side."

Arlene took a deep sip. "Is that a threat?"

Wilson looked at her. *You'll never ruin me. The network is mine for the taking.* "It's more than that, Madame Z, as you're called on the side. You either turn it around here, or I turn what I know over to the district attorney."

CHAPTER TWENTY-TWO

Tuesday, November 7

Fred stood in the office doorway of research whiz Ken McCrory. He hadn't slept well. After tossing and turning for most of the night, and finally realizing at four in the morning that his eyes weren't going to close, he got up and came to work. But his curiosity wouldn't let him go to his own office. So he watched now as McCrory stacked what appeared to be the results of his overnight study.

"Hey, Kenny," Fred said.

McCrory jumped. "Come on, Fred, don't do that. You scared the you-know-what out of me."

"Sorry, man. I know how you get lost in all those numbers you come up with."

McCrory had spent a lifetime turning audience research into usable information; he was an expert in polling the right people, asking the correct questions, and reaching the proper conclusions.

"It looks like you're going to meet Ruggles's deadline," Fred said.

"It was close, but I'll just make it about forty-five minutes before yesterday's ratings results come in."

"How many people did you call?" Fred asked.

"We got to five hundred, during the day and night."

"The usual sources?"

"Yeah, property owners, registered voters, and names from the phone book."

The Nielsen company had electronic meters monitoring TV-viewing habits in five hundred homes and apartments throughout metropolitan Los Angeles. The viewers' identities and exact addresses were confidential, but TV stations were told how many meters were in each zip code. The Nielsen families were selected according to age, race, economic status, and where they lived—more meters were located in heavily populated neighborhoods. So, with a map showing the general location of Nielsen meters, McCrory and his staff had programmed the station's computer to give them, as he called it, "The Fickle 500."

"What did you ask them?" Fred wondered.

McCrory stacked some papers as they came out of the copy machine. "You want to know all the questions?"

Fred nodded.

McCrory, who had a photographic memory, began to list each question. "Well, we had two parts to the survey. We asked if in the past six months they'd watched local television news more than once a week. If so, what was their preferred station and why? Had they stopped watching last Thursday, and if so, why? If they no longer watched TV news, what would it take to get them to do so again a regular basis? That's just the first part. You want the second?"

Fred nodded again.

"Okay, secondly, we asked what they thought of the Light the Night campaign. Did they think it was fully in place, and if so, why? And did they feel safer in the city? And finally, if so, how had that changed their lives?"

"So what did you find?"

"Sorry, Fred, can't give that to you. Wilson gets to see it first."

Fred understood and respected that. "Can you give me a hint?"

"You'll find some of the results shocking. I think there's a clear explanation as to what's happened to local television news and why, especially at Channel Three."

"You're the best, Ken," Fred said with admiration.

Assistant Police Chief Rex Ford stood in the offices of the crime prevention arm of the LAPD and looked at the crime numbers from Monday. When compared to a year ago, overall crime was so low, it bordered on the unbelievable. He'd been called in to look at videotape a surveillance team had taken the night before. A citizens' safety patrol in Eagle Rock had apparently shot a remarkable piece of tape.

"Okay, what do you have? You make this sound like a Hollywood blockbuster," Rex said as he sat in a chair in front of a television monitor.

A smiling woman sergeant in her mid-thirties stood next to the monitor. "Thanks for coming, Chief. This is a classic. What you're about to see is how to catch a car thief. Eagle Rock has really been hit hard with car thefts."

"Well, come on, roll the tape!" he said with a smile.

"I've got to set the stage, Chief. They had one particular bad guy we just couldn't catch. Locks, car alarms, and clubs on steering wheels—nothing worked."

"Okay, okay, what did you do?"

"We may want to keep this away from the media, especially Channel Three, but here's what we did." She punched the button on a tape player, and Rex saw a darkened neighborhood street. "We used a Jeep Cherokee—thieves love 'em. There it is, parked under a streetlight. It's unlocked, and the keys are in the ignition."

"I don't see any other cars on the block," Rex said. "Where's the camera?"

"We did that on purpose. The block was cleared of cars—except for the Cherokee and our van with a camera. Neighbors were clued in. The idea was to have the Cherokee stand out like a fresh hunk of cheese on a rat trap."

"Kind of obvious, wasn't it?"

"Yeah, we began to think so, too. Every night for a week, the bait was set, but the car thief was a no-show, until last night." The video showed a car with two men inside driving slowly by.

"Are those our rodents?" asked Ford.

"Yeah, watch, you'll love this."

The car, its lights off, drove to the end of the block and then turned around and came back, stopping beside the Cherokee. A man on the passenger side, about thirty, of medium build and wearing a Yankee baseball cap, got out and looked inside the Cherokee. He carried a tool for starting cars, but when he saw the keys in the ignition, he put the tool in his coat pocket. He signaled thumbs-up to the driver, who waved back.

He stepped into the Cherokee and turned on the ignition. A loud explosion and a huge puff of dust rose up from within the car, followed by screams of pain.

"Good night!" Rex exclaimed. "What did they do to that car?" He looked in amazement at those in the room.

"Well, Chief, like we said, it's probably stretching things, but this is war. Some guy on the citizens' patrol was an expert in air bags, and he rigged up the car so that when the ignition was turned on, the air bag on the driver's side inflated."

The camera now showed the thief inside the Cherokee. His Yankee hat was knocked off and his nose was smashed and bleeding profusely. Four safety patrol members, armed with golf clubs, stood next to the getaway car until the police squad cars roared onto the scene and blocked it.

The driver still had his mouth open in shock when a man looked in the window and said, "Hey, partner, you just stay put for the time being, you hear? See this five-iron?" He held the club in front of the suspect's nose. "We're not the greatest golfers in the world, but if you move, we'll kind of tee off on you—know what I mean?"

Rex Ford laughed and got up from his chair. "That's Oscar material, but let's keep the video in-house. We'll probably be sued on this—no more rigged air bags, understand?"

"Right, Chief," he heard around the room.

At the door, he turned. "But it sure felt good, didn't it?" He left to a shouting chorus of "Yes, sir!"

Wilson Ruggles walked into his office and saw a thick report on his desk. *McCrory did it—he got it done when he promised. The guy probably counts sheets on a roll of toilet paper for laughs.*

Wilson hung up his coat and then sat down behind his desk. McCrory's survey was neatly printed and enclosed in a plastic binder with the stuffy title, "Analysis of Viewing Patterns for Period 10-26 to 10-30." Wilson held it, unopened, in his hands, then turned to page one.

The survey showed that 90 percent of those called had watched local television news at least once a week, and 60 percent said they preferred Channel Three. Many said the reason they watched was to find out about Light the Night and see what Paul Thomas was reporting. They singled out Channel Three's exclusive video, including the burglar in the shed with the skunks, the supermarket robbers, and the murder of Grant Peters. The majority also said they liked seeing good things happening in the city. *We pay McCrory a hundred thousand dollars a year?* Ruggles thought. *Even Harvey Rose could have told me this.*

Those polled were apathetic to local politics. In addition, there was a lull in breaking national stories and political events with which local viewers could identify—more reasons to leave television sets turned off.

Wilson turned a page. *So far, this tells me squat.* He felt his stomach begin to tighten. This was not what he'd hoped for. *McCrory is supposed to give me something to tell New York. This is junk.*

More than half of those called said that as of last Thursday, they'd stopped watching local television news entirely. Many volunteered that it wasn't something they'd planned—it had just happened, and now they didn't miss it. *Come on, McCrory,* Wilson thought, *who are you calling for this survey? Where are the guys in the undershirts, belching and gassing with beers in their hands? These goody-*

two-shoes you called aren't our kind of people.

Wilson read on. When asked what would get them to watch television news again or more often, the responses were varied. People were happy to see positive stories coming out of Light the Night, but thought the station had only tapped the surface. Many still believed most of what was reported on the news had no direct bearing on their lives.

Some on-air people were given high marks, and others were perceived negatively.

"All right," Wilson muttered, "now you're giving me what I need." *Who's on the air that I can blame?*

At the top of the list in the favorable category was Paul Thomas ("trusted, honest, caring, and believable"). Wilson had hoped for just the opposite. *What about Randall? He's dead meat as far as I'm concerned.* When Wilson read that Bill Randall was considered a liability ("pompous, airhead, egomaniac, and superficial"), he said out loud, "He's gone." *New York will understand that. We had the wrong guy on the air, and I didn't hire him.* Wilson was feeling better. *Good going, McCrory.* Many said Randall lacked credibility, and some thought he was arrogant, but most of those who mentioned him believed he should be more friendly with Paul Thomas. *Well, Randall won't have a chance, 'cause he's gonna be canned.*

Wilson leaned back in his chair, feeling good about the survey. *Okay, what's next?* Under the heading, "Worst Reaction", he read the following: "The Channel Three employee who evoked the most negative reaction was described as a 'creep, fake, goon, slime, moron, nerd, idiot, and buffoon.' That person is Wilson P. Ruggles." A yellow stick-on note attached to the report read, "Sorry, Wilson, just reporting what respondents told us."

Wilson swore out loud, then reread the words used to describe him. *What New York doesn't know won't hurt them.*

He turned to the section on Light the Night. Wilson's eyes widened when he read that every person (95 percent) who said he or she knew about Light the Night thought the project was fully set and there was nothing more to do. Several reasons were given, including the mayor's citywide celebration Thursday night, Channel Three's print ad that morning that had stated that "all was in place," and Wilson Ruggles saying the same on the air that day and all weekend.

Thanks, Harvey. The print ad and the promo spots were all your stupid ideas. You sent us down the tubes.

Wilson read McCrory's conclusions.

"Summary: The overwhelming majority (98 percent) of the respondents believe their lives are safer than they were just two months ago. Most credit the change to Light the Night, which has prompted a reexamination of lifestyles. People have become reacquainted with their neighbors, have committed themselves to a more active role in their schools, and are spending more time with their families."

So what can we do to drive them back inside to watch us? That's what I want to know. Don't give me all this pop psychology.

"Hundreds of respondents have joined citizens' safety patrols or are on waiting lists to train for police and sheriff's volunteer reserves." *No more free crime-stoppers public service announcements for the cops from now on, that's for sure.*

"Churches and charitable organizations have been revitalized; street corner evangelism is up, and the homeless population seems to be going down." *Big deal.*

"Many formerly unemployed respondents are now working, having found jobs while meeting their neighbors during the Light the Night campaign." *Who cares?*

"Our callers believe that TV newsmakers are biased and that the news is sensationalized to get higher ratings. The more sensational, the higher the ratings." *One person's bias is another person's belief. You can't please everyone, so go for the ratings.*

"Forty percent of the respondents told us that TV news does not accurately reflect the religious feelings of people, nor does it understand the importance of religion in society." *Holy rollers!*

"Conclusion: The survey reveals a number of problems for local television, especially Channel Three. If we continue to reinforce residents' feelings of safety by promoting Light the Night, the logical outcome will be a further erosion of the viewing audience." Wilson reread that portion. *How do I explain that to New York?*

"We've done a great public service to our city, but in doing so have lost more than six million viewers. Do the people of LA owe us their allegiance? I think not. Can we ethically ignore the well-being of the city? Of course not. But if the current trend continues, we will 'public service' ourselves out of business." *Then we stop being the good guys.*

"If we're to regain the viewers we've lost, we have two choices: (1) Come up with a different news presentation approach, or (2) Convince people they aren't as safe as they think. The first alternative will take time and may be rejected entirely. The second brings into question ethical considerations, credibility, and possible fraud. Signed, Ken McCrory, Director of Research and Analysis."

Wilson liked the second conclusion. *You let me worry about ethical considerations, credibility, and possible fraud. I need ratings, and I need them quickly.*

"Bob, what do you mean 'indefinitely'? We've made a ton of money for your clients, and you're bailing out?" Arlene Zahn knew she was in a losing battle.

Moments before, she'd picked up the phone to hear that yet one more advertising agency wanted to cancel spots on the six and eleven o'clock newscasts—three of them.

"It's a new week, election results are tonight, people are going to be watching." She leaned back in her chair and grimaced, but then her attention was momentarily diverted, as across the room the laser printer began rolling out the ratings for Monday. She wanted to see the results, but she had to at least try to keep the station from losing any more money.

"We go way back, Bob. I can understand the bank and furniture people, but Cal Finley? We helped him sell more Dodges than Iacocca." Arlene paused. "Okay, they don't want to pay the new rate. Listen, just because of you, Bob—and you can't tell anyone—I'll let you have your thirties at six and eleven for half the going rate." *Buy them, please, buy them.*

"No." The answer was firm. "I already—"

"Huge mistake, and a disservice to your clients, Bob. The drop is only temporary. Your people can do all the rethinking they want. But when we're rolling again, don't come sweet talking to me to get your old spots back." She slammed down the receiver.

Three major accounts—poof, gone! Not in her wildest dreams could Arlene have predicted she would have any spots open on the news—now she had three that no one wanted to buy at any price.

The printer had stopped, and she could see the papers nestled in the bin. She slowly walked over to the machine, pulled the pages out, turned them over, and read the numbers for Monday, November 6:

	6 P.M. News	10 P.M. News
Channel 3	11	15
Channel 5	4	5
Channel 7	2	4

The ratings were in a full-scale meltdown. Things were clearly out of control. In three days, Channel Three had lost more than four million viewers at 6 P.M., and more than five million at ten. *Nine million people gone! That's nearly a hundred Rose Bowls.* Arlene felt like she'd fallen in the toilet. She'd stopped keeping track of how much money she'd cost the station, but tonight's revenues would be down another $425,000 from Monday. Had she totaled them up, the losses would soon be enough to pay for Wilson Ruggles's new estate.

Wilson Ruggles had put aside McCrory's survey and now

had a copy of Monday's ratings in his hands. His world was collapsing in front of his eyes.

His office intercom buzzed, and his secretary told him Dino Ballard, the *Examiner's* TV critic, was on line two.

"This is Wilson Ruggles," he said as gruffly as he could. He was tired of the abuse Ballard had heaped on him, and he felt like lashing out at someone, anyway.

"Good morning, Mr. Ruggles, Dino Ballard of the *Examiner.* Thanks for taking my call."

"Yeah, what do you want? Seems like you've written enough dirt on me and this station without ever talking with me."

"Well, I've tried to reach you and never could get through."

"I'm busy."

"Of course you are, so I'll get to the point. I'm doing a piece on the overnight ratings. I haven't seen the numbers for yesterday, but Thursday and Friday showed a huge drop-off for Channel Three. I'd like to know what you think the reason might be."

"Well, those were only two days out of twenty. We have a long way to go."

"I know, but the numbers say you've lost half of your audience. That's six million people. How can that happen?"

"We're still wiping out the other stations," Wilson replied defensively.

"You didn't answer my question. How can you lose six million viewers in two days?"

This guy sounds like Rolondo Burton. "Okay, Dino, I'll admit we're concerned. We've just run a survey to try to find some answers."

"What did it say?"

Get some excuses in print. Maybe New York will read them and understand. "Most of it is confidential, but we think we were hurt by Thursday's Light the Night celebration. Everyone in the city was out in the streets."

"But that was the first night of the ratings, and your problems carried over to Friday. You have Monday's numbers—were they up or down?"

"Down a little." Wilson wasn't about to tell him they'd lost nearly three-fourths of their audience.

"What about your on-air people? Are you going to make any changes to stop the slide?"

"I can't talk about personnel moves in advance." *I bet he'd like to know what those idiots in the survey thought of me.*

"But it sounds like you may be making some. Am I right?"

"I'm not telling you."

"Well, from what I'm sensing here, it seems like one of the changes may be you," said Ballard. "Is your job in danger?"

"It's as safe as the people of this city think they are," said Wilson.

"What do you mean by that?"

Wilson thought of Ken McCrory's report. "We think one reason the news has dropped off is because people think the LA area is safe now."

"Your station was the one behind extending Light the Night," said Ballard. "You almost sound disappointed that LA is safer."

"What I'm saying is the mayor and our station may have given the wrong impression."

"Like what?"

"That all was in place for Light the Night."

"What else has to be done?" Ballard asked.

Wilson saw a chance to do what the research suggested and get some potential viewers. "Los Angeles is not as safe as people think it is. Look at your own paper—the report by Marcia Willis about a gang war that's on the verge of breaking out. I'm not saying it—she is. She says well-known people are on a hit list. Should people think that problem is for someone else?"

"Is it?" he asked.

"It's everybody's problem, because when gang warfare breaks out, innocent people are caught in the cross fire. I think there's cause for great alarm, and people need Channel Three more than ever to keep themselves informed."

"You'd like to have all-out violence in the streets again, wouldn't you?" Ballard said with contempt.

Wilson was boiling. "Of course not. It's just that people can't afford to let their guards down."

"You don't care about the people, you never did," Ballard said. "You just can't afford to have their TVs off."

Wilson tried to compose himself, to make it sound as if he were taking the high road. "Dino, whether or not you believe me, that's your problem. But if Channel Three can help this city become a safer place, I'm willing to sacrifice ratings and advertising dollars to make it happen. Three cares, and so do I."

"Then I guess I have a problem," Ballard said, "because I don't believe you. Tell me yes or no: would your ratings improve if people in the city felt they were in danger?"

"Yes."

"Well," said Ballard with genuine surprise, "that may be the first time in your life you've ever been honest."

Wilson slammed down the receiver.

"Mr. Ruggles," his secretary said through the open door, "Mr. Burton on line three."

Wilson wiped his hand across his forehead, pushed the button for line three, and with every ounce of cheer, said, "Top of the morning to you, sir."

"It may be the top of the morning to you, Ruggles, but I just saw the numbers for Monday, and you're going to the bottom of a black hole."

"I know it looks bad, sir, but we just completed that survey you suggested, and my people think we've pinpointed our troubles."

"Well, in all my years, I've never seen or heard of a station's ratings doing what yours have done in just three days."

"I'm more upset than you are, sir."

"I would hope so, Ruggles, because right now I'm thinking you may not be the man we want to have running Channel Three."

"I can understand how you would feel that way, sir, but I promise you we'll turn this around. Remember how fast we went up—we can do it again."

"Okay, get moving. I'm not sure how much longer you can charge sponsors what they've been paying. Man, am I glad you locked in our sales contracts."

Wilson swallowed hard and managed a weak "Yes, sir."

Fred leaned back in his chair in the news department's conference room and looked around the room to make sure everyone was there—Tim Hires, Paul Thomas, Bill Randall, Nancy Chen, Carol Singleton, and the producers of each newscast.

Fred Taylor had called a special meeting in the newsroom this afternoon to go over the findings of Ken McCrory, and respond to the ultimatum that Wilson Ruggles had thrown down to the department heads in the morning. Ruggles was like a madman, ranting and raving, marching around the conference table and stopping behind each department head, where he would launch into a personal attack, accusing the person of being disloyal, incompetent, and gutless. Even the engineers, who had nothing to do with the news ratings, were caught in the cross fire. Phil Nelson, head of station maintenance, was ridiculed.

It was ugly—Ruggles's eyes were glazed, his hair was disheveled, and his shirttail was hanging out. The people who came under the most fire were Arlene Zahn, Harvey Rose, and Fred Taylor.

"Thanks for coming," Fred began. "I know it's a little early for some of you. And for you, Alex," he looked at the 6 A.M. producer, "you've been here since midnight."

Each person held a copy of Ken McCrory's survey results, minus the negative findings about Ruggles and Randall—those por-tions were blacked out.

Fred smiled. "As the engineer of this locomotive, I'm open to ideas on how to stop the train wreck."

"What was blacked out?" boomed Randall from his place over by the wall. "Did it have something to do with on-air people?"

"Yes, as a matter of fact it did," said Taylor, "but those findings are private and not part of our discussion now."

"They want to see more of me," Randall muttered loud enough for everyone to hear. "I told you Paul was on too much."

"Shut up," said the eleven o'clock producer.

"Thanks for speaking for all of us, Myrna," Fred said as he turned from Randall in disgust.

Paul was seated by the window. "Fred, this report shows that we were right." He flipped over a page. "Here, on page three, Ken is saying that we did give the wrong impression that everything was in place. Looks like we've got to 'unsell' them that idea."

"Why don't you come right out and say it was my fault?" said Harvey Rose.

"I didn't say that, Harvey," Paul answered, "but we're beyond putting the blame on anyone for this. We've got to give people new reasons to watch us again, and I have a few ideas."

"Fred, what's this stuff about convincing people they aren't safe anymore?" asked the assignment editor.

The discussion went on for an hour. Rose outlined some ideas for a new promotional campaign that centered around the theme, "The Battle Is Not Over." Fred wanted people on the assignment desk to concentrate more on actual crime than on crime prevention. He told Paul to see what he could find on the hit list that Marcia Willis had mentioned in her story on Sunday. He also announced that Light the Night would be cut back from two segments to one at 6 P.M. and one at 11 P.M., and that it would now be placed lower in the newscasts. Bill Randall clapped his hands when he heard that. He would be surprised to know that Paul was the one who suggested the idea to Fred before the meeting began. Paul had also given Fred a list of ideas that would radically change the way news was done. Included on the list were more interactive segments and ideas for telecasting the news live from various places in the city. He suggested having a regular segment on the impact of the religious community, and doing more investigative reports with hidden cameras. On the list were detailed suggestions for a promotional campaign.

Fred was overwhelmed when he saw all of Paul's ideas. "Paul, I wish I had ten of you in this newsroom. Let me look this over."

After a few more questions and comments, Fred told the group not to be discouraged, but to be creative and keep working hard. As the meeting broke up, Fred felt that it was time well spent. But he also knew the only measure that counted was outside of the newsroom and out of their control. It would come from the 500 Nielsen families who held the station's future, if not in their hands, at least in their remote controls.

Fred predicted strong competition from Monday night football, and he had reminded them of the part of McCrory's survey that showed citywide apathy for today's off-year elections.

"Right now the polls are open," he'd told them, "but for us, it's not ballots that count—it's buttons. Let's see how many will be tuned to Channel Three tonight. Go get 'em."

CHAPTER TWENTY-THREE

Wednesday, November 8

"Shut up! You fools, just shut up!" Mo-Jo Jones pounded on the paper-thin wall in his motel room. A man and a woman in the room next door were yelling at each other. He beat on the wall now with both fists. "Shut up, or I come over there and shut you both up for good!" He grabbed his Walkman and put it on, turning the volume up to drown out the couple, who were now banging on the wall in return and cursing at Mo-Jo.

Mo-Jo sat on the edge of his sagging, smelly bed, and stared at the three cockroaches on the floor that he had squashed earlier. He'd stayed out late the night before, but he had something to show for it. A wad of money—tens, twenties, and a lot of ones—and some change lay beside him on the threadbare blanket of his bed. A bottle of Seagram's Seven was on the bed, too. Mo-Jo had held up a liquor store in South Gate and grabbed a couple of hundred dollars from the cash register, money he could now live on. Someone he figured was-not living was the guy at the liquor store who tried to stop him. Mo-Jo had shot him. *I wasted him, man. Boom! Gone! Wonder if that fool made it?*

Mo-Jo tuned his radio to a station that might have news of his crime. He stopped the dial at the first voice he heard.

"It's 7:07 in the morning, you're listening to KFI. Here's what's happening in local news."

Mo-Jo nearly turned to another station as the newscaster began giving the previous night's election results. He had never heard of any of the winners or the losers. He pulled his black notebook out of his jacket pocket. *Here's my list of losers.* Mo-Jo wanted to know if the man he shot had died, and what his name was. He was ready to list him in his book.

"Los Angeles homicide detectives are still investigating a fatal liquor store holdup in South Gate last night." *All right, I got the dude. What's his name, man? I want to write it down.* "Dead is forty-six-year-old Ignacio Quinteres, shot by a lone gunman who got away with about four hundred dollars in cash. Police say Quinteres apparently tried to stop the armed robber, and was shot several times in the chest. He was pronounced dead at the scene. Witnesses told police the gunman seen running from the store may have been a youth." *A youth? What you talkin' about?* "They said he was short, barely over five feet tall, and further described him as scrawny, possibly black, and wearing a cap."

Mo-Jo picked up his .38 revolver. *I'll show you what scrawny is. Scrawny this!* He began to write a name in his book. *What'd he say his name was—Egg-noss-something Keen-tear?*

"Ignacio Quinteres was the father of five children. So far police have few clues and are asking for help." *I'll just put "I. Q." in my book,* Mo-Jo thought, as he wrote down his latest victim's initials. *That be good—'cause he didn't have much smarts to try to stop the Mo-Jo man.*

"In other news, there's reaction to a column by Dino Ballard in this morning's *Examiner*. In it he quotes the general manager of Channel Three, Wilson Ruggles, as saying that a sudden drop in the number of the station's viewers is due to crime in LA having gone down, and people feeling that the city is safe. He's also quoted as saying that ratings would improve if people in the city felt they were in danger. KFI spoke with third district council member Francie McMillan."

"I'm very troubled by the statement. It's highly irresponsible. There should be nothing but cheering when crime goes down. Think of Ruggles's implication. Following his logic, he's saying, 'All of you maniacs out there, call me at Channel Three. Let's do lunch and talk about a crime you can commit that will help our ratings.' The next thing we'll see is some shoot-out on the air, live in the studios of Channel Three. I believe Wilson Ruggles owes the people of Los Angeles an apology."

"That was third district council member Francie McMillan. Now here's the weather forecast for greater Los Angeles. Mild days and cool—"

Mo-Jo ripped off his headset. The couple next door was still arguing, but he smiled, in spite of it. Ever since Sunday's article by Marcia Willis, Mo-Jo had been following the story of Light the Night, looking for a way to carry out his master plan. The news just now had given him an idea, a way that would bring him face-to-face with certain people that certain other people wanted eliminated. His plan would need perfect timing and deception, and it carried the maximum risk—his life. But if he pulled it off— *No ifs in this plan, man. When I pull it off, I be in complete control of a criminal empire.*

It started with a phone call to Wilson Ruggles.

Wilson Ruggles had left his Pacific Palisades estate at the crack of dawn. He'd made the move over the weekend, but now, three days later, the place was still a four million-dollar mess. He'd let his wife straighten it out. *Maybe it would be better to just keep things boxed up; the way our ratings have gone, the bank may foreclose on me.* He wanted to call in sick, but he knew if he did, Rolondo Burton, or some honcho from New York, would still call him at home.

It was 7:20. His secretary wasn't there, the ratings were delayed, and now the phone was ringing. Wilson guessed the switchboard operator was putting calls through to pester him. *Beak-nosed hag.* The phone kept ringing. *She's going to let it ring until I pick it up.*

"This is Wilson Ruggles."

"You the man?"

The voice meant nothing to him. "Who is this?"

"Never mind. I know who you are, and right now you need me. I got a business deal."

Wilson began to hang up the phone without even replying. It was an obvious crank call. But when the receiver was halfway down, he pulled it back. "What kind of deal?"

"Now you talkin' some smarts. It's how I'm gonna help you with—what you call them—the rates?"

"The ratings," he corrected.

"Yeah, them—the ratings."

"Who is this—how can you help me?"

"Simple. You help me get close to some people. I bring in some heat, people get scared, and Channel Three is back on top. Like I say, simple, man."

"What do you mean, 'heat'?"

"You need people watchin', right?"

"Yes."

"More people, more money, right?"

"Of course." *Why am I staying on the line with this nut?*

"I can deliver both, in a hurry, and in a big way."

"What do you get out of this?"

"That don't concern you—I make out from someone else."

"I don't know you," Wilson said. "Our conversation is over."

"No, wait, man. Take my number—555-1754—until noon. Then I gotta check outta here."

Wilson couldn't believe he was writing down the number. "Who put you up to this?"

"You did."

"Me?"

"Yeah, what you said in the paper, about makin' people feel afraid so's they watch your news."

"I don't believe I'm still talking with you. Good-bye."

"You got my number?"

Wilson sighed. "Yes, I got it. Say, mystery man, if I should call, who do I ask for?"

"Mystery man—hey, I like that. Yeah, ask for Mo-Jo, the mystery man. Ruggles—don't let Mo-Jo down."

"Oh, of course not," Wilson said sarcastically. "Bye, mystery man." He hung up the receiver and shook his head. "I've lost it."

Paul Thomas knew it was time to level with his wife; he should have done it two mornings ago. The breakfast she'd prepared for the two of them made it even more difficult. She'd gone all out: waffles, sausage, coffee, two eggs over easy, and maple-strawberry syrup they had bought while on vacation in Hawaii.

He looked at the bottle. "This syrup brings back some sweet memories—pun intended."

"That was fun snorkeling."

"I'd never seen you that excited about something in a long time."

"Well, you don't normally see a jillion fish at one time. It was like being in an aquarium."

"Let's pray," he said, and took her hand. "Dear Heavenly Father, thanks for the night's rest, and for the food, and especially for Maddie." She squeezed his hand. "Now keep our thoughts focused on You for the rest of this day . . . " He paused. "And help me as I say something difficult. In Jesus' name, amen."

"You didn't sign your contract, did you?"

Paul dropped his fork. "How did you know?"

Her shoulders sagged. "Oh, different things—you didn't have much of an answer when I asked about it Monday. Care to fill in the blanks?"

"How do I say this? No blanks to fill in—I messed up." Paul looked at Maddie's flashing eyes. "Pretty stupid, isn't it?"

Maddie sighed. "Paul, you know I believe in you, but this is unbelievable. I'm supposed to be your helpmate, but right now I feel like you let us down. You were promised millions of dollars. Think of our family!"

"I tried to tell you, but just didn't know how."

"Can you go in tomorrow and get it settled?" she asked without much enthusiasm.

"What do you think? The numbers are going south faster than a three hundred-pound fireman on a greased pole."

Maddie tried to keep a straight face, but burst out half-laughing and half-crying. "Oh, Paul, this is no joke. How could you have done this?"

"I don't know." He reached for her hand, and she pulled it back. "Maddie, the only way I can look at this is that the Lord just didn't want the contract signed. What else can I say?"

She wiped a tear from her eye and took a sip of coffee. "Your faith is stronger than mine, Paul. I'm mad at you, and I'm angry at God for letting this happen. Sorry, but that's just the way I feel."

"I love you, Maddie."

"I love you, too. Right now, though, I'm just having trouble liking you."

Fred walked into Ruggles's office, and seeing that he was the last one to the meeting, closed the door behind him. Arlene and Harvey stood across the room, copies of Tuesday's ratings in their hands.

Ruggles stood at the window. He turned and walked over to his desk and picked up the morning newspaper, then looked at Rose.

"Harvey, I see your new promo campaign began."

Fred had never heard Ruggles call Harvey by his first name before.

Ruggles ripped a page out of the newspaper. "Very impressive—a full page. What did that cost?" He snapped his fingers. "Five thousand dollars?" He whirled in the direction of Zahn. "Why, that's nothing to Arlene—she loses that much in five seconds around here." Ruggles threw the paper on his desk. "I'll tell you what that ad should have said. It should have said: 'Your Jobs Are Over!' because I don't see any end to this stinking mess we're in!"

He walked over to Rose and rubbed the paper in his face. Ruggles's nose was now inches from Harvey's. "Read me the numbers, Rose. The boss wants to hear them again."

Harvey's hands were shaking as he held the paper Ruggles had given him.

"Read it, you idiot!"

"Yes, sir. At 6 P.M. the ratings were, Channel Three, a 9; Channel Five, a 4; and Channel Seven, a 3."

"Very good, Rose," Ruggles said in a mocking tone of voice. "Another quarter of a million viewers have gone bye-bye. Now, you be a good boy and read Professor Ruggies the eleven o'clock numbers. The class is listening."

"At 11 P.M., Channel Three had an 11; Channel Five did a 6; and Channel Seven came in with a 5."

"Oh, goodie," Ruggles said. "On election night, we only lost another half million viewers—not as many as before." He looked at Fred. "But then again, we don't have all that much to lose anymore. Right, Taylor?"

"You're dead wrong, Wilson!" Fred said in a loud voice. "We still have our integrity, no thanks to you!"

"You can't talk to me like that. I'll—"

"Stuff it. You can ridicule them, but don't try it on me, you miserable excuse for a human being. I can get a job anywhere I want, but I happen to care for the people upstairs. They're good news people who—"

"I don't have to take this—"

"Shut up! There's something really weird going on in LA that may never happen again. We've got to ride it out. Perhaps we change our approach to local news, I don't know, but your bully tactics won't get us anywhere. Try to give us some leadership. We're in a sinking ship, and we don't need a captain in a straightjacket, frothing at the mouth."

Ruggles wiped his mouth. "Okay, okay, but I'm getting it hard from headquarters. I gotta show some signs of stopping this. You want to know how bad this is?" He held up a piece of paper. "This morning, I took a call and actually listened to a guy—what's his name—oh yeah, here it is, 'Mo-Jo the mystery man.'"

"What did he want?" asked Zahn.

Ruggles laughed. "This clown said he could help our 'rates'. He meant ratings, which shows how stupid he is. Anyway, he gives me a phone number and says I should call him before noon today for more details."

"How did he say he could help?" she asked.

Ruggles gave her a puzzled look. "Oh, come on, Arlene, the guy's a nutcase. I don't know. He said something about us getting him near some people, then he'd bring in heat, whatever that means, and everyone would get scared and we'd be back on top. Like I said, a nut." He tossed the paper with the phone number on his desk. "That's it, meeting's over. I've got to call New York. At least I can tell them things aren't as bad. Arlene, you stick around. I want to talk with you alone. Rose, outta here."

Fred started to walk out of the room.

"Oh, Taylor, I'm not signing Paul's contract." Everyone in the room stopped in their tracks. "What's with the big surprised look? Not with what's happened to the ratings."

"He could sue us," Fred said. "We did have an oral agreement."

"He won't sue."

"How do you know?"

"If he gives me any static," Ruggles sneered, "I'll lay some of his own religion on him. It's not the Christian thing to do—suing your employer."

"As if you know all about Christianity," Fred said. "What are you going to pay him, then?"

"The same as he was getting before—no raise, no written contract. He's week to week until I can get someone else."

"Pretty shabby treatment, Wilson."

"Yeah, and what's he doing for us now? Zero! Put him back on the 6 A.M. And cancel his bodyguards. No one's watching him on TV—why should we pay someone to do it?"

"Both of them?" Fred asked. "Can't we at least keep the guy on the street a little longer?"

Ruggles shrugged. "Okay, only the one outside, and only for the rest of the week."

"You going to tell him all this, or you want me to do it?"

"I'll give you the pleasure, unless you want me to do it."

Fred shook his head. "No, I can just imagine how sensitive you'd be. I'll do it." Fred turned to leave. "This place stinks."

"I didn't appreciate the way you mouthed off to me in the meeting, Taylor."

"Too bad. You needed to hear it."

"Close the door on the way out, and give my regards to that pious pinhead."

Fred slammed the door, but then stood by the water fountain a moment and pretended to get a drink.

"Okay, Madame Z, do you know what a two-minute drill is in pro football?" he heard Ruggles ask Arlene through the door.

"It's something that happens at the end of the game when one team is running out of time."

"Correct. Well, you're that team, you've got the ball, and your time is just about up—only this isn't a game, it's the real deal. I'm giving you until Monday morning to come up with a miracle. How you do it, I don't care. But if things don't change, you're history."

Harvey Rose stood in front of his staff, brainstorming, pleading, and demanding new ideas. "We've got to stop the ratings from falling—"

The door to his office flew open, and Arlene Zahn stuck her head in. "We've got to talk. Meet me in my office."

"But we've just started our—"

"Now!"

Harvey ignored the confused looks and snickers, and went after her.

"What's going on, Arlene? I've got stuff to do." She was silent as they walked along the hall. "Come on, this is ridiculous."

When they arrived at her office, she picked up a piece of paper on her desk. "Here's the phone number of that Mo-Jo guy. Call him." She looked at the clock. "It's 11:15. I hope he's still there. Go ahead, call him. I don't want him to know a woman's involved."

"How'd you get the number?"

"I saw it on Ruggles's desk." She pushed the phone toward him and handed him the receiver. "Now call him! Find out what he wants."

He punched the numbers and waited. A rough voice answered on the third ring. "Yeah, who you calling?"

Harvey cupped his hand over the receiver. "Who do I say I am?" he whispered.

"Ask for Mo-Jo the mystery man."

"Mo-Jo, mystery man."

"Who's this? You don't sound like Ruggles. What's goin' on?"

Again, Harvey looked to Zahn for help. "He wants Ruggles. What do I tell him? Can't you do this?"

"No. Tell him you're calling for Ruggles and need to know more about his plan."

Harvey repeated what she'd said.

"I don't know who you are, man. You could be the cops, you could be a Ruler—you could be a lot of things."

Harvey had an idea. "Why don't you call me back at

Channel Three's main number, and ask for Harvey Rose? Then you'll see that I'm who I say I am."

"What's the number?"

"It's 555-3333. Ask for Harvey Rose, but give me a couple of minutes. I've got to get to my office. I'm with—I'm somewhere else at the station now."

"You Harvey Rose?"

"Yes."

"Okay, Harvey Rose—you got two minutes."

"Okay, talk to you later."

Harvey hung up the phone. "Come on, he's calling me back in my office. We've got two minutes."

They rushed out of Zahn's office and back into the promotions department's office.

"Everybody out!" Harvey shouted.

His staff was still seated in a semicircle, going over ideas for on-air promo spots. "Take a break, go to the newsroom, do something, but I want everyone out of here for the next half-hour." He practically pushed them out the door. "Out, out—private business. Out!" When the last one left, he closed the door and locked it. He and Zahn then went into his private office and waited for the call.

"What do I ask him when he calls?" he said.

"Find out what he wants from us. If he can do something, it has to be done fast—I'm out of time."

The phone rang, and Harvey picked it up. "Harvey Rose."

"This is the guy who just called you—what's my name?"

"Mo-Jo the mystery man," Harvey said.

"Okay, Harvey Rose, is Channel Three ready to make a deal?"

"What do you want?"

"I want to get into your station and do some payback for someone I know. You give me a few names and sneak me inside, I guarantee you'll have the whole city watchin' by Friday."

"What names do you want and what are you going to do here?" Harvey asked.

"That comes later. You interested?"

"Yes, but when will you call? Can we call you again at this number?"

"No, I'm checkin' out. I'll call you at eight tonight. You got a direct number?"

"I'll be at 555-7200," Harvey promised.

"555-7200. I'll call you at eight."

Harvey put the phone down. "He wants to get in the station—something about a payback. I don't like this at all. What could he do that would get people to watch us? I smell trouble."

"You don't smell trouble, Harvey, you smell your spine, 'cause it's melting under pressure. You just follow old Arlene—she's gonna save the day for everyone."

CHAPTER TWENTY-FOUR

Maurice Jones high-fived himself. The first phase of his plan had worked, but now the most difficult part was ahead. He had to somehow make contact with Jorge Escobedo, the gang leader he hated and wanted to kill. As Mo-Jo, he had sworn his allegiance to the Iron Claw, but things had changed. Mo-Jo was now a man without a gang, a man without a family. In a way, he was a fugitive from both the Iron Claw and the Insane Rulers at the same time. He was certain they both had orders out to kill him, but he had something the gangs wanted—a diary that could send Main Man to the gas chamber. He also had what he believed was a direct entry to the Channel Three studios, and that was what Escobedo was after. This could be the ultimate sting. Jorge Escobedo and Main Man would be convinced that he was working for each of them, when in truth, Mo-Jo intended to murder both of them.

Mo-Jo might be in exile, but he was not without information, and now he dialed a phone number given to him as payment for a gambling debt. It was the number of the home where Jorge Escobedo was staying.

Mo-Jo asked to speak with Escobedo and was told to wait. *This is great. I'm gettin' right to Jorge.*

After a few seconds he heard a voice. "Who's this?"

Mo-Jo recognized the voice of Tony "Big Ears" Romero, Escobedo's most trusted friend and number two Insane Ruler. "I know it's you, Big Ears. I wanna talk with Jorge. This is Mo-Jo."

"I'll talk for Jorge. How'd you get this number and what do

you want?"

"Tell him I got a book that'll put Main Man away for life—maybe to the chamber. But I wanna talk with Jorge, not you."

"What book? And what kind of a fool are you to be calling us?"

"Listen, I'm tired of talkin' with one of Escobedo's ugly flunkies–stop messin' with me and put the man on. I'm tellin' you, I'm ready to give you China white, Main Man, and get this, Paul Thomas."

"Hold on."

Mo-Jo took a deep swig from a can of beer in his hand and looked down at the black book lying on the bed.

A voice came on the line. "Mo-Jo, you know I'm talking to a dead man, don't you?"

"This Jorge?"

"Doesn't matter who it is, because the way I figure it, you're as good as dead. If we don't get you, your old gang will."

"Well, I'm still here. You interested in my deal?"

"I don't know about no deal. What's all this jive about Main Man, a book, China white, and Paul Thomas?"

Mo-Jo smiled. *He's nibblin' at the bait.*

"I got a record of all the hits I've done and who ordered 'em. I got names, weapons, and a lotta other stuff the police can use against Main Man. That's what's keepin' the Claw from killing me—they don't know where my book is. But most of all, I'm calling you now, 'cause I can give you Paul Thomas and the guy who shot the video of you murdering Peters."

There was no reply. Then Escobedo spoke, but his tone was different, more businesslike. "What do you get out of this? You got kicked out of your gang. Why you doing me this big favor?"

"No big surprise. I want Main Man to pay for what he's doin' to me, puttin' me out on the street, like an animal. I figure if I give you Paul Thomas and the video guy, then get close enough to

Main Man to kill him, maybe we can work out some other stuff, and you'll make me part of the Rulers."

"You know a lot about what I want," Escobedo said, his voice flat, sending a chill through Mo-Jo.

"Yeah, but I know what happened in prison between you and Main Man."

Main Man and Escobedo had been in prison together in San Luis Obispo, California. They'd been in the middle of two stabbing incidents; Main Man won the first, and Escobedo nearly killed him in the second. Now they were leaders of the two most powerful street gangs in Los Angeles.

"I got my contacts on both sides," Mo-Jo said. "I've always been good at that. You need me—to get Main Man and Paul Thomas."

"Do you know how I want to do it?" Escobedo asked.

"Yeah, I hear you want to kill Thomas while he's on TV. That's where I come in, 'cause I can get you in."

"Okay, Mo-Jo, maybe I'm interested, but I don't trust you for a second. I've got a little test to see if you can get inside Channel Three."

"What is it?"

"Give me the name of the guy who took the tape of me killing Peters and where he lives. Do it by tonight."

"I'll call you at nine," Mo-Jo promised.

"I'll be here."

Mo-Jo put down the receiver and high-fived himself again. "Yes!"

Another step in his plan was now completed. Next, Mo-Jo called the person he'd faced in terror just six weeks ago—only now he felt in control. Half of the sting was set in motion. Now he had to do a con job on Main Man. The phone rang five times.

A gruff voice finally answered. "Yeah?"

"Put Main Man on. It's an emergency."

"Who is this?"

"Tell him it's Mo-Jo. I got some heavy stuff for him."

"Yeah, and we got some heavy stuff for you, like breakin' every bone in your body. You was told never to call."

"Shut up, Dice Head. Get Main Man and tell him I can take out Escobedo."

"Yeah, right. What you mean, you can take out Escobedo? How can you do that if we can't?"

"'Cause you're stupid, Dice Head, that's why. Let me talk with him or he's gonna hear from somebody else that I had Escobedo, but you screwed things up. Now get him!"

Mo-Jo and Dice Head, whose real name was Willie Stevens, had been rivals within the gang for years; it was no secret each wanted to succeed Main Man some day. Their hatred for each other had escalated when Dice Head moved ahead of Mo-Jo in the Iron Claw leadership. Mo-Jo was furious when Main Man put Dice Head in charge of all gambling and loan-sharking—Mo-Jo wanted that and his enforcer role.

Mo-Jo heard voices in the background. He recognized Main Man's voice. " . . . Dice Head, if this is another one of your . . . Yeah, who is this?"

"It's Mo-Jo."

"Don't you mean, 'Doe-Doe'?"

He heard laughter in the background—the loudest was Dice Head's.

"Not Doe-Doe anymore," said Mo-Jo. "I think it's time you gave Mo-Jo some respect."

"Why should I do that? You're a loser, Doe-Doe. You've got nothing I want."

"How about Jorge Escobedo? How about Big Ears Romero? How about my little black book?"

"I know all about that book of yours. But if the cops get it, we both go to the chamber, so what good is it to you?"

"Let's just say the book is my insurance policy to keep you from killin' me."

"So what's this stuff about Escobedo and Romero?"

He took it. "I can't tell you how, but I've worked my way into Escobedo's gang. I found out that the guy from Hong Kong, the China White connection, is going to use Escobedo's gang. You're out, Main Man, unless Escobedo can be killed. That's where I come in."

There was silence on the other end of the line. "Go on," Main Man said finally.

"I know I can kill Escobedo and Romero, but I need your help. Do it, and this city is yours."

"So, what's in it for you? Why are you doing this for me?"

"I want back in the Iron Claw. You know I put my life on the line for my brothers for a long time, man. Okay, I made a mistake when I killed that Jackson guy, but you shouldn't have kicked me out. I want bigger responsibility and I got a way to show you I'm worth a second chance."

"Like what?"

"I'm gonna kill Big Ears. Then we'll talk about what you need to do to help me get Escobedo—agree?"

"Talk is nothin' but words. Let me see action, Mo-Jo."

He took it, and he called me Mo-Jo. "You'll see action, and you'll see me soon." He hung up the phone and clapped his hands.

Mo-Jo jumped off the bed, threw his meager belongings into a gym bag that said "Michigan State" on the side, picked up the box with the night-vision goggles, and headed out of his room. He was on a high, a natural high for a change.

Mo-Jo needed a different car. He'd left a stolen Nissan sedan on the street two blocks away. He moved slowly from car to car in the motel parking lot, looking for keys left in an ignition. He finally found some in a Ford Escort. It was a wreck, having been on the losing end of several fender benders, but it gave Mo-Jo a new set of wheels. He looked around, and when he didn't see anyone, he threw his stuff on the passenger seat, got in, and started the car. Mo-Jo peeled out, bouncing the car through the parking lot potholes and onto the street, nearly hitting a pickup truck whose driver yelled out an obscenity.

Mo-Jo congratulated himself for stealing the car, not paying for the motel, and executing a smooth plan so far. He had a good feeling about everything except dealing with Harvey Rose. *Fruity-sounding name.*

He needed to find a new place, in case his phone calls were traced and he was followed. He had money from the liquor store holdup, and with his plan on schedule, he decided to step up in class and look for a better motel. That's where he'd make his call at eight to Rose. He drove onto the Harbor Freeway and headed north.

The sound of thunder rumbled in the distance as an afternoon rainshower swept down from the San Gabriel Mountains. Mo-Jo was now on the Golden State Freeway. He turned on the windshield wipers, but the one on the driver's side didn't work. He had to get off the freeway, so he took the Western Avenue ramp. He was in Burbank now, and spotted a motel with a vacancy sign, but cursed the rain because he was going to get wet. He didn't want to park the stolen car at the motel. He'd leave it about a block away and walk to the lobby. He pulled up short of the motel and waited in the car for the rain to let up.

"Paul, I need to see you. Can we talk for a few minutes?" Fred was waiting for Paul as he arrived at his office.

Paul had been in TV news long enough to know that such lines as "Gotta minute?" or "Can we talk?" never meant good news. *Uh-oh. Good-bye, million-dollar contract.*

"Do I have to?" Paul said, trying to sound cheerful. A flock of butterflies had just attacked his stomach. "I try to run when I hear those words. They usually mean one of three things—you're fired, demoted, or about to be chewed out." Paul took off his coat and draped it over a chair in his office. "One of the first two, right?"

Fred motioned for him to follow, and they walked past Bill Randall's open office door. "It's about your contract. I've got some bad news."

Paul heard clapping in Randall's office. He felt like making a brief stop and punching his lights out. Paul tried to think of a Bible verse for comfort. *What did James write? Something about being "slow to speak and slow to anger." Yeah, right. James never knew Bill Randall.*

Paul followed Fred into his office and Fred closed the door.

"You mean the contract that's been lost in space?" Paul asked.

"Yes. Ruggles never signed it, and now he's taking back the offer," Fred answered.

So, this is how it feels to lose two-and-a-quarter million dollars. "The whole thing?"

"The deal is off."

"What about the handshake and the oral agreement? Worth anything at all?"

"Not with Ruggles."

"And you?"

Fred looked down at his desk. "I was just the middle man." He looked back up. "It stinks."

Paul expected this, but still felt like he'd been punched in the gut. *Lord, give me wisdom.* "Fred, it's not your fault. I don't believe God wanted me to have that contract."

Fred shook his head. "Well, neither did the devil, because I talked with him in Ruggles's office this morning."

Paul laughed. "So, what happens now?"

"This is rotten. Ruggles says no contract and the same pay rate as before."

"At least I didn't get a pay cut."

"There's more, Paul. No contract—you're here on a week-to- week basis."

"Whew. Sounds like he's just waiting to can me."

"I gotta be honest—that's exactly how he feels."

"Did he say that?"

"Uh-huh. He also wants you back on the morning news."

Fred leaned back in his desk chair, put both hands over his mouth, then moved them over his nose as if he were praying.

The guy is dying inside, thought Paul.

"I hoped we could ride this thing out," Fred said in a muffled voice. "We're just in a weird cycle. I liked your ideas for changes in our news coverage." He took his hands away from his face and leaned forward in his chair. "Do you want to see if Channel Five is still interested?"

Paul thought of the guaranteed deal he had turned down at Channel Five. Ten million big ones! He laughed. "Wellington's probably thankful that I didn't take his offer. No, I think it's obvious what his answer would be. But there may be a reason for all of this."

"What?"

"I think the Lord wanted me to stay here all the time."

"The Lord did this to you?"

"No, He allowed it to happen. There's a big difference."

Fred was silent for a moment. "What do I tell Ruggles, Paul?"

"Why don't I finish out the week and we'll shut down Light the Night on Friday? The captain of the Light Brigade already has the last line of his farewell speech: 'Old captains never die, they just have their lights turned out.'" But Fred's expression never changed. "Hey, Fred, lighten up! So, I just blew two, three, or ten million dollars. It's not the end of the world. For me, I wish it were the end—I'd be in heaven."

"Oh, come on, Paul, how can you give me that

garbage?"

"I'm serious. I'm ready for heaven, but you're not. Have you made that decision about eternity yet?"

Fred coughed. "I'm working on it."

"That's not good enough. What's there to work on? I've explained it, and you've heard it at your church."

"Yeah, I know what I should do, but I'm just not ready."

"Time's running out. Nowhere in the Bible can you find anyone who heard the message of Jesus, rejected it, and ever came back to follow Him."

"I haven't said 'no.'"

"Yes, you have. By not saying 'yes,' you're saying 'no' to Jesus. He wants to come into your heart."

"Give me more time, Paul. I don't know what to think. My mind is all messed up because of Ruggles."

Paul got up from his chair and opened the door. "That's a cop-out, Fred, and you know it. I'm praying for you. Thanks for being up front with me." As he left, he heard Fred pound his fist on the desk.

Now I've got to tell Maddie, Paul thought as he walked down the hall. *That should be a real downer. She'll probably change the locks before I get home.* As he approached Bill Randall's office, he saw him leaning up against the doorjamb, a can of pop in his hand. "Hi, Bill."

"How'd your talk go with Fred?"

"It went."

"New assignment?"

"It's none of your business."

"You see the ratings from last night, Captain Nemo?" Randall smirked.

"Yeah, I saw them. What's with the Nemo line?"

"Looks like you're taking us '20,000 Leagues Under the Sea'!" Randall let out a raucous laugh.

Paul jabbed his finger into Randall's chest. "Very, very clever line, Billy boy. Yeah, Captain Nemo has new orders. I'm going back to the early morning news next Monday. You're going to be the star anchor again." Randall grinned. "But, Bill, do you know what a big anchor does?"

"No, why don't you tell me, Captain Flash in the Pan."

"Big anchors have been known to take everyone to the bottom."

CHAPTER TWENTY-FIVE

Fred and Tim were brainstorming in Fred's office. The ratings and careers of many people at Channel Three were about to go down in flames, but before they crashed and burned, everyone wanted to give at least one last-ditch effort to pull out of the nosedive.

"You want to do what?" Fred cried in astonishment.

"A town hall summit between the Insane Rulers and the Iron Claw—televised live in our studios." Tim Hires grinned.

"You're nuts. Get out of here."

"Would you at least listen? We don't have anything to lose."

"Try our lives, for starters. But go ahead, confirm in my mind that my assistant news director is a complete wacko." Fred sat back in his chair.

Hires's idea was to hold the gang summit over the next two nights during the 6 and 11 P.M. newscasts. The threat of an all-out gang war in the city already hung over everyone's heads. "Maybe if they talk to each other during a public forum, we can keep the city out of their cross fire," Tim said.

"You want World War III to break out in our studios?" Fred didn't even want to think about what might happen. "Forget it. I'm desperate, but I don't have a death wish."

"I'm serious, Fred. We make studio five wall-to-wall cops, security like you've never seen."

Fred listened to the plan. It was risky and dangerous, but for every question, Tim had an answer. For every argument why the plan wouldn't work, Tim made a better case why it would.

"I still think you're crazy," he said. "But if you can get the gangs here, I'll bring in some movers and shakers—business-types, educators, politicians. How would the format work?"

"We open our news at six with a summit preview, have a short block of news–then spend the rest of the news on the summit."

Fred was skeptical. "I've heard of dumb ideas."

"We're already in the middle of a ratings catastrophe."

Fred let out a knowing sigh. "It's worse than that. What about the news at eleven?"

"Work on Ruggles. Get him to expand the news to an hour, then we follow the same format as the six o'clock news."

"Okay, you've got the cops and the gangs. I'll get started on the community leaders."

The familiar can-do grin came over Tim's face. "This is gonna work—just wait and see."

"Then prove it. Make a few phone calls and show me."

"Here? Now?"

Fred got up and pointed to his chair and the phone. "Here and now. There you go—you're in charge."

Tim sat down in the chair, looked at a paper he held in his hand, and began. He first called the LAPD gang unit; he had been given the names of former gang members who were working in the community, trying to keep young people from becoming gang members. Tim summarized his idea and asked that they contact their sources. Fred was impressed to see Tim not taking "no" for an answer.

After six phone calls, Tim looked up at Fred. "The message is on its way up the gang's chain of command. Word travels fast—it'll get to the top today."

Tim had asked the gang members: "If you were guaranteed no police interference, would you and members of your gang agree to take part in four live televised summit meetings at Channel Three?" Tim was overflowing with confidence and enthusiasm.

"Easy does it, Tim. Escobedo won't show up—he's wanted for murder. And there's no way the Iron Claw leader will be here either."

"I know that. But here's how we sell this to city hall and the police. Maybe lower-echelon gang leaders could start work on a truce, or at least make it look like they are."

"Aha. Now the truth comes out."

Tim looked around the room and smiled. "Do you have a tape recorder in here? I wouldn't want this to be like Watergate."

"No tape recorder—just you and me."

"Okay, come on, you know as much as I do that the main reason for this would be to get our audience back. But what if we somehow brought the gang violence to an end?"

Fred smiled. "You're a dreamer, Tim. But it's worth a try. After all, money always wins out over common sense. Let's talk about some ground rules for our summit."

The two agreed that there would be a weapons search, and they would limit the summit to ten members from each gang in the studio.

"What about those wanted by the law?" asked Fred.

"We let them wear masks—police would agree to make no arrests during the summit."

"Would the gangs believe that? Sounds like a great sting operation."

"Not if the mayor and police chief give their word."

"This will be live," said Fred, "but we've got to have some sort of protection from what these dirtbags may say on the air."

"No problem. The engineers have a seven-second delay to bleep out any language that needs bleeping."

Fred threw up his hands in surrender. "Okay, let me get started on the mayor and community leaders. You keep working on the gangs."

"Yes, sir!" Fred watched Tim run out of his office. *Did I ever have that much energy?*

As the afternoon wore on, Fred had a commitment from the mayor who promised to put pressure on Chief Morgan. But Fred knew nothing would happen unless the gangs were willing to take part.

Two o'clock passed, then three, then four. Fred kept checking with Tim, but neither gang had responded. It appeared that the great gang summit was dead before it started.

Then, just before five, as Fred watched the news, Tim burst into his office. "Guess what, Fred? We're on!" Tim jumped into the air. "They're coming!"

"Who?"

"Iron Claw and Insane Rulers. They both said 'yes'!"

Fred lurched forward in his chair and reached for the phone. "I'll tell Paul and he can announce it—"

"I already told him," said Tim. "He'll put it on at six."

Fred still had the phone in his hand; he punched in the mayor's number. "Mayor Bodine, please. This is Fred Taylor—she's expecting my call." He paused. "Mayor, Fred Taylor. It's on. You can notify Chief Morgan. We're announcing this at six. My people will get with yours for details. Gotta go. Talk to you later. Bye."

"Okay, what now?" asked Tim.

"Since we had police officers at the station checking out security in advance, we've got a good start on that." Fred stopped for a moment. "Tim, I have no idea why the gangs agreed to do this, or what's going to happen tomorrow—but I just want you to know, I'm impressed with you. This may still blow up in our faces, but for now, you have just pulled off the impossible. Well done!"

Tim grinned. "Thank you, Mein Director."

Wednesday's six o'clock news was well underway. Paul stood on the special effects set, announcing the planned summit. He walked to the area of the city where Channel Three's studios were located, and an explosion of video rolled toward the screen. A montage of scenes bombarded viewers—murder victims, weeping parents, funeral processions, suspects in handcuffs, and a series of gang hand signs and graffiti.

"We hope what you've just seen will stop in Los Angeles," said Paul. "We can't end the violence—we can only bring enemies together. Tomorrow at six and eleven, live in our studios, we've asked members of LA's two most powerful street gangs, the Insane Rulers and Iron Claw, to be here. There's a chance they can reach a truce and avoid an all-out war.

"We've also received promises from influential people in our city. These are top decision-makers in business, education, and politics. They'll be here, armed—not with guns, but with ideas. They have the means and contacts to put gang members on the right track. They can help them find meaningful and permanent work and become educated so we can stop the cycle of violence."

The special effect was dissolved, and Paul was shown in a tight shot. "You may be asking why we're giving gang members a chance to spread their hatred on television. Why waste our taxes to provide police protection for two groups of criminals who have terrorized our city for years? We asked ourselves those same questions and, frankly, we don't have a lot of answers. There's a possibility of violence when the two sides meet—we know that. But there's also a chance to stop it."

He turned to another camera, and a special effect put up the faces of Jorge Escobedo and Main Man, positioned so they were looking at each other. Main Man's photo was an old prison mug shot, and Escobedo's was taken from the video of Grant Peters's murder. "Unless they come with masks on, and that's part of the ground rules, these men will not be at the summit—but they should be. They're the leaders of two highly organized businesses. Their business is crime, and they are the chief executive officers of two operations that would rival any major corporation in our state in terms of distribution, sales, finance, market penetration, and profit. On the right we have Jorge 'Cruel Rule' Escobedo, leader of the Insane Rulers, and wanted for the murder of Grant Peters. On the left is a person with a long and violent criminal record who is called 'Main Man,' but whose real name is Shirley Hogg." Off-camera, Bill Randall began to giggle.

Paul tried to ignore Randall's laughter. "If either of these men had applied their abilities in a lawful way, there's no telling how much success and respect the two would have today. But they chose a life of crime. However, tomorrow they have a chance, perhaps for the first time ever, to do something positive in our city. It will never erase the violence and heartache they've brought to countless people—but it could be a start.

"Those who have faith in God believe the hardest heart can be changed. Well, right now, we've never had a greater need for a miracle." He walked to the anchor desk. "Bill and Nancy, I'll have more details on the summit tonight at eleven."

"What was Main Man's real name, again?" Bill Randall asked Paul, still giggling.

"Shirley Hogg."

"You're putting me on, right?"

Paul couldn't believe this. "I don't put anyone on, Bill. Perhaps if Main Man shows up, you can ask him about his name and see if he thinks it's funny."

"Oh, come on, can't you take a little joke? How dangerous is some guy with the name of Shirley?"

"This isn't a joke, and frankly, I'm embarrassed right now." He looked at the camera and shook his head. "Speaking for the station, I apologize for what was just said. Main Man, if you're watching, don't let that stupid comment change your mind about the summit. This is too important . . ."

The screen suddenly turned black, and a series of commercials began.

Paul, seeing that he was off the air, grabbed Randall by the shoulders. "You stupid, jerk!" He pushed him backward, and Randall fell over in his chair behind the news set.

On his back, the chair on top of him, Randall sputtered, "Was that live? Thomas, I'll sue you!"

Just then, Fred, Tim, and Rueben, one of the station's writers, ran into the studio. "Randall, you're suspended!" Fred shouted, then turned to the writer—a large man of at least two-hundred fifty pounds. "Reuben, put a headlock on that maniac and drag him to my office."

"Yes, sir—my pleasure," he said with gusto. He reached down and took Randall by both ankles, yanking him out from under the chair.

"Hey, what are you doing—ouch, that hurts!" cried Randall.

Reuben and the floor director, who'd jumped in to help, started pulling a kicking and screaming Randall along the platform. "Grab one ankle, I've got the other," Reuben ordered.

"Do you want to make a wish?" the floor director asked. "I always knew he was a turkey." Both of them were enjoying a rare moment for behind-the-scenes people.

Paul watched with a mixture of rage and amusement. I should have knocked his teeth out. "Was that live?" he asked Fred, but Taylor didn't hear him.

"Get that imbecile out of here!" Fred yelled.

The two men dragged Randall to the end of the platform. His head thumped twice on the two steps as they pulled him toward the exit.

"You'll hear from my agent about this!" he cried as he disappeared through the doorway.

"Thirty seconds to air," said the director over a loudspeaker to the studio. "Fred, I'll put on a couple of PSAs until we're ready to go."

Fred rubbed his hand through his hair and surveyed the battlefield. "Just give me a thirty to make sure he's outta here." He looked at Randall's co-anchor, Nancy Chen, who was frozen in amazement, then at Paul. "Paul, jump in the anchor chair. Take Randall's place."

"Yes, sir," Paul said as he picked up Randall's chair. The star's throne. He put on the microphone that had been stripped from Randall.

"Nancy, you and Paul are the anchors of this psycho ward." Fred glanced up at the studio speaker as if it could hear him. "Everyone got that?"

"Got it," came over the speaker. "Stand by—fifteen seconds to air."

Fred turned to Thomas. "Okay, run with it, Paul. I would have decked him on the air. I'll talk with you after the show."

"Stand by in the studio. Nancy, we'll start with you in five seconds," said the director.

Paul remembered Maddie's prediction. *You may get Randall's job, anyway. It looks like he's doing his best to fire himself.*

Nancy quickly composed herself and was back on-camera. "I'm joined for the rest of the newscast by Paul Thomas. Bill Randall isn't feeling well at the moment. . . ."

The call came at 8:05, and Harvey answered it. "Hello?"

"Who's this?" asked the caller.

"Harvey Rose. Who's this?"

"Mo-Jo. You ready with the plan?"

"What do you want?"

"The name of the guy who took the video of Jorge Escobedo killing Peters. Also, where he lives."

"Wait—stay on the line for a minute." Harvey cupped his hand over the receiver and repeated Mo-Jo's words to Arlene Zahn. "Do we know the guy's name?"

Zahn thought a second. "Tell him we'll call him back in an

hour. It's going to take some time."

"We'll call you back in an hour—what's your number?"

"No, I'll call you—nine o'clock. Remember—I want the guy's name and where he lives." He hung up.

Zahn immediately got on the phone to the 11 P.M. producer. "Hi, Myrna, Arlene Zahn here—got a question. I've had some people ask me if we pay for home video that gets aired. If so, how much?"

"Depends if it's really good. It varies, but usually about a hundred dollars."

"Is that cash on the spot? My friend wants to know."

"Not too often. Usually a check is sent the next day from accounting. Do you have something for us?"

"Uh, I wish I did, but not now. They just want an idea of whom to contact and what to expect. Thanks."

She hung up, opened her middle index drawer, and took out a key. "Let's go."

"Where are we going?"

"Accounting. They all leave at five. I've got a master key and want to try to get into their computer."

"Why?"

"They should have a record of payment and where we sent the check for the Escobedo video. Then we can give that info to our guy Mo-Jo."

Harvey began to understand what they were doing. "But that would put him in danger. You know what these street gangs do. They'll—" He lowered his voice. "They'll kill him."

"Move it, Harvey, we don't have much time."

They walked to the accounting offices where Zahn unlocked the door, went inside, and turned on a computer. She had a list of access codes to all computers at the station. Harvey watched as she searched the news department's menu. "Here it is—Payment for Freelance News Video," she said. "The check would have gone out on the fourteenth or fifteenth of last month. First, let me look at the fourteenth."

Just as she was about to call up the payment records, they heard a man's voice. "What are you doing in here?"

Zahn went rigid at the keyboard and turned around. Roger Gilbert, supervisor of the payroll department, stood in the doorway. He was a short man in his fifties, painfully shy outside of his world of numbers, but in command now. He walked in and looked suspiciously at her computer screen. "I asked, what are you doing in here?"

"Um, with the year ending, I need to start thinking about my taxes. I wasn't sure about the number of exemptions I've claimed, so I'm trying to find it in my personal file." Zahn gave a sheepish grin. "I guess I should have asked you instead, right?"

"You're darn right you should have. This is highly confidential, even to the sales department. You know better than to break into the system." He pointed to the screen. "I don't know what you're after, but this has nothing to do with W-4 forms."

Gilbert pushed the escape button and shut down her computer, then looked at Harvey. "What's your excuse? You some kind of tax consultant, too?"

"Me? Oh, I'm just with her. We're working on something together."

"How sweet. Well, both of you, get out of here." He sat at the computer and called up some functions. "Here, Arlene, before you go—you're currently claiming four exemptions on your W-4 form. Do you want to change it?"

Zahn was headed to the door but stopped. "What?"

"The exemptions—"

"Oh, yeah. No, Roger, keep it the same. Sorry to bother you—we're leaving."

The two disappeared out the door. "That was close," she said. "I've got another idea. Let's go to the newsroom. You have access to the archives there, don't you?"

"Yes, why?"

"We should have gone there first. I want to look up the stories on Grant Peters's murder. But don't tell anyone what we're doing. If they ask, just tell them you're working on some promotional things."

They walked into the newsroom where everyone was talking about the sight of Randall being dragged by his ankles into Taylor's office. No one paid much attention when they passed through the room and into an area used by those who worked on the morning news. Harvey sat behind a computer and turned on the power.

"Okay, call it up," she said. "We've only got ten minutes."

"What date should I start with?"

"Look at Wednesday, September 13, and put in the key words, 'Peters, tape, murder, 11 P.M., and Escobedo.'"

He did, and the computer showed that night's script. It was the story they wanted, but because Paul had ad-libbed over the video, the script had no details. All it said was, "Closed Captions Not Available for This Report."

"Now what?" Harvey felt a sense of relief, knowing what this would lead to.

"I've got an idea. Call up the 11 P.M. show rundown that night with the list of stories."

He did, and soon the presentation she wanted rolled onto the screen.

"Now select the story that's called 'Peters.'"

A list of information about the story appeared–graphics, length of the story, which newscast had aired it, the reporter, photographer, and editor.

"What does it say for 'photographer?'" she asked.

"It says 'Home Video.'"

"Nothing else?" She pushed him aside and sat down in his chair. "Let me look." She scanned the list. "Wait a second—what's this at the bottom?" She smiled. "Bingo—here it is, Harvey, under 'contacts.' Our video guy is Bobby Silva, and it gives his address, Erwin Street—even his phone number in Van Nuys." She pulled a scrap of paper out of her pocket and grabbed a pen from a nearby desk, then scribbled down the information. "Let's get back to your office. Mo-Jo should be calling in five minutes."

They rushed out of the newsroom. Harvey felt trapped. Ethics was one thing, but this was different.

"Why the silent treatment, Harvey?" Zahn asked as they walked back to Harvey's office.

"You know what we're doing?"

"Yeah, we're trying to save our jobs."

"If we tell Mo-Jo who shot the video, we're signing Silva's death certificate—that's what we're doing."

"Harvey, you've never worried about what's right or what's wrong. Don't start now. When Mo-Jo calls, just give him what he wants."

"I'm not going to get mixed up in a murder." The thought of prison or the gas chamber made his knees wobble.

Once inside Harvey's office, Zahn slammed the door, walked up to him, and pinned him against the wall. Both of her hands were on his shoulders, and her face was inches from his. "Listen, you hypocrite. Don't hand me that self-righteous crud—you'd sell your mother for a rating point."

His eyes opened wide, his mouth even wider. Arlene Zahn scared him to death.

"Listen to me on this. You're already in up to your neck. No matter what happens, the police will know that you were with me when we got Silva's name, and you're the one who first talked with Mo-Jo."

The phone rang.

"Answer it, Harvey, and tell him what we know." She handed him the piece of paper. "Here are Silva's name and address."

The phone rang two more times.

"Answer it!"

He did, and told Mo-Jo what he wanted to know.

"It's nothing more than a publicity stunt by Channel Three," Arthur Jackson said with disgust. He was referring to the gang summit planned for the next day.

"Why do you think the gangs agreed to it?" Marcia asked.

She had called to see if Arthur's investigators were ready to move in on Mo-Jo.

"They must think they can get something out of it, and I guarantee nothin' will be peaceful. Summit. Truce. What a joke."

"Any idea when you're going after that guy's notebook? My editor wants to know when I can blow this story open."

"Did you tell him?" Arthur asked with concern.

"No, come on, Arthur, you know me better than that. I've kept it to myself, but he's sure there's more."

"This is off the record, then, okay?" he asked.

Marcia groaned. "You're doing it again. Okay, off the record, go ahead."

"We've tailed this Mo-Jo lowlife for a week now. We think we can get into where he's staying tonight."

"Where's he at?"

"He's moved twice. First, he was in Watts."

"Wonderful neighborhood," she said.

"Right now, he's in Burbank—"

"Burbank? What's there?"

"I have no idea. But there's something else goin' down. We can't figure it out."

"What's Mo-Jo been up to?"

"My people tell me they saw him outside a liquor store in South Gate, the one where that clerk was blown away. We couldn't do anything to stop it."

"This is my exclusive story—don't let me down."

"This is for James, Marcia. That's what this is all about. Your story is just another story. Mo-Jo killed my son."

"I'm sorry, Arthur. Anything more on that hit list?"

"The people on it, including you, are still alive, so be careful."

Three men in a black sedan had watched the home on Erwin Street in Van Nuys for about an hour.

"If he's not out soon, we go in," Jorge Escobedo said from the backseat.

"He be out, don't worry." Mo-Jo was barely visible over the steering wheel. "He think he's big, ever since he shot that tape of you. He's out doin' it every night now."

"Who told you?" Tony Romero asked from the passenger seat. "We been here so long, I can't even move. You sure he even lives there?"

"Just keep lookin,' Big Ears. Mo-Jo's gonna deliver your man."

Tony didn't trust Mo-Jo. How could he? Jones had betrayed his own gang; what would stop him from doing the same now? This could be a trap. Tony was even having second thoughts about being there. Escobedo wanted to kill the person they were waiting for. Tony was the only one who could tell his friend when he thought something was off. "Jorge?"

"Yeah?"

"I got a bad feeling about killing this guy. Let's just mess him up, bust his face, trash his house, burn his van. Let his patrol pals see how we work him over. Killin' Peters didn't stop them."

Just then, a man walked out the front door.

"There he is!" cried Mo-Jo.

"Shut up, keep your voice down," Escobedo ordered.

Tony looked over his shoulder at Escobedo. "What about it,

Jorge? Rough him up?"

"We do it my way, all the way. I want him dead for what he did to me."

Tony turned back to the front. "If you do it, do it here, not where he's going. He won't be alone."

"We get him while he's taping. That's the way it's going to be."

The man was carrying a case.

"His camera's inside," said Mo-Jo.

Tony watched the man get into a tan, full-sized van, and back out toward the street. Two cars passed, and then he headed east, driving right by their parked car. Mo-Jo pulled away from the curb, swung a U-turn, and followed the van.

"Don't lose him," said Escobedo.

"Be cool, we'll get him," answered Mo-Jo.

The van turned north on Van Nuys Boulevard.

"Where's he going?" Tony asked.

"It won't be far," Mo-Jo said. "He tapes surveillance stuff close to his home." The van signaled a right turn, then pulled into the parking lot of the Van Nuys Senior Citizens' Center. "See, I told you he wouldn't go far."

Tony noticed that the graffiti had been removed from the building's north wall that day. He guessed this guy was setting up his camera here in case vandals returned.

"Keep driving. Don't let him see us," Tony said.

"Oh, yeah—I'm gonna start honkin' my horn to let him know we're here. Shut up, Big Ears. I got you this far, leave the rest to me."

"That's what I'm afraid—"

"Let him set up," Escobedo ordered.

Mo-Jo parked the car. The men watched as the driver opened the van's door, set up his camera on a tripod, then got back inside the van. The side door closed.

"That's the same van I saw at Peters's house," Escobedo growled. "Stinkin' one-way windows."

"At least he's alone," Tony said.

"He's making it easy for us," said Mo-Jo.

"I still think we should just break him in two and leave him for his patrol to find," said Tony.

Escobedo's silence was his answer. The men waited for ten minutes.

"He's been there long enough," said Escobedo. "Let's get him."

They got out of the car and approached the van from the rear, keeping low enough so they wouldn't be seen from either window. Mo-Jo held a crowbar. At Escobedo's signal, Tony walked out in plain sight of the van. It was a diversionary tactic; Tony knew the man with the camera would focus on him.

Slowly, Escobedo peeked in the passenger window of the van. He motioned to Mo-Jo to be ready. Somewhere a dog began barking. Escobedo crept in front of the van and then alongside until he was under the mirrored window on the driver's side. Tony stood in front of the van, as if he were casing the area.

Without warning, Escobedo rose from his crouch, and looked directly into the mirrored window and into the camera that quickly brought him into focus.

"Escobedo!" the man cried out.

Escobedo smiled into the camera the same way he did the night he murdered Grant Peters. "Do it, Mo-Jo!" he yelled.

Mo-Jo raised the crowbar over his head and smashed the driver's side window, then reached in and unlocked the door.

"Make sure he doesn't have a gun or a two-way radio," said Escobedo. "Tony, hold this guy. I want to make sure we got our man."

"No gun," said Mo-Jo, "and the radio's not on."

Escobedo took the man's wallet and found the driver's

license. He read, "Robert Silva." He looked at Mo-Jo. "Is this the guy?"

"Yeah," Mo-Jo said, "that's what I got from Channel Three."

Silva was stunned. "They told you about me?"

Escobedo smiled. "You're a famous guy, Silva. Remember me? I didn't say you could take my picture." Escobedo took a seven-inch switchblade out of his jacket pocket. He pressed a button and a gleaming blade flashed in the night.

"Jorge, let me at him for five minutes," said Tony. "I'll make him so he won't work that camera again."

"Don't kill me, please," Silva pleaded. "I have a family."

"Come on, Jorge, five minutes."

"Too long," Escobedo said. "I only need five seconds."

Escobedo looked at Silva; his eyes were open wide and his lips were quivering. "Please," he begged.

Escobedo was right. It was over in five seconds.

Minutes later, the three men were driving east along the Ventura Freeway. They were in a stolen car and needed to exchange it for another vehicle, but first they had to stop by Mo-Jo's Burbank motel room. He'd told them he needed to pick up something there.

"You did okay, Mo-Jo," said Escobedo from the back seat. "You gave me Silva. Next, you get me to Paul Thomas."

Silva was easy, Mo-Jo thought. *From now, it's gonna be tricky.* He looked in the rearview mirror. *That's one bad dude in the backseat.*

"Why you got to go back to your motel?" Escobedo asked. "We've got everything you need at my place."

"It's not clothes. It's some guns and stuff I took from an armory, but I gotta get the book I told you about—what's gonna get me close to Main Man. You want him dead, don't you?"

"Yeah, but I want to get someone else first. That guy back there was nothing—he was just a little quiz for you, Mo-Jo. Now we let you take the final exam."

"So, is Paul Thomas next?"

Escobedo nodded. "That's right. You gonna get him for me

Friday night, live on TV with the whole city watching."

Mo-Jo felt as if Escobedo were breathing down his neck. There were a hundred ways his plan could fail. One slipup and he'd end up just like Silva, probably worse.

"Well, how about it?" Escobedo asked again. "How you gonna get me Thomas?"

"I got a plan, Jorge—things are fallin' in place. You kind of delayed me with what we did tonight." They were now on the Golden State Freeway. Mo-Jo flipped the turn signal and steered the car toward the Western Avenue exit. "You just wait, man. I can put Paul Thomas in my book for you." Mo-Jo's motel was only a few blocks away.

"This book you keep talkin' about," said Escobedo. "How long you been keepin' it?"

"Two, maybe three years." *Oh, man, don't be asking me any more about it.* Mo-Jo didn't want to go into detail because most of the murder victims on his list had been members of Escobedo's Insane Rulers.

"You started a new list for us?" asked Tony.

With a nervous laugh, Mo-Jo glanced back at Escobedo in his rearview mirror, then looked at Tony. "Aw, no, Tony—you can trust me." He changed the subject and pointed ahead. "There's my motel."

Mo-Jo turned off of Western Avenue and into a Holiday Inn parking lot, then drove to the back of the motel and parked the car. "I'll be right out."

"Hurry up, we gotta get rid of the car—it's hot," Tony said.

Mo-Jo ran to a stairwell and then up three flights of stairs, nearly knocking over an older man and woman carrying their suitcases to their room. "Get out of the way," he said, as he pushed them against the side of a wall.

Mo-Jo was out of breath as he bounded onto the third-floor landing. He stopped in his tracks when he saw a man pushing a housekeeping cart out of his room a few doors down. Maid service at night—and a guy? "Hey, what you doin'?"

The man turned the cart in the opposite direction.

"Hey, man—stop!" The man started running. The cart's wheels were screeching now as they rolled along the cement walkway. Mo-Jo pulled a pistol from his jacket pocket and ran after the cart. He cursed and shouted, "I said, stop!"

The man reached an open elevator, pushed the cart inside, and the doors closed just as Mo-Jo reached them. A glance at the floor indicator told him the elevator was going down. He ran to the nearest stairway and down to the next floor, jumping two and three steps at a time. But the elevator was headed toward the ground floor.

Mo-Jo swore again and ran down the stairs, reaching the elevator as the doors opened and the cart came halfway out. He pointed the gun at the man whose face was filled with terror and confusion. His cart held the elevator doors open. "Why didn't you stop when I told you? What were you doin' in my room?"

The housekeeper held his hands up. He shook his head and begged for his life. *"No hablo Inglés, senor. Por favor, no me mata. Soy nadie."* (I don't speak English, sir. Please don't kill me. I'm a nobody.)

Mo-Jo had been on the streets long enough to understand the man didn't speak English and was pleading for his life. Some of his murder victims had used the same words before he shot them. On any other day, he would have killed the man just to be safe, but with Escobedo and Romero waiting in the car, he didn't want to draw attention with gunshots, and he had to get his notebook. "Get out of here!" he ordered, and as the man pushed his cart out of the elevator, Mo-Jo whacked him on the shoulder with the barrel of his gun.

"Lo siento, lo siento. No mas, no mas." (I'm sorry, I'm sorry. No more, no more), he pleaded. As he wheeled his cart away Mo-Jo got in the elevator and pressed 3. The doors slowly closed, and the elevator trembled and groaned and began to rise. First 2—*Come on, come on*—then 3. As soon as the doors opened wide enough, he slid

through and ran to his room. He fumbled with the key, opened the door, and turned on the light. The place was trashed.

Half the carpet was ripped up, the mattresses were torn apart, and the pillows were cut open. Air-conditioning ducts were removed, and the back of the television set had been unscrewed and opened. *The book, did they get the book?* Mo-Jo looked quickly up at the ceiling fan, grabbed a chair to stand on, and reached on top of one of the blades. Nothing. He rotated the blade and felt on top of the next one. Nothing. He turned the last one and rubbed his hand across the blade. He felt something. "It's here!" He ripped the diary loose from the blade, and took it down. The cover still had the three rubber bands around it, two green and one brown. Same order and spacing.

He grabbed his shaving kit and threw the book and a few clothes into his Michigan State sports bag. He looked around the room once more. The box with the night-vision goggles was still there. *Who knew I was here? Main Man? The cops? Well, you missed Mo-Jo, and you didn't get my book.* He ran out of the room and sprinted down the stairs three steps at a time.

Romero had backed the car up to the stairwell. Mo-Jo jumped in the front seat, and Big Ears made a screeching U-turn out of the parking lot. They were thirty minutes late for a rendezvous with gang members who were waiting for them with a clean car. "What took you so long?" Escobedo growled. "Why were you chasing that guy with the cart—what was that all about?"

Mo-Jo gasped for breath. *Don't tell them your room was searched.* "Some stupid Mexican was in my room, probably trying to rip me off."

"You got a problem with Mexicans?" asked Romero. "Last time I checked, that's what me and Jorge were."

"Shut up, both of you," Escobedo ordered. "Did you get the book?"

"Yeah, everything's cool." Mo-Jo reached for his sports bag, which was still unzipped, and pulled out the diary. He took off the rubber bands, one by one, looked at the cover, then the side of the diary with the alphabet tabs on the pages. He held it up for Escobedo to see. "This be it."

Satisfied, Escobedo sat back in his seat.

Mo-Jo opened the book and gasped.

"You okay?"asked Romero.

Mo-Jo cleared his throat. "Uh-huh," he said weakly.

The pages were blank.

Channel Three's eleven o'clock news was almost over.

"Paul, we're dropping the movie story at the end," the producer told him through his earpiece during the last commercial break. "There's a breaker. I can't get you hard copy in time. It'll be on TelePrompTer. Read it cold. Brace yourself—Bobby Silva was found murdered tonight."

"Silva! Wasn't he the guy who shot the tape of Grant Peters's murder?"

"Right. We'll roll that tape and you can talk over it."

"How did it happen?"

"Someone stabbed him. He was taping surveillance stuff at a senior citizens' center from his van."

"Was he alone?"

"Yes. The cops say his partner showed up late and found him dead."

"Thirty seconds to air," said the director.

Paul turned to Chen and explained what he planned to do coming out of the commercial.

"Stand by in the studio—take Paul on camera."

"We've just received word of a breaking story in Van Nuys," Paul began. "*Channel Three News* has learned that citizens' safety patrol member Bobby Silva was found murdered just a short time ago—the victim of a gruesome knife attack." Video of Grant Peters's murder appeared on screen and Paul ad-libbed over the footage.

"Silva was the man who took this incredible video of gang leader Jorge Escobedo murdering community leader Grant Peters on September 12. We had kept Silva's name confidential, in hopes of preventing something like this, but tonight, Silva has been murdered."

The camera came back to Paul on a close-up, and out of the corner of his eye, he saw the floor director giving him a one-minute cue. "Details on the murder are sketchy, but we've learned that Silva had set up his camera in the parking lot of the Van Nuys Senior Citizens' Center, which had recently been the target of vandalism. Normally, safety patrol members work in teams, but for some reason, Silva was alone at the time of his murder. His partner discovered the body when he drove up to the scene."

"While investigators search for suspects, it seems this crime is not a random act of violence. I believe Silva was murdered in retaliation for being part of a Light the Night citizens' patrol, and for taping the murder of Grant Peters. I say that, because we've learned from eyewitnesses that Silva's camera was found smashed in the parking lot. A trail of videotape led to the van, and his body was found with videotape stuffed in his mouth."

"Tomorrow at 6 P.M. the first of four summit meetings will be held at the studios of Channel Three. It will involve the leaders of the two most notorious street gangs in our city. Right now, just the thought of that makes me sick because of the possibility that Bobby Silva was murdered by one of them."

"Put up *Commentary* under Paul," said the show's producer. "This is good, but it's his opinion."

"Insert chyron," said the director.

Commentary was superimposed under Paul in the lower third of the screen.

"So what do we do—call off the summit?" he asked. "Part of me says, 'yes, nothing good can come from it.' Another part of me says, 'remember Raul Fernandez and his infant son. Remember

Grant Peters and James Jackson—and all the other victims of gang violence.'"

The producer turned to the director. "He's on a roll. Let him go another thirty seconds if he wants—we can drop the editorial."

"Here's what we do—we give it a last-ditch chance. We look the leaders of these gangs in their faces, and we say, 'Stop. Find another way to use your skills, however warped they are. Stop the killings and the drug dealings. Stop destroying your lives and the lives of our young people.'"

"We plan to have business, education, social, and political leaders in our studio tomorrow who are ready to begin a new chapter in Los Angeles—one that includes all who want to do things the right way. Not our way and not the gang's way, but the *right way*. Whether or not we succeed is almost entirely up to the gangs. If they're open and willing to join us and not fight us, there's hope."

"Give him a wrap," said the producer.

"Wrap him, Ray," said the director.

The floor director began waving his right hand slowly in a clockwise motion.

Paul began to conclude the newscast. "Right now, the body of Bobby Silva is on a cold slab at the LA county morgue. His death is a message to each and every one of us. But that message is marked 'Return to Sender.' We're not going to give up our neighborhoods again. These people can live with us, and work with us, but if they fight us, they'll lose." Paul felt a lump in his throat, and as he spoke his voice broke. "Our deepest sympathy—" He struggled to compose himself. "Our heartfelt sympathy to Bobby Silva's widow and their three children—our prayers are with you. I'm Paul Thomas—good night from all of us here at Channel Three."

CHAPTER TWENTY-SIX

Thursday, November 9

It was dark when Harvey Rose heard his morning newspaper land with a plop on the driveway of his Manhattan Beach condominium. Still in his underwear, he rushed out the door and bent down to grab the paper. Then he sprinted back inside.

Harvey ripped the paper out of the plastic bag and looked at the *Examiner's* front page. The headline was the murder of Bobby Silva; he stared at the photo of the smashed camera and the trail of videotape. *I knew it! I told Arlene they'd kill him.* Harvey scanned the article, not wanting to read any of the details. He hadn't killed Silva, but he knew he was responsible for his death.

Another story under the headline caught his eye: "Diary of Death Found." Harvey recognized the name of the reporter, Marcia Willis. That's the woman who had all the trouble with the Boss. Harvey read the article. Private investigators had discovered a notebook that could help solve the murders of at least twenty-five people in Los Angeles, including Raul Fernandez, James Jackson, and Grant Peters. The report suggested that when the notebook was turned over to police, it would result in arrest warrants for members of the Insane Rulers, Iron Claw and—Harvey's eyes widened, his knees buckled, and his hands began to shake—and employees of a local television station.

Harvey ran to his phone and called Arlene Zahn at home. "Arlene, did you see this morning's paper?" he whimpered.

"I've been expecting your call," she said, seemingly unconcerned.

"The paper said arrest warrants for employees of a local television station—that's you and me, Arlene. It can't be anyone else."

"No proof, Harvey—it's just a guess."

"Last night, you told me nothing could be traced to us."

"It can't."

"What about the diary? What's the reporter talking about?"

"Harvey, I told you last night, everything is under control."

"And I told you we shouldn't get mixed up with that guy, Mo-Jo. I knew what would happen when we gave him Silva's name. It's murder, Arlene. I don't—"

"Shut up! We can't be tied to this. There's no proof."

"I'm not taking this rap alone," he warned.

"There's no rap unless you panic. Get yourself together. I'll talk with you at work."

"I'm scared."

"Trust me, Harvey. Your old buddy Arlene's in charge."

Twenty-five miles northeast of Harvey Rose's Manhattan Beach condo was the Oaks Boulevard home of Main Man, the leader of the Iron Claw street gang. The home was in an older, exclusive part of Pasadena, overlooking the Rose Bowl.

Main Man had gotten up early; it was a habit since childhood. At first it was a necessity. He had dropped out of grade school, got mixed up in street gangs, and began stealing meal money from his ex-classmates to feed himself. As he grew older, he ran errands, acted as a lookout for drug deals, painted graffiti, and learned how to steal cars.

He was now close to forty years old, and others did his business for him—pushing drugs, handling juice loans, working prostitution rings, and stealing cars. When he gave orders to kill, people died. It was a million-dollar empire—the nickels and dimes he'd scrounged as a punk kid were now replaced with stacks of laundered money. But he felt troubled; he knew he was being squeezed out by the gang of his lifelong enemy, Jorge Escobedo.

Main Man was a quick study of people, able to make instant decisions. He was also a voracious reader and spent hours pouring over periodicals, newspapers, and books. The *Examiner* on his lap was one of several papers he read to start the day. He knew he was a paradox—a murderous, vicious man with a heart of stone, who had spent a third of his life in either juvenile hall, the LA county jail, or prison. He'd also educated himself beyond what anyone knew. Rather than sleep his time away, or spend hours pumping iron, he'd passed his high school equivalency test in prison, then had gone on to earn college credits through correspondence courses. He was fluent in Spanish and French, could quote the classics, and believed strongly in supply-side economics.

Main Man had watched Channel Three's eleven o'clock news and knew immediately who was behind the murder of Bobby Silva—the crime had all the bloody handprints of Jorge Escobedo.

He opened the morning newspaper now to read about Silva's murder and see how the *Examiner* was handling the so-called gang summit. He couldn't risk going to the television station in person, even if identities were concealed. No way. But he needed a way to gain the upper hand on Escobedo's gang.

He read the lead story on the Silva murder, but then saw the smaller headline, "Diary of Death Found," and the story beneath it. After reading the first two sentences he knew Maurice Jones was no longer a threat to him. But he also realized that he was now in terrible trouble. Mo-Jo no longer had the notebook that could link Main Man to murders of the past. But who did have it? *I've got to get it before the cops do.*

Jorge Escobedo sat on a sofa in the living room of his home in Bel Air Estates on Stone Canyon Road. He took a sip of freshly brewed coffee and listened to the rich, baritone voice of his lifelong friend, Tony "Big Ears" Romero, singing a love song in Spanish. Tony was making *huevos rancheros* and freshly-baked flour tortillas, giving their latest hideout a feeling of home. Jorge marveled at Romero's cooking skills; he often thought of what might have been had they opened the Mexican restaurant they talked and dreamed about as kids.

Lately, he'd grown weary of being a fugitive, but he hadn't talked with anyone about his plans, not even Romero. He would soon. His gang had made him wealthy; he had more money than he ever dreamed possible. Jorge planned to take Romero with him to Brazil, Costa Rica, or at the very least to Mexico—any country where the police could be bought. They would set themselves up in a large hacienda with servants, women, speed boats—perhaps a couple of planes for a new drug-smuggling cartel.

One of Jorge's four bodyguards brought the morning paper to him now. Jorge took it and walked to the dining room table where Romero was dishing out their breakfast. The bodyguard went to a kitchen nook and joined the others.

"Smells great, Tony."

"Thanks, man."

"Where's Mo-Jo?"

"I don't know, probably upstairs, still sleepin'." Romero sat down at the table. "I got a bad feeling about him, Jorge—really bad."

Jorge took some melons and grapes, then poured himself some freshly squeezed orange juice. "He did okay last night. He got us that guy's name and where to find him."

"I don't trust him. Let me do the job we talked about for today with someone else."

Jorge savored his first bite of eggs. "Tony, just take Mo-Jo with you, like we planned. We went over this with him last night. You're gonna do the heavy work—Mo-Jo's your lookout."

Romero shook his head. "He's gonna double-cross us."

Jorge sighed. "One day soon, you're gonna forget all about him. You and I are gonna have our own place, we'll have lots of women—but you gotta do the cookin'."

"Si, señor," said Romero, and they both laughed.

Jorge opened the newspaper and read about the man he had murdered the night before. "Hey, Tony, come here. Look, they got a picture of the tape you pulled out of the guy's camera."

"I'll take your word for it."

"You still sore about me killin' that guy?"

"Doesn't matter now."

Jorge took some more bites of his breakfast, then saw the story by Marcia Willis. Suddenly the food wouldn't go down; he'd lost his appetite. "Get Mo-Jo, now!" he shouted to his bodyguards. Two of them looked with confusion at Jorge. "Get him!" he screamed, and they headed upstairs.

"What's goin' on, Jorge?" asked Romero.

Jorge pushed the paper across the table. "Mo-Jo never got his notebook."

Romero grabbed the paper, read the first few lines of Marcia Willis's story, and pounded his fist on the table. "I knew it!"

"Jorge, he ain't here!" yelled one of the bodyguards from a second-floor landing.

"Mo-Jo's gone!" said another, running down the stairs.

"He was bad news, Jorge. I told you, you should have—"

Jorge held his finger up to his lips—a sign for Romero to be quiet. "Hey, don't worry, Tony. We'll find him and kill him, but we don't need him anymore."

"Why not?" asked Romero with a puzzled look. "He's got our names in that book, and now the cops may have it."

"So we're wanted for another murder—big deal. The book doesn't mean squat. We needed Mo-Jo for another reason—we had to have him to get Silva, right?"

Romero nodded.

"And we thought he was the only way I could get to Thomas. But yesterday, Tony—we got ourselves a personal invitation from Channel Three to come visit their studios and meet *El Capitan* in person. No questions asked, and we can even wear a mask."

Romero's face lit up. "You're right. We check things out tonight, look the place over—then Friday, Thomas gets it. Now I'm with you."

"I knew you could do more than cook." Jorge grinned.

"What about the job Mo-Jo and me was supposed to do this afternoon? He knows all about it."

"He ain't gonna show up, not with the book gone. Take Pepe with you this afternoon. You didn't want Mo-Jo with you anyway, right?"

"You got that."

"Just do the thing like we planned, only use Pepe. I want *El Capitan* all broken up, begging me for mercy when I put a bullet between his eyes tomorrow night on TV."

"You the man," said Romero.

"A hungry man," Jorge said. "Let's finish what you cooked."

The laser printer in Arlene Zahn's office came alive. Wednesday's numbers were coming through the bin, but Harvey Rose was thinking more about the prison number he might soon be wearing.

"Harvey, you look awful," Zahn said as she walked over to the printer.

Harvey sat in a chair, his head buried in his hands. "I keep thinking about Silva's family, his wife and children. We helped murder him, Arlene, and I think our names are in that notebook. I don't want to be part of this anymore."

"Harvey, shut up. You're in this up to your yellow belly." She removed the pages from the printer and looked at the ratings. "Well, well, well."

Harvey looked up. "Well, well, well, what?"

"Whatever it was—Mo-Jo, Bobby Silva, the gang summit,

Randall going nutso—who knows, but our ratings went up yesterday. I'm going to go see Ruggles."

"What about me?"

"Just wait here, and don't do anything stupid."

In his office, Wilson Ruggles held a copy of the ratings in his hands. "Betty, get me Rolondo Burton, now!" The ratings were up for the first time in a week. The numbers showed Channel Three with an 11 rating at six o'clock, two points higher than the day before, and a 17 rating at eleven o'clock—an impressive increase of six points from the previous night.

Burton came on the line just as Arlene Zahn walked into the office. She held a copy of the ratings and wore a smile.

"Mr. Burton, good news about our ratings last night." Wilson pointed to a chair for her to sit down.

"Yeah, we've seen the numbers, but compared to a week ago, they're still anemic."

"I think we're on the way up, sir. We've made some changes in our lead anchor."

"Paul Thomas, I hope."

"Ah—yes, Paul's a fine person. I've got big plans for him. I'm his biggest supporter."

"Well, that's good. Understand you had some problems with your other guy—what's his name, Randall?"

"Bill Randall—and he's out." Wilson then told Burton about the planned gang summit. "I think it'll really boost our ratings."

"How are your sales?" asked Burton.

"We've lost a few sponsors and cut some prices, but we're coming back."

"Hope so, Ruggles. These are the days that count. You got off to a rotten start. There's a lot riding on this book."

"I know, sir." *If you only knew.* "I know."

Wilson hung up the phone and looked at Arlene. "Wipe that

cheesy grin off your face and close the door." When she did, he held up the newspaper. "What's this article about—some kind of diary and a TV station?"

"Don't know what you're talking about," she shrugged.

"Are people here involved in a murder?"

"How would I know?"

Then it came to him. The answer was in front of him, on a piece of paper still on his desk. He picked it up. "You were the only one who asked about that Mo-Jo character. I think you saw his phone number." He paused. "Uh-huh. Of course. And I think you're the one who gave him Bobby Silva's name."

"Where's your proof, Inspector Clouseau?"

"Very cute, Arlene. Oh, I'll find it, and put it with the rest of the dirt on you. Keep the ratings up, Arlene, or you're going down."

"Have you seen the morning paper?" Maddie asked as Paul staggered into the kitchen. He rubbed his eyes, and she looked at him and laughed. "Good morning. I'm Paul Thomas, captain of the Fright Brigade," she said in her best news-anchor voice. He felt the stubble on his chin. He knew his hair was standing straight up, and when he looked down he saw that his nightshirt was on backward.

He wiped the sleep from his eyes. "I'm a mess. If we had a cat, he would have dragged me in."

"You want some coffee, bright eyes?"

"Yeah, that might help." Paul plunked himself down on a chair at the kitchen table. "Where's the paper?" Maddie brought it to him, and he began reading the front page.

"I'm sorry about Bobby Silva," she said. "What a shock, especially because you knew him."

Paul heard Maddie, but continued reading.

"Dino Ballard has a column about you and Bill Randall—seemed pretty fair, if you ask me."

"Okay, thanks. I want to read what Marcia wrote first." It

didn't take long for him to see what the station was getting itself into. Who are we trying to kid with this summit? "Oh, man, this is heavy stuff."

"What's the reporter writing about when she says people at a TV station are mixed up in murder? What station is she talking about?"

"Obviously, someone set up Silva. It wasn't just an accident."

"So, it's Channel Three?"

"Silva brought the tape to us. We were the only ones who knew. It's got to be us."

Maddie poured more coffee for herself. "Who?"

"I can't imagine anyone in the newsroom, but you never know. Last night after the show, some of us talked about that. We figured Silva's name could have been found in accounting—they paid him for his video."

"Somebody in accounting leaked it?" she asked in disbelief.

Paul shook his head. "Probably not. No, we think it came from the newsroom. Silva's name and address are in our computer archives."

"That's scary, Paul."

"Well, I've got some news that won't help."

"Like what?"

"No more bodyguards inside the house."

"No more Vinnie and his friends?" she asked.

"Yeah, Ruggles canceled the contract." Paul saw Maddie smile. "You won't miss Vinnie, will you?"

"Not really. I like my privacy."

"Well, you'll soon have it outside, too. Ruggles is pulling the outside rent-a-cop tomorrow. Do you want to take the kids and stay with your folks?"

"Nah, nothing's happened here in two months. Besides, starting Monday, you'll be here at night again."

Marcia Willis spotted Arthur Jackson and another man in a corner booth at Denny's in Reseda. Jackson waved at her, and she walked his way.

"Marcia, this is Ernesto Guitierrez. He's the private investigator we've been using. You talked with him on the phone when you were doing your story."

Marcia sat down in the booth, reached across the table, and shook his hand. "Pleased to meet you. Arthur told me you had a close call with Mo-Jo the day you got his diary."

"All in a day's work," he said with a smile.

"Well, Arthur says it almost got you killed."

A waitress appeared at the table and asked Marcia if she wanted anything to eat.

"Yes, do you have a carrot cake muffin? I'm really in the mood for one."

The waitress nodded.

"And some coffee, thanks."

The woman scribbled the order on a pad and left.

"That was a good story this morning, Marcia," said Jackson. "What a tragedy for Silva and his family. I know, I've been there."

Marcia shook her head and looked at Guitierrez. "Don't you think his murder was in the works for a while?"

The private investigator nodded. "They wanted to kill him ever since Silva's video of Escobedo was on TV. But until yesterday, I don't think they knew who they were looking for."

"I asked you this over the phone, but you wouldn't tell me. Who at Channel Three tipped them off? Mo-Jo keeps track of who orders his killings, or who is involved, right?"

"Yeah."

"Well, whose name is connected to Bobby Silva's murder?"

"This is still off the record," said Guitierrez, "but we think the trail goes back to Channel Three. We found two sets of initials."

"What were they?"

Guitierrez looked at Arthur, then back to Marcia. "W. R. and H. R."

Marcia thought for a moment, then started at the top. "W. R. Wilson Ruggles?"

"He's the only one at the station with those initials," said Guitierrez.

Marcia drew a blank with H. R. "And the other person?"

"Only three people at the station have those initials," the investigator said. "Harold Richards, an engineer; Helene Ralston, who works in accounting; and a guy who runs the promotions department, Harvey Rose."

A shiver went through Marcia. "Harvey Rose is a creep."

"Tell her about the Ralston woman," said Arthur.

"We looked at her first, just because she worked in accounting, but she's been on vacation and out of the city for two weeks."

"Not likely it's the engineer, so that leaves Rose," said Marcia. "I'm not surprised. He's slimy, but I never thought murder."

"Looks like he's the leak or is mixed up in it," said Guitierrez.

"When do you give the diary to the police?" she asked.

"Not sure—maybe after the gang summit. We're trying to locate Mo-Jo. He gave us the slip after we ran into him at the motel." He rubbed his shoulder. "He hit me with his gun."

"You've got to tell me how you got the diary," Marcia said.

Ernesto grinned. "Not for publication yet. I don't want Holiday Inn to sue us for the damage we did to his room. We really messed it up."

They waited while the waitress placed Marcia's muffin and coffee on the table.

"My partner was Mitch Bledsoe. We work really well together. We knew about the notebook and what it looked like—the size, thickness, and that it had alphabet tabs on the pages and three rubber bands wrapped around it—two green and one brown. We looked everywhere, even in the Gideon Bible, in case the pages had been hollowed out. We couldn't find it. Then suddenly, Mo-Jo shows up in a car. I turn off the room light, but accidentally hit another switch that starts the ceiling fan. Just as we're about to leave, we hear a thump against the wall."

"What was it?" asked Marcia.

"I get out my pocket penlight, and there at the base of the wall is a small black book with alphabet tabs."

"And three rubber bands, right?" asked Marcia with a smile.

"Yep, he'd taped his little 'diary of death,' as you called it, to the fan. Then things got hairy. Mo-Jo is coming up the stairs, so Mitch jumps in the housekeeping cart, and I cover it with bedsheets, open the door, and start wheeling the cart in the opposite direction." Guitierrez then told her about a chase down the hallway and an encounter at the bottom of the elevator. He rubbed his shoulder again. "I thought he broke my collarbone, but some good *barrio* Spanish convinced him I was a housekeeper."

Marcia was confused. "But the diary—did he—did you?"

Guitierrez smiled. "He found it, but I'd switched the pages and taped the notebook back to the ceiling fan. The little rat didn't know what happened until he and Escobedo took off in their car. There was no way he was going to tell what happened. We think Mo-Jo was with Escobedo the night Silva was murdered."

"I'd like to write something for tomorrow's paper. What can you tell me that's on the record?"

Guitierrez looked at Jackson, who nodded. "You know that videotape the police found stuffed in Silva's mouth? Well, my sources tell me the police put the tape together, and they have clear footage of two guys in the parking lot the night Silva was murdered."

"Let me guess," she said. "One is Escobedo, and the other is Mo-Jo."

"Yes, on Jorge—just like the night Peters was murdered. Silva got a great close-up of his face. But the other guy on the tape is Tony Romero, Escobedo's longtime friend. But we think Mo-Jo was there, too."

"Thanks," she said. "I'll see what I can get downtown." She took some money out of her wallet. "I gotta go. Let me pay for this."

As she began to slide out of the booth, Jackson reached out and took her hand. "Marcia, you be careful, girl."

"Thanks, I will. Give my love to Clarice."

"Marcia?"

She stopped and looked at him. "Yes?"

"Your name is on that hit list."

CHAPTER TWENTY-SEVEN

It was the perfect time for Tony Romero to pull off Jorge Escobedo's plan. It was a little after four in the afternoon. Children were no longer straggling home from school. Every weekday about this time, there was a lull until people began arriving home from work. Right now, the neighborhood on Camden Avenue was quiet.

"Okay, you ready?" Tony asked, and Pepe nodded. Pepe Velasquez was his partner on this little mission. "If you see the other bodyguard, let me know. That's the only thing I'm worried about."

They walked toward the parked car. A man sat behind the steering wheel. Tony pulled a gun with a silencer from his jacket pocket, and was about to move toward the car when he heard another car coming down Camden Avenue. He held the gun behind his back, and they watched the car drive by.

Tony then crept quickly from the sidewalk to behind the car and to the driver's door. The window was open. Tony shoved the gun against the ear of the security guard and squeezed the trigger—he heard a muffled *pfftt*, and the body fell to its right. Pepe opened the door from the passenger side and reached in to prop the security guard upright behind the steering wheel.

"Go get the car," Tony ordered as he put his pistol back in his jacket pocket. Velasquez went to get their car, which was parked a block away, and Tony approached the side door of the house. He heard a piano playing and knew it was Maddie Thomas. Gang members had watched the house for a while now and knew her pattern; just about every day at this time, she played the piano for an hour. On

Thursdays, the Thomas children had after-school activities until five. But his concern now was the private security guard, who, lookouts said, usually stayed upstairs.

Tony used a lock-opening device to gain entry into the house from the side door, but he could just as easily have broken a window—the woman was deep in concentration at the piano. As he moved through the kitchen, Tony heard Velasquez pull up in the driveway.

The piano was just off the kitchen. Maddie was playing a classical number—he knew a little about music and could tell she was pretty good. As he tiptoed across the wooden floor, his gun drawn, he looked around for the bodyguard. He'd been told the man was an oversized LAPD officer. The piano music continued as Tony reached the dining room carpet. Maddie's back was to him, and he walked slowly behind her. He held the gun with the silencer in his right hand and a strip of cloth in his left hand. He moved within three feet of her. Oblivious to him, she now reached a dramatic part in the piece. Just as she was coming down with her right hand, Tony put the cold muzzle of the silencer against her ear. She jumped at his touch, and the music instantly stopped.

"Don't move, or you're dead," Tony said in a monotone voice. "Where's the bodyguard?"

She didn't answer. She began to turn his way. "Don't even move," he said again.

Tony glanced at a wall mirror in front of him, and their eyes met. Hers were filled with terror.

"Who are you?" she asked.

"Never mind. Where's the bodyguard?"

"He's not here anymore."

Tony smiled. "So, it's just you and me, huh?"

"What are you going to do?" Maddie asked.

"It all depends," Tony said. "We can do this easy, or you can make me hurt you."

"My children will be home soon, and there's a security guy outside," she said in a trembling voice. "If you leave now, I won't say anything."

"Shut up!" He put the gun in his waistband, and wrapped a piece of cloth around her face and across her mouth, then tied it in back. "Now, we're gonna walk out the side door and take a little ride. No trouble and you don't get hurt." He pulled her off the piano bench, but she sat back down.

"I'll give you money—take what you want," she said through the gag.

Tony pulled out his gun and struck her over the head with the barrel. A cut opened over her right eye, and blood streamed down her face and began soaking the gag. Then she passed out.

"You took the hard way," Tony said, as he began to drag her toward the kitchen door. "Hey, Pepe, we're coming!" He spotted two plates piled high with gingersnaps on the kitchen counter and reached for one. Out of the corner of his eye, he saw a movement at the door. He looked up in surprise.

"Mo-Jo, what are you doing here?"

Maddie woke up in a tight, dark space. Suddenly, she bounced from one side of the small space to the other, and she knew she was in the trunk of a car.

I'm going to suffocate. I can't breathe. She felt like vomiting as the car turned another corner and she was thrown once again from one side of the cold, musty-smelling trunk to the other. She reached up to her head, which was throbbing, and felt the blood caked there. *Dear Lord, I'm scared. Give me courage.*

Who is driving the car? She tried to remember what had happened. *I was playing the piano. . . .* Then she could see his ugly face in the mirror. He had hit her with something. . . .

The car bounced over some kind of bump and came to a stop. *It's too quiet outside. What's he doing? Is he going to rape me? Oh,*

God, save me.

She heard the car door open, then slam shut. Maddie jumped when someone pounded on the trunk. "Be cool in there," a man's voice ordered. "My plan is workin' out just fine. I didn't expect you to be part of this, but you is what I call a bargainin' chip. I'll be back—got to make two phone calls."

It was 4:30, and Fred Taylor was briefing his producers, writers, and news anchors. The gang summit would dominate both newscasts, and he wanted everyone to be prepared—for anything. A sense of urgency and excitement could be felt everywhere in the station that afternoon. The format was set, community leaders were about to arrive, and police security was in place. Engineers, carpenters, and graphic artists had spent the past twenty-four hours turning studio five into a spectacular, futuristic tie-in with the summit's theme, "Doing the Right Thing." Of course, Fred had no idea if the two gangs would show up.

"This could go down the tubes if these thugs stiff us," said Fred. "What's the latest word from your police contact, Tim?"

"The cops say each gang will have ten guys here at least an hour before we go on the air, but so far, no sign of them. I have no idea who they'll be, or what they'll say—it's strictly a shot in the dark." The room went silent. "Sorry, bad choice of words."

"Mayor Bodine will be here," said Fred, and several people groaned.

"I smell Ian Thornberry," someone said.

"I know, I know," Fred said. "It's good politics for her, but I think it adds a dimension for us."

"And some votes for her, too," said someone else.

Paul Thomas leaned back in his chair. "Okay, the summit is in two parts—tonight at six and eleven we set the stage, get some ideas from gang members, and have business people tell what they're prepared to do."

"We'll be lucky to get that much," said Fred.

"Then tomorrow, maybe—just maybe—we can reach some kind of an agreement," said Paul.

"That would be a miracle," Fred said, knowing he sounded a little hopeless.

"Well, let's be ready for the best-case scenario," said Paul.

"What's the worst-case scenario?" someone asked.

"Oh, these animals could smuggle in guns," Fred said, "and have a war with each other on live television. I can see it now—'Gunfight at the Channel Three Corral'."

"Isn't that why the police will be here?" Paul asked.

"Something tells me they won't do much good."

Jorge Escobedo paced the floor in the living room of his Bel Air home. *Where are Romero and Velasquez?* "Trouble, man—we got trouble, I know it," Jorge told his top gang lieutenants and bodyguards. "They shoulda been back by now." He looked out the window to the iron gate and the end of the driveway. "If Tony and Pepe don't make it, I'm not goin' to that thing tonight—I got a bad feeling."

Jorge had decided he would go to the summit, along with Romero, Velasquez, and seven of his gang's zone leaders. Four of them, including Jorge, would wear masks—but now he was about to change his mind.

"Nothin' happens tonight, anyway," he said. Those in the room waited, ready to carry out his orders without question. "You guys find out what the security is, and how to get guns in tomorrow night." He walked to the window and looked out at the street. "Where are those guys?"

Mo-Jo recognized Dice Head's voice when he answered the phone. "Let me talk with Main Man."

"Who's this?"

"This is Mo-Jo. I said, let me talk to Main Man."

"Don't you know you was never to call again?" He snorted out a laugh. "You seem to forget your name is Doe-Doe."

"Shut up, Dice Head. Tell Main Man I got a way for him to get Escobedo and China White."

"How can you do that if we can't?"

"'Cause you're stupid, that's why. Now put Main Man on the phone—or he's gonna find out you were the one that kept him from killing Escobedo."

Dice Head yelled at someone to get Main Man, and a moment later he was on the phone. "Yeah, what's all this stuff about Escobedo and China White?"

"Some heavy stuff goin' down, man. I did what I told you I'd do."

"What are you talking about?"

"I gotta make this quick," Mo-Jo said. "Tony is dead. I killed him, and Escobedo is next—'cause I got something he wants."

"What's that?"

Mo-Jo giggled. "This is gonna blow your mind, Main Man."

"I got no time to play games with a loser like you."

"Sorry, man. You won't believe this, but I got that Paul Thomas guy's wife—I kidnapped her."

"You what?"

"Kidnapped her."

"Where is she?"

This is great. Mo-Jo, you the man. "She in my trunk!"

"Your trunk? You're crazy! Why'd you do that?"

"Escobedo wants to kill her and her husband. It's great, man. Don't you see? I use the woman—get close to Escobedo, and then kill him."

"I don't trust you—you and that diary of yours. Why are you doing this? What's in it for you?"

He's buying it. "I want back in the gang, Main Man. I know I messed up with that Jackson killing, but you shouldn't have kicked me out the way you did." Mo-Jo was making the sales pitch of his life. "Let me prove myself again. Give me another chance." *Can't you feel my pain? Ha, Ha, Ha.*

"If you got Romero, that's good, but Escobedo's the one I want. You do that—then we'll talk about a place for you." Main Man paused. "We're leaving now for that TV thing."

Mo-Jo high-fived himself. *He fell for it.* "Don't worry 'bout a thing, Main Man. I'll get Jorge for you, and it won't be long."

Jorge Escobedo turned from the window. "Okay, you guys get going. I don't know what happened to Tony and Pepe."

As his gang members began to leave, the phone rang. "Hold on, this has to be them." Jorge picked it up, sure it was Romero. "Where you been, Tony?" he barked.

"It's me, Jorge—Mo-Jo. Tony and Pepe are dead."

"Dead?" Jorge slumped in a chair. Those in the room stopped where they were and listened. "Where—what happened—how?"

"One of Main Man's guys killed them. I was over at Thomas's house—keepin' an eye on things, 'cause I knew your plans. I knew you'd be mad at me 'cause I lost my book, but I wanted to make things up to you by protecting Tony."

"How did they get killed?"

"I couldn't save 'em. Tony got shot. Pepe was smashed in the head. I saw it all."

"Mo-Jo, you're in this, I know—"

"No man, you're wrong. But listen, Jorge, I did okay for you. I got the woman—"

"Who?" Jorge was confused, angry, upset.

"That TV guy's wife—I got her."

"Where is she?"

"In my car trunk. Hey, man, I'm sorry 'bout Tony, but—"

"You said Main Man's guys were there, too?"

"Yeah, they just, well, they just showed up."

Jorge didn't trust him, not for a minute. "How'd you get the woman away from them?"

"Ah, I shot him, I mean, them, after they took the woman. Then I put her in my trunk."

"Who shot Tony?" Jorge asked.

"Ah, some new guy. I never seen him before. Listen, I got a plan for you to get Main Man and that Paul Thomas. You gotta believe me, I'm on my way back. Later."

The dial tone buzzed in Jorge's ear. A hundred thoughts flooded his mind. *Tony's dead. I can't believe it. Mo-Jo's behind this—I'll kill him.* Jorge knew he had to act fast. He looked at those who were about to leave for Channel Three.

"Who did it?" asked one.

"Mo-Jo says Main Man did it. I don't believe him. Go on without me. Don't say much, just check the place out." He paused, trying to clear his mind of Tony's death. "When you're done, stick around until the late news. See how we can get guns inside tomorrow night, because I'm gonna show up. I think Main Man will be there, too." *I'll get him and Thomas at the same time.*

"That's good, Jorge—but let us do it for you," said Felipe Manuel, a loyal lieutenant. "How do you know the cops won't bust you? It's too risky."

"You think I'm scared?" Jorge roared. His manhood had been challenged, but his anger was mostly because of his best friend's apparent death.

"You've got more guts than any of us in this room, Jorge," Manuel said, "but all you can think about is revenge and doin' this yourself."

Jorge walked over to Manuel. No one in the gang had ever dared talk this boldly to him—no one except Tony Romero. Jorge was just inches from his face. "No one but Tony talks to me like that."

Beads of sweat formed on Manuel's forehead. He was

breathing hard, but his jaw was rigid. He wasn't backing down. "Tony's dead, Jorge—you gotta hear the truth."

Jorge trusted Felipe almost as much as he did Tony Romero. "Felipe, you just showed me something. Here's where you and I stand. If Tony is dead, like Mo-Jo says, you're now second in command. You're my second Ruler."

Manuel looked stunned. "I—I—oh, man. Jorge, I know Tony was like a brother to you."

Jorge felt tears welling in his eyes. "Go on, get out of here."

"I won't let you down," said Manuel. "I promise."

"One more thing. Mo-Jo says he kidnapped the TV guy's wife—says he has her in his trunk."

"You think so?"

"He's crazy enough to do anything."

"What do we say if they ask us about that?" said Manuel.

"Tell 'em you don't know nothin.'"

"Anything else?" asked Manuel.

"Yeah. I'm goin' with you guys tomorrow night."

Homicide Lieutenant Ted Banks had locked his desk and was about to go home when his phone rang. "Homicide. Banks here." He listened and then, when he saw a sergeant in his office heading out the door, he cupped his hand over the phone. "Alice, wait." He turned back to the phone, "When?" Ted motioned for the woman not to leave. "Okay, we're on the way."

"What now?" she asked in a tone that told Ted she knew the answer.

"Call your husband. You won't be seeing him tonight. We've got a triple murder at Paul Thomas's house—let's get to my car."

Ted told his sergeant that two 911 calls had come in a minute apart—the first at 5:42 from a terrified teenager in her house, the second from a passerby. The person outside had seen the body of a security guard behind the steering wheel of his car, and had run to the nearest house to make the call. The police dispatcher had then sent four units to Paul Thomas's West LA home and notified the watch commander.

When Ted and Sergeant Alice Freeman arrived, yellow police tape was being unraveled and stretched around the security guard's car, and his body was covered with a yellow plastic sheet. Officers were coming out of Thomas's house. The first police units, Ted was told, got to the scene at 5:48. Elizabeth Thomas had met the two patrol cars.

"She and her brother are over there, in the backseat," said the officer in charge, who pointed to his patrol car. "His name is Travis. He got here just after our first people arrived."

"Who's inside?" Ted asked.

"No one. We checked to see if the kids' mother was home, but the place is empty, except for two bodies—one in the kitchen, the other outside by the door."

"Any crime lab people here yet?" asked Sergeant Freeman.

"They're on the way. You get the first look."

Ted and Alice walked to the side of the house. They stepped over a body near the open door.

"No problem with footprints," said the sergeant, pointing to the cement walkway. "Whoever did this ran right through the blood."

The open door led to the kitchen, and they entered the house.

"Look at that, Alice. Having a sweet tooth can be hazardous to your health." A body lay at their feet, on top of a platter of cookies.

The car was moving again. It made a sharp turn and scraped its bottom when it bounced over something, then screeched to a stop. Maddie was thrown violently against a panel of the trunk and struck her head on something sharp, reopening the cut on her forehead. She didn't want to think about what was coming. *Dear Lord, please help me.*

When the trunk opened, she expected to be blinded by the sun, but there was no need to shield her eyes—the sun was setting.

"Get out!"

She stared in confusion at a different face than she'd seen in the mirror. She started to climb out, but apparently not fast enough. The man grabbed her arm and began to pull her from the trunk. She struck her head on the trunk lid, lost her balance, and tumbled in a painful heap to the driveway. "Why are you doing this?" she said through the gag, then began to cry.

The man pushed her to the front of the house, and she looked up, catching just a glimpse of a smiling face through the living room window. She'd seen that face somewhere before.

Maddie's kidnapper shoved her hard toward an open front door where two ugly and mean-looking men stood waiting. They reached out, took her by the arms, and jerked her inside.

"My arm!" she cried out, as she fell onto the tiled entryway. She found herself staring at a pair of black shoes.

Her kidnapper walked in and smiled at the man in the black shoes. "There she is, Jorge—*Señora Capitan,*" he said.

Maddie gasped when she looked into the man's face. *Jorge Escobedo. It's him.* She'd never seen anyone with so much hate and evil in his eyes. He was much scarier in person than in his photo on TV.

Escobedo took something out of his pocket, and leaning down, held it to her face. She heard a loud snapping sound as the shiny steel of a switchblade flashed in front of her eyes. *Oh, God, help me—he's going to kill me.*

She felt the knife next to her cheek, then winced as the blade broke the skin. With one quick motion, Escobedo pulled the knife upward and cut the gag from her mouth. Maddie wiped her mouth, trying to clear the dirt and caked blood from her lips.

"You live for now," he said in a cold, flat voice. "Later

you'll suffer, and then you will die." His leering grin was inches from her face—the same leer she'd seen on television after he'd murdered Grant Peters. *I'll never see my family again.*

CHAPTER TWENTY-EIGHT

"This is *Channel Three News* at 6 P.M., with Paul Thomas and Nancy Chen, Andrew LaPointe with weather, and Eric Brock on sports. . . ."

Fred Taylor stood off to the side in studio five, watching the newscast's production open. He shook his head. If millions of people are expecting a gang summit, boy, are they in for a surprise. What a fiasco this is going to be.

". . . *News Three*, we report directly to you."

The camera showed Thomas and Chen on a two-shot. "Good evening," Thomas said. "Tonight our lead story is unlike any we've reported in the past. It's a story we hope will happen."

Marcia Willis stood next to Fred. She was there to cover the gang summit for the *Examiner*. "Pray, Marcia," Fred whispered, "pray like you've never prayed in your life."

"Tonight," said Chen, "you'll hopefully see the beginning of a new chapter in our city's history. In our studios will be . . ."

Fred looked at the community leaders seated on the platform. He held a walkie-talkie in one hand so he could make contact with his assistant, who was in the lobby waiting for the gangs to show up. The knots in his stomach grew tighter. *This is going to be embarrassing*.

Uniformed police officers stood rigid in each corner of the studio, and in the director's booth was Assistant Police Chief Rex Ford, who was connected by radio to his officers and Channel Three's security director, Phil Nelson. Despite maximum precautions, and Tim Hires's insistence that they could pull it off, Fred saw nothing but disaster ahead. This could be the biggest fiasco in TV news history. He could just see it now at the next Radio and Television News Directors' Association convention: Special RTNDA award to Fred Taylor, the man who enticed millions to watch his station and showed them nothing.

A robotic camera, at the far end of the studio, took a shot of the community leaders. They looked antsy.

Another robotic camera, to one side of the studio, was for close-ups and cut-away reaction shots from community leaders. A third camera was suspended overhead, and the fourth camera was in the other studio for the news set. An operator seated to the left of the director controlled the robotic cameras with a joystick. Chief Ford stood behind her, watching the monitors on the wall.

Paul walked behind the community leaders now. "These men and women want a better Los Angeles and have come here tonight with one goal in mind. They want to meet the leaders of two street gangs."

I'd settle for one gang member, Fred thought.

"Frankly, the odds are against us," Paul went on. "The gangs we've invited have tried to destroy what the people of Los Angeles have achieved during Light the Night." Paul glanced in Fred's direction with a look that asked, *Are they here yet?*

Fred shook his head, spread his arms, and shrugged. "Taylor to Tim," Fred said into his walkie-talkie. "Any sign of them yet?"

"Nothing, Fred," came a scratchy reply.

Paul explained how they'd planned the summit, leaving out the fact that, so far, there was no sign of the gangs. "The business, political, social, and educational leaders who are here have real solutions for those who are willing to—" He paused and pointed to the sign above the set. "—do the right thing." He was now shown on a close-up. "That's what we expect to take place." He looked Fred's way again, but Fred just shook his head. "And we're hopeful it will happen. But now, we want to bring you up to date on the latest news. Here's Nancy with that."

As soon as Paul was off-camera, Fred approached him. "Paul, we'll give this thing five minutes. That's what we have for the news summary."

"Then what?" asked Paul.

"We go to plan B. You come on and explain, as only you can do—nice and comforting—that this was a chance we took, and the gangs never showed up."

"You don't want to wait a little longer?"

"No, we've got some other news we can fill in with, and if they show up later, we'll break in. But let's pull the plug on this now—put the onus on the gangs, thank the community leaders, tell our friends at home how sorry we are, and leave the invitation to the gangs—"

"Fred, this is Tim," came a voice over Fred's walkie-talkie.

"Go ahead, Tim."

"One of the gangs just showed up!"

"Just one?"

"Yeah, it's Iron Claw. Ten of 'em—five in masks."

"Get them through security as fast as you can—then hustle them in."

"Okay. Hey, Fred, brace yourself—they came in two limos."

Maddie was thirsty, in pain, and terribly afraid. Escobedo's men had locked her in a large, empty closet in an upstairs bedroom of the estate-sized home. It was a huge house—when they'd pushed her up the stairs, she'd glimpsed a library and a black concert grand piano in an enormous family room. *Some family.*

For a while she'd heard voices, but now the only sound came from a television in a room directly below the closet. When she put her ear against the floor, she could hear it more clearly. Escobedo and his men were talking, but then someone turned the TV volume up, and to her amazement, the clear, comforting sound of her husband's voice suddenly filled her ears. Tears came to her eyes. "Thank you, Jesus, for letting me hear Paul's voice."

"Earlier, we introduced you briefly to members of the Iron Claw who came tonight," she heard Paul say. "It looked as if the other gang, the Insane Rulers, wouldn't make it, but as you can see, they're coming into our studio. . . ."

"Hey, Jorge, there's Felipe!" Maddie heard someone downstairs yell. "He look like a cool Rule!"

She heard laughter, then, "Shut up! I want to hear this."

"As you can see," Paul continued, "four of the ten men from Insane Rulers are wearing masks. Five Iron Claws have chosen to do the same and conceal their identities. This is part of the ground rules established with the LAPD and Channel Three."

Did Paul even know she'd been kidnapped? *He's on the air. Does that mean Elizabeth and Travis were taken, too? Elizabeth would have been the first one home.*

Once again, she heard Paul's voice. He couldn't know; his tone was too upbeat. "We've arranged the chairs in a triangle. We have community leaders on one side, and the two gangs on the other two sides. Police officers are standing by throughout the studio, and I'll be in the middle moderating our discussion. It's half past six. We need to take one final break, then we'll begin the summit."

As a commercial for Right Guard deodorant began, a key turned in the closet door. The door opened, and she shielded her eyes from the light. The man who stared down at her had a pockmarked face, pencil-thin eyebrows, and a thick moustache. *He's uglier than the goons at the front door.* "I'm—I'm thirsty," she said. "And I need to use the bathroom."

The dull expression on the man's face never changed. "Get up."

She winced as she put weight on her cramped feet. "Where are you taking me?"

He pointed down the hall. "Go that way."

She walked out of the closet and found the bathroom a few doors down on the right. On the vanity was something to eat—a sandwich, two cans of soda (a Pepsi and a 7-Up), and an assortment of fruit. Some clothing was folded up next to one of the double sinks.

"Jorge says you've got thirty minutes. Shower, put on some clean clothes, but don't try to get away." He pointed to the bathroom window. "It's two stories down and we have guards outside." He closed the door.

Maddie looked at herself in the mirror. *Not as bad as I expected.* Her face was bruised and dirty, her hair was caked with blood, and the knife cut on her cheek was more than a nick. *At least I can recognize myself.*

She opened a can of Pepsi and took a bite of a surprisingly delicious chicken sandwich. She turned the water on in the shower and took off her clothes. The steam was soothing, and the warm water felt wonderful. With her back against the tiled wall, she slid down the side of the shower and sat on the bottom. The water beat on her head, and she watched the caked blood go down the drain. *Oh, God, what's going to happen? I need a miracle.*

"Mr. Thomas?"

"Yes?"

"This is Lieutenant Banks, LAPD Homicide. We need you to come home right away."

Fred had pulled Paul off the news five minutes early and told him the police wanted to talk with him on the phone. He had picked it up in Fred's office.

"Homicide? What's going on?" he asked.

"I'm at your home. There's been a shooting here."

"A shooting?" Paul said in disbelief. "What do you mean a shooting? Is my wife all right? What about my children?"

"Your children are fine. Do you know where your wife is?"

"Ah, no—she should be at home. What's happened?"

"Mr. Thomas, we can't locate your wife, but I'd rather talk with you in person—"

"You said there was a shooting—who got shot?"

"We've got three male victims—two in your house and one outside."

"Who are they? Is one Vinnie? And who did it?"

"We're still trying to learn what happened. Can you leave now?"

"I'm on my way." Paul hung up the phone and looked at Fred.

"I only heard half the conversation," said Fred. "Fill me in."

"Three guys were shot at my house. I can't believe it." He ran out the door. "I'll call you from home."

During the thirty minutes it took to drive home, Paul played out every possible scenario in his mind. He had flashbacks of the afternoon Maddie was attacked. What would he see when he got close to his home? A block before his house, he saw a police barricade. He drove his car up to an officer who was directing traffic and rolled down his window. The officer seemed irritated and directed him to make a detour. When Paul didn't, the officer approached his car.

"You'll have to turn around, sir, there's been a—oh, I'm sorry, Mr. Thomas. I didn't recognize you at first. Let me move this barricade and you can go ahead."

Paul waited for him to clear a path, and he waved his thanks as he drove on. They always gave him a chill—a police car's flashing red and blue lights. As did the marked vehicles and live minicam trucks of news crews at the scene of a crime. Only this was his home.

An officer asked him to park in the street and he saw why—a coroner's van was backed into the driveway. At that moment, two men wheeled a sheet-covered body out of the house.

"Daddy!" Elizabeth and Travis ran out the front door to

meet him. He wrapped them in his arms, and Elizabeth began crying.

"Where's Mom?" Travis asked.

"I don't know, Trav. I don't know."

The six o'clock news was over, and Wilson Ruggles was doing what he enjoyed most—acting like a big shot, schmoozing among top business, educational, and political leaders.

"Brenda, thanks for coming," Wilson gushed at the mayor. "We want you to know Channel Three is here to serve the people."

"Thank you for putting this together. It was—"

Before she could finish her answer, Wilson turned to council member McMillan. "Francie, excellent comments—great to have you here. You're a credit to the city and the minority community."

"Well, it's much more than one segment of—"

She, too, was cut off in mid-sentence. Wilson had spotted Preston Cesario, the head man at Regal Brothers. He'd never met him before, but slapped him on the back now. "Press, a terrific start to the summit with your million-dollar job training idea." Cesario opened his mouth, but Wilson moved on. He felt a tap on his shoulder and turned to see a tall, Hispanic young man—one of the gang members. *Which side is he on? Who cares?*

"Mr. Ruggles?"

"Yes?"

The gangs were there to boost the station's ratings. Wilson never thought he'd actually have to talk with any of them. Is he with Iron Claw or—what's the name of that other gang? "Are you—ah, with the Insane gang?"

The young man squinted and cocked his head to the right. Then his eyes seemed to soften with sincerity. "Insane Rulers," he said. "Sir, my name is Felipe Manuel." He pointed to a table of food prepared for the guests remaining at the station between the early and late newscasts. Members of both gangs had now gathered around the table and were helping themselves. "Thanks for having all that great food for us. It's not often people treat us with respect."

"Well, we're all brothers under the sun, right? What did you say your name was?"

"Felipe—Felipe Manuel, sir."

"Flip, just let us know if there's anything we can do for you."

"Yes, you can. I'm real impressed with your TV station. I've never been inside one before—or met someone as important as you."

Wilson looked around to see if anyone had heard Manuel. He beamed and tried to sound humble. "That's very nice to hear, Flip. This is a country with opportunities for people of all races, creeds, and colors." His voice rose. "I've dedicated myself to public service and am always interested in helping young people like yourself."

"I was wondering—this is really asking a lot, and if you can't, I'll—"

"Now, now, I'm never too big to help young members of our minority community. What can I do for you?"

"Do you think someone could give me a guided tour of your station and the news department? I know you're busy, but do you think you—"

"Why certainly!" Wilson was ecstatic. He was eager to get away from this gang member, so he would be free to talk with more important people. "I know just the person who can help you." He spotted the person he wanted across the room. "Harvey! Harvey Rose. Get over here!"

"Do the police have any idea where Maddie is?" Marcia asked.

"I don't think so." Fred closed his eyes and rubbed his hand over his face. "I feel responsible—"

She'd known something was wrong the minute she saw Paul and Fred walk out of studio five a few minutes before. But by the time she'd squeezed past the police officers, private security guards, and others in the crowded studio, the two men had disappeared into Fred's office and shut the door. She'd waited outside until Paul came out, but when she tried to talk to him, he rushed past her without a word. Now she was in Fred's office and knew as much about the shooting as he did.

"It's not your fault."

"It might not have happened if the bodyguard were still there."

"Who took him away?"

"Ruggles. He would only let us keep the guard outside." Fred got up from the sofa and turned off the television with the remote control. "I should have kept Paul's house guarded until after this stupid summit was over."

"What are you going to do now?" she asked. "Off the record, if you want."

Fred smiled. "Marcia, I want to put something on the record between you and me."

"What's that?"

"I love you." He walked back to the sofa and sat down next to her. "I know I told you that once before. Any chance of an answer now?"

Marcia touched her finger to his lips. "You're a sweet man, and I do care about you. Those are beautiful words, but something needs to happen before we can go any further."

"Jesus, and all that other stuff?"

"That's one way of saying it." She laughed.

"Couldn't we just move to the next step and take care of the religion later?"

"What did I tell you about religion, Fred? It's a—"

"I know, it's a relationship, not a religion," he said. "What about our relationship? Does it just stop?"

"No, but it can't get better until you become a Christian. If you don't, I'm not the one for you."

"Tell me about Tony," said a stone-faced Jorge Escobedo. "None of this makes sense."

He and Mo-Jo were seated across from each other in Jorge's living room. The newscast had ended, and the television set was off.

Mo-Jo knew this would be a tough sell. If he wanted to pull it off, if he wanted the sting to work, he had to sound confident. "It happened, man, just like I told you."

"How could one person kill both Tony and Pepe?"

"I didn't see the shooting," said Mo-Jo. "I was hidin' behind a bush. All I saw was the guy hit Pepe over the head—"

"What did he look like?"

"I never saw him before. He went into the kitchen. He musta shot Tony right away, 'cause I heard the gun."

"How do you know it was the kitchen?"

Mo-Jo's heart skipped a beat. "Ah, I just thought the side door would be to the kitchen. I don't know, maybe it wasn't."

"Yeah, maybe it wasn't," said Escobedo, as he paced the floor. "What you haven't told me is, why would another gang decide to kidnap the same woman we wanted?"

"To mess up the summit?"

"But on the same day we planned to do it?" Escobedo roared.

"Jorge, I don't know. What you askin' me all this stuff for?"

Escobedo crossed the room and pointed his finger in Mo-Jo's face. "'Cause Tony was like a brother to me, man—and I don't trust you for nothin.' What are the odds of Main Man and me wanting to kidnap a woman on the same day—and the same hour?"

Mo-Jo's mouth felt dry—he tried to gulp something that wasn't there. "I got no answer for that, Jorge—only that without me and the woman, you don't get Thomas." Escobedo didn't say anything. "Look, I'm sorry about Tony." Mo-Jo looked into Escobedo's eyes, hoping to break through, hoping a lust for revenge would replace reason.

Escobedo got up from his chair, walked to the window, and looked into the night. "Yeah, me too," he whispered.

Hit with the plan, now. "Listen, Jorge, I was gonna tell you, but I got back into Main Man's gang," Mo-Jo said in a rush.

Escobedo turned from the window. "You double-crossed me."

"No, no—I did it for you." Mo-Jo was near panic. *Make up the biggest lie you can come up with, man, or you dead.* "Listen, Main Man had his guys watchin' Paul Thomas's house, just like you were. They told me, so I knew they'd do somethin' when Tony and Pepe showed up." Escobedo showed no sign he was buying this, but Mo-Jo went on. "They gonna pay for how they treated me. I keep tellin' you, I got a plan. It won't bring Tony back, but it'll work."

"You keep talkin' about a plan, but I ain't heard nothin' I can believe."

"You can kill Paul Thomas and Main Man on the same night and do it on TV with everyone in LA watchin.' You'll be gone before anyone figures out who did it." Mo-Jo pulled a paper from his pocket and spread it out on the coffee table. "Listen to me for ten minutes." Mo-Jo took a deep breath, then laid his gun on the same table. "If you don't think my plan will work," he slid the gun toward Escobedo, "then put a bullet between my eyes."

"You that sure?" asked Escobedo.

"I'm puttin' my life on the line for it, man."

"Start talking."

Back in his office, Harvey Rose swept some papers off of his desk and put them in his briefcase. He considered where he wanted to eat dinner tonight; stuffed pizza sounded good. He was eager to get away from the station.

He'd just taken Felipe Manuel on the strangest tour he'd

ever given. Most people were interested in the studio where the newscast was broadcast, the control room, and the newsroom. But Manuel was interested in where the news vehicles were parked, how many entrances there were into the newsroom, how the lights in the studio worked, and whether or not the fence around the station was patrolled. Manuel explained that he was just taking precautions to protect himself and his gang. Twice, Manuel wandered away from Rose, returning both times and apologizing for not paying attention. He kept repeating how much he appreciated that such an important person like Rose would take time to show him the station.

The phone rang. *Let it ring. No, better answer it.* He picked up the receiver. "Hello, this is Harvey Rose."

"And this is Mo-Jo."

A chill shot through Harvey's body. *Mo-Jo? What does he want?* "You're getting nothing more from me, not after what you did to Bobby Silva."

"You mean after what *we* did, Harvey—you and me. So shut up and don't tell me what you ain't gonna do. I want to see you tonight, in an hour, at your condo. Manhattan Beach, right?"

"How do you know where I live?"

"I know plenty about you. Someone's gonna tail you, and if you don't go to your place, you a dead man—you understand?"

Harvey was paralyzed with panic. "Someone else is in on this."

"Wilson Ruggles, I hope," said Mo-Jo.

"No, Arlene Zahn."

"A woman?"

"Yes, she's the one who got Silva's name—she knows about you. She's been telling me what to do from the start."

"Well, it looks like you better have—what you say her name was?"

"Arlene Zahn."

"You make sure she's at your house, too."

"What if I can't find her, or if she's busy?"

"Let me put it this way—if the two of you don't show up, there's gonna be a double funeral at Channel Three—closed caskets."

"We'll be there."

"You got exactly one hour." It was 7:50.

As soon as Harvey heard the *click,* he punched Arlene Zahn's three-number extension and counted the rings. *Be there,* he pleaded, but there was no answer—only a voice mail greeting. At the signal he said, "Arlene, I'm gonna look for you in the studio, but I'm leaving this message. You must be at my condo in one hour. This is life or death—I'm serious. That guy Mo-Jo called. He wants to see me, and I told him about you." His voice cracked. "Please, be there—he says he'll kill us if we don't come."

Harvey slammed down the receiver and sprinted out of his office to studio five. He prayed and pleaded that Zahn hadn't left the station for home. As he rounded the corner leading to the studio, he ran headlong into Wilson Ruggles, knocking him into a young woman carrying a tray of hors d'oeuvres.

"Rose, you idiot."

"Boss, I'm sorry—I've got to find Arlene. Have you seen her?" Just then he spotted Zahn and ran in her direction, leaving Ruggles with quiche on his coat and bacon-wrapped weenies at his feet.

Zahn was talking with four clients whom Harvey Rose knew had recently canceled ads on the newscast. She told him she'd invited them to the summit, hoping to convince them to once again become sponsors.

"Arlene, we've got to go to my house now!" Harvey said, as he tugged on her arm.

The four men looked at each other and smirked.

"What are you talking about?" she demanded in an irritated tone.

He pulled her away from the group and tried to lower his

voice. "I'm really scared. Mo-Jo wants to see us, and we've got to be there in less than an hour."

She pulled him farther away from the group of men. "How does he know about me?"

"I had to tell him, Arlene. I can't carry this thing alone anymore." His voice became louder. "It's all because of Silva—"

She looked over her shoulder. "Shut up, you fool," she hissed. "Why does he want to see us?"

"I don't know, but he said he would kill us if we don't do it—says there's someone outside who's gonna follow me home. Arlene, we've got to leave now, or we'll never make it in time."

"Okay, settle down. I'll meet you at your condo." She put her hands on his shoulders. "Harvey, don't worry, this is going to work out—you let me take care of Mo-Jo. Now go on, get out of here."

He turned and ran out of the building to his car.

Harvey Rose gunned the accelerator of his car as he approached his condo. He was seven minutes late. He looked up and down the street to see if a car was parked anywhere, but didn't see one. He turned into his driveway, pushed the button on his remote door opener, then drove inside the garage. Just then, Arlene Zahn's car pulled up along the curb. Harvey got out of his car and walked to the street to meet her.

"Is he here, yet?" she asked.

"I just got home. I don't think so."

"Well, I raced like some crazy woman to get here. You sure it was Mo-Jo on the phone?"

"Positive. Let's go inside."

They walked through the garage, and Rose pushed a button on the wall to close the garage door. Then he opened the laundry room door. The house was dark, and as they walked into the family room, Harvey turned on a light.

Harvey sighed. "Looks like Mo-Jo is a no-show."

"Nope," said a voice nearby.

Harvey whirled in the direction of the voice. *The guy's nearly a midget.* "How did you get in?"

In response, Mo-Jo pulled a gun out of his pocket. He walked toward Harvey and jammed the barrel of the gun in his chest, causing him to gasp for breath. "Never mind—I'm here and you late. Mo-Jo don't like that." He eyed Zahn. "You Arlene?"

"The one and only," she said matter-of-factly. "What's all this about?"

Harvey was amazed at Arlene's nonchalance.

"I need some information." Mo-Jo walked into the kitchen, opened the refrigerator, and took out a can of beer.

"What kind of information?" asked Zahn.

Mo-Jo opened the beer and took two long gulps. "I already got Harvey's phone number. I need four more numbers, a gate pass into the parkin' lot, and a key to the station."

Harvey's stomach knotted once more.

"What do you need all that for?" asked Zahn.

"I ain't through. I'm gonna need some help gettin' a box full of heat into the TV studio tomorrow."

He wants to bring guns into the studio.

Mo-Jo handed Arlene a piece of paper. "Here are the names—you write down the phone numbers for me. I figure Harvey can give me his gate pass and a key to the building." Mo-Jo looked at Harvey and winked. Harvey felt sick to his stomach.

Harvey glanced at Zahn, then at Mo-Jo. "I'm afraid to ask what you mean by 'heat,' and what you plan to do to the studio."

"Guns, Harvey—AK-47 semiautomatics, Uzis, and handguns. I promised I'd get people watchin' your news again, didn't I, and tomorrow they gonna see us blow away ten Iron Claws live on the six o'clock news."

"No way. I'm out." This was something out of a bad movie. "A lot of other people could get killed—including me."

"I don't care what you think, Harvey," Mo-Jo said. "I own you now—remember, Bobby Silva's murder began with you." Harvey felt light-headed and slumped into a chair at the kitchen table.

"How can you get guns into the station?" asked Zahn.

"Arlene, are you going along with this?" Harvey asked in disbelief.

"What other choice do we have, Harvey? We're probably dead meat either way, but there's a chance Mo-Jo here can pull this off—and if he does, we're liable to do a 60 rating."

"Well, count me out."

"Wrong, my partner in murder." Zahn leaned over and put her face just inches from Harvey's. "Okay, Harvey, time to bring out the heavy artillery, time to use the 'A' material. You, me, and our new friend Mo-Jo, all have the blood of Bobby Silva on our hands. You don't have a choice." She looked at Mo-Jo. "Mo-Jo, my pal Harvey here will give you all the help you need."

"That's cool," he said. "I gotta leave now and make some phone calls, but before I do, here's the plan."

When Mo-Jo finally left fifteen minutes later, Zahn was excited about what might happen, and Harvey was morose about what he felt was certain disaster for all of them.

"Let's go over this again," said Arlene.

Harvey was convinced his life would soon be over. Through bloodshot eyes, he watched Zahn pour herself another drink. It was 10:45 and she had just asked him for the tenth time—or was it the twentieth—what she wanted him to do tomorrow.

"I know, I know," he said. "I call in sick in the morning—which I will be anyway—and wait for that maniac to bring his guns over here. I put them in two boxes marked 'Channel Three Promotions,' take them to the station, and lock everything up in my office." He staggered to the kitchen for another drink.

"Don't pass out on me now, Harvey. We need each other to get out of this mess."

Harvey grabbed a bag of corn chips and poured himself a fresh drink. "If Mo-Jo has my gate pass," he said as he came back into the room, "how do I get into the parking lot with the guns?"

"I'll meet you out front with a new pass and a building key. Come on, Harvey, show a little confidence in old Arlene." She picked up the remote control and turned on Channel Three.

Paul stood in the kitchen with Lieutenant Banks, Sergeant Freeman, and a police technician, waiting to record any call that came to the house. It was 10:50. Six hours had passed since the kidnapping, and police had put in phone taps at Channel Three, as well as at Paul's house. Elizabeth and Travis were across town with his parents.

A Channel Three crew was set up in the living room, ready to broadcast live from the scene. A reporter had been at the house earlier to put together a report for the eleven o'clock news. Paul had convinced Fred to let him do a live segment from his home; he wanted to make a personal appeal for his wife's safe release.

The phone rang.

"Let it ring three times," Banks said, and Paul and the technician exchanged glances.

Paul lifted the receiver on the third ring. "Hello?" He could hear traffic in the background.

"This is the guy who gonna get your wife back," a deep voice said.

Paul's heart pounded. "Who is this, and how do I know you have my wife?"

The caller described Maddie's clothing, but Paul wanted more details.

"Okay, try this—she had cookies in the kitchen."

"What kind?" asked Paul.

"Gingersnaps. I know, 'cause my grandmother used to make 'em."

"I believe you. Now, why did you kidnap her?"

The caller told him he was the go-between for a rogue gang that had kidnapped his wife in hopes of sabotaging the summit and grabbing some new turf in the city. Paul didn't believe a word, but went along with it. "So, why are you involved? What's in this for you?"

"I got contacts with the kidnappers and Iron Claw and Insane Rulers. They all interested in a business agreement with the city—and by givin' your wife back, it shows they serious about changin' for the better. I get a percentage of the deal."

"Yeah, right. When do I see my wife?"

"Sometime tomorrow." And the man hung up.

"He's lying through his teeth," Paul said. "Did you trace the call?"

"A pay phone in El Segundo," said the officer. "I don't think we can get a car there in time."

"Hey, Paul," a member of the TV crew called. "We're about five minutes away from air time."

"Good evening, I'm Nancy Chen. Because of extraordinary events this evening, Paul Thomas isn't here at the top of our newscast, but will be in a few moments."

"Hey, Harvey, come on, the news is on. No more booze, okay?" Arlene Zahn waved at Harvey in the kitchen. "Get yourself in here, now!"

"Yeah, yeah, I can hear it." Harvey staggered into the family room and dropped onto a sofa. Half of his drink sloshed on his pants, and he cursed.

"Our lead story was to have been the gang summit this evening, but we have a breaking story that's personal and difficult to report. There has been a shocking triple murder at the home of Paul Thomas. Channel Three reporter Kirk Addison has been following that story and also what appears to be a kidnapping close to us all.

Kirk, what's the latest?"

Addison looked from Chen to another camera. "Nancy, we can now report that Maddie Thomas, the wife of Channel Three news anchor Paul Thomas, was kidnapped late this afternoon from her home. Paul will be joining us live at his home shortly, but let's bring our viewers up to date on what happened earlier." A taped report began with video of the bodies of Tony Romero and Pepe Velasquez as they were wheeled out of the Thomas home. "Police believe the two dead men were surprised by a gunman and were murdered while trying to kidnap Maddie Thomas."

"You know we caused all of this," Harvey slurred. "None of this would have happened if we hadn't given Silva's name to Mo-Jo—Mo-Jo!" he repeated with drunken contempt.

The video now showed the security guard's car. The driver's door was open, and his left hand dangled out from under the sheet. "How long before they put us in body bags, Arlene?"

"Harvey, you're drunk."

Harvey shivered. "Just so we don't end up together." He laughed. "Now, that's a horrible thought—Zahn and Rose in the same body bag."

"Shut up!"

"It may be the last night to imbibe." He struggled to his feet. "I shall pour myself another liquid libation."

He felt himself being pulled back down. "You've had enough."

The report was over. "Thanks, Kirk. We're now going to switch live to the home of my co-anchor and friend. Paul, we're all shocked at this—any word on Maddie?"

Thomas was seated on a sofa. "Nancy, I talked with a person who claims to have contact with Maddie—"

Harvey turned to Arlene. "Did Mo-Jo call Paul already?"

"Sounds like it."

"She may be released tomorrow," Paul was saying.

"That's great, but who did this, Paul—and why?"

"That's confidential—we hope to say something tomorrow."

His co-anchor seemed to search for words. "Paul—you seem so—well, you look so calm. Are you?"

He smiled. "Nancy, I'm hurting, and I'm praying that Maddie's all right, but as a Christian, I know that God's in control. He just wants me to trust him a little extra tonight."

"Would you, ah, like to make any kind of appeal?"

"Yes. I don't quite know how to say this." Thomas took a deep breath. "To the kidnappers of my wife—please don't hurt her. I'll take her place if you want. I don't know why you've done this, but please—" He paused. "Don't harm her. If this can bring peace to LA, then start it tomorrow with her safe release. Now, to you, Maddie—my friend, my wife—I pray for you. You're in the Lord's hands. Elizabeth, Travis, and I love you dearly."

With that, Harvey Rose passed out on the sofa.

CHAPTER TWENTY-NINE

Friday, November 10

A distant sound brought Wilson Ruggles out of a deep sleep. It was his phone. *What time is it?* He reached up to turn on the lamp by his bed, but knocked the porcelain lamp to the floor, shattering it. He swore and looked at the digital clock—5:07 A.M.. "Hello," he growled into the receiver.

"Ruggles?"

He was instantly awake. "Speaking."

"This is Mo-Jo, the mystery man. Remember me?"

"Yes."

"I got your news guy's wife."

"Maddie Thomas?"

"Live and in person."

"Why are you calling me?"

"Here's what you gonna do for me today. You gonna bring the woman onto the news tonight. . . ."

Wilson listened. Mo-Jo made his skin crawl, but he liked the idea of being in the spotlight for everyone to see. "But this ties me to the kidnapping," he said when Mo-Jo finished with his instructions.

"No way," said Mo-Jo. "Who gonna even know that I told you 'bout this? Just be on the lookout for Harvey and the woman—then bring her up on the platform."

"Is Rose in on this?"

"Yeah, and one other person."

"Who?"

"Arlene Zahn, and she gonna need your help to bring some

guns into the station."

"Guns!" Wilson cried. His wife was now awake and listening. "You didn't say anything about guns."

"They won't be loaded. It's part of our plan for peace. Who knows, you may get—what do they call it—the No-something Peace Prize?"

"Nobel Peace Prize."

"Yeah, that's it."

Mo-Jo said that each gang member would place a gun at the feet of a community leader. "It'll be great on TV—I told you I'd get more people watchin' your news."

A knot had formed in Wilson's stomach. He felt trapped; he was getting too deep into something he wanted no part of. "I will not be part of any kidnapping, or bringing guns into the station."

Mo-Jo was silent for a moment. "You want me to go to the papers or the other TV stations with what I know?"

"What do you know?"

"How your station helped us find Bobby Silva."

Wilson wanted to hear no more. "Okay, I'll talk with Arlene when I get to work. Is that all?"

"Yeah, just do what I say. You won't forget tonight, believe me."

Paul Thomas, not fully awake, stretched his arm across the bed, expecting to feel the warmth of his wife. Instead, he touched the bedspread, flat and cold.

"God, why did You do this?" he yelled with all of the fury he felt inside.

He felt like a hypocrite for what he'd said on television the night before—"He just wants me to trust Him a little extra tonight." *Yeah, right, just like Mother Teresa.*

He threw back the covers, turned the light on, and sat on the edge of the bed. He looked down and realized that he hadn't even taken off his clothes. He rubbed his face with both hands, then looked up. *Oh, Maddie, I miss you. Lord, please take care of her.*

Paul tried to remember what had happened before he had leaned back in bed for what he thought would be a catnap. He'd stayed up until three or four in the morning; he wasn't sure what time officers finally told him to get some sleep. The police technician had spent the night on the sofa near the phone in case the kidnapper called again. But the only calls the rest of the night were from Maddie's parents and Elizabeth and Travis, who called just before they went to bed at their grandparents'.

Paul glanced at his Bible on the night stand, then got out of bed and walked to the bedroom door. He stopped and looked back at the nightstand. *No—forget about the Bible. I need to do something about Maddie.* He walked out the door, then turned back. *Lord, you know I'm not the person others think I am. Let's see what You can do with me.* He returned to the bed and sat down. He opened up his Bible and looked for verses of comfort. As he flipped the pages, he came to the words of David in Psalm 40:

Be pleased, O Lord to deliver me;
Make haste, O Lord, to help me.
Let those be ashamed and humiliated together
Who seek my life to destroy it;
Let those be turned back and dishonored
Who delight in my hurt.

Sorry, Lord, that just didn't cut it. Let's see what Your guys in the New Testament can do.

Paul turned to James, chapter one. "Consider it all joy, my brethren, when you encounter various trials, knowing that the testing of your faith produces endurance." *Joy? Was your wife ever kidnapped, James? Then go ahead and talk to me about faith. I want to read what Jesus said.* Paul turned back to the words of Jesus in Matthew 5. "Blessed are those who have been persecuted for the sake of righteousness, for theirs is the kingdom of heaven."

The phone rang then, and Paul jumped to his feet and ran to the door.

"We have the tracer ready," the police officer called out from downstairs. "Pick up the phone."

Paul ran back to the nightstand and lifted the receiver. "Hello."

"This Paul Thomas?" It was the same voice he'd heard yesterday.

"Yes, who are you?"

"You don't ask no questions—just do as you're told and you might see your wife alive again."

"When are you going to let her go?"

"You don't listen, do you? Now get this—I'm gonna say it only once. If you wanna see your wife, here's what the people who have her want you to do."

Paul looked anxiously at the police officer who now stood in the bedroom doorway making a circular motion with his hand, the signal to keep stalling. "Tell me about my wife—is she okay? Can I talk with her? Where is she?"

"Shut up. I know you tryin' to trace this call—and it's gonna be too late. The only way your wife stays alive is for you to be on the six o'clock news tonight—live in studio five. Got it?"

"Yeah, but what about my—" The caller hung up. They had not had enough time to trace his location. Paul looked at the officer. "How did he know about studio five?"

Arlene Zahn had been a gambler all of her life, and now everything was on the line. The odds were against her, and her biggest handicap was Harvey Rose.

She'd put Harvey to bed after midnight and set his alarm. She was unable to sleep herself, and had arrived at the station before sunrise. It was the only place she felt any meaning in life.

She looked at her list of things to do. Step by step, she went over the sequence of events. She shook her head—she saw more ways that the plan could fail than ways it could work. *You've gone this far, Arlene, it's too late to turn back.*

Beside the list lay a revolver. She picked up the loaded gun, felt the end of the barrel, and looked at the safety lock. She touched the trigger with her finger, switched the safety off, then put it back on and slipped the revolver in her desk drawer.

The laser printer in her office came to life, and Arlene glanced at the clock on the wall. It was that time again—last night's ratings results were coming her way. She picked up her phone to call Harvey; she had to make sure he got up on time.

"Hello?" he answered groggily.

"Harvey, wake up."

"Ohhhh, my head—that you, Arlene?"

"Yeah, get yourself out of bed and get cleaned up. Your visitor should be there soon."

Harvey moaned.

"Get up! I'll call you again in ten minutes. You'd better be ready."

"Okay, okay—I'm up."

"Remember, boxes to the station—I'll have your new gate pass out front. Got it?"

"I guess so."

"You know so, Harvey. Do it!" She hung up the phone and walked over to the printer. In recent weeks, the numbers had been her daily fix, but this morning, it didn't really matter. Her world was about to change radically—either for the good, or it could be over altogether.

She removed four sheets of paper from the printer, and slowly she began to smile. "Weee'rrrrre baaaaack," she said out loud. "Are we ever!" Channel Three's six and eleven o'clock news had more than doubled their audience from the night before. *Good old Maddie. She does wonders for the ratings—who else can we have kidnapped?* Arlene looked at the numbers and felt a rush.

	6 P.M.	11 P.M.
Channel 3	25	41
Channel 5	4	5
Channel 7	2	3

Nearly five-and-a-half million people had watched the eleven o'clock news the night before. *Wait until they see what happens tonight at six. We could have ten million!* Arlene jotted down some numbers on a piece of paper—*why, the newscast could bring in more than a million dollars a night.* She looked at the sequence of events again. *It's a long shot, but what a jackpot.*

"This is *Channel Three News* at 6 P.M., with Paul Thomas and Nancy Chen, Andrew LaPointe with weather, and Eric Brock on sports—*News Three,* we report directly to you."

Paul watched the production open and saw the smiling faces of the anchor team. *Will I ever see Maddie alive again? Will it be during the newscast, like that maniac promised? How can he get her here? How can I look in control when I feel so helpless?*

"Stand by, Paul," said the floor director.

Paul was in studio five to open the newscast and saw his cue to begin. "Good evening. At the top of our news tonight, we have hope and a promise—hope that peace can begin in our city."

The overhead camera showed the two gangs and the community leaders seated in a triangle. Paul walked behind the chairs of the Insane Rulers and stopped next to a masked man at the end of the row. *Which one of you murderers has Maddie? If I had a gun, I'd blow you away right on camera.* "We've invited the same people back to our studios tonight who were here yesterday." He motioned to those in masks. "We don't know—these people could be different—it doesn't matter. What does matter is that we're ready to get down to business. We're ready to go beyond just saying we have problems." He pointed to a wall at his right, and the camera took a shot of a banner that spelled out the summit's theme. "It's time we start, as our banner reads, 'Doing the Right Thing.' It's time for all sides to find answers."

Paul walked from the Insane Rulers to Iron Claw. A masked man, who was seated at the front of his gang, stared at Paul with unblinking eyes. "The promise I mentioned," said Paul, "is the release of a hostage—my wife, Maddie. We were told it would happen today—so far it hasn't." Paul was supposed to toss back to his co-anchor for news headlines, but he chose to keep going. He looked at both gangs. "If you're behind this kidnapping, and I think you are, I want some answers!" In a mocking tone, Paul said, "Look at you, sitting there, high and mighty—cocky and cool."

"We don't have to take this from you!" one of the Insane Rulers shouted.

"Oh, yes you do." Paul pointed to the camera. "You're not about to walk out of here, not in front of millions of people. What's your name?"

"Felipe Manuel."

"Well, pleased to meet you, Mr. Manuel." Paul turned to the camera. "Ladies and gentlemen, Felipe Manuel of the Insane Rulers, and all of these gang members, are going to stay right in their seats." He looked back at the gangs, and with a sweep of his hand, said, "Otherwise, it'll look like they didn't have the guts to take a little heat. We'll begin the summit, after this break."

Maddie sat in the backseat of the taxi and wondered where they were headed. It was pouring down rain, and she heard a rare rumble of thunder in the distance. The car's wipers made a dragging, squeaking sound as they tried to clear the raindrops.

The driver, a man in his early thirties, with Middle Eastern features, was fidgety and kept looking out the windshield, or into his rearview mirror at her and the man on her left.

The person next to her had kidnapped her less than twenty-four hours earlier. *It seems longer than that,* she thought. "Where are you taking me?" she asked.

"Channel Three."

She waited for him to say more, but he didn't.

"What happens there?"

The car traveled several blocks. "Okay, we're close enough. A guy named Harvey Rose is gonna meet you. You know him?"

"Unfortunately, yes."

"How come you say that?"

"It's none of your business. What does Harvey have to do with this?"

"And that's none of your business. If you want to see your husband alive, you do what Rose tells you. Our driver here knows what'll happen if he don't deliver you to the front door." Mo-Jo poked the cabdriver in the back of the neck with his finger. "Right, Saddam?" The cabbie nodded, but kept looking straight ahead. "Rose will take you inside. Just stay close to him."

"Where will you be?"

"Never mind, you just look for Rose." Mo-Jo looked out the window, then poked the driver in the back again. "Okay, Saddam—let me out here. Right by that curb." The cab kept going. Mo-Jo slapped the back of the driver's head. "I said, stop! Don't you understand English, camel jockey?"

The taxi stopped, and Mo-Jo got out of the car. "You got your money," he said to the cabdriver, "and a hundred-dollar tip. Get her to the front lobby, or you never get on a camel again—got it?" The driver nodded, and Mo-Jo turned to Maddie. "Do what I told you, or your husband is dead meat." He grabbed a gym bag off the seat, closed the door, and walked away.

The cabbie put the car in gear and drove on. Soon Maddie

saw the studios of Channel Three; the station was surrounded by police cars, and people were lined up on the sidewalk. "You can drop me off here, and I'll walk the rest of the way."

"No, you stay there. I have my orders."

The cabbie drove closer to the station, passing an officer who had held up his hand for the car to stop. The officer shouted at the driver, who continued. After moving past another officer who waved at him to stop, the cab couldn't go any further. Harvey Rose ran toward the car, arms in the air. *He looks crazy.*

He rushed to the side of the cab and opened the back door. "Come with me," he yelled, "and don't ask any questions. We're running out of time!" He grabbed Maddie's arm and pulled her out of the cab. She stumbled briefly, regained her balance, and ran with Harvey into the lobby.

"Open the door!" Harvey shouted at the receptionist. A buzzing sound released the lock, and soon they were in a hallway.

"What's going on?" Maddie asked, as Harvey rushed her through a door and up a flight of stairs. Paul had talked about Harvey many times, and she had met him a few times, but she had never seen him like this before. His hair hung in his face, he hadn't shaved, and he smelled like alcohol.

He kept moving while he held onto her arm, but he avoided looking directly at her. They burst through a door to another hallway and nearly knocked over a woman. "You must do what I tell you. Ruggles will take you to meet Paul in the studio—just stay with him."

"What about the man—"

"Never mind, hurry up!" Rose walked faster. "We've got to get inside."

She stopped in her tracks and pulled her arm free. "Harvey, the guy who got out of the taxi stuffed me in a trunk and kidnapped me!"

Harvey's eyes were desperate. "Maddie, please, you must

come with me, now!"

Fred Taylor and Marcia Willis sat in an area reserved for the media in studio five. All was in place for the newscast—Fred had left the details up to others. He reached over and gently took Marcia's hand. She looked at him and winked.

"I'm dreading what comes next," he whispered.

"I thought you were the news director," she teased.

"This part is Ruggles's baby."

That morning, Ruggles had told Fred that he wanted to give a gift to each gang member during the live broadcast. Ruggles had insisted on handling the presentation and was now entering the studio, followed by the station's security chief, Phil Nelson, who was wheeling a large box on a dolly.

"Here it comes," Fred warned.

"Just before we start the summit," Paul said, "our station's general manager, Wilson Ruggles, would like to make a presentation. So, at this point I'll turn things over to Mr. Ruggles. Wilson?"

"Thank you, Paul." Ruggles stood near the gang members and held a hand microphone. He looked into the camera. "Channel Three is privileged to host this historic moment in our city's history, and as a way of expressing our appreciation to the gangs, we have a gift." He walked to the box that Nelson had wheeled in and pulled out a black nylon jacket with Channel Three's logo on the front. He held it up for all to see. "We'd hoped to monogram each member's name on his jacket." He glanced at the gang members who were wearing masks and laughed nervously. "However, some of our guests prefer to remain anonymous. So, let me give these out, and then we'll get on with the summit." Ruggles reached into the box, removed two plastic bags, and gave one to each of the masked men seated at the front of each gang.

Fred watched. So far, so good—he hasn't embarrassed himself. Fred leaned toward Marcia. "The two guys he gave the bags to are supposedly the leaders," he whispered. "That's what Ruggles told me."

"Jorge Escobedo and that Main Man guy?" asked Marcia with disbelief. "Do you think they're both here?"

"I don't think so, but who knows?"

Ruggles and Nelson handed the remainder of the jackets to the others, who then put them on.

"It was nice of Ruggles to do this," Marcia said.

But Fred knew Ruggles didn't do something for nothing. *What was up?*

Mo-Jo pushed the card into the slot in the metal box, and the chain-link gate slid open. The taxi had dropped him off a block from the station, and now he'd made it inside the gate without anyone seeing him. He wore a beige uniform—the kind worn by security officers, and he walked along the building now to a door just off studio five. He clutched his gym bag; inside were the night-vision goggles he'd stolen from the National Guard Armory and a nine-millimeter Uzi carbine, loaded with a 30-round ammunition clip. The switch was set for full automatic firing, making it a machine gun.

Mo-Jo reached in his shirt pocket for the map Felipe Manuel and Dice Head had drawn for him. It was a sketch of the area that led to studio five's side entrance. He walked past two doors on the east side of the building. *So far, so good—no one's in sight.* Just then, a door opened a few feet in front of him, and a young woman carrying a news camera stepped outside. Mo-Jo stopped in his tracks.

"Hi, I haven't seen you before," she said. "Need some help?"

Mo-Jo shoved his left hand into his jacket pocket and gripped his switchblade. "No, I'm security for the summit."

"Well, it's about time. We've been trying to get some protection here for months." She set her camera on the ground. "My name is Katie LaPointe. Everybody knows my brother, Andrew LaPointe, the guy who points the pointer at the weather." She laughed. "I'm just the LaPointe who points the camera at the news. What's your name?"

A long conversation was the last thing Mo-Jo wanted. He needed to get into the studio before Maddie Thomas was escorted in. "Stanley," he said. "Sorry, but I gotta go."

"Sure, no problem. Keep us safe, at least for tonight."

Mo-Jo walked past her and turned the corner of the building. He checked his map, then headed west down an alley. *If Felipe and Dice Head are right, I should enter the building at the third door.* He chuckled as he thought about both gangs helping him with the map. He smiled when he saw the van parked outside the door, exactly where he told Harvey Rose to have it. Mo-Jo opened the van's door and saw that the keys were in the ignition. *Just like I asked.* He put down the sports bag, reached in his pants pocket, and pulled out the key Rose had given him that morning at his condo. *Click*—he turned the key, opened the door, and slipped into the building.

The dimly lit hallway was obviously used for deliveries. It smelled of stale cigarette smoke and cardboard boxes. Boxes of what looked like paper were stacked along the wall, and two broken desk chairs were turned upside down on the floor. Mo-Jo checked his map, then began walking toward what he believed would be studio five. He passed a light stand, some old computer keyboards wrapped in cords, and a wooden ladder on wheels. He turned a corner and bumped into a uniformed police officer.

"Sorry, man, didn't see you," said Mo-Jo.

The officer, a man in his thirties, looked suspiciously at Mo-Jo's uniform and then down at his bag. "What are you doing here?"

"Extra security. My supervisor told me to go into the studio. I just sneaked outside for a smoke." Mo-Jo smiled. "Bad habit, man."

The police officer pointed to the sports bag. "What's in the bag?"

Mo-Jo's hand once again gripped the switchblade in his jacket pocket. "Gonna play me some hoops tonight, man. I been here since this morning—got my basketball stuff in the bag. You want to see if I got a gun hidden in my jockstrap?"

The officer frowned. "Naw, I wouldn't touch that." He hesitated. "Basketball? You're kind of short, aren't you?"

"I'm fast."

"And you smoke?"

"Like I said, bad habit. You gonna let me do my job?"

The officer nodded to his left. "Go on inside."

Mo-Jo sighed with relief and continued walking until he saw a high double door. He remembered from the map that it led to the back of studio five. One of the doors was open and he heard voices in the studio; he recognized one of them as Paul Thomas.

Mo-Jo walked into studio five and saw a brightly lit platform. Paul Thomas was leading a discussion between police officers and a member of the Iron Claw gang. The background, the lights, the audience, and everyone on stage looked much smaller in person than on television. He felt confident that his plan would succeed, even with police officers in the studio. He looked to his right for the panel of switches that controlled the studio lights—there it was, exactly where Felipe Manuel had said it would be. A private security officer and a policeman stood next to it; they looked bored. Mo-Jo looked closer and spotted the switch that would throw the entire studio into pitch darkness. Felipe had learned how the studio lights worked during his tour of the station, and he'd relayed the details to Mo-Jo. Everything was where it was supposed to be—all was going smoothly. So far, no one seemed to care that he was there.

Paul Thomas was still talking. "What assurance, Mr. Dice Head, can you give police—"

"Wait a second!" shouted Wilson Ruggles from the side of the room. "Stop!"

Thomas shielded his eyes from the glare of the lights. "Ladies and gentlemen, something seems to be happening off-camera. Our general manager—he appears to be bringing a woman—"

Ruggles was pushing a woman through the crowd.

"Yes, he's with a woman, and—oh, it's Maddie!" Mo-Jo watched as Thomas dashed from the platform and grabbed his wife, lifting her several inches off the ground. The two were crying, and many in the studio were cheering and applauding.

Ruggles picked up the hand microphone that Thomas had dropped and looked into the camera. "What we're seeing here is proof that the leaders of these two gangs can be trusted. Without their efforts, Maddie Thomas would not have been released safely. How about this? Isn't this great?"

Mo-Jo gave a subtle wave to the two gang members wearing masks at the end of each row of chairs. They reached to their faces and quickly signaled back.

Ruggles motioned to Thomas and his wife. "Paul, Maddie—come on back up here." They returned to the platform, but Ruggles held onto the microphone. "Can we handle any more good news?" He laughed. "We have another surprise. And since I'm the boss of this television station, I'm going to handle this. So, Paul, you and Maddie just stand there and watch."

"Take camera two on a tight shot of Ruggles," said the director. A camera snapped to life and focused on Ruggles.

Mo-Jo watched. Thomas seemed confused about what was happening. He looked to the side and gestured to someone that he didn't know what was going on. The person just shook his head. Mo-Jo knew exactly what was next.

Ruggles pointed to a door next to where Mo-Jo stood. "Okay, from the back of the studio, bring in the boxes." Two men wheeled two large boxes on dollies to the platform. "Ladies and gentlemen, while our men are bringing these boxes forward, I'd like to ask two gang members to explain what we're doing. From the Iron Claw, Mr. Dice Head, and from the Insane Rulers, Mr. Felipe Manuel—come over here, fellows." Dice Head and Manuel moved over next to Ruggles. "Tell these people and those watching at home what you're about to do."

He held the microphone for Dice Head. "Okay, in these boxes here, are guns, rifles, handguns—you name it."

Gang members lifted the boxes to the platform. One box was placed next to the Insane Rulers leader and the other next to the Iron Claw leader. A security guard took a knife out of his pocket and cut the packing tape around the boxes, then walked off the platform and stood along the side of the studio.

Ruggles held the microphone for Manuel. "It's your turn, Mr. Manuel."

"Like the other guy said, the boxes have guns, but they aren't loaded. We're all gonna take one gun, and give it back to the community."

"How come?" asked Ruggles. "Explain to our viewers, Flip."

Manuel frowned. "It's Felipe, not Flip." He continued, "We're giving up our guns as kind of a peace offering—a way to show we're ready for change."

"Well, I think that's just great." Ruggles looked into the audience. "Don't all of you, too?"

"Take the overhead camera," said the director, and a shot of people applauding was shown.

"I see council member Francie McMillan," Ruggles said, peering into the audience, "and there's Arthur Jackson, the guy who grabbed my tie that first day." He laughed. "A lot has happened since that first protest, hasn't it, Mr. Jackson?"

"Get me a shot of Jackson," the director barked. The camera turned on Jackson, but he wasn't smiling.

Ruggles then launched into a speech about Channel Three's role in Light the Night.

In the back, Mo-Jo knelt down out of sight, reached into his bag, and pulled out his night-vision goggles. In a few seconds, he was ready.

"All right, gentlemen, now pass out the guns," Ruggles instructed.

The two gang leaders looked at Mo-Jo, and seeing that he had his goggles on, they reached into their boxes and pulled out matching Uzi carbines. *They think I'm going to lead them out of the darkness,* thought Mo-Jo. Escobedo and Main Man removed their masks and stood—they looked at each other for two, maybe three seconds. Ruggles droned on, and then everything seemed to shift into slow motion.

"Take camera two on a two-shot of those guys," said the director.

"They took their masks off!" someone in the control booth shouted.

Mo-Jo watched Escobedo and Main Man reach into their jacket pockets and pull out ammunition clips, then insert them into their weapons. They both smiled, and Mo-Jo knew each of them thought the other's ammo clip was filled with blanks. The two men pointed their guns at each other, swore vengeance, and pulled the triggers.

Not everyone could see what was happening, but everyone heard the explosion of gunfire. Escobedo's arm recoiled from the jolt, as did Main Man's, and Mo-Jo grinned at the shocked look on their faces. They stared at their guns, then at each other.

Mo-Jo reached for the main studio lightswitch, and pulled the handle down. Screams rose as the room went dark, but it wasn't pitch-black, as Mo-Jo had expected. He'd forgotten about the open studio doors. Police officers, guns drawn, rushed toward the platform, ordering the gang members to drop their weapons. Escobedo and Main Man immediately obeyed.

There was pandemonium, but with his night-vision goggles, Mo-Jo could clearly see through the confusion.

"Give me a shot from the back on three," yelled the director.

A police officer in the control booth, apparently watching the monitors, yelled, "I see him! He's got an Uzi!"

Mo-Jo raised his weapon and took aim. *Who should I shoot first, Escobedo or Main Man?* But he waited a split second too long to decide.

The camera next to Mo-Jo, with its pointed metal hood, pivoted hard. "I got him!" someone yelled.

Mo-Jo felt something slam into his gun hand, just as he pulled the trigger. A burst of shots fired wildly. Something sharp then cracked him on the side of his head, and he saw bright flashes of light. His vision cleared. He'd missed Escobedo and Main Man, and he saw Paul and his wife diving for the floor.

"Where are the lights?"

"I've been shot!"

"Help me!"

"Get an ambulance. She's been shot!"

Mo-Jo's perfect plan had fallen apart. Dazed by whatever had struck his head, he ripped off his goggles and tossed them aside. *Get to the van—save yourself. Get away!*

Everyone was diving for cover or running for the exits, and the police were moving in on Mo-Jo in the back of the room. Mo-Jo had stayed in studio five too long. The lights flashed back on, and he bolted for the door. As he reached the hallway, he turned toward the back delivery door he'd used to get into the building. He sprinted around the corner and smacked headlong into the same policeman he'd collided with earlier.

"Hey! What are you—" The officer looked at the Uzi in his hands, then started to draw his service revolver. Mo-Jo never gave him a chance to get it out of his holster. He shot him at point-blank range. People in the hallway screamed, then dropped to the floor or scrambled for cover.

Mo-Jo spotted the exit that led to the alley and the waiting van. *I'm outta here,* he thought as he threw open the door and saw the van. He reached for the van's door handle and tried to turn it. *The door's locked!* The window was rolled up. He jerked on the handle, thinking the door might be stuck, but it was locked. Through the window, he could see the keys still in the ignition. He pointed his Uzi at the window to blast it open, when he felt a crushing blow across the back of his shoulders. His gun clattered to the pavement, and he screamed in agony. A large man stood over him, holding a pipe.

"That was for J. J.," said Arthur Jackson. "You locked out of your car, too?"

Before Mo-Jo could say anything, Jackson swung the pipe and connected a bone-smashing blow to Mo-Jo's kneecaps. Mo-Jo fell on his face, writhing in pain. Jackson dropped the pipe and picked up the Uzi. "I ought to fill your empty head with lead right now, but I'm going to let the state do the killin' for me."

Mo-Jo was in excruciating pain, and as he rolled on the ground, he saw Arlene Zahn rush out of the building. She pointed a gun at him. *I'm dead*, Mo-Jo thought.

But then Jackson said, "Lady, we got enough guns goin' off 'round here—why don't you drop yours?"

CHAPTER THIRTY

Paul and Maddie made their way through the hospital's intensive care unit to Marcia's room. Once inside, Paul shook his head at the endless string of tubes connected to her. Fred sat at her bedside, holding her hand.

"How's she doing?" asked Paul.

Fred turned, a look of surprise on his face. "Paul, Maddie—with all you've been through, I didn't expect you here."

"How's Marcia?" Maddie asked.

"She lost a lot of blood, and the surgery was more complicated than they thought, but the doctors say she'll make it. She's stable and off the critical list. You guys all right?"

"Just thankful to be alive," said Maddie.

Paul nodded toward Marcia. "How did it—"

"I don't know. When the first shots went off, I looked at her—she started to say something, then I guess the guy in the back got her. Hit her right in the chest."

Paul and Maddie walked closer to Fred and sat down in the two chairs next to him. "Did you have a chance to talk with her before the surgery?" Paul asked.

"Yeah, just before they wheeled her in."

Paul thought for a second. *Lord, give me the right words.* "Listen, Fred—remember our talk about how we never know when it might be all over?"

After a moment of silence, Fred said, "Yeah."

"You know, that bullet Marcia took could very easily have

had your name on it. You could even be dead right now."

"In so many words, that's what she told me, too."

"And what did you say to her?"

"I told her it was time to make that 'decision for eternity' the two of you have been bugging me about."

"And?"

"Just before she went into surgery, I prayed with her, and received Jesus Christ into my heart—I'm a Christian, Paul. And Marcia and I are getting married."

Paul looked at Maddie and grinned. "Fantastic! Now I can go over to Channel Five." He let the words hang in the air for effect. Then he laughed out loud. "Fred, I'm just kidding—that's great!" Maddie gave him a playful punch on the arm.

"Thanks, man—and thanks for praying for me, and not giving up when it seemed like I wanted nothing to do with God and Jesus, and all that stuff."

"Hey, forget it. I can't wait to see the two of you walk down the aisle."

"Don't know when that's going to be. She's got a long recovery ahead. But about tonight—I talked with Tim, and he says everything is under control for the eleven o'clock news. You sure you want to do it?"

Paul looked at Maddie. "Yeah, we're going to pick the kids up after the news and have a little reunion. It's Friday, and I've got the whole weekend to recover."

"What about the cops and the investigation?" Fred asked.

"That's going on in studio five. They'll be in there the rest of the night, but nothing happened on the regular news set, so that's all clear."

"Were we rolling a tape during the shoot-out?" asked Fred.

"It's all there—wait till you see it. Tim's putting together an incredible piece."

"Okay, what about the other stations?"

"They're going crazy, asking to use it at eleven, but Tim told them it's our exclusive until tomorrow."

"I agree," said Fred. "Give me a call if you need me, but it looks like you've got things under control."

"No, Fred, what's most important is that now you have eternity under control. That's what counts."

Paul and Maddie tried to relax in his office before the newscast, but every few seconds the phone rang with yet another call from a viewer, a news reporter, or a friend. After talking with one man who claimed he was a Hollywood producer and was interested in making a movie about the shoot-out, Paul got up from his desk. "This is ridiculous." He picked up a copy of the eleven o'clock news script. "Come on, I've already checked the script. Let's get out of here and go somewhere we can be alone for a few minutes."

"Where?" Maddie asked.

"The news set. The lights are out, and we can just sit alone—who knows, I might even steal a kiss."

She laughed. "Lead on, captain of the Dark Brigade."

As they made their way to the studio, Maddie asked, "What about Ruggles, Arlene, and Harvey?"

"The cops are talking with Ruggles. From what I understand, he'll probably be charged as an accessory to murder."

"Arlene?"

"Arrested. People in the newsroom say the guy who kidnapped you and did the shooting implicated her—says she masterminded the whole thing. Looks like she was the one who gave Bobby Silva's name to Escobedo."

Paul and Maddie approached the door to studio four. "How about Harvey Rose?" Maddie asked.

"So far, he's a question mark. But the desk just told me there was a three-alarm fire at his condo tonight. His car was in the garage, but there was no sign of him."

"And the gang leaders?"

"No surprise—Escobedo and Shirley "Main Man" Hogg are behind bars. But there's a twist in all of this."

"What's that?"

"Remember that guy who came up to me after everything had settled down?"

"Felipe-something?"

"Yeah, that's the one. You didn't hear what he told me."

"What did he tell you?"

"I couldn't believe it. He said that he and Tony Romero, the guy Mo-Jo apparently killed at our house—Felipe says they tried to talk Escobedo out of doing a lot of what went down."

Maddie gave him a look that said, *You're putting me on.* "Come on, he really did." Maddie's expression didn't change. "Okay, don't believe me. As corny as it sounds, he told me that Light the Night was a good thing."

"Yeah, right. I suppose Felipe told you that he has 'seen the light.'"

"I didn't say it, you did."

Maddie raised her eyebrows.

They walked hand in hand into studio four's semidarkness. "Welcome to the tunnel of love," Paul said. "Sorry, I forgot our boat."

"Don't worry, I'd get seasick."

A bank of lights had been turned on across the room, and a camera was pointed at a test pattern. Paul assumed some engineers were inside the control room shading the robotic camera.

"Come on, let's sit up on the set." They walked onto the platform and found their way to two chairs on the dimly lit news set. "You know what chair you're in?" Paul asked, smiling.

"No."

"That's the one I sit in, when I do the news."

"I'll be the lead anchor tonight," she said.

Paul laughed. "Good—then lead me astray."

"That is such an old line, Paul—but it works."

He leaned over and kissed her. At that moment, the lights in the studio flashed on.

"Looks like our tunnel of love has lost some of its romantic atmosphere," he said.

"Who cares? How about another kiss?" They embraced, oblivious to everything around them.

"I thought I'd never see you again, Maddie." Paul held her face gently in both hands. "More than a couple of times, I lost faith, but God answered my prayers."

"I had my doubts, too. But the Lord brought us back together."

"I love you, Maddie," They kissed, took a deep breath, and kissed again. It was an intimate moment, or so they thought. Ten million people across Los Angeles were watching on television. The woman in the control room, who'd smashed Mo-Jo with her camera, had struck again. She had put them on live.